NINE NOTCHES

TJ SPENCER JACQUES

NOVELS BY
TJ SPENCER JACQUES

NINE NOTCHES

BURGUNDY DOUBLOONS SERIES

INFALLIBLE SERIES

This is a work of fiction created by author TJ Spencer Jacques. All the characters, organizations, and events portrayed in this novel are either products of the author's imagination or used fictitiously.

I dedicate this book to my mother,
who gave birth to me in 1971 and 2007.

AUTHOR'S NOTE

In the novel *Nine Notches*, I tell one story that takes place in the 1800s and current day. After the slave auction scene in Chapter One, the story shifts to current day, but don't worry—the 1800s are woven throughout the novel.

Enjoy.

NINE NOTCHES

TJ SPENCER JACQUES

CHAPTER 1

November 18, 1835
Mandeville, Louisiana
Marigny Plantation
8:15 a.m.

It was a shotgun blast, she was certain of it.
Threatening words became flesh and arrived on black
horses.
Her time was up.

In her hands she held a purple satin gown that was eight threads from becoming the best dress she'd ever created. It was the newest of many dresses she had made for her mistress; all assembled with an expert touch. The man who had fired the rifle was just below her balcony—the shot caused her delicate fingers to freeze in mid-stitch.

On a typical day, the picturesque scenery outside her large bedroom window provided a view of workers moving about like ants—a single organism obsessed with production, hurried by demand. Today had been no different . . . until the birds fled the trees. She approached the window with slow, timid steps, struggling to breathe.

Suddenly, he came into view, mounted on a fire-breathing horse, a smoking shotgun in hand, the brim of his cattle hat set across the bridge of his nose.

"Boys, let's make this quick! Every nigger, and I mean every one of them you see, is now the property of the New Orleans Canal & Banking Company. Old Benedict Marigny . . . *that fool* . . . has defaulted on his obligations to the bank. This sugar mill and all the niggers are collateral, and we've come to enforce this judgment of repossession. Round up everything that's breathing! Shackle each one to the other, by hand and foot. I expect to head back across the lake by noon," the sheriff ordered.

His deputized gang scurried about, indiscriminately evoking chaos among the terrified field hands. The sheriff was a man she recognized. He had been a guest at many of the fancy parties hosted at her master's home. She knew him to be pleasant, always in good spirits—quite jovial, but not today. The petrified damsel hid in the drapes and watched as the sheriff fired into the air again, seemingly for no reason. Several of the men who accompanied him did the same. A chorus of gunfire rattled the bedroom walls. A treasured family painting crashed to the floor and ejected from the frame. The usually tranquil chandelier that hung above the bed clattered in fear, in perfect sync with her teeth.

The sheriff had certainly earned her undivided attention. Judging by the cacophony of frantic screams that ensued, he had earned the full attention of the entire plantation. From her hiding place within the drapes, she watched as screaming toddlers were separated from their mothers, emasculated men were sundered from the tight embraces of their wives, and all the babies being nursed by midwives were placed in several large baskets. In that one instant, all unions were shattered and shackled individually, in full compliance with the orders of the sheriff. Only cries of sorrow and terror remained united, bonded together by the uncertainty of the morning.

The sole remaining truth she knew for sure was her name was still Beatrice. But for how long? She alone was the pride of the plantation; her master's perfect teenage product, the envy of all the other slaves. But she was a mystery to them, one they whispered about while they cut the sugarcane. She wore the best dresses, ate the best food, and never held a shovel in her soft, fragile hands—only needles that slid through elegant fabrics. While the other slaves labored twelve hours a day in the sugar-cane fields, Beatrice enjoyed the comforts of a spoiled puppy, one who only endured the Louisiana humidity when it was time for a walk.

Her master was a third-generation colonial who indulged in a lifestyle filled with Southern decadence. Beatrice was his fifteen-year-old daughter, a product of his overindulgence conceived with a free woman of color in St. Dominique: a French island that served as his destination of pleasure. During the Haitian Revolution, he moved his lover to New Orleans and housed her on the corner of Rampart and St. Roch. He soon relocated her to his plantation in Mandeville to avoid the slave smugglers in Orleans Parish. Not long afterward, she bore him twin girls. When the girls were barely out of their toddler years, the smugglers' harassment of their mother every time she left the plantation became too much for Benedict Marigny to handle. He eventually sent her back to St. Dominique, insisting she leave the twins behind.

Beatrice was born in the time of slavery, but she wasn't a slave; she was something in between. She was her master's daughter—sort of—but not entirely.

Such was the life of a mulatto offspring.

Her pale skin allowed her inside the home of the master, which caused the field workers to brand her a *house nigger*. The consequence of her pale skin was that she was hated throughout the plantation, but the blessing of her high yellow complexion was a silk-upholstered pedestal that towered her above the others. It was both evident and obvious. Beatrice's bedroom was directly next door to her father's, while the rest of his kids slept in rooms down the hall. Whenever he argued with his wife, she heard every word. Beatrice knew the sheriff was coming that morning, and she knew why.

For weeks she had heard them arguing through the peach plastered walls that separated their bedrooms. Every night she listened to her mistress pleading with him to accept the offer, but he always refused. Every night started out the same: with intense yelling. This was followed by the sound of sobbing, and then the shattering of a wine glass on the dark cypress floor. Finally, she would hear the thumping sound of her master marching down the stairs and conclude with certainty that he wouldn't return until morning.

The offer he had repeatedly refused to accept was a loan from his father-in-law to repay New Orleans Canal & Banking Company and recover the deeds to his estate. The only problem was that her master was Benedict de Marigny de Mandeville, thought to be one of the richest men on both sides of Lake Pontchartrain. The truth was, he was flat broke. Benedict Marigny was a very proud man, a famous New Orleans developer credited with subdividing the residential area just below the French Quarter—the Faubourg Marigny neighborhood. Benedict de Marigny was also credited with introducing the high-stakes game of dice to the United States, a dubious honor that landed him upside down in debt. From a lifetime of eavesdropping, Beatrice knew enough about her master to know he would never accept help from his father-in-law. To do so would be an admission of failure.

Many nights when Beatrice pressed her ear against the cold, plastered walls, she heard strings of foreign words. She heard them so often she learned the approximate meanings of them all. Words like *foreclosed, collateral*, and *bankrupt*. She also discovered the meanings of words like *auction, sold*, and *shackled*, as well as the exact title of the wagon driver who delivered newly purchased servants: Mason, the slave trader.

Mason was a third-generation merchant of human beings. Mason's daddy and grandfather were both known as Louisiana privateers for their naval commissions in the Gulf, but peel back the fancy labels and they were nothing more than smugglers of Africans. After the United States banned the import of slaves in 1807, Mason's family made a fortune kidnapping and trafficking Africans from Dutch traders. After hijacking Dutch ships in the Gulf of Mexico, they smuggled that same human cargo up through every swamp in Louisiana until they arrived in New Orleans. Mason's grandfather referred to their family business as *speculating*—which was just another way of saying, "we sell people."

Beatrice had often watched Mason from the same upstairs window, as his dual horse-driven wagon delivered servants several times a year. Disoriented souls she often referred to as the *new folk* spilled from the wagon when it arrived; people she pitied but never felt any relation to. Beatrice could hear her heart beating in her chest as she counted the wagons that followed Mason onto her master's property—a total of twelve, all empty. Out of the same window, Beatrice watched as Mason and the other drivers tied their horses to the wooden fence that bordered the fields across from her home and grabbed their shotguns. Mason walked in a straight line toward her front door. Just as he entered the house, her bladder released right where she stood. Mason was there for the servants; it had been whispered last night through the peach plastered walls.

"All you niggers better get down here now! If I have to come find you, your ass getting strapped to the pole."

Beatrice had never experienced getting strapped to the pole, but she'd witnessed it enough times to know what it meant—getting whipped while tied to a pole. Mason's angry voice vibrated the floor beneath her feet as he demanded all servants to appear before him. On her way to the bedroom door, Beatrice passed a mahogany Georgian dresser and mirror that she had stood in front of on many a day, fitting gowns for her mistress. She paused for one last look. Her skin looked like a muddled cup of coffee that was mostly cream. Her eyes were as blue as the clearest day in spring, her hair like the sands on Flamenco Beach in Culebra. In a perfect world, Beatrice would be seen as a perfect blend of everything lovely and pure. Her lips and nose were African, but her head and shoulders were something on loan from France.

Letting out a deep sigh, she continued toward her bedroom door. The room she left behind was more than just a bedroom; it was her sanctuary and observatory. With trembling hands, Beatrice slowly opened the door and peeked through the railing, down toward the foyer. There he was—with his shotgun cocked. Beatrice slowly stepped out of the bedroom and hurried as best as she could. Paralyzing fear weighed down her thin legs. She inched along like a rake across a thick Persian rug. *I pray Mason only came fo dem maids*.

An hour earlier, the aroma of freshly baked bread blended with the herbs of potpourri to provide the fragrance of the morning. Mint, cedar, cloves, jasmine, lavender . . . but that was before the slave trader entered her home.

As she slowly descended the staircase, she could see and smell Mason. He was a short, dusty man with midnight eyes, cruddy fingernails, a bird's nest of a beard, and a hat that certainly doubled as a washcloth. She could see that he desperately needed a bath, but halfway down the stairs, her nose confirmed it. Mason stunk—like a musty cattle herder, or, better yet, a bucket of urine that had simmered in a hot barn for three weeks. The scented herbs and hot oven bread conceded. With each downward step she took, his body odor become increasingly more nauseating, a foul stench so strong she could almost see it. Today was the closest she had ever come to Mason. She had always watched him from the window upstairs, now he stood only ten feet away. His eyes were as black as a moonless night, as was the gun he aimed at her head.

"Hurry your ass down those stairs before I drag you down!"

"Yes, suh! Yes . . . sir."

It all happened so fast for her; only yesterday she had been steam-pressing hems onto dresses inspired by the pages of *La Belle Assemblée* and patterned out to perfection. What was once so important to her day-to-day life now seemed picayune in comparison; beautiful silk gowns were the furthest things from her mind. Directly outside the front door was an empty cart, with more than enough space to carry her across the lake to the auctions in New Orleans.

"Are there any other niggers in this house?" Mason yelled while pulling the hammer of his gun into firing position. "You lie to me and I will blow your head off!"

"No, suh! It's . . . just us."

"All of you, head out to that wagon."

". . . oz no slave, suh," Beatrice tried to explain.

"Fancy niggeress . . . you mouth off again, you will swallow those teeth. Get your ass in that wagon."

Mason grabbed a fist of her hair and shoved Beatrice onto the porch. The cooks and the maid stepped over her on their way to the wagon as she frantically glanced around for her father or any of the foremen. No one stepped forward to explain that she wasn't a slave—no one cared.

Mason and the sheriff had successfully executed a plantation foreclosure that included all the land, livestock, sugar mill, homes . . . and every slave. With Mason's shotgun aimed at her back, Beatrice and the four other housemaids—all elderly women—stepped off the front porch and directly into the full atrocity of America's Greatest Sin. The fifteen-year-old seamstress was shipped south across Lake Pontchartrain. Benedict de Marigny de Mandeville had spared his family the horror of the morning. He had thought ahead and shipped them safely North to Amite.

The next morning, hours before the sun clocked in, Beatrice was awakened by the same abrasive voice she had heard in her foyer. It wasn't a nightmare, she wasn't in her bed, and this wasn't her house in Mandeville—not even close. Beatrice opened her eyes in one of eight auction houses in New Orleans: the Saint Louis Hotel, a preferred marketplace for those who could afford her kind. The angry voice approached from down the long hallway and marched in her direction, growing louder and louder all the way to her cell.

"Wake your asses up! Wake up!" Mason barked as he banged on each cell door. "All of you are going on the block today, and if any of you act out, it will be hell for you! Wake your asses up!" His voice echoed from cell to cell.

The wooden floor of the holding cell was damp and slippery. The moisture on the floor entered from a roof that regularly leaked wintry precipitation; an annoying, continuous drip that saturated all the cell's inhabitants. There were no windows; only Beatrice's internal clock knew the precise time of morning. Her source of water was a rusty metal bucket where a dead roach floated on top, along with other thirsty bugs. The only place to relieve her weak bladder was a black chamber pot that sat in the corner of the room, next to a woman who appeared unfazed by the nauseating stench. The woman looked slightly familiar to Beatrice, but the poor lighting and constant shuffling of anxious mothers reduced her to nothing more than a silhouette.

Moments later, Mason entered the cell carrying a bundle of dresses. He dropped the garments in the middle of the floor, then slid in a washtub with a few pieces of soap.

"Take off the rags you have on. Put on these gowns and comb that nappy hair! Make yourselves look decent, and I may just give you some extra butter bread for breakfast. If you don't look presentable, then you will sit outside buck naked until your black ass sticks to the ground. Y'all understand me?"

"Yes, suh!" the slaves replied.

Beatrice watched as her cellmates shuffled through the pile of wrinkled dresses; a few even welcomed the change in attire. The gowns in the middle of the floor were far finer than the sackcloth material female slaves usually fastened into garments. The women quickly disrobed, but not Beatrice; she cherished every minute in the dress she wore. Her fitted, sky-blue camp dress with a matching wool petticoat was a gift from her mistress when she turned fifteen years old; she had only worn the dress twice since September. To disrobe meant she would no longer be exceptional, and Beatrice loved the feeling of being an exceptional Negro resident of the plantation. In a symbolic act of defiance, a disgusted Beatrice allowed the degrading gown to slither through her fingers down to the floor.

Just hang me, hang me now.

Despite being deposed from her elite lifestyle, in her lowest moment of despair, she retained her dignity as a child of Benedict de Marigny de Mandeville. Her camp dress with the matching petticoat was more than just a birthday gift from her stepmother; her dress was the equivalent of a gem-laced tiara worn by Queen Marie Amelie of France.

I will not wear this. I ain't doing it. That smelly little man will just have to beat me. I ain't wearing it.

The other women quickly stepped out of their tattered work clothes and slowly fastened Mason's gowns around themselves.

"It's been a long time since I had a dress that wasn't full of stalk from the cane," one of the younger girls said.

Beatrice listened as the women wept for their homes back in Mandeville. They cried for the husbands they had grown to love and the dreadful possibility of being forced to produce children for a new owner. Despite their daunting reality, punctuated by their pouting and watery eyes, they still dressed for the occasion. In between their sniffles and moans, Beatrice could hear infants crying in the cell next door. Their wails caused several of the mothers to press their ears and bodies against the brick wall, each listening for the cries of their own, some even trying to hug their babies through the wall. The senior women, who were veterans of slave auctions, sought to console many of the weeping mothers, but to no avail. They were all inconsolable in their grief.

Beatrice knew she should change clothes like the others, but she firmly refused to pick the inferior gown off the floor. It was the one clear thought in her mind that kept her from jumping out of her skin. *I hate that dress.*

Her disgust was evident, and her facial expression made it even more clear. The other women took notice of her disdain for the dingy garment. A few of the female slaves who were about the same age as Beatrice seemed in awe of her. Many of them had never seen her up close, only through the view of the second-story window. But there was one woman present who was not impressed at all—one who seized the opportunity to express her deepest antipathy.

"Yo' high yellow ass just like one of us dark niggas now," a woman said in a raspy voice that sounded clogged with sugar-cane husk. "Master sold yo' ass too."

Beatrice looked around and saw that the verbal assault had come from the dark-complexioned slave sitting in the far-right corner of the room near the chamber pot.

"Hanging around Master and his wife, you forgot you were one of us?"

Beatrice looked closer at the woman and finally recognized her. It was the midwife of the plantation, a slave with the foulest of dispositions—the one called Clarice. She hated Beatrice, and all the field workers knew it. Even as Clarice urinated in the chamber pot, she never took her eyes off the plantation princess from the second-floor bedroom window.

"You ain't nothing but a nigress, just like us! Masta care nothing if you his chillum. You still one of us. Got beside yourself up in that big house but you 'bout to get a bid on you—like me, and her, and old mammy over there." Clarice laughed out loud. "Ha, ha. Sold down the river like the rest of us. How about that?" Clarice seemed to find a tinge of joy in the irony of it all.

"You hush yo' mouth," an old woman named Tempie Durham said. All the slaves on the plantation referred to her as Big Ma Tempie. A seasoned elder who had been bought and sold more than twenty times, Big Ma was seventy-five years old and had gray hair plaited into pigtails. Her eyes were dark gray due to cataracts, but her mind still functioned like that of a woman half her age. Big Ma was the matriarch of the Mandeville Plantation, and the one slave that was mother to all.

"No need to keep needling her, *Clayrice*. We need to pray for our mercy ova da chillun. Mercy dat new massa keep us with our chillun. Don't none of us know where we gonna end up," Big Ma Tempie chided.

"Big Ma, why you takin' up for that house nigger? She never cared nothin' bout us. Not one day did she tote a bucket of water to us in dem hot fields or soup in the winter. I hope they sell her to a hoe house rite here in N'awlins."

"Clarice, hush!" Big Ma pointed down at Clarice on the chamber pot. "Ain't none of us no betta than the other. So just hush yo' mouth! Yo' mammy would turn in her cold grave if she heard such talk out of you. Hush dat talk right now."

Clarice looked up at Big Ma from the chamber pot. "Masta Marigny worked my po' mama like a mule, while this half-white watched from that window. She didn't even come pay respect when we buried my mama, so I care nothin' for her. I hope the new masta make a whore out of her!"

Big Ma placed her small-framed body directly in front of Clarice, trying to shield Beatrice from the furious woman's glaring stares. But Clarice wasn't done with Beatrice.

"Where is yo' mistress at this morning? Don't look for dem

to buy you back 'cuz they never buy you back." The heckling continued as Clarice stood upright to adjust her dingy, ruffled dress.

Beatrice turned her back to Clarice. "My mistress will come for me! She will not sell me off. You will see! Mind yo' business, Clarice."

Beatrice was trained to be a seamstress for Mrs. de Marigny, while Clarice was forced against her will to be a midwife and field hand. In between pregnancies, Clarice had to return to the fields, only getting a break when it was time to deliver another baby. Clarice was a mere ten years older than Beatrice, and ten shades darker due to many summer days in the sugarcane fields. A life of hard labor and unrelenting Southern heat had roasted her appearance into the illusion of a woman three times her age. Suddenly, the tension between Clarice and Beatrice was interrupted by an odor reminiscent of someone who had just walked through a mile of manure. It was Mason.

The room fell silent except for a few stifled gasps of hyperventilation. Even Clarice suppressed her resentment for Beatrice in the presence of Mason, who walked slowly into the middle of the cell. Beatrice welcomed the silence. In Mason's hands, she saw links of chains fitted with bracelets—not like the expensive bracelets in Mrs. de Marigny's jewelry chest, but rather rusty iron bracelets like the type shackled on the new folk. They were the same bracelets she had worn for the first time when Mason kicked in her front door and repossessed the life she once knew.

Mason bound each of them individually by the wrists, then singularly along a twenty-four-foot-long chain. All the women clamped to the chain appeared emotionally devastated—all except Clarice. At the exact moment Beatrice was clamped to the twenty-four-foot chain, a smile appeared on Clarice's face. The female slaves were then led in a single file line into the main hall of the auction; Beatrice was last on the row of fourteen women, linked behind the three elderly slaves.

"Is that one of the dresses from the pile I placed in your cell?" Mason asked Beatrice once he noticed she hadn't changed her clothes.

"No . . . no, suh."

"You high yellow wench. What is your name?"

"Beatrice . . . suh."

"So . . . you're one of those house niggers who feels like you're better than the rest of the niggers on this chain?" Mason yelled.

"No, suh," she replied as her left ear rang.

"I have a good mind to slap the taste out of your mouth for disobeying me. Nothing makes me fightin' mad like a hard-headed nigger. Good niggers stay in their place, you hear me?"

"Yes . . . suh."

"Good niggers do what they're told, you hear me?" The indoctrination continued.

"Yes . . . suh."

"Well, I consider you to be disobedient, and I'm known to severely punish those who are disobedient. You better hope one of those gentlemen places a bid on you this morning. If not, then I plan to beat that dress clean off your ass." Mason turned to walk away.

"Mr. Mason, I'm good—"

Mason returned to her left ear. "Who told you my name?"

"Sir, I heard your name from my fathaw."

"Your father?"

"Mastaw Marigny is my fathaw."

"Because your master said my name, you feel you can address me directly? So, you feel you can disrespect me because your master raised you in the house?"

"No . . . suh! No, suh!"

With the force of a punch, Mason grabbed a fistful of Beatrice's sandy blonde hair so hard she felt the follicles ripping away from her scalp. He slammed her to the floor, then dragged her petite frame out of view of the bidders. Releasing her hair only long enough to place his hand around her neck, Mason lifted Beatrice to her feet. His hand vice-gripped her throat against a splintered partition.

"The only thing saving your ass right now is time. The auction is about to start." Mason snarled, releasing a gust of rotten breath. "I will teach you a lesson about talking back. No nigger has ever disrespected me, and you will know why right after the bidding is over."

Mason released his chokehold, allowing Beatrice to breathe for the first time in what felt like an hour. She started to pray for a buyer who would save her from returning back to the cell with Mason. The buyer she prayed for was Mrs. de Marigny, or better yet, her father.

"Hee, hee, better hope you get a bid," Clarice said from a few chain links ahead. "I'm prayin' you don't."

The auction block was nothing more than a platform of shipping crates arranged to form a stage. The auctioneer and his assistant stood in the middle of a circle of buyers, while the banker sat off to the far left at his table, to assure the correct price once the bidding got underway. Despite the frigid air that chased the southerly flow of the Mississippi, the sale today was expected to draw wealthy buyers from as far away as Kentucky; buyers with pockets full of cotton profits. Beatrice had never experienced a slave auction, nor had she ever been touched by any man except her master.

Unlike the women she was chained to, Beatrice had been born on the plantation. She was born a twin, but her father had shipped her sister to the auction when she was eleven years old because his wife accused the girl of stealing a necklace. After that day, she never saw her sister, Marietta, again. Today, it was her turn to experience what her sister and so many others repeatedly suffered: a demoralizing rite of passage reserved for American slaves, the act of *bringing a bid*.

Beatrice was startled by the pounding of the auctioneer's gavel, signifying the end of all inspections. It was time for the bidding and selling to begin. The treasure of the estate was up for sale first: the twenty-three repossessed male Negroes. They had been her father's most valuable possessions.

The male slaves entered the room. Beatrice had seen most of them from a distance, but she never knew they carried such value until that morning. They stood just as powerfully as prized workhorses. The males were the reason for the huge crowd. As Beatrice gazed at the crowd of well-dressed plantation owners, she couldn't help but notice how they seemed to salivate over the male slaves, but not so much over the females. No one even noticed her at all. Eight of the males were masters of their own sugar mills; none of the buyers cared about a half-white seamstress. The twenty-three black men were the stars of the show.

When they were first led into the room, all of the male slaves were dressed in black tuxedos, as if they were going to serve as butlers. Then, all of their clothing was removed. There they stood on the auction block completely naked, at an average height of six feet, two inches, with chiseled muscles and thick penises. The bidding for most of these males reached as high as 1,600 dollars each. The absence of whip scars made them even more valuable, as this was an indication of a well-mannered slave.

The bidding battle for the males went on for about two hours, as Beatrice watched the plantation owners place their highest bids in a forum of organized chaos. The most coveted Negro was a nineteen-year-old male who stood at six feet, four inches tall and weighed in at 225 pounds. This Negro was a skilled carpenter and had fathered eight children by three different women. He was bought for a final price of 1,900 dollars by an ecstatic bidder.

The auction of the male slaves seemed to be over as quickly as it had begun. Beatrice gasped for air when she realized the bidding had commenced on the females. The first woman sold for nine hundred dollars to a plantation owner from St. Charles Parish. The next two women were offered as a package deal because one of them was deaf and the other one was needed to help her communicate. They were sold together for 1,275 dollars.

The fourth female to hit the auction block was an absolute jewel. She'd just given birth to a set of twins with her first pregnancy. This attribute put her value close to that of the nineteen-year-old male. The bidding for her was nearly as intense as for the men, and lasted just as long. She sold for 1,650 dollars. Next up was Clarice.

When the auctioneer announced that she was a trained midwife, the bidding for her intensified. Beatrice watched as two men launched into an intense bidding war for the right to own Clarice. To Beatrice, the first bidder appeared just a cruel as Mason, but the second bidder appeared more polished and pleasant. He was clean-shaven and looked no more than thirty years old. The clean-shaven bidder won Clarice. Once the auctioneer announced she was sold, Clarice and Beatrice made eye contact. Clarice poked her tongue out at Beatrice, taunting her even as she stepped down off the block.

The next female in line was a young girl, about thirteen years old, who had already been impregnated by Benedict de Marigny. Pregnant slaves were often avoided because it could take as long as ten years to recoup a return on investment—not to mention they could die during childbirth. The pregnant female only brought a price of 465 dollars. The three elderly ladies were all sold together for 350 dollars, leaving Beatrice as the last girl connected to the twenty-four-foot chain. In desperation brought on by despair, her eyes scanned the crowd, hoping to see her father's face. Beatrice hung onto a thread of hope that he would reclaim her. That's when the auctioneer stopped the bidding to make an announcement.

"Gentlemen, I have to pause the bidding for one brief moment to allow the chairman of the board from New Orleans Canal & Banking Company to record a slave swap on the official record. It will just take a moment, so feel free to help yourself to some warm coffee."

Beatrice became instantly excited when she heard that someone was requesting a swap. She hoped in her heart to see her father step forward. She held onto her faith that her mistress had sent a rescue, if for no other reason than her talent as a seamstress. Her eyes frantically scanned the room in search of Mr. or Mrs. de Marigny, but there was no sign of either. Over by the banker's table, Beatrice noticed a fair-skinned black woman signing her name to a document.

"They talk to her eye to eye?" Beatrice whispered to herself.

The woman was impeccably dressed, just like Mrs. de Marigny, and was not accompanied by a master or overseer. She wore a bonnet with a partial veil that covered her face, along with matching gloves. She presented a folded sheet of paper to the auctioneer and was then allowed to move and speak freely throughout the auction. Beatrice could also tell the woman knew how to read, because she saw her examining the ledger of slaves who had been sold and the poster describing all the auction terms and conditions.

Moments later, all of Beatrice's questions were answered when the auctioneer called the bidders back to the floor.

"Thank you, gentlemen, for your patience while we resolve a swap from a New Orleans Canal & Banking Company sale that took place last week. Please let the record show that bidder number seventy-two, Harriett Green, a free woman of color, has requested to trade one of her male slaves, age eighteen, for two females around the same age. If any of you are interested, please step over to the banker's table where our notary officer, Felix Grima, will witness and certify the swap. The loan officer from the New Orleans Canal & Banking Company of Louisiana also has to sign off on the trade. Keeping all things in decency and order, I will approve the conditions of the transaction during the next break in bidding."

A plantation owner from New Iberia quickly expressed interest in the swap. Mason was already in possession of two females, who were locked away in a holding cell. Moments later, Mason returned from the cell escorting two fair-complexioned females. He handed the two women over to Harriett Green for inspection. One girl was about seventeen years old; the other appeared about two years younger. Both had the same skin tone as Beatrice. After the inspection, the swap was approved by J.L. Carpenter. Harriett Green delivered the male slave to Mason, and once the deeds exchanged hands, she quickly departed with her purchases.

It was now Beatrice's turn to hit the auction block. Without a word, Mason positioned her on the block, quickly unsnapping the buttons that fastened the top of her camp dress. He exposed her fifteen-year-old body from the waist up for all to see and judge in the worst way. Her skin flushed in the open air, bruising with each gust of wind. Her pores seized as if she had slipped into a frozen pond. Her quivering jaw chattered her teeth. She trembled uncontrollably.

Beatrice was afraid. Once again, she emptied her bladder right where she stood. She now fully accepted that she had gone from first among the slaves to the least of them in less than twenty-four hours. It was now her turn. As with the others, the auctioneer stood in front of Beatrice. He cleared his throat, raised his right hand over her head, and opened the floor for bids.

"We have this fifteen-year-old Negress who has not produced any children as of yet, but you know that can quickly change. Bidding starts at two hundred dollars. Can I get two hundred dollars for this light-skinned house Negress? She cooks. She cleans. She can sew a beautiful dress for your lovely wife. Can I get two hundred dollars?"

"My wife would throw me out of the house if I brought that half-white nigger home with me. I'll pass!" a bidder screamed out at the auctioneer as the crowd burst into laughter.

"Can I get two hundred dollars?" the auctioneer continued. He beckoned to Mason. "Hey, trader, would you strip all of her clothes off, so these kind gentlemen can see what they're getting? Maybe someone will buy her to keep their bed warm tonight."

Mason strutted over and ripped a huge tear down the lower back of her beautiful camp dress. Beatrice was mortified—and her dress was destroyed. From the rear, Mason held her arms behind her back, twisting her left to right, causing her small breasts to jiggle for the amusement of the bidders.

"There can't be enough milk in those tits for a cup of coffee," someone yelled out, bringing on another wave of laughter.

By saving her for last, the auctioneer had made her the laughingstock of the auction. The only bidder who did not look amused was the pleasant-faced man who had purchased Clarice. Beatrice lifted her head to make eye contact with him. She could see concern in his eyes; his face was as gentle as her father's. Unfortunately for Beatrice, the bidding ended—no one wanted her. While they had fought over the male slaves and the darker-skinned female slaves, the wealthy cotton plantation owners all rejected Beatrice. Some never even looked in her direction. With the conclusion of the comedic portion of the auction, the jovial bidders walked away from the auction block. Only one stayed behind.

"Back to the holding cell for you, half-breed!" Mason yelled at Beatrice in disgust.

"Let her be," the gentle-faced man called as he hurried over to the table where the banker sat. "I will give you one hundred dollars for her."

The banker scoffed and chuckled. "Sir, I appreciate the offer, but we plan to send her to Virginia. We can get at least three hundred dollars for this half-white Negress. But thank you for the offer." The banker stood, and he and the auctioneer turned to walk away.

"Then I will raise my bid to 150 dollars. That is my final offer to take her off your hands," the gentle-faced man yelled at their backs.

"She has no children and looks like she might not even survive the week-long wagon trip to Virginia. You will never get three hundred dollars for her, and you know it. I offer 150 dollars for this Negro woman. That is my final offer!"

The banker and the auctioneer came to a complete stop; they knew they had the man hooked with this last slave girl. The banker took another minute to check his bottom-line price. "I can't accept a bid of 150 dollars, but if you would consider paying me the asking price from the floor, then we have a deal."

"Just one moment." The gentle-faced man walked over to Beatrice.

There she stood, a demoralized female with her entire teenage body exposed, frostbitten, shivering, and weeping. Beatrice slowly raised her head once more, allowing her sandy blonde hair to fall back and reveal her dark blue eyes—as deep as the Atlantic Ocean, and just as wide.

"You have a face more deserving of a convent. Your eyes are like none I have ever seen, even in some of the most exclusive opera houses in France," the man whispered to Beatrice as she trembled.

Then he removed his cloak and draped it over Beatrice. The remaining warmth from his body that was trapped inside the wool felt like the arms of God had wrapped around her. In that fragile moment, Beatrice spoke to his soul, appealed to his decency, and pleaded for his compassion.

"B . . . buy me!" she said as another gust of wind burst

through the open doors of the auction house. *"Buy me, and I will serve you!"*

The gentle-faced bidder held true to his expression, and he smiled. "You have a deal," he told the banker, never once looking away from her eyes.

Once the transaction was complete, he placed Beatrice in the back of his cart along with Clarice. However, only Beatrice wore his cloak and gloves. Clarice had only the dingy ruffled dress to protect her from the cold. Beatrice didn't say a word to Clarice; the auction block had humbled her into silence.

On the way home, Beatrice's new owner stopped at a little cottage house on Royal Street and leaped off the wagon to tie up his horses. The cottage door opened and out came a female slave followed by five light-complexioned little girls, none of whom appeared older than six years old.

"At least oz out the sun," Clarice said

"All right, Clarice, you're getting off here. This is your new home, and Mable will help you clean up and get you into some warm clothes. I will drop by later this afternoon to speak with you."

Clarice obeyed and stepped down off the wagon. Beatrice lifted her head from inside the warm cloak long enough to see Clarice standing right below her, on the same side of the wagon. Gone were her smirk and the harsh words she'd spoken inside the holding cell. Gone was her short-lived arrogance. Gone was her sense that she was better than Beatrice. Their eyes met like two colliding weather fronts. A simple wool cloak and gloves demoted any sense of accomplishment felt by one woman—and re-established a sense of normalcy for the other.

"You will be his whore and nothing more! I will see you again, you heifer, you!" Clarice whispered. Then she followed Mable and the five children into the house on Royal Street, and the door closed behind them.

The man then climbed back aboard the wagon, and in less than five minutes, they arrived at his residence: a beautiful brick home in the middle of the French Quarter.

Beatrice was grateful. During the short ride from the auction house, she had resolved to serve her new master and his beautiful home for the rest of her life. Whatever he desired within the walls of 1005 St. Peter Street, Beatrice vowed to provide.

THE MASTER'S WIFE DIARY ENTRY ONE

November 20, 1835

Dear Diary,

Today was a horrible day—simply awful from the moment my husband arrived home, and it's only noon. My Lord, what have I done to deserve this? Today of all days, my husband returned from the market with a woman and presented the frail, trembling soul to me. This woman is not entirely Negro—she's closer to my complexion. Close as kin, but a little too close. She's a few years younger, but we're about the same height and weight. This is quite troubling to me, indeed.

Did I mention that she's very fair? Much lighter than any of the other servants who clean the house and much lighter than Delicia, who works in the kitchen. At first glance I thought my eyes had failed me in my youth—this Negro woman is nearly as white as I am. She's my assistant, he says, and a highly skilled seamstress. He says her talents are a gift to me. Imagine that! This girl he referred to as Beatrice will keep me adorned in beautiful gowns, he says, but all of it seems far-fetched considering the rags she was wearing today. If my husband desired to surprise me with a gift, he should have laid with me in the noon hour. It would be naive of me not to notice her beauty, which makes me feel very uneasy. My husband vowed to me that she is not a slave woman, but a servant he rescued from the auction. But why her, of all the Negresses in distress? Why her?

This new servant is different in ways that are uncomfortable, threatening, and imposing. How could a gift cause so much doubt? Am I wrong for wanting him to hire servants that all look the same? Preferably much older, like Lucille, my beloved nanny in Amite who cared for me as a child. Lord, please forgive this heart of mine, but I cannot suppress the truth of how I feel. I am deeply troubled by this . . . Beatrice. Like the unmerciful cold winds from the north, so is condition of my heart. I want to repent, but in this hour, I can't bear it.

Diary, I know I should pity her, but she doesn't resemble the other servants. I doubt if any of them could tempt my husband, but this Beatrice girl most certainly can, even if she lacks intent. My mother once warned that the origins of adultery are always innocent, but over time and with nurturing, they grow into something scandalous. I refuse to have my marriage become the subject of some salacious hearsay, printed on the back pages of *Le Pressee*. Not my life, not with my husband. How wretched are my thoughts, but is it not my duty to protect my perfect union? He is mine, and she cannot have him. I'm troubled terribly by the sight of her in my living room. This Beatrice has the kind of appearance that could attract attention from my husband, and deep down I feel it is very probable.

Though I harbor no ill feelings for the Negro people, we have never had servants in our home that possessed the same characteristics I possess; the same stature, the same build. My brown hair and eyes hardly compare to her blue eyes and sandy locks. I hate myself for feeling this way! I know I should welcome this girl with open arms and make her stay with us as comfortable as possible, yet I want her gone in the worst way. She's prettier than I am, I fear, even with weather-whipped skin and dressed in rags. Nevertheless, my husband says he loves me, and that should pacify all of my fears. Do you agree? At least I believe he loves me and only me, but I can't compare to Beatrice.

Woe is me . . .

CHAPTER 2

New Orleans
Current Day

Sherman and Brandon were seated at their favorite table at Café Du Monde, more interested in social media than the majestic scenery of midday New Orleans. Unlike the tourists who inhaled every nuance of Jackson Square, Sherman and his best buddy wanted one thing only—hot, sugary beignets. This world-renowned treat was like a donut on steroids: sizzling out of the fryer, then baptized in a tub of powdered sugar. The intoxicating aroma of something hot and sweet coerced everyone who walked by. After a brief investigation of the source, the passerby usually continued on their way with white bags filled with the heavenly delicacies.

Café Du Monde beignets were Sherman and Brandon's drug of choice.

The locals were known to eat beignets hot, within twelve feet of the cashier. Most sat around one of the street-side tables, where they could be serenaded by Richard the Sax Guy.

Sherman raised his head just for a moment to watch a couple swinging out to Richard's rendition of "Right Place Wrong Time" by Dr. John. The guy wore a crimson shirt and matching hat with

Roll Tide inscribed across the front. This couple—obviously from Alabama—was comprised of the kind of tourists that were bitter-sweet for the city. They were excellent because they traveled well with the team, but they were horrible if LSU lost. The trash talk after the games was always brutal. Last night, LSU had lost to Alabama, ten to three. The couple from Alabama was performing a two-step victory dance on the sidewalk while a few LSU fans tried their best to ignore them. The annual ridicule was a conse-quence of losing a football game in the South, and Alabama fans were legendary for being horrible winners.

"I still can't believe LSU dropped that game last night," Sherman said.

"What do you mean, you can't believe LSU lost that game? Have you forgotten we're grad students from Tulane? I couldn't care less," Brandon replied as his eyes reconnected with a music video on his cell phone.

"You're right, I never attended LSU, but I still wanted them to win. And besides, every time LSU loses to Alabama, their fans camp out until Monday! Go home, already!" Sherman sighed.

"That's your problem right there. You care about too many things."

"And you care too little about everything."

"I care about the things I should care about, but you're sit-ting here upset about a football game that didn't involve your alma mater! Who does that?"

"This entire state! The whole freaking country! Not to men-tion, my brothers are on the team. It's like the older you get, the more detached you get," Sherman retorted as he sent a call from his girlfriend to voicemail.

"Exactly, unlike you, Mister Carry-the-Cross," Brandon re-plied. "If it's not football, it's the unarmed black man who was shot by the police, then the location of the protest march, and the obsession with the backstory of the victim. Once that contro-versy dies, you emotionally attach to the next shooting victim—there is always another one—and then onto the next. After you run out of shooting victims, then it's politics and the hypocritical Republicans, and how you hate *Fox News*. It never ends with you. You will catch a heart attack before your twenty-seventh birthday . . ."

"Brandon, the difference between us is you live life on a lollipop stick, and I don't. There is more to life than rap beats and trying on one girl after another in search of the perfect fit."

"The fit matters!" Brandon laughed.

"Laugh now, Mr. Privileged, but when your little white bubble pops and life kicks in, I don't want to hear the whining." Sherman's eyes reconnected with his cell phone.

Brandon leaned across the table. "*White bubble? White bubble!* Sherman, you're black, and your skin is whiter than every member of my family. You attended a predominantly *white* high school, *white* Tulane, and you're dating my *white* sister. Your parents raised you in the *whitest* neighborhood on the Lakefront! The only time you step foot in a 'hood is when you visit your grandmother! On a daily basis, I interact with more black people."

"That's only because you have that recording studio and sell bullshit dreams of record deals, convincing a bunch of ninth-grade dropouts they can be the next Lil Wayne."

"Call it what you want, but I could knock on at least twenty doors in the Ninth Ward right now and enjoy a plate of beans. Can you say the same? I have real relationships with real people. When it comes to lily white, you're the *whitest* black dude I know . . ."

"Whatever." Sherman waved at Brandon dismissively.

Brandon continued. "Just because I haven't joined one of your fake Twitter revolutions doesn't mean I'm not aware. I'd rather focus on what I can control, and I have no control over the multitude of issues you care about."

"Because you're asleep at the wheel of life." Sherman shot him a look of pity.

". . . And you're suffering from Colin Kaepernick Syndrome."

"Colin Kaepernick . . . ? Because I'm standing up for social justice? Thanks for the compliment."

"It's not a compliment." Brandon's head shook in rebuke. "You just hatched out of an egg, now all of a sudden you hate America and the police?"

"I don't hate the police . . ."

"Well, I never hear you praise them for the good they do, either."

"It's hard to see the good because of the killing of unarmed African Americans."

Brandon's lips fluttered in exasperation. "Sherman there are nearly five-thousand police officers in this city. If they wanted to kill black people it would only take them until next Friday to do so. Dude. Stop blaming all cops for the actions of a few."

"Brandon, that's where you miss my point every time. I never said it was a Black Problem—it's an American crisis anytime an unarmed person is killed by the police. Race is irrelevant. Wake up."

Brandon smirked "You do know you've just lost this debate . . . don't you?"

"B, you have never beaten me in a debate . . . ever." Sherman chuckled.

The song was over, and the dancing Alabama couple returned to the table next to Brandon and Sherman. Sherman could tell Brandon took offense to being called Mr. Privileged, because the sides of his face and ears were as crimson as the hat worn by the Alabama fans. Sherman was equally bruised because he didn't appreciate Brandon's jab at him, but all of it was true.

His mother was an OB-GYN.

His father was an attorney and New Orleans councilman-at-large.

His parents immersed themselves in the least diverse communities in New Orleans, all in the name of adding diversity . . . but he was always the token black kid.

Brandon, on the other hand, was a musician, and more culturally in tune with New Orleans. In Brandon's world, race didn't matter because he was an artist, and artists only discriminated against those who lacked creativity. Nevertheless, Brandon's family had accumulated the kind of wealth that eluded any indication of vastness, otherwise known as old money. His last name was Fortier—as in Fortier International Shipping. His father, Steven Fortier III, was a fourth-generation CEO but looked more like the guy who sanitized the restrooms and stripped the floors at the end of a workday.

Sherman could tell Brandon was ready to end their lunch, but the reason for their meeting hadn't been discussed: the topic of their joint dissertation. Tomorrow was the deadline to notify Professor Davis, and they couldn't agree on a theme that would provide enough content to cover ninety-thousand words. If they failed to agree on a topic, they would miss the annual deadline and their doctorates in U.S. History would have to wait another year. Sherman couldn't wait another year. He was exhausted with his life as a professional student and desperately needed the distinction of being addressed as Dr. Campbell.

"How did we get on this subject anyway?" Sherman asked while ignoring another call from Ronelle Fortier.

"I can't remember. Poor memory is probably a side effect of living a privileged life," Brandon simmered.

"My bad . . . that blow was a little too low."

"A little? Bro, you know how much I hate being called privileged." Brandon pointed at himself. "Look at me, do I look rich?"

"No, B, but—"

Brandon cut him off. "My family is rich, but I'm trying to make my own name in this world. Privileged is when you can decide the path of your life. My mother dominates my world, and Ronelle's world. All of this money you think I have is controlled by Brenda Fortier, and the moment any of us veer off the path she has mapped out, we're cut off. So, you're right. I don't care about a lot because I'm not allowed to." Brandon reached for his backpack.

"My dad and your mom are one and the same. It's the type of tough talk all parents preach to their college-aged students to keep them focused."

"Did your dad add that clause to his will?" Brandon asked.

"Ummm . . . no. But he has said it . . . repeatedly."

"Well, my mother has that clause in her will. If I don't finish . . . *I better start selling CDs at the corner store because I will not see a dime.* Those are her exact words."

"Wow, B, you never expressed any of this before. I had no idea."

". . . You assumed my life was easier because of the Fortier fortune, but my mom will cut me off if I don't get this doctorate. So . . . let's pick an easy topic and knock out this dissertation so I can get on with my life as a producer."

"So, you've given up on the idea of teaching?"

"I can't say one hundred percent, but I have fallen in love with my music."

Like Brandon, Sherman had launched his own project that could benefit greatly from obtaining his doctorate. The previous year, he had launched a free genealogy website that allowed students to track their history based on a DNA profile. The website also provided students with a detailed historical breakdown of their family's journey to America in the form of a lecture from a college professor. After Sherman received an endorsement from the nation's largest homeschool network, the traffic on his site exploded. It was then that he started to dream of obtaining a regional accreditation and perhaps opening a charter school . . . but first, there was this issue of a dissertation.

"I got it. The elimination of race," Sherman suggested.

"Huh? What!"

"You just said it, about twenty minutes ago. I'm the *whitest black guy* you know. I hate rap and could listen to Nirvana twenty-four hours a day."

"I'm still not following you. How are we going to get ninety-thousand words out of Nirvana and Lil Wayne?"

"Brandon, that's just it. We simply tell a story, but we start from the early origins of our families. I hit it from the perspective of my family, and you do the same. We will then prove that race is no longer a valid identifier of who we are. Is it time for America to do away with black and white? Let's make that argument."

"Okay, I see where you're going. Don't like it, but I get it."

"B, you said it earlier, my skin is lighter than your entire family. How could that be? How did that happen? Why am I so pale when neither of my parents are Caucasian, and neither was my grandmother? The things that are commonly associated with being black are more embraced by you. *Does that make you black?* And your skin color is not exactly the color white.

The darkest person I know is not the color black. We are only considered black as compared to European skin tones. Is it time to do away with race and just identify as Americans? That is our dissertation."

"Sherman, my brother from another mother, if you take this topic to Professor Davis, he will chew us up and shit us out! The dude wrote textbooks called *Chronicles in Louisiana Black History* volumes one through fourteen! I don't think so! Nope! That topic would only bulk us down."

"But that's just it! We can produce something that would shake up the historical debate as it relates to race. I'm African American. You are European American. Most importantly, we are Americans. After we complete the ancestral overview of our families, then we lead off with the question, 'Do race classifications hinder racial acceptance?'"

"Sherm, I don't know about this one. I think we should focus on something less controversial. I want to hit this and quit it."

"And you will, I promise you. Conclude your research by showing how your parents didn't raise you to hate black people, how your sister and I can date without fear of me getting lynched. Do you see it? In the future, race will become obsolete. So why not start now? B . . . trust me on this, it will blow Professor Davis away."

"I can't see this working, but I'll sleep on it."

"No problem, but let's not reach for the low-hanging fruit. Let's write something that will land us on the *Today Show*!"

"Or land us on the news, shot up by some white-power skinheads," Brandon chuckled.

As they got up to leave the café, Brandon dropped some bills in the saxophonist's case while Sherman helped the Alabama couple by snapping a few photos to remember their trip by—all while Richard blew "We are Family" by Sister Sledge.

CHAPTER 3

After leaving Brandon, Sherman decided to pay a visit to his grandmother, Mrs. Susan Campbell. Her home was a traditional New Orleans shotgun house, with a cement porch and a green screen door. The houses were called "shotgun" because if you stood in the front doorway and fired a shotgun, the bullet would pass through the entire house without hitting a wall. In fact, shotgun homes in New Orleans were so perfectly aligned, neighbors could open their windows and walk from room to room in perfect step with one another.

Mrs. Campbell's home was elevated about three feet off the ground to reduce the risk of flooding, which worked quite well until Hurricane Katrina. Sherman's grandma and her next-door neighbor, Ms. Vera, were the type of Ninth Ward residents who wouldn't think of living anywhere else in the world—and they had been friends for well over fifty years. After Katrina, as soon as the city allowed residents to return, they wanted back into their homes.

Standing on the porch, Sherman heard a familiar tune; a song that revealed exactly where to find his grandmother. Through the front door, he listened as she fired back with answer after answer to Alex Trebek's questions. The second Sherman entered the living room, he spotted her seated in her favorite chair, watching one of her favorite television shows. After a moment, she noticed him.

"Puddin', that's you?"

"Yes, Grandma, it's me."

"Boy, you graduated yet?"

He kissed her on the cheek. "No, Grandma, I graduate this year." He braced for the upcoming comparison to his cousin Jynika.

"You sure? Because you have been over there a while. Jynika started after you and finished before you. Makes no sense to me, it don't." Sherman's grandmother stared at him sideways.

"Grandma, I promise, by this time next year I will be Dr. Campbell."

She giggled. "I sure hope it's before God calls me home."

". . . before God calls you home, I will graduate."

Inside his grandmother's renovated home, on every available wall space, were pictures of uncles, aunts, and cousins, as well as a memorial wall for all the deceased family members. Obituaries were squeezed securely into the picture frame of each photo. His grandma took great pride in those obituaries.

Susan Campbell's meticulous care of her household items spilled over to her furniture. And yes, the sofas still had the plastic covers on all the seats and armrests. The grandkids all joked about the age of her sofa and loveseat. Though the material under the plastic had long since shown normal wear and tear, she cherished every piece as if it were a historic antique, fitting enough for a museum display.

"Grandma . . . I have a few questions for you."

"Well, you gonna have to wait . . . the Final Jeopardy is coming up."

"Okay, Grandma."

Sherman sat quietly while his grandmother watched her favorite show, but he could still hear Brandon's voice. *You're whiter than my entire family*. Today was the first time he noticed just how much his grandmother resembled an elderly Caucasian woman, with her frail mocha skin that hung off the back of her arms and her partly cloudy blue eyes. The white hair at the base of her scalp moved liked fog toward the dyed sections and slowly swept across her eyebrows. She wore pink cat-eye frames that sat on the tip of her nose while she peered over the top to watch television.

Sherman noticed another missed call from Ronelle, followed by a text, but it was time for the Final Jeopardy answer.

In 1934, the lease for this place was increased to 4,085 dollars per year. Since 1959, the checks have not been cashed.

"What is Guantanamo?" Mrs. Campbell answered before the TV contestants. "I was cooking at the Woolworth's back then, and the cafeteria manager, Mrs. Emma Gene, her son was sent to that base. Just about every woman in the cafeteria had a son in the service back then." With another *Jeopardy* victory under her belt, she giggled her way to the kitchen.

"Ya ate?" she asked.

"I had some hot beignets at Café Du Monde, but you can pack me a plate, please."

"Puddin', you keep on eating those greasy beignets, you gonna fall out with a heart attack like Mr. Benson next door. He worked down there and ate four of those grease balls every morning. It caught up with him. It's going to catch you, too. Better start eating grits again and leave those beignets alone. You hear me?"

"Yes, Grandma, but I'm addicted now."

"Well, you better get addicted to some grits and eggs! Grits ain't never gave nobody a heart attack. I eat grits every day, and I am . . ."

". . . ninety-four years old."

"That's right. Ninety-four years young, and I thank the Good Lord first and grits second." His grandmother was very proud of her longevity.

"Okay, Grandma, I'll lay off the beignets if you answer a question for me."

"A question about what?"

"Brandon and I decided, for our final assignment, to research our families, to learn more about our ancestors. I figured the best place to start was here . . . with you. What can you share about Big Mama?"

Mrs. Campbell turned from the kitchen sink and took a seat

at the table. She had very few wrinkles on her face for a woman in her nineties—only the frailness that hung off her arms. Her dentures featured two solid gold teeth in the upper corners of her mouth; custom dental work she often referred to as her "fancy teeth."

"Something like what, Puddin'? You already know all there is to know."

As her arms folded on the table, Sherman immediately noticed her confused expression and saw that his window of opportunity was slowly closing. "What I mean is, do you remember much about your mother? Did she share any stories with you about her father?"

Grandma leaned back in her chair to reflect. It was then that Sherman decided it was the right time to bring out the old photo book and obituaries she hid in a not-so-secret place: her cherry oak-stained chifforobe. Sherman returned to the kitchen table and slid his chair next to his grandmother's. After sifting through decades of family memories, he stumbled upon a time-worn cardboard photo of a teenage girl. The girl stood next to two ladies, but only one of the ladies held the girl's hand. The woman holding the girl's hand in the photo appeared to be in her mid-forties. The other lady was elderly; in her seventies, at the very least. Written on the back of the picture was: *1929 Mc-Donogh 35 High School Graduation.*

"Grandma, who are the women in this photo?"

"Well, let me see here. Look at that." Her hand covered her lips. "I have not seen this one in years."

"So, you remember this picture?"

"Oh, yes, good Lord God—"

She stopped in mid-sentence as if a ghost had entered the kitchen and sat beside them at the table. From that moment on, she stared at the photo, holding it high as she looked over her glasses. The photo was so old it was faded beige, and it seemed to hold his grandmother suspended in time—as if someone in the picture was speaking on a frequency only she could detect.

Sherman knew the journey to discover the history of his family was going to start with the two women in that photo. He also knew the more he probed, the less Grandma would reveal. She was a woman who talked from the time her guests entered the door until it was time to for them to leave—the type of host that walked her visitors to their cars carrying plates of food wrapped tightly in love. But one of the women in this photo had rendered her speechless.

"Grandma, who are the women in this photo?"

She finally looked down through the lenses of her glasses. "The woman holding my hand is my mother, Momma Glenda."

"And who is the other beautiful lady?"

"That is my dear grandma. I made a promise to her many years ago, a promise I have kept until this day. She was so fair and beautiful. Terrible times those were for those who didn't fit in nowhere. She was too colored for the white folk and too white for the colored. Such terrible times, Puddin'." Mrs. Campbell turned from the table and stretched her back until she was upright.

Silence. Avoidance. Disconnect.

Sadness engulfed her as she twirled in a memory that was hidden far away, a time-stamped moment that was locked away deep in her soul. Mrs. Campbell returned to her place of solace, the area of the house where she sang old spirituals—healings songs that helped her cope. At the kitchen sink, she descended into a tearful song, "I Won't Complain," as she washed a few pots. Once she finished the remaining dishes, she prepared Sherman a plate of mustard greens and cornbread, wrapped it in aluminum foil, and placed it in front of him. Sherman knew the interview was over, but he tried for one more question.

"Grandma, did your mom happen to tell you where she lived as a child?"

"Yes she did, Puddin', down in the Quarter on Burgundy Street, then she moved to St. Peter."

The singing continued, but it was now louder and more sorrowful. With his plate in hand, Sherman followed his grandmother back to the front of her shotgun home where she returned to her chair, just in time for the five o'clock news.

"Puddin' . . . you put my photo album back in my chifforobe?"

"Yes, Grandma," he said as he kissed her on the cheek.

"Tell your daddy to call me."

"I will, Grandma. I love you."

"I love you too, Puddin'."

Another missed call from Ronelle.

The Fortier estate was a far cry from Sherman's grand-mother's house. It sprawled through a Garden District community that boasted beautiful, bold residences, and it was one of the most beautifully restored Victorian mansions in New Orleans. Yet, it was completely gated from adoring eyes. This house was the residence of Steven Fortier III, his wife, Brenda, their son, Brandon, and their daughter, Ronelle—the angry one who had been trying to reach Sherman for most of the day.

Ronelle loved everything about Sherman except his inconsiderate nature and forgetfulness. She also hated that he was a repeat offender of the worst kind—quick to throw himself at the mercy of the court only to repeat the same crime three months later.

Sitting on the living room sofa in a pair of dark purple dance tights, she hid her angry eyes behind a curtain of naturally blonde hair. Today was the second time this week her boyfriend had pulled a disappearing act until the end of the day. From the corner of her eye, she watched the kitchen door swing open. Her brother entered the house reciting rap lyrics—an annoying habit that always disturbed the peace of the entire home. Brandon whizzed through the kitchen and made his way to the refrigerator.

"Hey, sis. I didn't know you were home. What's good with you?"

"I've been trying to reach Sherman all afternoon," she said from behind her blonde veil. "Have you seen him?"

Brandon spoke into the fridge. "We had a late lunch today at Café Du Monde, but I haven't seen him since."

"Hmm . . . interesting."

"We had a meeting about the topic for our dissertation, which hopefully we can complete before the next presidential election."

"Is that right? So, what did you settle on?"

"I don't think you want to know. I still can't believe that I'm considering it."

"Well, what is it?"

"We decided to tell a story tracing the history of our families, and ultimately make the argument that racial classification is irrelevant."

"Ha! Good luck with that."

"I know, right?"

"Seriously, if you go with that topic you're never going to finish," Ronelle warned.

"Yeah, we've got our work cut out if I can't convince him to go a different route," Brandon said with a mouth full of grilled chicken breast.

". . . but why do a joint dissertation? Why not go at it alone?"

"Because Professor Davis has a big thing about collaborative research and how scholars produce better results when they work in groups. Beats the hell out of having to write ninety-thousand words by myself."

Ronelle was only half-listening to Brandon as she redialed Sherman's number. The call went straight to voicemail. "I'm going to kill him."

"Come on, Ronelle, you know if he hasn't answered you, it means he's in the middle of a heated discussion. Sherman is an attorney trapped in a teacher's body, but he's in denial."

Ronelle called again and decided to leave a message. "You had better be kidnapped, hogtied, and stuffed into the trunk of a car. Otherwise, I will kill you for ignoring me all day." She tossed her phone aside in a huff.

THE MASTER'S WIFE DIARY ENTRY TWO

January 12, 1843

Dear Diary,

In the morning I depart for Amite to spend a few days with my mother. I have received word she is a touch under the weather. I miss her terribly. I'm still without child, but not due to any lack of effort on my part. I labor with all my might to please my husband, but it is my husband who lacks the passion and desire for me, his beloved wife. When we make love at night, it's over before our lips touch. Some nights he rolls away without a kiss. The emptiness is dreadful. Then there are the restless nights that are only salved after he takes a long walk alone through those feverish roads in the *Vieux Carré*. His restless nights have become more frequent, and more confusing to me. He is becoming increasingly distant.

What has made my husband so anxious?

What would make him desire me more?

I crave him so. I have even tried to take on the likeness of a brothel girl—I even had Beatrice make me a few seductive garments—but his eyes are blind to me. He commits little effort to pleasing me. Maybe this short time away will cause him to miss me? Maybe when I return he will throw me over his shoulder, like he did in the weeks after our wedding, and make love to me all night? Oh, Diary, these are the things I share with only you, because these are the things that trouble me most.

I pray for better thoughts to record in my next entry. Hopefully, my next entry comes after a night filled with unquenchable passion.

Sincerely,

Submissive & Lonely

CHAPTER 4

Sherman quickly parked and hurdled over the three steps that led to Ronelle's front door. Before his knuckles could make contact, the door swung open. Her eyes tightened and glowed like two coals plucked from under a grill, her lips were thin and hidden, her breathing slow and heavy. There they stood, face-to-face, close enough to kiss, but he was smart enough not to try. Only then did he notice she was dressed to go out without him.

Ronelle tried to step around him, but he blocked her path. He lowered his eyes and fixed his gaze on her red heels with rose-painted toenails, her blue jeans shrink-wrapped around her every curve, her white blouse that struggled to conceal her cleavage, and her full lips that matched her heels. The fragrance that escaped from under her red leather jacket was Marc Jacobs Decadence, one of the gifts he had given her last month for her birthday.

"Where do you think you're going without me, *Mrs. Campbell?*" he joked.

"Well, first of all," she whipped her hair to the left side of her shoulder, "I don't see a ring on this finger."

"I know you're angry, but . . ."

"I'm asking you politely—please step aside. I have plans."

She tried to waltz around him again, but he held her arm.

"I know I missed a few of your calls, but . . ."

"A few?"

"Ronelle . . . I was headed here once I was done."

"I see, so I should've waited for the most convenient time for you?"

"Ronelle, I didn't say that."

"I get it now . . . I'm something convenient—"

"I didn't say that."

"You didn't have to."

"Look, I'm sorry. I know I should have called you back sooner, but the day got away from me."

She tried to free her arm. "Sherman, I can understand if you're too busy to text me back . . . I get that. I can understand if you're too busy to call me back . . . it happens. And even though it makes me angry when you forget our plans, I understand you're busy."

Sherman looked up and studied his girlfriend's face. She appeared empathetic.

"Baby, thank you for understanding. I was just caught up in this new project we're—"

"I am not finished."

"I'm sorry. Please continue."

"Sherman, sweetheart," she murmured, "I can understand your life is too busy for me. So, when you happen to see me with someone else, I hope you are . . . just as understanding."

Ronelle pulled away from his grip, hurried in a straight line to her white BMW convertible Roadster, and backed out of the driveway. For the first time that day, Sherman tried to call her, but the call went to voicemail on the first ring. As Sherman watched her car disappear into the darkness between the streetlights, only then did he accept responsibility for another argument. Turning to leave the porch, he looked down and noticed two white pieces of paper—two reminders of why Ronelle was so angry.

I can't believe I did it again.

Ronelle had purchased two tickets, fourth-row center, for a performance of *Ain't Misbehavin'*, a musical she had waited eight months to see at the Mahalia Jackson Theatre. The show had started an hour ago.

CHAPTER 5

With a chilled glass of red wine elevated in her left hand, she turned the familiar pages of *Gone with the Wind* as if for the first time, trapped in an antebellum fantasy she wished would never end. Brenda Fortier was every bit the upscale New Orleans socialite, obsessed with days gone by, possessive of everything old and nostalgic. She was a symbol of wealth and had many affluent friends, but her children deliberately rejected her tastes and sentiments.

She lounged on the living room sofa as though she were waiting for a photographer to adjust the lighting. Her short black hair appeared freshly feathered to the left, and the makeup she'd applied that morning remained flawless. But there was no photo shoot; she was just Brandon and Ronelle's mom, Mrs. Fortier until the curtain closed on the day. The pores on her face never had a day to breathe or a cream-free night, and the few wrinkles around the corners of her eyes were constantly harassed by smoothing serums. What Nancy Reagan was to the White House, Brenda was to the Fortier home—she acted in a First Lady role she relished and wore like a crown.

Though her children were born with the proverbial silver spoon, in her mind, they were rebellious. She couldn't stomach how Brandon submerged himself in rap music twelve hours a day, or how her daughter enjoyed a blended culture of Broadway and pop but rejected the rules of her society. In Brenda's society, all the participants matched in class, wealth, and lineage. It was an elusive clique in which every unspoken governing facet was adhered to verse after verse according to a doctrine of regional elitism, a bleached social order.

It wasn't advertised, but *white only* was implied. Those who cried foul were condemned as progressive liberals who sought to destroy Brenda's way of life, a way of life she fought to preserve. Her daughter, on the other hand, was more of a hippie as far as the diversity of her closest friends, the places she chose to hang out, and her relaxed points of view. Fueling Brenda's outrage was Sherman, a source of endless arguments between her and Ronelle. The more she protested their relationship, the tighter her daughter clung to him—a black man.

She had exhausted every controlling tactic in her arsenal to keep her daughter's relationship with Sherman from flourishing, but it had all been in vain. Ronelle was madly in love, and Brenda was madly in opposition. Her daughter's feelings for Sherman were the crisis of her life, and of far greater urgency than Brandon's dreams of owning a record label. *Maybe she will grow tired of him*, Brenda mused as she took another sip.

A little before midnight, Ronelle entered the front door, causing Brenda's eyes to rise from Margret Mitchell's novel and greet her only daughter.

"Why are you still up, Mom?" Ronelle said as she dropped her purse on the kitchen table. "I sure hope Dad didn't eat my gelato."

"How was your night out with the girls?"

"About the same." She searched the freezer from shelf to shelf. "We decided to meet at Port of Call Bar and sip the night away." Ronelle finally spotted the gelato behind a bag of frozen asparagus.

"Any . . . cute guys tonight?" Brenda hoped.

Ronelle blew a lock of hair from her eyes. "No, Mother, nor am I available." She plopped down on the sofa.

"But you are . . . available."

"No, I'm not." She licked her spoon. "My night out was just like any other night out. We complained about *our* boyfriends . . . typical girl stuff."

Brenda sat up. "Since you mentioned boyfriends," she bookmarked her novel, "have you ever considered that the reason you're having so many problems with Sherman is because you're not compatible? I mean, he does . . ."

"Mom, not now."

"Ronelle, it's just a thought."

"Our issues aren't any greater than those of my friends and their *white* boyfriends."

"Ronelle, I never said anything about race."

"I know you." Ronelle stood. "Goodnight, Mom."

"But you just got here. Don't go. Sit and talk to me."

"Tomorrow. I'm tired. After I devour this gelato, I'm going to bed."

"Why is it every time I mention his name, you run away?" Brenda stood. "Why is it we can discuss every little thing in your life except this temporary relationship you've developed?"

Ronelle scooped up her dessert. "Because you have made up your mind about Sherman, and that will never change. You don't like him. I get it. The good news is, I'm twenty-five years old. No parental consent required. The minor issues I have with my boyfriend are my problems to sort out."

"But you do know that is all this will ever be . . . right? Just boyfriend and girlfriend?" Brenda said in a concerned voice. "You're at the age where I would prefer you to think about your future, and I don't see Sherman in your future."

"And I don't need a psychic friend . . . just my mom." She kissed Brenda on her cheek. "Goodnight, Mommy. Enjoy Scarlett and Rhett."

"Goodnight, darling. Enjoy your anger food," Brenda snapped.

Once Ronelle's bedroom door closed, Brenda settled back into the couch, curled her legs underneath her, and sighed. "I will find a way to break up this thing she has with Sherman," she whispered to herself as she sipped her wine. "This has gone on long enough."

CHAPTER 6

October 6, 1842
1005 St. Peter St, New Orleans
10:30 p.m.

B eatrice paced back and forth in the throes of unrelenting labor, gaining no relief from holding her womb,
nor any comfort from constant deep breaths. The
birthing quarters was a room that lacked any décor or warmth.

Nothing to see on the walls.

Nothing to see on the floor.

A rotted oak table, covered with a white cotton sheet, served
as the birthing table. At the foot of her bed, alongside the wall, a
wooden chest was stocked with clean rags and blankets. To the
left of the chest was a large pot, covered with rust on the outside,
filled to the top with soapy water. On top of the chest were herbs
and healing oils; a thick cloud of fresh cloves hovered above her
nose. Only one window allowed a view into the courtyard; on
the other end of the yard was the green screen door that led to
the kitchen. Above the birthing quarters was the room where Beatrice slept—a room with four windows and fresh air—but the
air in the birthing quarters was stale, like a closet packed with
old clothes.

The attending midwife was named Delia; a woman about seventy years old. The skin on her face was pulled tight like plastic. She had perfectly white teeth, a caramel complexion, and hair that looked like it had been doused with flour. She walked slightly bent over from a herniated spine, but age had yet to rob her of strength. Delia was also the primary cook when she wasn't delivering babies. The skin on her arms was paper-thin and revealed protruding biceps. She rocked babies to sleep for a living, carried her own water pots, mashed her own potatoes, and manhandled fifty-pound sacks of wheat like they were pillows. Her dress wasn't quite white but far from beige; more or less the color of eggshells. Hers was the type of dress worn by old housemaids; it completely covered her feet and swayed left to right as she moved about, like a large bell without the clapper. In between hymns, she glided gracefully around the room, awaiting the baby.

The servants all called her Momma. She was a labor and delivery specialist, an age-old expert in childbirth. Academically illiterate, yet still an expert. She was also a slave owned by the same man who had purchased Beatrice. Delia had been a gift to her master as part of his inheritance. She had been a little over sixty years old when she first arrived at her current residence, 1005 St. Peter Street.

Over the course of her career, the old midwife had delivered more than two hundred babies, including two of her own on the floor in the middle of the night. Delia was a master at her craft who synchronized her urgency in perfect alignment with the threshold of her patient's pain.

Suddenly, Beatrice could no longer walk. The pain would not allow her to take another step. She had just hit that threshold. Instinctively, Delia placed her on the rotted birthing table.

"Lord, let it be a boy child. Don't give me no mo' girls," Beatrice gasped as the contraction briefly subsided.

Suddenly the baby slid into its lowest position of the night. The loudest scream of the evening quickly followed. Beatrice's face was drenched with sweat and tears. She prayed that a cool breeze would visit through the lone window to rescue her from the cloying tropical heat, but the air that entered was the breath of Satan, both foul and relentless. None of this seemed to bother the old midwife as she instinctively got into position and prepared to receive another baby in her soft, padded hands.

Delia tried to distract Beatrice from her pain. "Do you think it's a boy child dis time?"

"Momma, I pray to God for a boy, but God keeps makin' girls," Beatrice replied, struggling to control her breath.

"Good Lawd will give what you need . . . not what cha want."

Another wave of contractions. *"Oh, Lawd! Help me, Lawd! Help me!"*

"Beatrice, you know what to do now. Start pushin' it on down." Delia placed her steady hands inside of Beatrice's thighs.

"It hurts so bad . . ."

"Beatrice, I can see the head. Do yo' part and push."

"That's all I got, Momma. I can't."

"Don't you quit. Push some mo'!"

Beatrice took a deep breath and pushed with all her might until the baby's head appeared up to the neck. Then she collapsed from exhaustion. In a swift, single motion, Delia leaned over her and pressed down on her stomach, right below the ribcage.

"Dis baby is stuck! If you don't push, the baby will die in your womb. Push, I tell you . . . push!"

With a sudden gust of determination and strength, Beatrice pushed with all her might, causing her baby to make a slow entrance into the world. As Beatrice lay on the sweat-soaked bed, panting for air, she heard Delia mumble dreadful words as she cut the umbilical cord.

"Look at all dat pretty hair on her head."

Beatrice's hands covered her face. "Lord, no! *Not another girl.*"

"Yes, it is a girl. And a fat one, too."

"I didn't want another girl."

"Beatrice, she is still a blessin'. She's beautiful, let that bring you some joy. Rejoice, Beatrice. She has all her toes and two blue eyes."

"But Momma, I didn't . . ."

"But nothin'! Go on and give praise for a mighty fine baby,

and let God worry 'bout the rest."

"Yes, ma'am."

"I done cleaned a many chilluns' in my day, many like us and a few like them. None of them chillun' knew nothing 'bout this world 'cept what we teach 'em. Just figured if we taught all the white ones to love, the world be better off for us colored folk. White babies never care what color a tit is, long as it has warm milk. Yes indeed, one day the good Lord gon' deliver us free, and then deliver us from color. One day, I believe that."

After the midwife cleaned and prepped the infant, she walked alongside the bed and gently handed her to Beatrice.

"Sweet Jesus!" Beatrice murmured in a voice soaked with tears. "She mighty fine, mighty fine indeed. And look at all that hair. A whole head of hair."

Then her smile turned down toward her chest. The moment the thought entered her mind, she knew what was about to happen next. It had happened four times prior, like four simultaneous hurricanes. The realization that it was happening again caused her to hide her baby beneath her breast. Every slave in the house had a particular talent and skill set that made them valuable to the master. Beatrice's talent was giving birth to healthy, light-skinned girls, and in the seven years since he purchased her, she had adjusted well to her role.

Beatrice was his *plaçage* without the freedom of mobility.

His whore without compensation for services rendered.

His fancy girl purchased at a discount.

His lady friend without the flowers.

His property.

Unfortunately for Beatrice, her master had discovered a niche market for half-white girls known as quadroons, and Beatrice possessed the perfect gene pool for his new venture. Beatrice's fertility added to his wealth. Her reward for producing healthy babies was extra clothing handed down from his wife, as well as fewer chores than the maids. Nonetheless, her job was to remain pregnant with every passing season. Like a prized heifer, she was a slave to the expectations of her master: *produce a child every other year*. This year she was exceptionally profitable for him. The baby Delia delivered was Beatrice's second of the year.

The only perk she enjoyed was the weekly opportunity to attend a church service of her choosing, unaccompanied by an overseer. All day on Sunday until about four o'clock, she would visit the religious assemblies of the *Gens De Couleur Libres* (freed people of color) in a section of town known as Congo Square. There, she was able to worship, interact with other women who were forced into her lifestyle, or simply sit and listen to the bongos that filled the air. Congo Square gave Beatrice her only glimpse into her stolen heritage, and it also served as her happy place.

It never got any easier, and today was even harder than her other five pregnancies because she had prayed night and day for a boy. Her master had allowed Beatrice to keep her twins, Timothy and Lawrence, because male slaves were treasured, but not her daughters. Right after birth, sometimes within the first twenty minutes—before she could nurse—the one she hated would appear.

On cue, a woman stuck her head through the birthing room window. Delia turned to acknowledge her presence. A black headscarf matched the top of her black dress. Her eyes were bloodshot red, her skin was like hot tea, and she spoke in a deep, raspy voice.

"Dat half-white bitch had dat baby yet?" the woman asked.

"Yes, she done had it," Delia replied.

"Well, what she got?"

"Anotha girl," Delia replied as she walked alongside the bed. "Beatrice, you know I hate to do it, but we have to hand her over to Clarice."

"But so soon?"

"If it were up to me, she would never leave your arms, but Clarice is here. Go on and kiss her one mo' time," Delia said.

Beatrice tried to hide her baby as she turned toward the window.

"Can I have a little more time with her, please? Massa don't even know I had her yet so he ain't expecting no baby right now anyways. I'll be right here, *Clayrice.* Can I hold her a little while? Please?"

"No! Why would I do anything for you? I'm here to take this baby back with me, as Massa tell me to. I work fo' him, not you. I have to nurse this one and one otherin. Delia, you wrap that baby, so I can go," Clarice yelled.

"No! No! Just a little while's all I ask. Please don't take her. Let me nurse my baby. Just this once."

"White heifer, is you hard of hearin'? I am tired of fiddlin' around with you." Clarice reached into the room. "Delia, if I have to come in there none of you gon' like it. Hand over that baby, so I can get on back to the house."

Beatrice realized Clarice would not grant her wish, so she pressed her lips against the head of her baby until Delia lifted the newborn from her arms.

"I's so, so sorry, but Beatrice, yo' baby got to go with Clayrice," Delia said.

The pain Beatrice felt was like someone had peeled away her skin like an orange and taken huge bites. Just like that, another baby was ripped out of her arms and thrown into to an evil system that determined occupation according to the pigment of one's skin. The day should have been celebratory, with family and friends gathered around a precious newborn. Instead, Beatrice was left with the afterbirth from a child she kissed only once. Clarice vanished, her daughter was gone, but her broken heart remained.

"I wish my skin was as dark as the others, then Massa wouldn't lay with me. At least the others get to nurse they own babies," Beatrice sobbed aloud as Delia applied the healing herbs and cloves. "With Massa blessin', the others have the grace to fall in love and to marry who they loved, even if it was just for a little while. Why not me, Lawd? Why not me?" she cried.

"The Lord will make this right somehow; I know in my heart he will." Delia wiped her own tears as she wiped Beatrice's womb.

Beatrice cursed the day she was born with Caucasian skin, sandy blonde hair, and blue eyes. She wanted to trade it all— even the handed-down gowns and her private bedroom—just to be dark like the maids who cleaned the house and washed the clothes. Suddenly, a smile appeared as a ray of light and cleared the clouds from her face.

"I name my baby Alaina, no matter what they call her, and Momma, even if i have to run away and crawl on my knees through the swamp, I will see my daughters again."

CHAPTER 7

For the Saints vs. Atlanta game each year, Brandon's father hosted a huge tailgating event for the off-duty workers from Fortier Lines, an annual warehouse party that lasted well into the night. It was Brandon's job to provide the music and assist with the seafood boil. This was his tenth year, and his participation was mandatory. As Brandon poured out the last batch of crawfish, he received an incoming call from Sherman just as a group from the Fortier office in Atlanta arrived. The Saints fans quickly surrounded the guests.

Who dat! Who dat! Who dat say they gonna beat dem SAINTS?

"B! Don't tell me you're at the Saints game with all the work we have to do. Come on, man!" Sherman complained.

"Hey! I never told you I was going to work on a dissertation every single day without enjoying some of my life. And besides, this is my dad's event." Brandon set the empty boiling pot to the side. "My only question for you is what time are you coming out to enjoy all this good tailgating, bro?"

"I couldn't join you if I wanted to," Sherman yelled into the phone. "Brandon, we have less than eight weeks to get this first draft to Professor Davis."

"Dude, when you were fighting the powers that be, I didn't bother you . . ."

"Whatever, Brandon," Sherman huffed. "How many words have you written thus far?"

"What kind of question is that?"

". . . how many words have you written?" Sherman demanded to know.

"Bro . . . we just settled on a topic the other day."

"That's my point. You know the direction we're headed, but you have yet to type a single word."

"Sherm, you are blowing my high, so I'm ending this call."

"Brandon . . . go finish fuckin' off and give me a call when you're ready to work."

Just as Brandon ended the call, his dad walked over with a drink that appeared to be in a forty-ounce bottle. "Since when do you drink malt liquor, Dad?" Brandon asked, laughing at his father's attempt to fit in with his crew.

"One of my guys reached into his chest and handed me this beer. It's pretty darn good, ha, ha, ha!" His dad took a swig from the bottle.

"Dad, the other day I asked you to dig up some juicy details about our family. I'm not trying to be pushy, but Sherman is on my case big-time. He thinks I'm goofing off."

"For what it's worth I did look into it, but there's not a whole lot outside of the info in your grandfather's estate registry."

"I'm doom . . ."

"Although I did discover there was a really bad warehouse fire in 1862. Union soldiers started it. They accused your great-great-granddad of financing the Confederate Army, which led to them commandeering our docks and burning everything else to the ground."

"Well, was he guilty of helping the Confederacy?" Finally, his dad had delivered a starting point for his dissertation. "Dad give me the whole truth and nothing but the truth . . . I can handle it."

"Unfortunately, that part of our past is true. It was the custom of the day to support the home team, and the Confederate

Army was our home team. Is it something I am proud of? Hell, no, but it is a fact of history that played out in our family. Since then we have gone far beyond to correct a wrong that none of us had anything to do with," Steven Fortier explained.

"I appreciate it when you trust me with details. I never knew our family had a controversial history, but let me ask you this, Dad. In your honest opinion, was Bernard Fortier a racist?"

Steven took a swig out of the Old English forty-ounce liquor bottle. He closed his eyes in search of the correct words to say.

"I would say yes and no. Here's why. On the one hand, he went along with the slave culture of the day, but on the other, he never owned slaves. He had the means to own slaves, but never took advantage of that opportunity. That much I know for sure. He did, however, employ a lot of Irish immigrants that he paid right above slave labor rates, but that too was the custom of the day. I don't think you will find any other juicy details outside of that, son. Now, I need to get back to the crew."

Brandon could tell his dad didn't want to spend his NFL Sunday talking about the Confederacy and slaves, so he tried to sneak in one last question before letting him off the hook.

"Can you confirm that Fortier Lines has never imported slaves?"

"Brandon, I can say with all certainty that we have never imported a slave! I have bills of landing in our archives that date back to 1820 when Fortier Lines first set sail, and no human cargo was ever recorded. There would've been no reason to hide it at the time or lie about it, because human cargo was a routine occurrence. That concludes this interrogation. I'm going hang out with my guys, they only care about the game and beer."

"All right, Dad, I didn't mean to disturb your forty-ounce, but thanks again for being honest with me. I plan to check out the archives in the morning. Where should I start digging to get more information on that warehouse fire?"

"Go see Mrs. Jacques. She'll provide you with all the details."

As his father turned away to rejoin the party, Brandon felt for the first time that he wouldn't have much to contribute to this paper other than a warehouse fire. Nevertheless, he had to tell the whole story, regardless of its blandness.

"We dat! We dat say we're gonna beat them Saints!" the Falcons fans chanted.

Brandon knew in that moment it was going to take a lot of creative writing to keep his side of the story interesting, and it was a good thing he had his sister. Ronelle had a Master of Fine Arts degree in Creative Writing and could bring any topic to life, so he figured this was a good time to tag her in. He took out his phone and dialed her number.

"Hey, sis, I need to ask you for a small favor right quick. You have a minute?"

"Depending on what it is," Ronelle replied.

"I was wondering if you could help me put some spin on our family's past for this dissertation?"

"So, in other words, you're asking me to write the paper *for* you?

"Not exactly."

Click.

"Hello? Ronelle? Hello?"

On Sundays, it was a tradition in the Campbell family to meet at Grandma's house for oven-baked ribs and Saints football—every week Sherman set a goal to arrive before his father. Melvin Campbell could devour an entire pan of ribs like a caveman, leaving Sherman a few scoops of potato salad and a slice of cornbread. As Sherman parked, he noticed his father's car arriving at the same time, along with vehicles belonging to several other family members.

"Hey, hey, hey, everybody, whatcha say?" his dad shouted out as he made his entrance, followed by Sherman.

"Melvin you ain't shit!" a voice yelled out. It was his Uncle Clarence. His dad and uncle typically greeted each other with insults of affection.

"And who invited your drunk ass?" Melvin snapped back.

"Oh, it's the big-time councilman and son," his cousin An-

NINE NOTCHES / 63

thony said.

"I saw your monkey-ass on TV last night, looking just like Daddy with that fat head," Clarence roasted.

"Hope you greedy bums didn't eat up everything, the ribs were a secret." His dad started the procession of hugs.

"You know the rule in this family . . . sleep late, you lose weight," Clarence replied as the room burst into laughter.

Sherman found his grandmother in the kitchen and went over to give her a kiss. He noticed her mood toward him was dry, but he still wrapped his arms around her and squeezed.

"Boy, you're going to squeeze the wind out of my little lungs," she laughed.

"I can't help it . . . I love my granny so much." He held her until she pulled away.

"I love you, too. Yank that pan of ribs out the oven, Puddin'."

"Yes, ma'am, I got it."

His dad made his way to the kitchen after hugging and kissing every family member in the house, as was the Campbell custom. If you failed to acknowledge one person, you could spark a ten-year grudge just like that. His dad was a pro at embracing everyone. Without the support of his large family, there was no way he would've been elected twice by landslides. For that reason, Melvin Campbell always went out of his way to acknowledge every relative who campaigned for him, and even those who refused.

As they struggled to find a place to sit with their plates of oven-baked ribs, Clarence, Melvin's elder brother, followed them with a beer in hand. Sherman's uncle was one of those family members who made it big-time in the NBA, then blew out his knee in 1984, ending his career forever. Clarence was the alcoholic of the family. His slump was legendary. Melvin was always bailing his brother out of jail, mostly for drunk and disorderly conduct. He couldn't keep a job because of his committed relationship with Miller Lite, but the one thing everyone could count on from his uncle was the truth. He would just let you have it without a second thought, and, for the first time, Sherman needed to hear the whole truth.

Sherman sat back and allowed everyone to catch up over a case of beer. He was biding his time. Once Uncle Clarence was up to beer number six, Melvin started looking for another chatting buddy. That was Sherman's opportunity to move in like an investigative reporter.

"Uncle Clarence, do you remember much about our Grandmother Annette?"

"Yeah, but only from pictures."

Sherman knew there was only a twenty-minute window before the beer took over his uncle's cognitive abilities. Like a skilled prosecutor, he asked questions designed to get Clarence to spill it all.

"Uncle Clarence, what did Grandma Annette look like?"

"Boy, I tell you she was the Lena Horne of New Orleans, and just as pretty. I had a picture of her up until Hurricane Katrina. She died before I was born, but all folk talked about was how pretty she was, even in her old age. Why . . . all these questions?"

"Well, I'm doing a little research on our family, and I'm having a hard time finding info about our great-grandmother. I was hoping you could tell me something that could connect the dots. I can't get Grandma to open up."

"Don't count on Mama to ever talk about dead people. That's not her thing."

Sherman sighed. "Yeah, I know, but I was hoping she would tell me something, at least."

"Well, did she tell you about cousin Abigail?" Clarence asked.

"Cousin who?"

"Ole wanna-be-white Abigail." Clarence opened another Miller Lite. "She even called the police on me once when I knocked on her door—she never owned up to us." Clarence drained his Miller Lite in record time and popped open another.

"Uncle, please tell me more about Abigail?"

Clarence took another deep swig of his beer. "See, boy, we have a section of our family that has passed for white for so many years, the last thing they want is someone connecting them to us. They didn't just turn white, they *been* white. Some of them were so far on the white side that all of the children look like Vanna White. The other half of them who live in Metairie hate black people. Your daddy doesn't know them, but your grandma made sure I knew them all. She knows their little secret. They're all black! But she made me promise to not talk about it to nobody."

"Wow! I had no idea. We have white relatives? Wow." Sherman said.

"Do we ever! Back when they were bussing the Negro kids to the white schools, she used to tell us how some of the women who shouted racist bullshit at her were her cousins. They didn't even know they had the same grandma."

"Uncle Clarence, are you completely sure about that?"

"Lil' nigga, I put that on everything I love, and I love this Miller Lite."

"So that explains why this entire family is bright-skinned."

"Nephew, these families don't talk about it because back in the day there was a big falling-out."

"So how did we get a white side of the family? Do you think Grandma would tell me?"

"Your grandma ain't tellin' you shit. *Haha!*" Clarence took a swig of his beer and crossed his legs.

"So, how do you think the white side of our family entered in?"

"Well, my momma don't like to say nothin' about it, but I don't give a rat's ass . . . I'm gonna tell it. My grandmother was Glenda, and her mother was Annette—that is as far as I could trace it back, but you're good with that computer, so you figure out the rest of the story. Grandma Glenda had a sister named Gladys. From what I can tell, that's where the white part comes from."

"So, the black half of the family never spoke to the white half ever again because of a falling-out in the 1940s?"

"It went down like a pair of sweaty drawers. There are plenty of families around New Orleans who swear to God they come from overseas, but if you shake the tree in their backyard, a *nigga* will fall out. Haha!"

"Huh?" Sherman asked.

His uncle laughed. "That's too heavy for you." Clarence

stood up from the table. "We'll talk some more another day. Got plenty more stories where that one came from, but nephew, you're going to have to excuse me . . . I got to piss out some of this good beer." With that, he staggered toward the bathroom.

"Thanks . . . Uncle Kool."

"No problem, no problem . . . let me hold twenty dollars."

Sherman knew it was coming. No conversation with his uncle ever ended without a request to let him "hold twenty dollars," but the payment was well worth it. Sherman couldn't believe his good luck. What a gift. What a treasure from the most unlikely source: his Uncle Kool. Sherman took advantage of his time alone in the kitchen to eat as much as he could before the next wave of cousins rolled through. From the front of the house, he could hear his father's voice above everyone as he shared behind-the-scenes stories from City Hall and cracked jokes about the mayor.

When his plate was clean, Sherman signaled to his father that he was ready to leave. Melvin nodded, then repeated the process of kissing and hugging everybody as they made their way to the front porch of Grandma's house.

"Dad, why didn't you tell me about Abigail?"

"Let me guess. You jammed your Uncle Clarence in the corner, and he shared his theory about the blacks and whites in this family."

"Dad, he said he heard it from Granny."

"Well, son, that's all speculation and rumors that none of us can prove because none of the remaining people involved will ever talk about it. Clarence claims he got those stories from our mom. But she denies telling him the stories. Who do you think is telling the truth, your grandma or your Uncle Clarence?"

"I don't know what to believe now, Dad."

"For that reason, you can't just go running up to a bunch of white people telling them you're their black cousin."

"But Dad . . ."

"Son, what you heard today from your Uncle Clarence wasn't the truth talking; it was the Miller Lite. This is all part of the many dead ends I encountered when I tried to research the history of this family. Look, a better investment of your time will be to find the identity of our great-grandfather, instead of chasing Abigail."

Melvin Campbell's cell phone started to ring. "Hold that thought, son. It's your mom."

Sherman felt what his Uncle Clarence had shared was the truth; it was the only thing that made any sense to him. It also became apparent that ground zero for his research was Abigail and her residence. He was intrigued to learn that Abigail was, in fact, a black woman passing for white for well over seventy years.

I have to meet her. Maybe she'll welcome me if I approach her the correct way.

CHAPTER 8

January 14, 1843
9:45 p.m.

B eatrice agonized about her beautiful little girl every minute of every day—the daughter she had named Alaina, the one Clarice had stolen six months ago. Every second of every hour, she missed Alaina and her sisters. She still remembered their birthdays, though she had only held them each for less than an hour. Like age-progression software, a grief-stricken Beatrice mentally progressed all her daughters to their exact ages, with vivid attributes and defined features as if painted on a canvas. She saw it all: their eyes, noses . . . she could even hear the pitch of their giggles. Her heart was a living portfolio of their faces—all taken from her, but none forgotten.

Alaina would have been six months, with curly hair like mine, and eyes like mine.

Rose.

Sophie.

Phyllis.

Delicia.

She let out a sigh so deep it caused a wrinkle of waves in the tub. Her grief was so deep she hoped to drown where she sat.

Her oldest daughter, who she had named Rose, was sold eleven years ago this month. The scar never healed. Beatrice knew this for sure because the water told her; it's where she looked to see their faces, reflections of the babies who were stolen from her breast and sold. Once the water in the tub was perfectly still, they appeared one after the other. On Sundays, all of them appeared at once.

In the stillness of the water, she combed their hair, dressed them, and led them down St. Phillips Street to her happy place; that fascinating revival she loved, a place where bongos carried prayers up to God. In the stillness of the water, her master loved her daughters and cherished them as his own, and not as a return on his investment. Her tub was therapeutic, medicinal, and the place she escaped to when her heart was heavy. Suddenly, a bell tolled.

It tolled for Beatrice.

Her master had placed a little service bell right above her bed with a line that ran to his bedroom. If he pulled it once, she was to remain in bed— he was coming to her. If he drew the line twice, it was her notice to meet him in the guest room. She knew he would pull the line today, because his wife was away visiting family in Amite. The ringing of the bell above the door startled the water and one by one, her daughters waved goodbye. She could not ignore the bell because she had made a vow when he became her owner. That day she had quivered in pain with each gust of wind. That frigid morning, when he had wrapped her in his cloak, she made a vow to the bell. On this night, he pulled the line twice.

Ding, ding.

That meant less than thirty minutes to bathe and hurry to the guest room down the hall from the kitchen.

Beatrice removed the scarf from her head and pulled her long, sandy blonde hair forward over her breasts. She then slid into a halter-top gown, rubbed some scented oil on her neck, and hurried off to the appointed room. To get to his room, she had to pass through a courtyard filled with the eyes of the maids. On her way up the staircase, she couldn't help but feel the silent judgment, the stares of ridicule and pity. Some even looked jilted; jealous because their master preferred Beatrice above all—even above his wife.

Beatrice knew he loved her, because he whispered the words in her ear late at night when it was just the two of them. She loved that part of him; that palatable morsel of humility he showed in those quiet minutes after he released, when he was free from his role as her owner. When he confided in her, she held his attention in the center of her full breast and grooved her soft fingers through his hair. Her bell tolled at least four nights a week, leaving only one night for his wife, and two nights to recoup. After she pleased him, Beatrice returned to her duties as his property, and nothing more.

During the day she was his servant. At night she was his lover. Though he was master on paper, she was his master in bed. There, she controlled his body, his mind, and every whispered word.

Beatrice possessed something the master needed. Likewise, he hoarded something far more valuable to her. She wanted to see her daughters,

So, the enslaved mistress stepped out of the tub that evening with a plan. Beatrice walked into the guest room and dropped her gown in the middle of the floor. Then, she positioned herself in his bed. Opening and closing her legs for him. Inviting and teasing him. She caressed herself as she waited. He undressed in front of her, slowly. He loved to watch, and she knew it. He stood over her for a moment.

"I am in awe of your beauty."

"Kind . . . of you," she replied, but she knew it.

"So much more beautiful than my wife."

"Thank you . . . suh." But, she knew it.

"Beatrice, you are just as beautiful as the day I first laid eyes on you." Smoothly, he slid into her pond of pleasure.

No matter the lighting, her skin was radiant. Like a chameleon, Beatrice transformed according to his desires. At some angles, she was his shy Southern belle. In the blink of an eye, she became his exotic goddess. Tonight, he wanted the goddess.

"Wanna watch me some mo'?" Beatrice asked as she fingered herself with one hand and rubbed both of her breasts with the other.

"Not tonight, your body is so warm."

"Slow . . . please."

"If possible, I will try."

"Massa, can I ask?"

"Can it wait until the morning?"

"Massa, may I?"

"What is it?" He sipped her nipples like the finest oak-flavored wine.

"Massa, can I see any of our girls? Can I see any of 'em? One day? And take 'em to church?"

Just like that, he deflated. Her question had killed his mood. But, he attempted a partial explanation. "All of your daughters are well."

"Our," she reminded him.

"Yes, and I assure you, they are being cared for, but my wife can never know. We have discussed this many times before." He sat at the edge of the bed. "Do you believe I have taken care of them?"

"Yes, because you kind, Massa, but I just want to see 'em, and hold 'em, suh."

Like an unexpected storm on a sunny day, his anger was instant. He rolled off her like a barrel, stood, and pointed at the door.

"Get out of here," he screamed. "Get the hell out of here!"

Beatrice immediately grabbed her gown off the floor and ran back toward her living quarters. As she passed all the other servants in the courtyard, she avoided all eye contact, but she couldn't avoid the ridicule.

"Guess she didn't do it right tonight, huh?" one of the maids yelled.

"That sho' was quick!" another one joked as they all laughed at her from their windows.

On that night, Beatrice resolved to find her children, no matter where they were in the world. She was going to hold them all again. In her bed, tears flowed to her ears as she stared at the bell. It was a constant reminder she was not his wife, but his slave.

I must be a fool to think he love me. What am I? Clayrice cursed me a whore. Take his lust, Lord, and return him to his wife, she prayed.

Anger consumed Beatrice, causing her pale face to fluster and her nostrils to flare. The night didn't go as planned, and she still didn't have a clue where he had shipped her daughters. She didn't concede to failure, because he had confirmed her daughters were well, but she did concede to anger.

He done sold off our daughters. His own blood.

With a tight fist, she punched her mattress, imagining it was his face. She punched him until exhaustion. Her pounding of the bedding and her heart rate slowly reached a level of calm. Eventually, a smile appeared on her face.

He need me. He gon call me. But he gon be lookin.

Beatrice blew out her candle, said another prayer for her daughters, and wrapped herself tightly in her blanket.

Ding, ding.

The bell tolled for the second time that night.

Ding, ding.

It rung again above her head, but she didn't respond.

Stop my heart, Lord. Take my breath, God, Beatrice prayed as she continued to ignore the bell for nearly an hour. It sounded about every ten minutes.

Ding, ding!

"*Gal he callin fo you!*" Delia finally stuck her head through the door. "He never beat you, don't give him a reason. Get yoself up and go tend to him," she coached.

"I will, Mama . . . I will."

Beatrice couldn't stop the tears from flowing as she forced herself out of bed, repeated the process of preparing herself, and made her way back to her master's guest room to fulfill her duties. She kept her vow to the bell, even if she hated him on this night. Her vow to the bell was her way of honoring her master for the day he rescued her from the auction block.

If not tonight, he WILL talk soon. He will lead me to my daughters!

When Beatrice returned to the guest room, her master was naked, standing in the center of the room, pointing at the bed.

Her gown slid to the floor like a single cut of silk. Then, she positioned her body to his preference. Up above, on the candle-lit ceiling, she searched for a place to focus her eyes and thoughts; after a few short moments, she found one. An abstract chip in the paint appeared as a basket of fruit—her favorite fruit. For the rest of the night, until he was done, Beatrice thought of a basket full of huge, juicy oranges. In between breaths, she murmured to herself:

Alaina.
Rose.
Sophie.
Phyllis.
Delicia.
I will see you again.

CHAPTER 9

March 11, 1853
New Orleans French Market

Whenever the master's wife came to town from Amite, he would have Beatrice make sure all of the servants were presentable and clean. Then they would all line up, and he would give them twenty-five cents each for food items and whatever else they wanted to buy for the week.

"I need everybody to line up now, line up! Time to go to market!" Beatrice yelled.

As the servants scrambled to be first in line, Beatrice continued to yell at them like a drill sergeant. Whenever the slaves saw the master's wife, they knew it was allowance time, and all of them looked forward to it. Very few slaves received any compensation for services rendered. Therefore, to get twenty-five cents a week was unheard of in New Orleans in 1853.

Another rarity the master granted old slave women was the opportunity to profit from the sale of their desserts and *calas,* Creole rice fritters. On Sundays, their master allowed Momma Delia to sell her *pralines* (pecan candies) in front of the door on the corner of St. Peter and Burgundy Streets, as long as she left a tray for him on his nightstand. It was whispered around the house that Momma Delia freed four of her granddaughters with proceeds from her popular pralines.

When Beatrice and the others exited the house, Momma Delia was seated out front next to a stand loaded with her delectable treats.

"We will see you when we get back, Momma," Beatrice kissed her on the line of her cheek.

"Make sho to get some yeast and a sack of suga if y'all want calas fo breakfast. Ya hear?"

"Yes, Momma, I will make sho to let massa know. Anything else you need?"

"That'll be all . . ."

The entire group of slaves followed the master and his wife down Chartres Street toward the French Market. Other slaves would always gawk at them in envy, due to the perceived kindness of their master. Once they arrived at the market, the slaves were allowed to shop on their own, as long as they remained in pairs. The master's wife would always request Beatrice to accompany her on the trip, which Beatrice hated because she never had time to shop for herself. Saddened, Beatrice remained obedient.

All the slaves, including Beatrice, referred to the master's wife as *Queenie*—but only amongst themselves. Beatrice wondered why Queenie never asked her if she was laying with her husband. Deep down, she felt as if Queenie knew, but accepted it as a trade-off for the lavish antebellum lifestyle she enjoyed.

Queenie made her way through the crowds at the market, only stopping to inspect imported fabrics or any other novelty that caught her attention. Beatrice started to lag behind. Someone was watching her, and she felt it. Not how the other slaves watched her, with eyes of curiosity and jealousy—not at all. Something very dark with harmful intent was watching her, with eyes that felt like hot wax dripping down her back. Oscillating as she moved through the crowd, Beatrice searched for the nefarious gawker. Someone was tracking her every step. She continued to look over her shoulder, and that's when she saw him. A short, white gentleman was trailing her—only feet away—and gaining on her fast. Her nose soon confirmed what her eyes registered. It was Mason.

He made direct eye contact with her as he walked past—dark, black eyes she hadn't seen in more than twenty years. Eyes that still invoked the same fear she had felt when she was fifteen years old. She was relieved when Mason walked past her, but moments later, her fear returned. Mason caught up to Queenie, removed his hat, then formally introduced himself as Mason, the Speculator.

"Greetings, Madame, is there a cost you would accept for this beautiful Negress you have here? We're having a hard time finding females of her likeness. Name your price . . . right now."

Beatrice's bladder released.

"Sir, she is not for sale," Queenie said to Mason. "Now please excuse us." Queenie attempted to walk in the opposite direction, but Mason blocked her path.

"Madame, I will give you seven hundred dollars for her right now and take her off your hands." Mason reached into his pocket and retrieved a wad of cash, then counted out seven hundred dollars in notes from New Orleans Canal & Banking Company. Queenie looked down at the money Mason held in his hand, and then directly back up at him.

"I made my position perfectly plain the first time you asked—Beatrice is not for sale."

"I mean no offense, but everything has a price."

"She is not a thing, she is head maid of our household, and no amount of money would suffice. My husband would agree with me. Beatrice is priceless to us!" Queenie flicked him away with her wrist, but Mason refused to step aside.

"I see . . . Well, is your husband around? Maybe he would consider my generous offer?"

"No, he's not. I ask that you step to the side and allow us to pass," Queenie demanded.

As Beatrice and Queenie walked past Mason, he grabbed Beatrice by the arm, pulling her close to his face.

"Beatrice! I remember you. You were one of my niggers from that plantation up in Mandeville."

Beatrice struggled to free herself from his grip, but she could not pull free. Queenie also tried to pry her away from Mason by pulling her other arm, which held a basket of oranges, but Mason refused to release her. The basket of oranges fell to the ground, as did Beatrice.

"Nigger girl, don't I owe you something?" Mason yelled as he dragged Beatrice through the crowd by the crown of her head. Queenie stumbled behind him, holding onto Beatrice's dress.

The ruckus attracted the attention of the shoppers and merchants as Mason refused to release Beatrice. He seemed determined to drag them both to his wagon. Suddenly, her master walked up from behind and patted him on the shoulder. When Mason turned, her master landed a vicious right hook in the middle of his jaw.

Whack.

Mason fell flat, barely missing Beatrice as he plummeted to the ground. Queenie took hold of Beatrice and hid her behind the bell of her dress as her master jumped on top of Mason and repeatedly jabbed him in the face. It took several merchants to stop her master from killing him with his bare fists. Once the two were separated, Mason appeared lifeless on the ground, a trickle of blood flowing from his mouth and nose.

"Don't ever disrespect my wife! Do you hear me?" her master barked down at Mason. "Don't you ever place your filthy hands on a member of my household!" He tried to break free of the merchants. "Touch her again, and I will shoot you in the face, you son of a bitch!" her master warned in a voice that flamed in anger.

After about five minutes, and with assistance from the merchants, Mason rose to his feet, battered and bloody. He staggered in place as he surveyed the crowd for Beatrice, as if she were the only slave in the city that day. His eyes finally focused enough to spot her, and he sneered as her wide eyes met his.

It was then that Beatrice remembered the bidders; how they had mocked her on the auction block, how she was too white and too skinny, and how many of them would rather have purchased a goat instead. But those days were gone.

Thanks to her master, New Orleans had become the premier market for half-white women, who were purchased for long-term sexual arrangements. Since 1835, the sticker price for a light-complexioned slave like Beatrice had tripled in value, and Mason was in the business of buying low and selling high.

"I have been speculatin' a very long time," Mason spat out blood. "If I don't get what I want the right way," he placed his hat back on his head, *"I will get it my way."*

Mason winked at Beatrice, then disappeared into the crowd of French Market shoppers. It was over, but Beatrice was left disturbed and distraught.

His coal eyes, prune wrinkles, and toxic breath wrenched forward a memory of the first day he blew into her life, like a hot wind across a mound of manure. The grueling years of transporting slaves had left him with a hunch, and he was much weaker than the last time he had ripped her hair at the scalp. His hatred, however, hadn't aged a day.

"Beatrice, did he harm you?" the mistress asked as she inspected her ripped gown.

"I'm . . . fine," she replied, her voice filled with trauma.

"Is she hurt?" her master asked in a concerned voice.

"There's this horrible bruise on her arm, but other than that she appears fine." Queenie was incensed as she inspected Beatrice's arms and clothing. "We must get her and the other servants home. This market is crawling with *slave traders*—I can smell them from a mile away."

"I need to grab a few more supplies for Delia, and then we can leave." Her husband hurried to the yeast merchant.

"Please hurry . . . I would like to get Beatrice home as quickly as possible, so we can treat her arm."

With Mason no longer a threat, Beatrice searched the feet of the dispersing crowd for her basket. She eventually found it, with only two oranges left inside. At a frantic pace, Beatrice moved about salvaging as many oranges as she could before Queenie ended her search.

"Beatrice, don't worry about the oranges, we will purchase more on the way out. I'm done with this place for the day," Queenie said as her master led the way through the crowd, the other servants trailing behind them. Such was the order of things: first the master, then his wife, then Beatrice—who at times walked shoulder to shoulder with his wife, like they were two friends on a stroll.

As they were crossing Chartres Street, Beatrice heard the sound of teenage girls giggling off in the distance. When she looked around, she saw a street performer entertaining onlookers with a monkey routine. A group of adolescent girls stood around him, completely enthralled. They wore beautiful, full-bell silk gowns with bonnets to match. She realized as she drew closer that who she thought were three white girls were, in fact, three mulattos. One of them in particular captured her attention. Beatrice was captivated; she had to get a closer look.

Once she was close enough to make eye contact with the girls, Beatrice dropped her basket of oranges.

"Oh, my lord . . . my precious lord."

For the second time, her oranges rolled in all directions as her master continued to St. Peter Street. The three girls rushed to help Beatrice pick up her produce, and she instantly recognized the one who had captivated her soul. She recognized her eyes, her nose, her hair, and her neckline. Beatrice knew this girl.

She's beautiful.

This girl needed no introduction, but Beatrice wanted to know her name.

"What is your name?"

"Cecille." The girl replied.

"Cecille. That's a very pretty name. How old are you, Cecille?"

"I'm sixteen."

"You so pretty in dat gown. May I . . . touch it?"

"Yes. I made this dress myself. I also made their gowns." Cecille pointed at her two housemates as Beatrice folded and caressed the satin fabric in her fingers.

"You sewed these gowns all by yo'self?" Beatrice was amazed.

"Yes, madame. I do a lot of sewing. I can sew all day," Cecille said.

"Me too." Beatrice was overwhelmed to learn her daughter was also a seamstress. "I love to sew. I can sew from sun-up 'til sundown. Where are you chillun' headed all pretty like this?" Beatrice asked, but she already knew the answer.

"My housemates and I are on our way to the ball."

"*. . . the ball?*"

"Yes, ma'am . . . the Debutante Ball."

That quadroon filth, she recognized with resentment. Part of the travesty of being a slave was having to accept a slew of insulting names and titles. Beatrice hated the word *quadroon* and how white men who visited the home complimented her master.

"What a stunning quadroon you have there, I must have one just like her."

The word smacked so hard, it felt like her nose might bleed. Every time she heard it uttered, it made her feel like an ornament in the courtyard, or a piece of furniture. *My name is Beatrice! Beatrice . . . Beatrice . . . Beatrice!* She was the daughter of the richest man in the city of New Orleans for most of her childhood, therefore she knew her full name. Though her father had never lifted a finger to find her, she still maintained a sense of belonging—unlike the other slaves, she had arrived with a full name. A name that once serenaded off her mother's lips: *Beatrice Marguerite de Marigny.*

Not gal.
Not Creole.
Not whore.
Not wench.
Not quadroon.
My name is Beatrice Marguerite de Marigny.

Her honed skill of eavesdropping frequently gave her access to conversations between the maids—and she had heard many bittersweet accounts of how their daughters conceived with slave owners were sent to the ball and matched as mistresses with wealthy lovers. *Nothin mo than a meat market of black women for white men . . .* that's how she felt about the ball. The quadroon ball was truly the only reason young biracial girls with cake batter complexions would have to enter the grand doors of Theater de Orleans at 717 Orleans Street. Beatrice also knew there was a strong possibility that if Cecille were selected tonight, her lover would relocate her to a neighborhood that was well known for mistresses, one that bore her father's name: The Faubourg Marigny.

"And how old your housemates?" Beatrice asked, wide-eyed.

"We're all sixteen," Cecille replied as they finished gathering up the oranges. "Madame, you have very beautiful eyes."

"So do you." Beatrice blushed as she looked into a face that was like looking into a vanity mirror. "You very pretty, so all da nice menz will be kind to you . . . all of you."

Just then, an impatient voice called her from a distance. Beatrice lowered her eyes. Her mistress was looking for her.

With a warm smile, Cecille turned to join her housemates. As the debutantes jotted away in the direction of the quadroon ballroom and into a life of *plaçage*, they took the air in Beatrice's lungs with them. Before leaving, Beatrice inhaled several more breaths of their perfume cloud, and was left with no doubt that the girl who introduced herself as Cecille was none other than the baby Clarice had snatched out of her arms sixteen years ago.

Cecille is my daughter . . . Rose.

Across the street, Beatrice could see Queenie moving through the crowd of shoppers in a panic. She wanted desperately to follow the debutantes, but being the ever-so-obedient servant that she was, Beatrice hurried to calm a distraught Queenie.

"There you are! Beatrice, I was so worried because I thought that slave trader had taken off with you. The thought of losing you again . . . I would've never forgiven myself."

"If funky Mason would have grabbed me . . . Lawd Jesus! I would have screamed so loud. Folk woulda heard me on Canal Street," Beatrice laughed. Queenie smiled.

She could tell Queenie was very shaken, so Beatrice made sure to walk right beside her back to St. Peter Street. As they hiked it home under the French Quarter balconies, avoiding the constant drip of urine and gutters packed with slow-moving bowel, she fragranced her mind with thoughts of her daughter. Beatrice was enraptured by Cecille.

She had to see her daughter again.

Mason could be out lookin' for me, but I don't care. Mason or no Mason, I will see my daughter tonight.

Everyone was settled.

All the chores were completed.

Less than an hour remained before the bell.

Beatrice slipped out through the side door of 1005 St. Peter Street and hurried to the quadroon ballroom. She was dressed in a three-layer lavender ball gown with white trimming at the hem, a little something her mistress had passed down after a single outing to the opera. If she desired, Beatrice could have passed for a typical duchess from France, but she was always mindful of her race and the societal mandate that all non-white females cover their heads—if for no other reason than to identify who was, and who wasn't, born of two full-blooded European parents.

A curtsy to legitimate wives.

A courtesy to appear less intimidating.

A constraint shared by freed and enslaved females.

Nevertheless, it was a mandate she obeyed. Beatrice wrapped her hair in a white cotton cloth and merged into the crowds of slaves commuting that evening. Balanced on her head was a wicker basket of purple sheer and three yards of floral Indienne. She was hoping to gift the extra fabric to her daughter.

Once inside the ballroom, she assumed the demeanor of a debutant's mother and followed the other mothers to the balcony. At the entrance to the second-floor balcony seating, Beatrice was greeted by an attendant of her same complexion—dressed in the same type of attire. She had hazel eyes and two locks of golden hair that playfully draped the sides of her face.

"De cette façon, Madame." A graceful hand ushered Beatrice to a separate set of stairs provided for mezzanine seating. *"Voulez-vous que je prenne votre panier?"* The attendant reached for the basket.

"No, thank you," Beatrice smiled. The maître-d curtsied away. People often assumed she spoke fluent French because most women of her complexion were in common law marriages with men from France. Beatrice, however, spoke French just well enough to get by, though she practiced her vocabulary in front of her vanity every morning.

Her view of the ballroom floor was privileged enough to see the paisleys in the sleeves of Cecille's gown, the glitter in her eyes, the blush in her cheeks, and the curls that hung off her shoulders. The isle that gave way to the floor allowed the debutantes to draw attention to themselves and entice potential suitors. Once their names were called, a lot was riding on the line. If a girl was selected tonight, it could be the start of a life of comfort as the mistress of a wealthy lover—or perhaps the status of a wife if she was selected by a romance tourist. It was also a ticket out of slavery for the girls' mothers, who sat in the balcony watching. They could potentially assume new roles as servants for their daughters.

If a girl wasn't selected after multiple appearances, there existed the possibility of making a final debut in an exclusive brothel for the rich and famous. A brothel assignment was the worst-case scenario for the debutantes. Since the age of ten, they had dreamed of catching the attention of a handsome man who would take them away to the mysterious lands hidden in the wrinkled pages of the Madame's library.

Some of the men in attendance had come prepared to pay as much as three thousand dollars for the perfect quadroon.

Lover.

Mistress.

Concubine.

In many ways, the ball reminded Beatrice of her auction experience, only more elegant. In the far corner of the room, a quartet began to play songs Beatrice recalled from Queenie, as she often strummed them throughout the house. The soft, eloquent whine of the violin caused her skin to shiver and speckle with goosebumps. Then, another soothing violin joined in and massaged her with a melody. Finally, the chorus of a weighty cello awakened her soul and carried her up to the cherubim.

Suddenly, the debutantes started to dance.

Like floating flower pots of white roses, like wingless angels that waltzed in a roundabout, like daughters of one king presented to another, festooned as gifts. She watched as Cecille pranced around the ballroom floor in a single-file line. Innocently she seduced them; eloquently she teased them with sapphire eyes.

The mezzanine suspended Beatrice between two tiers. Above her sat the mothers of mulattos, their faces the color of coffee beans. On the floor level were four rows of prospective white suitors—an assortment of black and royal blue top coats with matching hats. In the middle was Beatrice, who was not completely Caucasian, and not completely African. She often wondered if she had been conceived in love. She usually concluded that she came from an interaction that settled somewhere right above lust, but either way, her parents' brief romantic episode equated to an endless drama in the mezzanine of her life.

Not since Mandeville had Beatrice felt such prestige. Like proud peacocks, the freed women preened next to her in multicolored gowns and beautiful, expensive hair wraps—fabrics she knew to be imported because she ordered the same materials for her mistress. The woman to her left wore a gown Beatrice was very familiar with, because it was one she had made for the boutique inventory. It was a teal-green silk gauze dress with tan trimming and three cascading layers in the bell, with five-inch tan hems on each. Beatrice remembered each stitch of the skirt and how it took most of the day to get the cartridge pleats wrapped seamlessly around the waist.

Tonight was the first time the enslaved seamstress had ever sat next to a woman wearing one of her gowns, and it was also the first time she'd sat next to a free woman of color.

I want to be free, she craved.

While Beatrice slouched, the free women presided on thrones, with stiff backs and broad shoulders. While she scented herself with generic oils, the free women permeated the redolence of freshly picked flowers from the sweetest gardens in heaven. Fragrances her nose couldn't identify. Beatrice couldn't help but eavesdrop, but the free women spoke in an unknown tongue: French. She wanted so desperately to join in their conversation, to be one of them in stature and posture, but she only looked the part. Beatrice was just as attractive as they were, but in her mind, she wasn't. Though she appeared as a free woman of color, in her reality, she wasn't.

For a brief second, a thought entered her mind: at the conclusion of the ball, she would disappear into the fog of night. *But where to?* And then what about Timothy and Lawrence? *I can't just walk out of their lives.* And how would she find the rest of her kids without the help of her master? Slowly, her fantasies of freedom fizzled under the strain of uncertainty and buckled under the bulk of slavery.

I can't leave. Not now—but soon.

Suddenly the hostess entered the room, and Beatrice was immediately taken back to that frigid morning when she stood on the auction block for what felt like an entire day. The hostess was none other than the woman who had spoken to the auctioneer as an equal—the one who had swapped the male slave for two females. She was introduced to the audience as Courtier d'amour Madame Harriet Green de Marquette. It all made sense to Beatrice now—why the auctioneers had treated Harriet Green with mutual respect sixteen years ago. *Courtier d'amour* was a fancy way of saying she was a sex merchant; a brothel owner, a quadroon broker.

It wasn't too long ago that Harriet had been a debutante in the same ballroom. The date was August 21, 1827, to be exact. She had entered into an arrangement with Louis de Marquette, a wealthy exporter of sugar to France, and structured a deal that freed two of her family members—her mother and sister. Louis de Marquette moved Harriet into an apartment on the corner of St. Roch and Rampart Street, where she bore him five children. In return, he provided her with a life of comfort. But Harriet wanted more. She wanted his wife out of the picture entirely. Shortly after Harriet gave birth to her fifth child, Louis de Marquette's wife became gravely ill. After four months, she died for reasons unknown. Unknown to most, that is—her illness was no mystery to Harriet.

Douce Mort. Sweet Death, as it was commonly known

among the sisterhood of enslaved cooks—it was Harriet's mother who had taught her the recipe. It was comprised of all the ingredients of a normal cake, plus one toxic oyster diced into the flour and laced with the lemon icing. Harriet baked two lemon cakes six months apart—one for her master's wife and another for his brother. The cooks were careful to discard the poisonous cakes after the first slice was served—somehow, the cakes mysteriously fell off the table both times. Not long after his wife's death, Louis de Marquette married Harriet Green, unknowingly progressing her plans.

There was no need to feed her husband *Douce Mort*, because he was one of the earlier victims of yellow fever. By the time Harriet's youngest son Ulrich was five years old, she was the heir to the Marquette estate in New Orleans, heir to an eighteen-slave sugar plantation in New Iberia, and heir to the Marquette Export partnerships in France. None of those entities in her inheritance excited Harriet like the opportunity to tap into the niche market of quadroon women, so she sold the slave plantation and used the export business to build a wealthy clientele for her new venture.

Harriet reinvested a portion of the sales from the plantation into four brothels in the area of New Orleans which later became known as the Red Light District. Her brothels were staffed with women she purchased off the auction block, but the rare finds—the blonde haired, blue-eyed types—she housed in her Burgundy street townhouse. There, she trained them for a distinct purpose—Harriet's Debutantes.

Harriet Green was the wealthiest free woman of color in New Orleans, and the only Negro to have an account at the same bank that foreclosed on Bernard de Marigny—New Orleans Canal & Banking Company.

Her business was sex.

Her commodity was Creole consorts.

Her clients were men who could afford her cost.

The girls offered through Harriet's Debutantes were guaranteed virgins—all of them were strictly supervised under her boarding and tutelage. Her debutantes received a liberal education in literature, business math, and the history of France from the House of Bourbon monarchy through the Revolution all the way to modern-day. Her girls were submerged in French language studies, because bilingual quadroons were offered at the highest prices.

At every ball, at least six of the girls where premium debutantes, but she also offered fair-complexioned companions for every budget. Tonight, Harriett would feature sixteen girls, six of whom were premiums. She expected to earn at least 2,700 dollars for each of them, and the time to collect had just arrived.

Around eight o'clock, Harriet took to the floor in a sparkle of diamond earrings, a ruby necklace that strobed through the candlelit room, and a studded tiara that beaconed like a crown. Harriet was just as desirable as her debutantes with her full eyes, peachy lips, and pampered face. Her lustrous, curly, black locks rested on her shoulders. She constantly groomed her curls with her fingers, to prove she wasn't wearing a wig. It was her stunning beauty that established the value of her debutantes and seduced her gullible gathering of successful men into spending more than they intended.

To exploit their anticipation even further, Harriet invited one of the men to the center of the floor with the wave of a finger. As he approached, Harriet unfastened the center of her dress, exposing her full, rounded cleavage. Without instruction, the patron kissed her between her breasts while she held him by the back of his head. Then, Harriet made eye contact with every man she had invited to her ball.

"My girls have mastered the art of pleasing you, and once you have entered one of my virgins, you will desire no other. Gentlemen, you have earned this pleasure for the way you have provided for your families. The time has come for you to treat yourselves to one of my Debutantes, because you have earned her in every way."

Harriet separated the eager patron's lips from her breast, then sucked his bottom lip as the room erupted in applause. She then ordered him to refasten her buttons, and with a flick of her wrist, returned him to his seat.

"Tonight, you will leave with a woman who will take care of your every need . . . well into your old age. Whatever it is your wife can't do or is not willing to do, my girls will gladly do for you. Who knows, you may come back next year for one more."

"I'll take two right now," a voice joked from a dimly lit area.

The drinks were on the house, and every glass was spiked with a potion that was the Viagra of its day. Harriet knew from the way her guests adjusted their erections in their trousers that she could ask any price. She saw their painful throbs. With the wave of her white-gloved hand, her girls made one final prance around the room while she stood in the center of it all—confident and concise as a carousel of beauty swirled the room. The procession revolved around the ball at the pace of an ice wagon and allowed each guest less than a minute to fall in love before the next debutant strolled into view. As the men watched the girls, Harriet stalked their lust-filled eyes for their reactions, and for any signs of weakness. During the prance, she discovered which girl each patron couldn't resist—his eyes followed her around the room. And so, they teased.

From memory, she passionately recited the bio of each debutant and took as long as she needed to highlight her talents and romantic perks. She also identified the broker who would handle the young lady's *la cour laterale* (side court) negotiations at the conclusion of the evening. That was the time she longed for— that intense hour when she recouped her entire investment, with generous profits for her partners.

"Honey Bees . . . I did not forget about you." Harriet pointed toward the hall. "When you're ready, I have placed ushers in the foyer who will escort you to my private viewing boutique. There you will find the desires of your heart."

Honey Bee was a special category of clientele who preferred adolescent males, who Harriet branded as Fancy Boys. In a side room, dressed in the same gowns worn by the debutantes, with the same makeup and perfume, were five boys ranging in age from twelve to fifteen, trained in all manners of homosexual relations. Harriet's bidders for Fancy Boys were just as aggressive as the men in the main ballroom, and all five boys were listed at premium prices. Non-negotiable!

In the furthest corner of the room, Beatrice couldn't free her eyes from a gentleman in a tan coat with a matching top hat in hand—she recognized him. *Oh no, I must hide.* Like the owner of a prized thoroughbred, he was fixated on the debutantes. Beatrice sunk below the brass banister to conceal her face.

"Next up is a lovely little pearl I am very excited to present," Harriet announced with an endless smile. "Gentlemen, this next young lady was raised to please a king." Taking Cecille by the hand, Harriet gracefully glided her around the entire ballroom. "Isn't she beautiful?" Harriet asked her wealthy guests. "She is the premium beauty of the night, the rarest of them all. I promise you will not find *whiter skin* on a Negro anywhere in the world." Cecille bowed to the gentlemen in the first row. "Gentlemen, this sixteen-year-old New Orleans beauty is in perfect health, both inside and out. She is ripe for child-bearing. She's an excellent cook, a gifted seamstress, and has hands as soft as cotton. Every part of her body is soft. She smells like the most expensive French perfume." More suitors stood and gave hand signals of interest.

I am looking at myself, Beatrice thought as she watched Cecille make her debut. *My Lord, she has my everything! Cecille is my child.*

Only Cecille's full lips and nose remained from her Haitian grandmother, and just as Beatrice had predicted outside of the French Market, the men were very kind to her. The premium beauty of the night won their hearts. Several of them even stood to express serious interest. It was time for Hostess Harriet Green to announce the broker for Cecille. That announcement was the reason Beatrice had risked everything to attend the ball, even at the risk of getting kidnapped by Mason and smuggled to Virginia. Even at the risk of getting beaten by her master for leaving his home without permission. Beatrice wasn't leaving until she knew the name of Cecille's representative.

"Representing this stunning beauty is one of my preferred brokers. A broker who only delivers the best companions found anywhere in this city. Tonight is no exception. This young lady standing next to me is special for so many reasons, and some lucky man will open this precious gift later on this evening."

"Back off boys, she's coming with me," a man joked.

"First, you will have to kill me. I have a house waiting for this one," a shipping baron roared in laughter.

"This debutante has been in my care since birth, nurtured by her mother and educated by the best tutors from France. Her mother is here tonight."

The freed women in the mezzanine were starting to become distracted by Beatrice. She was panting uncontrollably and rocking nervously in her seat.

"Please give a warm round of applause for Lady Clarice and her lovely daughter, Cecille."

"What! Clarice!" Beatrice gasped "Damn you, Clarice!"

"Shhh," a free woman tried to calm Beatrice.

"That is my daughter!" Beatrice hissed. "That bitch! She kept my baby! She had her all dis time!"

Beatrice could barely contain her anger as she realized the midwife who had carried away all five of her daughters now held the hand of her oldest in a quadroon ball. She wanted to leap out of the mezzanine to the bottom floor and choke Clarice until her last breath. But she was out of time.

He will ring that bell soon.

As Beatrice made her way down from the second floor, she spotted Clarice. Laughing and giggling. Wheeling and dealing away the future of her daughter . . . but Beatrice couldn't blow her cover, not tonight. Her hatred for Clarice intensified like a firestorm. Before leaving, she mentally recorded the faces of the men who surrounded her sixteen-year-old daughter, vowing to seek revenge on the system that had separated her from her screaming babies. Infants who only wanted to nurse but were denied that God-given right. Denied by Clarice.

Beatrice left the quadroon ballroom and hurried home, leaving a trail of tears down every street corner. Devastated, she entered the home on St. Peter undetected and hurried to the tub. Beatrice slid into a form-fitting yellow sleeping gown with a yellow scarf, oiled her skin, and perfumed her body. Just in time.

Ding.

The master of the house was en route to her room, seeking pleasure in her bed. In her arms. Inside that warm place Beatrice only opened for him. However, tonight was different. Tonight, she wanted answers.

How could you?

Why didn't you tell me Clarice had my babies?

He will answer me tonight, or my legs will not open.

THE MASTER'S WIFE DIARY ENTRY THREE

May 11, 1853
9 p.m.

Dear Diary,

My husband just departed for an evening walk; he appeared restless. His evening walks are a source of great worry for me, especially with this yellow fever outbreak. God forbid if one of us should fall ill. Speaking of worry, around noon today, a dreadful-looking man with filthy hands and black fingernails attacked my dear, sweet Beatrice. I have yet to calm down from our awful encounter at the market. The audacity of him to touch Beatrice!

What made him think he had the right to disrespect us like that? In front of the entire market, no less. Oh, the humiliation we suffered. I didn't know the man, but Beatrice knew him—a slave trader she thought she would never encounter again. The temerity of one to think he could buy and sell another merely based on the color of skin! Sometimes it feels like the slaves in this city outnumber the free citizens. I thank God I have a husband who feels the same way I do about this horrible institution of chains and whips. To the glory of our Lord, all of our servants are compensated fairly.

I have never been prouder of my husband for his defense of our household. What a powerful statement he made—it was quite pleasing to me. Though I have heard stories over the years of his many fistfights and duels over trivial matters, I had never seen him act in any way that was violent or threatening until today. I would have preferred the matter to be settled with a gentlemen's handshake, but I must say, there was something very comforting in his retaliation. His physical display of devotion was quite reassuring.

Beatrice seemed to appreciate the protection of my husband as well; the poor girl was scared frozen. I pray the Lord will steer that man far away, but should we cross paths again, it would be wise of him to stay clear of us. What a wonderful husband I have. When he returns from his walk, I will give him what he deserves—a night of passionate love, and even more at dawn.

I hope.

CHAPTER 10

It was the end of another busy day for Sherman, and for Ronelle, it was frustratingly typical. Not one call all day. Only when the day was done did he finally remember her and think to get in touch. It was ironic, she mused, how a quality she admired so much—his goal-driven focus—was also the same quality that made her feel irrelevant. It was obvious that he was falling back into his normal pattern of forgetting about her until the end of the day, but little did he know that when he stood her up for the play at the Mahalia Jackson Theater, he had blown his last chance. It had to be his last chance, because of his promise that no matter how hectic his schedule became, he would at least take five minutes to call. Tonight was the second night in a row he had failed to keep his promise.

I have to do this—if I don't, he will continue to treat me like shit.

Ronelle peeked out of the window as Sherman's BMW 6 Series rolled into the Fortier driveway and parked behind her car. She knew he would come tonight because she knew him, in the way a woman in love becomes in sync with all the intricacies of her lover. She knew Sherman perhaps better than he knew himself. And so, she sat in the living room on pretzeled legs in a pink cotton sweat-suit with a pink hair tie at the base of her ponytail and waited—the voice of her mother echoing in her ear.

Have you ever thought that the reason you're having so many issues with Sherman is that you're not compatible?

Have you ever considered that the reason you're having so many issues with Sherman is because you two come from different worlds?

Since the earlier days of her relationship, she had noticed that her mother always stopped just inches short of the *black* line, but never crossed it. Ronelle's issue with Sherman wasn't as complicated as her mom made it out to be. In fact, it was quite simple: he suffered from severe tunnel vision. He could only water one flower at a time while the rest of the garden withered. Unfortunately for Ronelle, this was the driest point of their relationship—a drought that would take more than a garden hose to saturate back to life.

Maybe it's time to go our separate ways.

I love him too much.

Her thoughts tumbled like weeds, and as he approached the front door, she didn't give him a chance to ring the doorbell, nor the pleasure of a greeting and a smile.

"Hi, beautiful! I missed you!" Sherman leaned in for a kiss.

"We need to talk."

"Okay . . . but can we at least kiss first?"

She stiff-armed him a "no."

"Ronelle, are you still angry about the play?" He asked in a confused voice. "When we talked on the phone earlier, I thought we agreed to move on? I thought you forgave me?"

"I am tired of forgiving you for who you are. I can't do this anymore."

"You can't do what anymore?"

"Us."

"So, you're breaking up with me because I forgot about a play?"

"First of all, it's always *hi, beautiful* after blatant disregard, but never before. It's always several calls after I bitch you out for ignoring me, but never before. It's always this convenient amnesia. It's always a new you for a few days until I fall for it—then it's back to the same inconsiderate bullshit." Ronelle took a step back from the door into the house, and her eyes made it clear that he was not welcome to follow.

Her normally glossy lips were bare, her face was plain, and her body was scentless. She had no motivation that day to put any effort into looking pretty.

"So . . . you're saying it's over? Just like that . . . it's over?" His palms beckoned for her hands, but she took another step away from him and reached for the doorknob. "Ronelle, I am trying to get better, but I keep making the same mistakes."

"Goodbye, Sherman," Ronelle said as she narrowed herself into the elbow of the door.

He stuck his foot in. "Ronelle wait . . . please."

"Goodnight, Sherman."

"It's the Adderall."

"The what?"

"The Adderall, I know it is." He forearmed the door as Ronelle shoved. "Ronelle please hear me out. I get into this tunnel that has no light at the end, no sound, only the thought that I must finish, and everything else has to wait. I don't eat, sleep, or even think about sex until I complete the task at hand, or until it burns out of my system. Trust me baby, it's the Adderall."

She shook her head in exasperation. "So now you're on Adderall? Goodnight, Sherman." Only half of her body was visible.

"I'm not making this up; it's the Adderall." A size twelve Oxford shoe was the only thing that prevented Ronelle from slamming the door; a black leather shoe Ronelle scuffed with each attempt to shut Sherman out of her life.

She slowly rolled her eyes. "So, you're taking meds?"

"I'm not bullshitting you, Ronelle. I have been on it now for a month because I was struggling. I would sit down in front of a blank screen for hours without typing any words, only to end up on Twitter fussing about things that were out of my control. Then I would get depressed." Sherman leaned into the narrow door space.

"So, you have been seeing a psych and didn't feel I needed

to know?"

"I was going to tell you, but . . ."

"When?"

"I know how this looks . . . but there was a good reason I waited to tell you."

"A good reason to keep me in the dark about your health? What are we? Facebook friends?"

"Ronelle, please hear me out. It was my mother who suggested I pay a visit to Dr. Naeem Mohammad. At first, I didn't like the feeling of going to see a psychiatrist, but I'm glad I did. Brandon was right; my mind was all over the place." Sherman's voice softened. "The medication helps me get shit done, but sometimes a little too much."

"Sherman, you were *forgetful as fuck* before Adderall . . ."

"You're right, but I wasn't as productive as I am right now. Ronelle, I'm adjusting to life on this medication. I am much more productive. I can concentrate on the things I need to focus on, and . . ."

Ronelle pushed him in the chest. "Well, I guess I'm not one of those things!" She slammed the front door.

When she turned away from the door, she saw her mom in the kitchen, leaning against a counter. In Brenda's hand was a celebratory glass of sparkling chardonnay—*I told you so* reflected through the wine glass.

Not even an hour had passed since Ronelle slammed the door on her relationship and left the only man she'd ever loved standing on the porch. It was over. She was tired of taking him back and tired of forgiving him, but when it came to Sherman, her anger phase didn't last long enough to get her past the loneliness. She missed him already, but hated that she felt so weak.

Tonight, I took back my life from him; he can no longer treat me like I don't matter, she tried to convince herself.

But now I have no one.

Flopping down on her bed, she stretched diagonally and cried into a giant teddy bear Sherman had given her when they first started dating three years ago—that once-upon-a-time moment when Ronelle felt like the most important person in his life. Her tears soaked the plush of the bear, but he never complained or passed judgment. Ronelle wished her mother were more like her giant bear.

Her anger suddenly returned when she relived one simple sentence Sherman had uttered:

I can concentrate on the things I need to focus on.

I can concentrate on the things I need . . .

I can concentrate on . . .

I can concentrate . . .

But not on me!

Adderall, my ass—It's amazing he can concentrate on things that are important to him, but I'm not one of those things.

His words changed and rearranged in her mind and cut deeper each time she relived their porch scene. *He will never hurt me like this again*, she murmured into the belly of the bear. Suddenly, the cruelness of his words were interrupted by a song—her favorite song—from outside of her bedroom window. He sang in a soft falsetto:

Until the end of time
I'll be there for you
You own my heart and mind
I truly adore you
If God one day struck me blind
Your beauty I'd still see
Love's too weak to define
Just what you mean to me.

She sat in her bedroom window, listening. The window was open just wide enough to allow the song to dry her tears, but not enough to let him back into her heart. Down below in the yard, Sherman was smiling from ear to ear. Ronelle sighed deeply and stuck her head through the window.

"So, you recruited Prince to get you out of the doghouse?"

"Without you, there is no me."

"Goodnight, Sherman."

"Please don't quit me. Please!" Sherman reached behind his back and presented a plastic spoon and a pint of banana pudding ice cream, which he hoisted up to the window.

For the first time that night, Ronelle smiled. She raised the window enough to receive the ice cream that he held like a bouquet of flowers. She snatched the container and the spoon out of his hand, smiled down at him, waved *bye-bye*, then quickly shut the window.

It takes a minimum of twenty days to form a habit.

The words of Maxwell Maltz appeared on Ronelle's phone from a quote app; today marked the twentieth day since her breakup with Sherman. There was something about this time around that was different from her previous attempts to go on with her life—this time, she hadn't given in so quickly. The old Ronelle would have bolted out of the house and jumped into his arms from the porch after the serenade and her favorite ice cream—but not this time. Since the breakup, she had allowed Sherman to remain in her life at the friendship level, but no higher. However, she was miserable.

In her attempts to prove that it was really over, a part of her died each day. It wasn't like Sherman was gone for good—two nights a week she would come home to find him at her kitchen table with Brandon pecking out their dissertation. In fact, everywhere she turned he was there in one way or another—even his dad was her dad's best friend.

Ronelle wanted Sherman back, but not the person who pushed her to the back of the line and used Adderall as the excuse. She wanted the man she had fallen in love with three years ago, the one who sat on her porch until midnight and spoke poetic words of love. To make matters worse, while she bled out from the heart, she had never seen her mother happier. Over the past two weeks, she had attended two events with her mother only to find herself seated next to Jared Joseph; a marriage her mother would have arranged if the year were 1750 and the city were London.

Finally, Ronelle did what she had worked so hard not to do: she typed a text.

If you're not too busy can you come over later tonight?
She pressed *send.*
Moments later, he replied.
I can come right now . . .

Sherman enjoyed growing up on the north side of New Orleans in the area known as the Lakefront; it was full of lifelong homeowners. People had relationships with their neighbors. Sherman's parents still lived on Leon C. Simon Boulevard in an all-white contemporary-style home near the lake. It was a very well-manicured neighborhood occupied by upper middle class residents—financially secure families like the Campbells who could afford the ridiculously high property taxes and ever-increasing insurance rates.

The alarm chirp notified Sherman's dad of his arrival. Every wall in the living room was more like a trophy case; every accomplishment his dad could hook to a nail was on display. Sherman's younger brothers—twins—attended LSU. Both were seniors and SEC all-American football players. One of the twins played quarterback; the other was a wide receiver. His brothers were projected to go in the first round of the NFL draft.

Sherman's high school basketball trophies were buried under his brothers' accomplishments, but he didn't mind at all. Their brick house was a five-bedroom two-story on a corner lot; it had a large swimming pool out back. The landscaping was flawless, and the interior furnishing—a mixture of vintage and contemporary seating—was a page torn out of *Southern Homes* magazine. Due to an empty nest, only the birds enjoyed the large backyard swimming pool and patio.

Before he arrived, Sherman had given his dad a heads-up that there was something important he wanted to speak to him about, so Melvin came walking from the back of the house with a huge smile that said he was excited to see his son.

"My little man, what brings you by?"

Sherman didn't make eye contact. His father's smile re-shaped to reflect immediate concern.

"Dad, you know I have been dating Ronelle for a while . . ."

"Hold up right there." Melvin stopped Sherman in mid-sentence and walked over to the base of the staircase. "Yvonne, get down here."

"Melvin I'm busy . . . what is it?"

"Yvonne!" His dad yelled.

His mom huffed as she moseyed down the stairs. "This better be important more important than the season finale of *Scandal*."

She entered the room and took a seat on the sofa while Sherman and his dad stood on opposite ends of the coffee table.

"I'm ready to ask Ronelle to marry me."

The smile returned to his father's face while his mother wore a blank stare.

"Son, are you sure?" his dad asked proudly.

"Yes, Dad. I am one hundred percent sure. I plan to propose to her this Friday, on her birthday."

"Well, son, if you're sure about it, then I support you."

"Thanks, Dad, I appreciate that. How about you, Mom?

"Puddin', I'm happy if you're happy," she said as she fanned her face. "This has caught me off-guard, of course, but I do support you. Ronelle is a precious young lady. I like her. I didn't think in a million years you two would end up in a relation-ship, but stranger things have happened." His mother continued to fan. "Have you asked Brenda and Steven for their blessings yet?"

"I plan to, tomorrow. After I buy the ring."

"Boy, don't buy that girl no aluminum ring and get your feel-ings hurt! You know she's rich. She comes from old money!" Melvin joked.

"Dad, Ronelle is so over it when it comes to being rich. So down to earth. So perfect for me."

"Like I said, Puddin', if you're sure, then I'm happy." His mother kissed him on the cheek and returned to her upstairs bedroom.

"Looks like we have a wedding coming up soon," Melvin said. "Son, I am very proud of you and will be here for you every step of the way. Let me know if you need to talk."

"Thanks, Dad." Sherman felt relieved.

"How's the research coming?" Melvin asked as Sherman headed to the front door.

"We're finally getting somewhere; I'll call you in the morning and update you. Love you, Dad."

Sherman left his parents' home. He knew they'd be up all night talking about the wedding. Next, he wanted to get the approval of his best friend, Brandon. Sherman's stomach filled with butterflies at the thought of asking Brandon for his blessings to marry Ronelle, but he wasn't sure why.

Café Dauphine
The next day

Brandon and Sherman had one strictly enforced rule: whoever was late for the meeting had to pay for the entire meal. Sherman was thirty minutes late, and Brandon ran up the tab every time Sherman arrived late. Pulling up at Café Dauphine, Sherman could see Brandon already seated at their table near the large window on the side of the building. He could also see Brandon's grin of victory as he combed through the menu.

"What's up, man? Sorry I'm running a little late today," Sherman said as he sat down.

"A little late? You might as well give the waiter the pin code to your ATM card, because I'm starving!"

Sherman stood to acknowledge Keisha Henry, the owner of Café Dauphine, who stopped by their table to say hello. Sherman and Keisha embraced; they were old friends.

"Keisha, I'm so proud of what you guys are doing here," Sherman beamed.

"People are lovin' our menu, and that makes me very happy.

Cha-ching!" Keisha said, grinning.

"What's good today?" Sherman asked.

"Everything," she said, handing him a menu.

"He doesn't need a menu, Keisha. He never changes his order. Bring him a cut of catfish, the charred oysters, and two of the stuffed bell peppers," Brandon said.

"How about some of my Lizardi egg rolls?" Keisha asked. "And what can I get y'all to drink?"

"Lemonade, and we'll take an order of those, too," Brandon said.

"Lemonade works for me as well," Sherman added as she gathered their menus.

Once Keisha was out of view, Sherman turned to Brandon. "Well, this will not be our ordinary lunch. I need to get your approval on something very important and urgent."

"Uh oh." Brandon stopped scrolling through his phone and raised his head. "Whatever this is, it sounds serious."

"It is . . . very serious," Sherman replied. "On Friday, I plan to ask your sister to marry me. May I have your blessings?"

The waiter dropped off their lemonades and Lizardi rolls without interruption. Sherman leaned back in his seat and smiled.

His best friend pounded an angry fist on the table. "Aw, hell no! No way! Not happening," Brandon replied with a frown on his face.

That was not the answer Sherman had expected. Seconds went by . . .

"Gotcha!" Brandon finally shouted, standing to embrace Sherman.

"Dude, you play too much."

"Well, it's about time. I can't imagine anyone else with my crazy-ass sister. And then there's you," he laughed.

"Whatever, dude."

"I'm just saying, two crazies tied together will only make crazy-ass kids!"

They both picked up their lemonades and clinked their glasses in a toast.

"Well, after dinner I'm off to ask your parents. Perhaps my toughest approval will be asking your mom if I can marry her only daughter. Man, my stomach is in knots."

"Dude! Relax! Despite her tough outer appearance, she knows it's coming; no surprises there. Mom and Dad have always liked you, so relax," Brandon said as he chomped down on a Lizardi roll. "These are good."

"They sure are," Sherman said with his mouth full.

Moments later, two waiters arrived with all the food Brandon had ordered. Sherman stared at five full plates with everything from crawfish stew to a rack of ribs. "I should kick your ass."

"It's your fault. Those are the rules," Brandon said as he began munching on stuffed shrimp. The waiter returned shortly with Sherman's entrée. After their feast, Sherman paid the 104-dollar check, and Brandon left a tip that made the waiters smile. Keisha stopped by to thank Sherman and Brandon as they were leaving.

"Hope all was good for you fellas tonight," Keisha said.

"Delicious as always," Sherman replied.

"I'm stuffed!" Brandon added.

"Awesome. You guys have a good night, and we'll see you next time. Make sure to tell Councilman Campbell I said thank you for that city hall catering order!" Keisha said as she moved onto her next guests.

"I sure will, Keisha. Thanks again for another great meal."

Next stop for Sherman was the home of Steven and Brenda Fortier.

CHAPTER 11

In the rearview mirror, Sherman checked the knot in his classic black necktie and brushed the shoulders of his classic black blazer. The last time he was this nervous about his appearance was when he had escorted Ronelle to her senior prom—Brenda Fortier gave him anxiety attacks back then, and little had changed. It wasn't that she treated Sherman in a discourteous manner, but she consistently spoke only five words beyond hello to him, and not much more. But tonight, tonight was bigger than a prom date or a weekly dinner night with Ronelle—tonight he would ask for one of the most precious jewels she possessed.

Her only daughter.

Ronelle volunteered at the New Orleans Recreation Department as a theater instructor. Her classes ended at nine thirty, so Sherman planned to capitalize on a narrow window of time before she arrived home. If things went well this evening, he would propose at their favorite park, the River View. It was there on a little bench overlooking the bending Mississippi River where they had first kissed, and first dreamed of a life together. The little bench was also the location of their first discussion about race and romance.

Sherman could feel his nerves and sweat glands kick into

overdrive as he pulled up to Ronelle's house, and his urge to pee reached the painful point of *right now. I can't hold it*, he thought to himself as he reached down toward the passenger floor for an empty Gatorade bottle. One of the privileges of being a man is the ability to urinate anywhere at any time. Sherman made it a point to never throw away empty Gatorade bottles for times such as this one: a piss crisis. After a long groan of relief, he firmly capped the bottle, then hid it behind the passenger seat. It was a necessary habit that Ronelle hated, but his overactive bladder couldn't care less.

Brandon had made it home just before Sherman arrived. Seeing his best friend's car, he stood outside his window just as Sherman tucked the full bottle of urine under the passenger seat. Brandon banged the window as hard as he could without shattering the glass.

"What the fuck are you doing?"

Sherman nearly hit the ceiling. "Bro, are you trying to give me a heart attack?"

"Still pissing in bottles, huh?"

"Dude, mind your business," Sherman said as he zipped.

"You do know they make large Pampers for men with your problem? You can walk around pissy all day and no one will notice," Brandon continued to roast.

"Whatever, dude!"

"Look at you; you're sweating like a pig invited to a barbecue! You have to relax."

"Easier said than done, but I can't turn back now."

Sherman pressed the door lock on his keychain, then he reached inside his blazer jacket and retrieved a damp towel. Inside of the same pocket was the engagement ring for Ronelle. This was it, and tonight was the night. Sherman couldn't catch his breath. As he and Brandon made their way inside and into the living room, Brandon called out for his mom and dad to meet them at the kitchen table.

As Mr. and Mrs. Fortier entered the room together, Sherman saw himself running out the front door, leaping off the porch, and making a fast break down the street until he reached the levee, but he resisted the urge. Brenda Fortier entered the room with a portrait face, wearing a pair of black slacks with a red satin blouse. Her pearl necklace and earrings completed her royal persona, while her husband wore a pair of Walmart jeans with a beige flannel shirt. This was it; there was no turning back now.

Sherman decided to make direct contact with Ronelle's mother. He figured his best chance of success was to focus on winning Brenda Fortier. So, he cleared his throat.

"Good evening Mr. and Mrs. Fortier. Thank you for giving me a few moments of your time before Ronelle makes it home." Sherman reached into his blazer pocket, pulled out a jewelry box, and opened it to reveal a beautiful marquis-cut diamond ring. The ring had little princess stones on both sides of the platinum band. He handed it to Brenda. She gasped and covered her mouth.

"I've been saving every dime for nine months just to purchase this ring. Your daughter is the perfect woman for me, and I wanted her to have the perfect ring. I stand here tonight and ask you for your blessings to marry Ronelle. I promise to love her, protect her, and to provide for her a life filled with joy, laughter, and commitment. May I, please, have your daughter's hand in marriage?" Sherman asked.

Steven Fortier laughed out loud as he recovered from his shock. "For a minute there I thought you were about to propose to my wife," he bellowed, with several hard coughs in between.

"Dad, I was thinking the same thing," Brandon joked.

Steven walked over to his wine cabinet in search of a bottle he'd saved for a moment such as this. "Son, I like you. I mean I really like you. Not just because you're Melvin's son and he's my source for free LSU football tickets to watch your brothers play. That doesn't play a factor at all."

"Sherman, if you believe my dad, then I have some beachfront property to sell you in the Lower Ninth Ward," Brandon laughed.

"I admit, the LSU football tickets may have played a small part in giving you my blessings," Steven blushed red with laughter. "But . . . but, I like the man you've evolved into. I like how you carry yourself. Yes, your father and I are buddies, but you have earned my respect individually. I just knew you would follow Melvin into law. I lost that bet, by the way."

Steven placed the vintage bottle on the kitchen table with four wine glasses. Then he continued. "My daughter really cares about you. She's spoiled beyond repair, but you have accepted that challenge. If you're sure, then you have my blessings."

Sherman rushed over to Steven, and the two of them embraced in a big, warm hug. Immediately, all eyes turned to Brenda. Even with all the makeup she was wearing, Sherman could still see that her face was completely red underneath.

"Oh, my, I'm not sure what to say." She handed the ring back to Sherman as tears welled in her eyes. "Sherman, I'm sorry, but I can't give you my blessings to marry Ronelle. I'm so sorry!" Brenda turned on her heels and hurried to her bedroom, leaving a breeze of perfume wafting through the kitchen.

Sherman was shocked. All of them were shocked. No one spoke. It was not the response any of them had expected.

Steven Fortier followed Brenda into the bedroom where he found her collapsed across the bed weeping, her face buried in a satin pillow.

"What was that about?" Steven yelled. "How could you do that to Sherman? He is an exceptional young man. They have dated going on four years now!" Sherman listened as Brenda continued to cry out. "Brenda, you had ample enough time to prepare yourself for this night. You knew it was coming; we knew it was coming. How could you?" Steven waited for her to respond. "Brenda, you're not getting off that easy. You will talk to me!" Steven roared, but she only cried louder.

"Sherm, I'm so sorry about this," Brandon apologized. "None of us saw that coming, but my dad will get to the bottom of whatever is going on."

All of a sudden, Brandon and Sherman heard an ear-piercing yell from the master bedroom as the argument escalated.

"You better start talking, Brenda. This better not be because he's black!" Steven stood near the side of the bed where Brenda could not avoid him.

"Get the hell out my face, Steven. How dare you accuse me of being a racist? How dare you!"

Back in the living room, Brandon and Sherman heard the sound of jingle-bells as a key slid into the front door lock. The time was nine forty-five. Ronelle was home.

"Hey, guys, what's going on?" she asked as she walked over to kiss Sherman. "What's all the yelling about?" Ronelle leaned into the hall but kept her distance. "Brandon, what did you do this time?" she asked as she dropped her bags and walked over to the refrigerator.

That's when her mother screamed again. "I have my reasons for not agreeing to this, and I'll be damned if I allow you to insult my character by insinuating that it's about his skin color!"

Ronelle froze. "Okay, what's going on? Why are they arguing like this?" she asked her brother.

Sherman placed the ring in his pocket before Ronelle could notice and made his way out the door. She followed him and screamed his name, but Sherman continued to his car. She pursued. Sherman refused to roll down the window. He started the engine. With two fingers, he touched his lips, then touched the glass. With tears rolling down his cheeks, he slowly reversed out of the driveway with Ronelle pulling on the door handle.

"You better roll down this window and talk to me!" Ronelle banged on the window. "I know this involves my mother. What did she say to you? Why are you crying? Sherman, open this door! Sherman!"

Sherman lowered the window just a little bit, so she could hear him. "I love you, no matter what, and I want to spend the rest of my life loving you. No matter what."

He slowly drove off, leaving Ronelle standing under a triangle of light from a streetlamp. Ronelle ran back into the house just as the argument in her parents' room escalated.

Loud!

Intense!

Confrontational!

"Brandon, please explain what just happened here. Did Mom say something inappropriate to Sherman? What did I miss here tonight? What's going on?"

"Ronelle, Sherman asked Mom and Dad for their permission

to marry you. Dad said yes, but Mom . . . but Mom said—"

"Brandon, what did Mom say?"

"I'm sorry. Mom said no!"

"Mom said what?"

"Sherman stood right there and asked to marry you. I was so proud of him because I knew how scared he was to approach them, but he pulled it off. Just when I thought we would have a celebration tonight, Mom flipped out! She handed him the ring back, then ran to her bedroom. Dad was about to pop open a bottle of wine when he took off after her. They have been back there fighting ever since. Ronelle, I am so sorry! Sherman didn't deserve what happened here tonight."

Ronelle's face turned as red as a candy apple. She raced down the hall toward her parents' room and kicked it in like a drug bust.

"Mom, I cannot believe you! How could you?" Ronelle pointed inward as she approached the bed. "This was the night I have dreamed about, and you ruined it! How could you do this to me?" Ronelle asked, a thunderstorm of emotion.

Brenda Fortier did not acknowledge her daughter's questions.

"Mom, why won't you accept him? He's a really good guy and a man that I love and respect. Why isn't that enough for you?"

Brenda didn't reply.

"Mom, answer me!" Ronelle demanded. "Sherman is a freaking PhD grad student at Tulane, for God's sake. The only reason I can see for you not giving him your blessings is because you don't want your white daughter married to a black man!"

Brenda said nothing as Ronelle's tirade continued.

"Dad has accepted him, but you can't? And you give no reason for it?"

"Ronelle, I don't expect you to understand, but I have my reasons," Brenda finally replied.

"Then share those reasons with me! I want to know why you rejected him!"

Brenda exercised her right to remain silent. Ronelle walked over to the far corner of the room and sat in her dad's recliner. "I'm not leaving until you talk to me."

Steven threw up his hands and left the room.

Ronelle lowered her voice for the first time.

"Mom, you owe me an explanation, don't look away."

Ronelle's words bounced off her mother like the back wall of a racquetball court. Like an indicted politician, Brenda offered no comment.

No elucidation.

No clarification.

No justification.

"Mom, I know what this is about, even though you're avoiding my questions. When I was passed over for Queen of Carnival three years ago, you never got over it. As much power as you have in the Krewe of Rex, the fact that they never selected your daughter as queen has made you hate Sherman. Well, I never wanted to be queen. That was your dream, Momma. You had your turn as queen. You did everything the *right way*, according to those stiff bitches in that society, but I just want to live my life."

Ronelle stood over her mother. "If his proposal still stands after the horrible way you've treated him, then I will be honored to be his wife. With or without your blessings! I will marry a *black man*." Ronelle said as she headed for the door.

"Ronelle this has nothing to do with the Rex Organization, and I ask that you leave them out of it," Brenda said.

"Bullshit, Mom. If it's not about Rex, then it's about your racist heart!"

"I AM NOT A RACIST!" Brenda screamed. "I am not going to allow you and your father to accuse me of being one. If you want to marry Sherman, then do so. But just know this: I am one hundred percent against this marriage!" Brenda approached Ronelle in a full-blown rage. "And another thing, young lady, you will not use words like 'bullshit' when speaking to me. Not in my house! Are we clear?"

"Well, I guess the time has come to vacate your house because this is bullshit! Are we clear?"

The sound of hangers crashing to the floor rang through the hall as Ronelle packed her things. Brandon and her father watched as she carried bundles of clothes to her car, then burned rubber out of the driveway.

After his failed marriage proposal, Sherman returned to his apartment alone, accompanied only by the engagement ring. He couldn't resist the pressure to pee, so he bolted for the bathroom, leaving a trail of clothes on the floor that included his black tie and blazer. Standing at the toilet for what felt like an hour, Sherman couldn't get her out of his mind. Not Ronelle, but Brenda. How she had said no without a bit of hesitation. How she had frowned when he asked to marry her daughter. How she had thrust the ring back into his hands and hauled ass to her bedroom.

So, I'm not rich enough?

So, I'm not white enough?

So, you reject me? Well, fuck you, Brenda!

Before leaving the bathroom, Sherman opened the medicine cabinet and there it was on the second glass shelf—his Adderall. *If I take this pill, it's going to be an all-nighter, but fuck it, I might as well get some work done.*

Sherman lived in an upscale building that was formerly the old Blue Plate Mayonnaise Factory at 1315 Jefferson Davis Parkway. After Hurricane Katrina, the building was converted into luxury condos. He loved his two-bedroom apartment with the high industrial ceilings and oversized windows. Unit nine was the ultimate bachelor pad, but the only problem was that Sherman no longer wanted to be a bachelor. He wanted Ronelle.

At the kitchen table, Sherman powered on his laptop and opened the file that contained his thesis, but the words were far away. Less than a paragraph in, his focus detached.

That bitch! That bitch! That racist bitch!

Sherman tried again to focus on his paper, but his anger wouldn't allow a single thought that wasn't associated with Brenda Fortier. After several deep breaths, he finally managed to calm, but could only manage a few fragmented sentences before his fingers stiffened like twigs. *I can't concentrate on this tonight*, he conceded to his thoughts about Brenda.

But I must get some work done.

Suddenly there was a warming feeling in the curves of his ears, and a blast of cool air through his nostrils. Like dark clouds that parted to make way for a rejuvenated sun, his rage against Brenda was swept away by a euphoric breeze. Brenda no longer mattered, tonight no longer mattered, and the engagement ring no longer mattered. But the thesis mattered. The reason the thesis still mattered was because of the thought he had at the exact moment the Adderall entered his bloodstream: *Fuck Brenda, I must get some work done.* And so, his fingers attacked the keyboard and transcribed each thought at a rhythmic pace that continued for thirty-five hundred words. He typed fiercely until he was distracted by tiny bells outside of his front door. It was Ronelle and her keychain of trinkets.

She entered the apartment carrying a bundle of clothes up to her chin and dropped it on the sofa. Before Sherman could ask if she needed help, Ronelle was out the door. She returned several times until every available space in the living room held piles of clothes, bags, and purses. Whereas Sherman had managed to regain his composure, Ronelle was still in the heat of the argument with her mother. After she locked the door, Sherman watched as she paced around the coffee table, smoke shooting out of her ears. Finally, after about ten minutes, she managed to join him at the kitchen table, and it was then that her anger made way for tears.

"Baby, I'm so sorry. I have no words to express how bad this feels."

"It's not your fault . . ."

"But it's my mother who ruined this night for us."

"Ronelle, I'm over it."

"But I'm not. She had no right to treat you like that!"

"But she does have every right to her feelings, whether I like it or not."

"Well, how she feels doesn't matter, because this is my life, and she will not control or dictate who I love."

"I agree, how your mother feels about me doesn't matter," Sherman said as he walked around the table and kneeled. Ronelle's hands came together in front of her lips.

"I was going to do this on Friday, but tonight feels perfect."

Sherman presented the ring. "Ronelle, I've loved you since our first date three years ago. I'm happy we are alone, so I can ask you a very important question. Make me the happiest man on earth: *Will you marry me?*"

"Yes, yes, a thousand times, yes!"

Sherman slid the ring onto her finger and stood. Ronelle kissed him deep and long. "Yes! Yes! Yes! I will marry you; it's all I ever wanted."

⚜

The room was just starting to steam, and her body was on the verge of shifting into disclaimer mode when Ronelle first noticed it: his erection died. It was a strange occurrence because his penis was always swollen and hard like her jumbo curling iron, but not tonight. Tonight it deflated deep inside of her. As he apologized, she figured his mind was probably distracted due to the events of the evening and the ugly way in which her mother had treated him. *That alone would make it difficult to concentrate on making love*, she thought.

"Sweetie, I'm sorry my mother ruined your plans. But I'm flattered you suffered it all for me," she said as he rolled off her.

His breathing was heavy. "I'm over it, trust me I am. And besides, your dad said yes, so I'll take that as a partial victory."

"I know, but tonight would have been so perfect if not for my mom."

"Tonight is still perfect because of you, and it looks like you've just moved in, so it's all good," he laughed.

"Yes, I have moved in and I will plan my wedding right here." Ronelle sat to view her ring in a beam of moonlight. "Wow, I'm going to be your wife. Mrs. Ronelle Campbell!"

She didn't remember dozing off, but when she reached for him in the middle of the night, Sherman wasn't there. Her head raised in alarm as her eyes verified the time; it was an hour past midnight and Sherman was gone. Just as she was about to call him, she heard the sound of frantic typing coming from the kitchen. Sherman was so intensely immersed in thought as he typed that he didn't notice her leaning halfway in from the bedroom, but she noticed him. Shirtless, in his boxers. Lean and ripped.

She loved his military bald fade haircut, his razor-thin eyebrows that he inherited from his father, and even his paper-thin ears. His golden skin and athletic shoulders made her want to sit across his lap, but she didn't want to disturb his groove on the keyboard. *I could stare at him forever and never get tired, and never say a word, like a stalker . . .*

That's when he felt her eyes, and his fingers froze immediately. "Sweetie, I didn't see you standing there . . ."

"I didn't mean to bother you, but I reached over and no longer felt your sexy body, that's all."

"Yeah, sorry about that, but I couldn't sleep."

"I have something that will help you sleep, it's waiting on you when you're done."

"Thank you, baby." He reached for her. "As soon as I'm done we're going for round two."

He caressed her hips as she leaned down for a quick kiss. Then, Ronelle and her pink lace panties slowly left the room.

It was the clicking that woke her up the second time, at around five o'clock in the morning. Ronelle reached for Sherman, patting her hand under the sheets only to discover that she was alone. For the second time, she leaned halfway into the kitchen from the bedroom, but Sherman never noticed. His fingers collided with the keys like this was his last morning to live, like he only had until dawn to complete his memoir. Periodically, he would pause to proof what he had written, pound the delete button about ten times, then resume typing like a gun was held to his head.

Ronelle had never witnessed anything like it; not from Sherman before, or in any of her creative writing classes. Ronelle was in awe of how effortlessly he moved words from his mind down through his fingertips and then onto the white page on the screen. As much as she wanted to make love to him, she respected the creative process enough to keep her distance. And so, she returned to their bed and allowed the clacking from the kitchen to rock her back to sleep. *Leave it all on the page, my prince.*

The bright morning sun opened her eyelids one at a time. She was alone. The digital clock on the nightstand with the neon green numbers left little doubt of the time; it was a quarter after eight.

"Where is my future husband?" she asked in a whiny voice. "No . . . way!"

From the kitchen table, she heard Sherman's fingers colliding with the keys on his laptop like cords on a Steinway. She opted not to disturb his rush of creative energy, so Ronelle made her way to the shower.

He's going to need a new laptop after the completion of that paper; my babe is killing it in there. Ronelle gathered her towels. *Hopefully he wraps it up by the time I'm done with my shower.*

An hour later, Ronelle entered the kitchen to find Sherman in the same spot, with the same intense look, typing at the same frantic paste, and it was then that she remembered something he had said:

I don't eat, sleep, or even think about sex until I complete the task at hand or it burns out of my system. Trust me baby, it's the Adderall.

Ronelle walked past where Sherman sat, placed a coffee pod in the Keurig, and peeled a banana. It wasn't until he inhaled the roasted beans that he finally noticed Ronelle standing to his left in front of the coffee machine.

"So, you wrote the entire dissertation in one night? Brandon will love you for it," she joked.

"I didn't write his section, only fine-tuned my opening and a few chapters in the body, that's all."

"A few chapters?"

"That's all it was . . ."

With her coffee mug and banana in hand, Ronelle asked, "Sherman how many words did you type last night?"

"Somewhere around ninety-four hundred words, I think . . . but I'm done."

"Interesting," she said as she reached into her bathrobe pocket to retrieve her cell phone. "And did you take an Adderall pill last night?"

He looked at her with a suspicious expression. "Yes, why do you ask?"

"About what time?"

"Right before you arrived . . ."

"So around, nine o'clock last night?"

"Yes, give or take a few minutes. Why do you ask?"

"Just wondering, that's all. Can I make you some breakfast?"

"No thank you, I need a quick shower and a nap. Maybe around lunch time I will have an appetite for breakfast." Sherman kissed her on the forehead on his way to the shower.

Then, the search results appeared on her cell: *The side effects of Adderall.*

The time on the microwave was 9:15 a.m.—a total of twelve grueling hours since he had swallowed that pill. The pill that caused him to deflate inside of her.

Sherman was telling the truth; the tunnel is real. But I wonder if he's addicted?

THE MASTER'S WIFE DIARY ENTRY FOUR

May 8, 1854
Breakfast Entry

Dear Diary,

Over the years I have grown to love her like a sister. It was surprising even to me, but we have just become as close. With the attentiveness of a lifelong companion, she listens without judgment—unlike my husband, who barely listens with half an ear, who waits for a long pause to signify the conversation has concluded. Not Beatrice; she takes in every word. What a valuable quality to have in a friend. I just wish she would talk more about her life and share more of her feelings. Does she have a long-lost love? She never talks at all about the father of her boys. She withdraws the moment I bring up the subject. From my perspective, life for Negro women must be unbearable. I only wish God would impart some of her resilience and determination on me. There was a time when all I wanted was to be as attractive as Beatrice. My recent prayer was for her strength.

Oh, how I long to know her thoughts. For now, I'm content with having her around on those days when I need a shoulder to cry on.

Dear and faithful Diary, I would be remiss to conclude this entry without a mention of her incredible skills as a seamstress.

Only yesterday, the Opera House of New Orleans ordered twelve more dresses for upcoming performances. It is safe to say my little boutique has become their preferred vendor. None of this would have been possible without Beatrice, but she refuses to take one dime in compensation, always reminding me of the fine home we have provided for her and the boys. I don't know what I would do without her by my side at the boutique or in this house. Beatrice has heard my every complaint, including my grievances with my husband and my feelings of emotional abandonment.

All the ill disdain I once held for her, all the jealousy, has vanished. How silly of me to think such a kind spirit would do something to hurt me or jeopardize our bond. That's all for now—until my next entry.

Content & Enduring

CHAPTER 12

May 11, 1854

Beatrice completed the five-inch hem on an evening gown she had designed for Queenie: "And done . . . it's beautiful!" The gown was emerald green with a black empire waist and floral embroidered print. She was very pleased with her work on the midsection, particularly on the eighteen-inch waistline. Despite being academically illiterate, as a seamstress, Beatrice knew just enough math to go from pattern to completion within three days. The ability to read was not a prerequisite; only vision, focus, and cutting skills were needed. After a few last-minute alterations to the portrait neckline and the bishop-style sleeves, Queenie's new dress was a completed masterpiece of stitched fabrics, interwoven with Beatrice's refined expertise.

I should keep this one for myself.

An internal voice suggested she swap it out for something less appealing and far less stunning. Then she was reminded of that frigid morning on the auction block—how icy winds had cut across her exposed skin like razor-sharp fingernails. Beatrice recalled how all the other bidders had laughed at her tiny breasts and diminutive waist, and clearly remembered that she had been the last Negress presented, right before the hogs. That was all before he saw her and stepped forward. Though nearly twenty years had passed, she could still hear his bid above the octaves of ridicule; few took him seriously, not even the auctioneer. Beatrice did not care if he had bid out of pity or a need to end his vicarious humiliation. She was grateful to step down off the auction block. This dress was for his wife.

Beatrice resolved in her spirit to give the dress away, if for no other reason than gratitude. And so, she surrendered it; the most gorgeous creation her calloused fingers had ever sewn. It was not her gown to keep. After applying a lukewarm iron to the hem, she stoically hung the dress full-length on the upper railing between the wooden bedposts in her master's room.

Tonight, her master and his wife had plans to see Gioachino Rossini perform at the Théâtre d'Orléans Opera House. Beatrice was very excited that her latest design was finished just in time. A deep sigh blew a lock of hair away from her eye, giving her a final view of a gown that had become her companion over the past few days. She wished she had more time to add this or that, and pouted at the thought of letting it go. Such was the way of things: as it was for her first mistress, Mrs. de Marigny, it continued for Queenie.

Suddenly, there was a soft knock on the front door. Beatrice headed downstairs to answer. It was the hairdresser for Queenie. Beatrice greeted her with a smile and a gesture to follow. Marie was the most sought-after hairdresser in New Orleans, and Beatrice was the most sought-after gown designer. Unlike Beatrice, however, the hairdresser was an exclusive member of *femmes de couleur libres*. Envious, Beatrice dreamed of becoming a free woman of color before she was elderly like the midwife. For the time being, she settled for being an ornament.

"Good seeing you again, Beatrice," Marie said.

"Good seein' you too, Marie. Follow me. She's waitin' fo' you."

Beatrice escorted Marie up the stairs. Queenie was waiting for Marie in a salon room her husband had designed as a fifth-year anniversary gift. It featured a large mirror in front of a vanity styling chair. The custom-designed room had white walls with pink crown molding just below the ceiling. An ottoman in the back corner held a vase with freshly-cut tulips. The room also featured an east-facing window that allowed the maximum amount of light and breeze on cool autumn days.

When Beatrice and Marie arrived at the salon on the second floor, Queenie was already sitting in her chair in front of the large mirror, writing in her diary.

"Thank you, Marie, for coming on such short notice, and thank you, Beatrice, for escorting her up. That's all I need for now, until it's time to get dressed."

Beatrice partially closed the door behind her as she left the room, leaving just enough of a crack for her to eavesdrop on their conversation. As soon as Marie started the hairstyling process, Queenie began gushing about everything from local gossip to romantic suggestions to spice up her marriage.

"Some nights he doesn't touch me. No matter what I wear to bed or how I caress him, he has no passion for me," Queenie said to Marie.

"Passion starts in his head. If you're in his head during the daylight, he will enter you in the night," Marie replied.

"But how, Marie? How do I get into his head? Please tell me," Queenie giggled.

"With your words, Madame, with your words. Not touch. Speak the passion you want. Say what you want in the morning, and he will bring that passion to your bed at night."

"Sometimes I feel like he has lost all desire for me. Some days I wish he would grab me like a sailor who has been at sea since autumn. I want him to pull up my dress and take me like a cheap whore. I wish he would have his way with me—just once! I want him all the time. But he has no desire for me."

Marie reached into her bag and handed Queenie a small jar, the kind used for jelly preservatives. In the jar was a dark red liquid that resembled red wine, but thicker—like strawberry syrup. Queenie opened the jar to smell the liquid. "What is this? It has no fragrance, none at all."

"*Verser un peu de desir dans son vin,*" Marie replied.

"I'm sorry, but I don't speak much French—not as much as my husband."

"'*Verser un peu de desir dans son vin'* means pour desire into his wine," Marie explained. "Young bulls need little help. Old bulls *besoin de beaucoup*."

"Old bulls need a lot?"

"*Oui*, Madame!" Marie replied. "*Verser un peu de desir dans son vin* and speak the passion you want. He will hunt you down," Marie said, adding a few words of caution.

"Thank you, Marie. You may have saved my marriage."

"There you go. I'm done with your hair. How do you like?"

"It's beautiful! Thank you for everything!"

"*Merci*, Madame," Marie replied.

Queenie paid Marie generously for her services. Then, she yelled out into the hallway. "Beatrice, please escort Mistress Marie Laveau to the front door. Thank you kindly."

Beatrice was only a few feet away. She had heard every word of their conversation. As she escorted Marie Laveau to the front door, she was completely enamored. She was especially in awe of how she spoke to Queenie; like an equal, not with the required vernacular of slaves. Beatrice opened the door for Marie, studying every detail of her face. She counted every freckle, recording her movements, her posture, even the gracefulness of her walk. She wanted to be Marie: both free and respected.

Once Marie stepped down onto the pavement, she gestured for Beatrice to step outside. "I have someone I would like for you to meet. Her master is not kind to her. Not kind like your master. He is very cruel. A very evil man! His name is Mr. Lafitte. He lives next door to me, but there is someone in the rear of his house I would like you to meet."

"To meet? Who?" Beatrice asked.

"You will see for yourself. Come to my house when your master is at the opera. I live on St. Ann Street. The yellow house you pass on the way to Congo Square. I will sit outside and wait for you."

"I will be there," Beatrice replied.

The following day
Around 9:15 p.m.

About halfway up the block on St. Ann Street, Beatrice could see a yellow house; a lady was sitting on the front porch. Walking the streets of the French Quarter after dark was extremely dangerous for slaves because of kidnappers, but her curiosity was a powerful motivator. With every step that brought her nearer to the yellow house, more questions entered her mind. Beatrice wanted to meet the woman Marie told her about; it was all she had thought about that day. She also wanted time alone with Marie because she had issues of her own to discuss.

Beatrice arrived at the yellow house. Marie smiled.

"Who is the woman you want me to meet?" Beatrice asked.

Marie placed a finger over her lips. "Listen!"

From the house next door to Marie, Beatrice heard the faint sound of a woman screaming in intervals. The house was a single-story red brick cottage with two attic windows on top. There was a wooden fence that led down a narrow alley along the left side. The red brick house sat very close to the yellow house where Marie lived; less than six feet separated the homes.

Every two minutes, they heard another scream. Beatrice listened for ten minutes.

"Wrap your face in this cloth," Marie said. She handed Beatrice a sheer purple scarf to wrap her face. Beatrice obliged, then she took a seat next to Marie.

The screams continued—one following the other—louder and louder. Marie reached for Beatrice's hand and began to pray in French. Beatrice prayed in broken English. After about thirty minutes, the screams inside the house next door ended. The house fell silent.

The moon was full. Turning off Rampart Street onto St. Ann, a mule and buggy rolled by. In the back of the buggy was a large cube of ice.

"Good evening, ladies," an elderly black man said as he guided the mule down St. Ann Street.

"Good evening, sir." Marie replied.

They watched the ice wagon slowly roll in the direction of

Bourbon Street, a late-night delivery for an all-night bar. Marie reached for Beatrice's hand once again. They locked fingers as a woman traveled at a hurried pace in their direction.

The woman wore an all-black maid's dress that swept the ground, and her hair was wrapped in a matching black cloth. Once the woman reached the middle of the block, Beatrice recognized her. It was Clarice.

"What she doin' here?" Beatrice asked.

"Quiet!" Marie replied.

Moments later, Clarice entered the red brick house next door—the same house where the screams had come from. The house remained silent for a moment, and then the screams started again.

"No! No! You can't have her! No!" a woman cried out. "Bring my baby back! I beg you! Please bring back my baby girl! Please! Stop her!"

Beatrice watched as Clarice exited the house carrying a baby that was less than an hour old—still crying—wrapped in a black blanket. Clarice walked at a steady pace back in the same direction she had come from, while the mother of the baby cried out from behind her. "Clarice! Clarice, come back here! Clarice, I hate you! I hate you!"

Once Clarice made it one block up St. Ann Street, she made a hard left turn and vanished into the night.

"Why did you bring me here?" Beatrice asked Marie. "Why you made me watch this? This too much for me!"

"Because there is someone I want you to meet. Follow me. Don't remove your scarf."

Beatrice followed Marie to the red brick house. As they entered the front door, a scratchy-faced man adjusted his vest and shirt in front of a wall mounted mirror. He and Marie knew each other well.

"Mr. Lafitte, you're leaving out?"

"Yes, I am! I always need a drink after a delivery," he said.

"Well, I just want to check on her. We won't be too long. Just want to make sure she heals well," Marie said.

"Sure, take your time. I will be out until morning," Mr. Lafitte said as he walked out the front door.

Marie continued to the back of the house. Beatrice could still hear a woman crying—not as loud as before, but continuous.

"Why did you bring me here? Why?" Beatrice asked Marie again, but this time, she didn't answer. Marie continued in a straight line to the rear of the house, to the room where the wailing flowed like a current in the Mississippi.

Hearing the woman cry ripped open a scar Beatrice knew could never heal on its own, nor could she find anything to soothe the pain. The sorrow was all too familiar; the way Clarice appeared in the middle of the night after a full day of labor pains and vanished into the night with her baby. Even if she hadn't heard the woman's pleas, Beatrice would have been certain that she had also given birth to a girl.

In the short distance from the front door to the back of the house, Beatrice wondered how Clarice could do it. How could she take a newborn baby out of her mother's arms over and over again? Then, her mind shifted back to the woman Marie wanted her to meet, the woman in the rear of the house.

They entered the back room to find a midwife caring for a woman crying under a dingy bed sheet. The weeping mother paid no attention to the midwife as she applied healing oils to her vaginal area, nor did she notice Marie and Beatrice standing just inside the doorway. The midwife acknowledged Marie with a nod of the head only. She also had tears in her eyes. Beatrice did not know the teary-eyed midwife, but Marie knew her well.

Marie walked over to the mother and whispered, "I know this is hard for you. I know this is the seventh time Clarice ran off with your baby."

"I will kill her! I will kill him, too. I will cut both of their throats!" the mother said. Beatrice also wanted to kill Clarice, but never could bring herself to utter the words.

"May I remove this sheet?" Marie asked. "I have someone I'd like you to meet."

"Leave me now! Leave!" The mother cried.

"But I have someone here who understands your pain—that witch also took her babies. I know this to be true, because Harriett Green confessed one day when I was curling her hair for a ball. So, I brought her here just for you, so she can help you.

Please remove the sheet."

Marie stood between them as the woman slowly removed the sheet from her face. Marie turned to face Beatrice and asked her to remove the purple scarf. Marie Laveau stepped to the side, out of their line of sight, and formally introduced them.

"Beatrice, I would like you to meet Marietta, your sister. Marietta, meet your twin."

Beatrice fell to her knees.

THE MASTER'S WIFE DIARY ENTRY FIVE

May 14, 1854
Breakfast Entry

Dear Diary,

Several times this week I have followed Marie Laveau's instructions and added a few drops of her love serum to my husband's wine. Marie is wise beyond her years. My husband has become a sex hound of a sort, but it's not for me. We are indeed making love more than before, but he appears to be in a hurry. I can almost watch the serum moving through his body. First, he starts to sweat, and then he complains about a stuffy nose. Finally, he attacks me. When I say my husband attacks me, it is not my intent to insinuate a complimentary act, like a man returning from a long voyage. It's more like I am a crevice.

Pound!

Pound!

Pound!

Then he's done with me. Just like that, without a kiss goodnight, he leaves our bed. Detached and dismissed. I asked my husband last night if he had a scheduled appointment somewhere more important than in my arms.

Of course, he took offense, but what else am I to think? Every night he pulls me to his side of the bed, carries on like a rabbit for a few minutes, then heads out the door to Lord knows where.

When my husband returns from his walk, there is always this slight grin, a look of relief—a suspicious calmness that he never achieves in our bedroom. I wonder if he is smoking those plants from the tribesmen. My husband vowed that day, two years ago, never to smoke those plants again. He said he felt like the room was spinning. Now as I recall, he took a very long walk that night, as well.

I am purely baffled.

He says the walks help him calm down and relax, but I feel there is more to it. I do not think it is another woman my husband hurries to, because he is home every night, but I do believe he's not completely open and honest with me. As far as the serum is concerned, it was worth every dime I spent, but I doubt if I will purchase additional bottles. Unfortunately, I have the right remedy, but it grieves me to admit I'm enticing the wrong type of man. That serum would work best for a man who is excited about his wife but needs a little spark, not for a man who has a penis the size of a candlewick. Please forgive me for my anger, but I can't help it—this marriage is not what I dreamed of in my mother's house.

Frustrated.

CHAPTER 13

After his shower, Sherman and Ronelle decided to take a trip to the grocery store to fully stock the cabinets and pick up a sleep aid to help him calm down. He was nowhere near sleepy and appeared to talk more than normal—about the first thought that came to his mind. *I can do this forever*, she thought as their fingers intertwined on the center console.

She had no ill feelings about last night because Sherman had recently committed the effort required to make her feel relevant: he included her in his daily life and remembered the little things that were so often forgotten before. He was different; far more affectionate outside of sex, and first to initiate public displays of intimacy. He released her hand long enough to survey the inside of her soft thighs, as if he'd lost familiarity and needed to relocate every curve.

Ronelle also noticed he was more relaxed when they discussed their future as husband and wife. It was a noticeable difference from the way he once scurried like a crab at the first mention of adult things like a baby and buying a home together.

I don't know if this change in Sherman is due to our engagement or the Adderall, and I don't care. I have fallen in love again.

"Hey, Uncle Clarence, it's too early in the morning for beer, isn't it?" Sherman laughed. His uncle turned around as the car pulled to a stop beside him.

"It's my favorite nephew! Puddin'!" Clarence said as he leaned into the passenger side window.

Clarence acknowledged Ronelle. "Good morning, Fortier gurl with yo' rich-ass self! Give me twenty dollars!" Clarence took a swig of his beer. "Boy, I was just thinkin' bout you two."

Sherman put the car in park. "Jump in, Unc. Let me give you a lift."

"You see, that's why I love you, Puddin'! You not jive like your so-phis-tic-cated-ass pa."

Ronelle laughed. Sherman agreed. "Where are you headed?"

"I'm headed up here to the Day Labor Office. Make me a quick lil' four-hour hustle. Mo' money for the beer!" he laughed.

"You know, Uncle Clarence, I appreciate the conversation we had last week. It really got me off to a good start. Before I spoke with you, I was getting nowhere. Now we know we're looking for Grandma Beatrice."

"Nephew, I'm happy to help. Everybody considers me a wino, so nobody asks me for my opinion no more. But what I know I know and beer can't take that from me." He took a long gulp of his beer. "Now what you oughta do is borrow some of your girlfriend's whiteness and go over by Abigail's. Ronelle can get it, but not your black ass!" Clarence slapped his thigh in laughter.

Ronelle interrupted him to show off her new ring. "I would have you know I am no longer just a girlfriend, Uncle Clarence!" Ronelle flashed her ring again "Hello! I am now the future Mrs. Sherman Campbell."

"Well, excuse me, Mrs. Campbell. Congratulations! See there, ain't nobody told me nothing!"

"I just proposed last night, Unc, so looks like you're actually the first to know she said yes."

"So, my brother don't know yet? Karma is a bitch," Clarence joked. "As I was saying, have your future wife go knock on the door and ask Abigail to let her take a look at that slave quarters. When I was a kid, I heard my momma talking to her sister about Abigail's house. She said that if you go into the roof of that house, you'll find a beam with nine chips of wood missing for every child our great-great-grandmother delivered into slavery. Trouble is, none of us in the family has ever been able to get into that house to know for sure."

"Wait, you're telling me Grandmother Annette had eight brothers and sisters? What happened to all of them, and why has Grandma refused to talk about them?"

"It's simple! If it could be proven that Grandma Annette is one of those wood chips that's missing, or shall I say one of those notches in the wood up there in that attic, then we have some money coming to us."

Sherman's interest in this story increased one hundred-fold.

"You see, we come from money, a lot of money. We just got cut out of our share of that money. Back then, no one believed our black asses was related by blood to the old wealthy slave master. But when he died, he left money and property to our great-great-grandmother." Clarence took another swig, then continued. "Her children who passed for white couldn't let it be known they had black blood mixed in their white blood, so with a lot of under-handed deals at the civil court, we got cut out."

"So, what you're suggesting is for Ronelle to go to Abigail's house and rummage up in her attic looking for those nine notches?"

"Not just that, nephew! I'm saying to you to put all that fancy Tulane education to use and help us take back what was stolen from us, our birthright," suggested Clarence.

At that very moment, Sherman knew his Uncle Clarence had just given him another gift.

"Hey, you can let me out right here by this liquor store. I need one more beer and some breath mints before I get on the job site," he laughed. "Lil' niece-in-law, let your uncle hold two 'til the loot through."

"Hold what?" Ronelle giggled.

"He's asking you for two ten-dollar bills until he gets paid."

"Okay. Hmmm . . . Thanks for translating," She laughed. Uncle Clarence smiled. Sherman took out his wallet and handed his uncle a hundred-dollar bill.

"See, that why I love you, Puddin'! You're not jive like your pa! Thank you!"

"Uncle Clarence, now you know you have no business going on that job site drunk."

"Who you callin' drunk? From two beers? Boy, this is my coffee. I'm ready to work now. Take this pretty little wife of yours and get over there to Abigail's and get our money." He turned to Ronelle. "Sweetheart, let me be the first to welcome you into our crazy-ass family. Love ya."

"Awww, thank you, Uncle Clarence!" Ronelle said. "I see why Sherman always refers to you as his favorite uncle. I love you too, Uncle Clarence." She kissed him on his cheek.

The car slowed to a stop. Clarence got out and headed down the street. Sherman and Ronelle sat for a moment, joking about how cool it was that Clarence walked like he was headed to a Funkadelic concert in 1977. As he watched Clarence walk away, Sherman suddenly felt an urgency to follow his uncle's advice.

"So, Ronelle?"

"Yes, my future husband?"

"Can I borrow some of your whiteness?"

"Sure! Anything for you, darling." Ronelle made sweet eyes at Sherman.

Sherman and Ronelle laughed. It was a beautiful morning!

Jackson Square
The Plan

"Okay, here's the game plan," Sherman said to Ronelle. "You'll pose as an architectural design student from Tulane and ask Abigail for permission to study the historical relevance of her French Quarter home."

"Sherman, I think it's a great plan because the residents in the French Quarter are always accepting requests to view their historic homes. All the homeowners in the Quarter love maga-zine features. Get a front-page spread in *Better Homes and Gar-*

dens and your property value could double. I think it's a great strategy to get inside Abigail's home."

"While on site I need you to view the attic over the main property and the attic over the rear slave quarters. If Clarence is right about the marks in the attic, then everything else he said is more than likely true."

"I think it's the first step in confirming your family is related to Abigail. And her side of the family cutting your great-grandmother's side out of their inheritance."

"Correct! You sure you're up for this?"

"Am I ever! This is exciting stuff! And I don't like what they did to your grandmother. Everything we have comes from an inheritance. Without it, my life would look completely different. I'm all in. The worst thing she could say is no, but we'll never know unless I ask."

They decided it was best that Sherman park the car and wait for Ronelle at the old Jax Brewery Mall, which sat on the outside of the French Quarter, directly on the levee bank. Ronelle would take her camera and ask if she could view the house as part of a photo documentary. Once they were both clear about the plan, Ronelle exited the car and walked through Jackson Square in the direction of Abigail's residence.

CHAPTER 14

A visit to the red brick house
May 17, 1854

Today marked the second evening since Clarice stole Marietta's baby, and Beatrice was paralyzed with worry for the well-being of her sister. From the many dinner conversations she had overheard between her master and Mr. Lafitte, she knew him to be a very cruel man—one who took sadistic pleasure in the inhumane treatment of slaves that didn't return a profit.

I must take care of her, I must, and Queenie will help me. I know she will.

It was Marie Laveau who cared for her sister during the mornings, in between salon clients, but during the evening hours, Marietta was alone. It was in the evenings that she wailed in the pain of post-labor.

Barely able to stand.

Stretched and torn.

Healing . . . poorly.

The top of her gown was soaked from a constant drip of milk, while the bottom was rouge from a determined flow. Her sandy locks—sweaty. Her blue eyes—reddish.

For the first time, Beatrice confided in Queenie and asked for permission to care for her sister until she recovered. To her surprise, she was granted permission for the evenings after the completion of alterations and chores. Beatrice was very grateful.

She finished her last gown for that day just as Delia entered her room with a basket of healing herbs and cloves and placed the basket at the foot of her bed.

"Mamma . . . thank you so much," Beatrice said as Delia tucked a white cloth over the top of the basket.

"I put a bottle in the basket for sufferin; it got a red ribbon. Take some in yo hand this way . . . and rub all around like so." The old midwife's hand moved like she was trying to clean the inside of a jelly jar. "Make sho you clean her good and tell her imma come see her in the morning." Delia said, her head tied in a dingy scarf that matched her dingy kitchen dress.

Beatrice's eyes watered with gratitude. "I will do as you say. I love you."

"I love you too, like one of my own, so you don't have to thank me. I also put some calas and pralines in the basket. Issa *shame* how that evil Mr. Lafitte got yo sister sufferin *like-a-dog*. But I *leaves* him to God."

Beatrice scooped the basket in her arm, kissed Delia, and hurried to her sister.

Once at the red brick Creole cottage on St. Ann, she knocked on the door. A deep, groggy voice invited her in; it was Mr. Lafitte. Beatrice had spotted him at the quadroon ball; he had stood in the far corner in a tan coat and top hat. He was the one who watched the debutantes like an owner of prized thorough-breds. Mr. Lafitte was her master's business partner, and both were partners with Harriett Green.

"Does your master know your whereabouts?" His voice was threatening, like a falling pine in the woods.

"Yes . . . yes, sir, my mistress said I could bring these herbs for Marietta to help her pain. I just came to clean her up, and I will be on my way."

"Then make it quick! I'm headed out to dinner, don't be here when I return. Do you understand?"

"Yes, sir," Beatrice caught her bladder just in time.

"She's back there," he pointed.

"Thank you, sir."

As Beatrice trotted to the rear of the house with a bowed head, she heard the front door slam shut as Mr. Lafitte departed for the evening, without any care or concern for her sister. *Thank God he's gone*, she thought. Her excitement over his departure was short-lived once she heard the hymn of moaning that resonated from the back room. It was the sound of one wailing beyond the threshold of pain, with no hope of remedy or relief—only a muttered prayer for death.

In a room with no windows or candles, Beatrice found Marietta crumpled on her hay-stuffed mattress, facing the wall. The wooden floor was still damp from the aftermath of her pregnancy, and Marietta's inability to care for herself. Beatrice lit some candles and saw her sister's body shaking from sobs.

After making quick use of an empty chamber pot, Beatrice placed her basket at the foot of Marietta's bed and went into the kitchen to boil some water. Once the water was the perfect temperature, she filled her sister's tub and helped her out of the soiled gown. After the bath, Beatrice dressed Marietta in a pink nightgown she had made that morning and was surprised to see that it was a perfect fit.

Back on the hay-stuffed mattress, she parted Marietta's legs and applied medicine to her womb area as she was instructed by Delia; a womb that was all too familiar. Then, she oiled coconut skin that felt like her own and reached for Marietta's brush to tame the same tangled strands. It was like staring down into a mirror except for the scar on the side of Marietta's jaw—a scar left by their first mistress's rocking chair. Finally, the moaning stopped.

"I always wondered where you were," Marietta said as Beatrice continued to brush her hair.

"I thought about you every day," Beatrice replied.

"Thought about you, too. I've been on this side of the lake since daddy sent me to the auction. Then that no-good bastard bought me."

"I know Lafitte too, he's very mean. Even when he comes to visit my master, he looks at me like a dirty rag."

"He started visiting my room as soon as I got here, late in the middle of the night, as soon as his wife was asleep. I couldn't have been no more than twelve. Then he got me pregnant with my first baby two years later. It was a boy."

"What happened to your boy?" Beatrice asked.

"Yellow fever took my boy and Mrs. Lafitte. She was very kind to me. She even taught me to read. She taught me in secret, and I still act like I can't read when he's around."

"You can read!" Beatrice was astonished.

Marietta continued, "His wife was a school teacher, so I guess she couldn't stand having me around and not able to read. When she died, he started drinking every day—all day—and beating on me. Mrs. Lafitte was my angel, but her husband is the devil."

"How many times you been with child?" Beatrice asked.

"Counting the one that black bitch Clarice took last night, I had eight—seven girls, one boy," Marietta said in a broken voice. "What about you? Marie tells me they sold all your children to the concubines."

"Clarice took my chillum—all the girls."

"*Child-ren* . . . it's children," Marietta corrected, but Beatrice took no offense. "You are too pretty to speak like you're still on the plantation. Now say it with me." Marietta encouraged Beatrice to repeat the word several times before she continued.

"Clarice took all my ch-child-ren. I got one boy named Timothy and one name Lawrence, twins."

"How old?"

"Twelve, one travels with master while the other works around the house. All my girls Clarice stole from me and raised for the ball. With your babies, too, I reckon." Tears began to race down the sides of her face as she reflected on her girls. "Was it true that daddy sold you off because you stole his wife's necklace? The pretty ruby red one?"

"Yes, that's true."

"You did steal it?"

"I did, and I still have it all these years. I hid it from mouth to hand, and they never could find it." Marietta chuckled with a sense of accomplishment.

"I knew it, too. I knew you had taken it," Beatrice giggled.

"You know I'm going to kill Clarice the first chance I get," Marietta said as her hands appreciated the nightgown Beatrice had made for her. "This is nice, real nice. Did your master's wife hand this down to you?"

"No, I made three gowns for you last night." Beatrice walked over to her basket. "This, for you." Beatrice handed Marietta the basket full of medicine and garments.

"Beatrice, you didn't have to!" Marietta reached inside the basket and pulled out a stuffed doll with sandy hair, blue eyes, mocha skin, and blushed red cheeks.

"Somethin' for you to hold at night. When Clarice took my babies, it hurt real bad havin' nothin to hold. Hold dis baby at night and rest."

"Oh, Beatrice!" Marietta cradled the doll beneath her breast.

"Massa and Clarice will pay for what they did to us. God will see to it. None of dem gon' see heaven," Beatrice asserted.

"Beatrice, I'm not waiting until Judgment Day to make them pay. Clarice will pay soon as I'm well enough to walk. And then that no-good bastard Lafitte will get what's coming."

"No, Marietta, don't do nothing to Clarice! Not now!"

"Why not? Don't you want revenge for selling your daughters?"

"Yes, I do, but Clarice work for my massa. She do what he tell her. My massa. Yo' massa. And Clarice sold our ch-children. I will get my massa to talk, and we'll find where them are first, then both of us will deal with Clarice. Don't need you getting sold off again."

Beatrice sat on Marietta's bed facing her, then leaned forward until their foreheads touched. She grabbed a small hunk of her sister's hair and a small hunk of her own and started to braid the hair into a single plait.

"I remember we used to do this as little girls back on the plantation in Mandeville whenever we made a promise," Marietta said softly. Then, she began to cry.

"Will you teach me how to read?"

"If you teach me patience."

Once their hair was locked on both sides by the two braids, they said together: "I make a promise that will never break, until God comes, for my soul to take."

⚜

Beatrice departed Marietta's house and headed home as quickly as she could without attracting the attention of a slave catcher. She knew the bell would toll for her soon because he wanted her every night, sometimes twice. The passion stimulant Marie Laveau had sold Queenie to increase his desire only resulted in him making more trips to Beatrice's bedroom. It happened nightly; once Queenie was sound asleep, he ran across the balcony to her room, and tonight was no different. No sooner had she stepped out of the tub and scented her breast, the rope from his bedroom sounded the bell above her bed.

Ding!

Within twenty minutes, he burst through her door with eyes that said *you belong to me.* He panted like a bull, forced his tongue into her mouth, and before she knew it, her back was pressed against the wall next to her bed as he gripped her delicate breasts in both hands. The heat from his nostrils felt like he had run three miles to get to her living quarters, but she was where she had always been—on the other end of the balcony, just an arm's throw from where he slept with his wife.

Against her leg was an erection as hard as a bedpost.

Beatrice knew this sex-starved madman was not her master, but a man under the spell of Laveau. Until Queenie was completely out of the red substance in the preservative jar, she would have to endure the sole responsibility of pleasing him; it was her duty. Suddenly, Beatrice pushed him backward onto the bed and allowed him to slowly enter her, forcing him to go slower than he wanted to. Then, she stood above him on the bed—just to drive him wild.

"Haven't I always laid with you the right way, Massa?"

"Yes, Beatrice, please come down!" he begged.

"Don't I make you feel good, Massa?"

"Yes, Beatrice!" She slowly lowered and allowed him to

re-enter.

For nearly an hour, Beatrice teased and pleased him until he was a helpless dove in her hands. The potion from Laveau caused throbbing erection pains, and she was his only source of relief.

"Please, Beatrice I am begging you to finish. I can't take it anymore." He pulled her chest to his. "Fuck me, Beatrice!"

"No!"

"Please, Beatrice . . ."

"Say it louder."

"Please!" he yelled.

Beatrice allowed him to enter her again, then stood with her arms folded. She seized the opportunity to get the answers she craved; when she had tried to ask him about Clarice and her daughters on the night of the quadroon ball, he had shut her down swiftly and left her with nothing. *Tonight he will talk*, Beatrice decided.

"Will you let me see my daughters?" she asked as he humped the air.

"Yes, I will let you see them," he panted.

Beatrice knew he was now her slave. The potion from Laveau was working like a psychoactive truth serum; it opened every door in his mind and allowed her to roam like a gazelle through his thoughts. He spoke without consciousness.

Beatrice allowed him back inside as the interrogation continued. She tightened her gripped on his swollen penis and stroked away his remaining defenses. In a soft voice, she implored, "Tell me, my king. Clarice got my girls?"

"Only two, Beatrice."

"My last two?"

"Yes! Yes, don't stop. Oh, Beatrice."

"My last two she still have at dat house?"

"Yes, my love! Your last two are still with Clarice," he moaned.

"And Cecille? Is she my daughter?"

"Yes! She's yours."

"Where is Cecille?"

"On . . . on . . . on . . . *Ram . . . parrt!*"

"Where?"

"On Rampart Street! Ahhhhhhh!" he moaned as he released inside her.

Trembling! Convulsing! A pleasure-induced seizure. He shook for five minutes. Then, she released him from the warm, wet hug, and he dozed off promptly. The sound of snoring trembled the walls of her quarters; it was a little past midnight when Beatrice decided her master had slept long enough.

"Massa, wake up! Massa, wake up befo' she come!" Beatrice shook him until he opened his eyes, then watched as he staggered out the door. Once he left her room, Beatrice replayed in her mind everything she had forced him to admit, careful not to forget a single detail.

"Clarice still has two of my girls and Cecille is on Rampart Street."

The next day, as her master and his wife sat at the breakfast table in the courtyard, the cooks in the kitchen cooked and the servants of the house served. Her son Timothy waved as he headed off for his first day as a carrier apprentice. Beatrice waved back from her window; she was very proud of Timothy.

The morning was still cool. The skies were clear and blue. While Queenie wrote in her diary, her husband glanced upward Beatrice's living quarters. Beatrice sat in her window stitching a gown. They made eye contact, and he tipped his hat. She smiled.

"He is my slave now," she whispered.

After her master and Queenie finished their breakfast, they departed to visit friends in Destrehan, Louisiana. Their departure gave Beatrice the perfect opportunity to visit Clarice. She placed the unfinished gown on her bed, wrapped her hair, grabbed a basket full of fabric, and blew out the door. Clarice lived on Royal Street, which was only a few blocks away from her house. Her master never allowed her to go anywhere near Royal Street. Beatrice was authorized to walk in the direction of the French Market and the opposite direction to Congo Square, but she was forbidden to travel down the street where Clarice lived. However, the usually-obedient Beatrice needed to see her daughters—even if it meant breaking one of his oldest rules. She walked in a straight line toward Clarice's.

She remembered the house where her master had delivered Clarice after he purchased both of them from the auction. She remembered the house like it was yesterday. Clarice lived in a single-story wooden house with two windows on each side of the door, an orange Spanish tile roof, and a narrow walkway on both sides. There was no way to see if her kids were in the house, because there was no indication anyone lived there. The dark green shutters were locked tight, like a shop owner had reached the end of the day. The two narrow walkways both had six-foot-tall wooden gates that looked more like doors, blocking any view of the side of the home.

There were no sounds of children playing in the backyard, nothing like one would hear during recess at an elementary school. The house was silent, determined to withhold all secrets from the outside world. It offered no comment; the house refused to satisfy her curiosity. Nevertheless, Beatrice stood across the street from the tan, wooden house wanting to knock on the door, but neither one of her legs would approach. She knew two of her children were inside, and the answer to the whereabouts of her other daughters was inside, but she was outside. Like a grieving statue. Stiff with timidity. Motionless like a stagnant pond.

Suddenly, Beatrice noticed that the door was opening. She immediately started walking away from the house before the door swung completely open. Beatrice looked carefully over her shoulder. Clarice stepped out, followed by four girls. They all walked in the same direction, Beatrice a few paces ahead and Clarice on the other side of the street with the children trailing behind. Beatrice set her basket on the ground and pretended to arrange the fabrics, allowing just enough time for Clarice and the kids to pass. Clarice never noticed Beatrice, but Beatrice saw her and the four girls who followed.

The two girls who walked directly behind Beatrice appeared to be in their early teens, and the two behind them seemed to be a couple of years younger. The teens' skin complexion and sandy blonde hair were the same as Beatrice's. Both girls resembled Rose, who Clarice had renamed Cecille. The two girls in the rear wore bonnets so Beatrice could not see their faces, but the two older girls she could clearly identify.

My babies! Those are my babies she stole.

Once the group was a few houses ahead, Beatrice picked up her basket and continued to follow from the other side of the street. Once they reached Burgundy Street, Clarice turned right at the corner, with Beatrice following a block behind.

I wonder where she's taking them?

Once Clarice reached the corner, the group stopped and faced a huge two-story gray home. The home had black, custom wrought-iron fencing that allowed a street view of the courtyard. The interior of the court was an example of the most amazing Audubon landscaping Beatrice had ever seen, with a circular, free-flowing Spanish fountain in the middle. The entire courtyard was royal grand, including the covered patio which complemented the fountain.

A lady walked through the yard to greet Clarice; the two hugged. Beatrice placed her basket down again, directly across from where Clarice and the woman were talking. The woman was Harriett Green.

Harriett appeared very excited to meet the four girls. Beatrice watched Clarice smile at her daughters like a proud mother. She wanted to run across the street and grab her children and escape, but she was too afraid. In the bottom of her basket of fabric was a cutting knife. There she stood with the basket at her feet and the seven-inch cutting knife in her hand, waiting for the right moment to kill Clarice and Harriett.

"Both of dem bitches gon' die today," she said softly.

Then she realized she wasn't holding a knife after all.

Only the basket.

Only paralyzing fear.

Only a fantasy of stabbing Clarice and Harriett.

Once she snapped completely out of her murderous hallucination, she saw the last of the children enter Harriett Green's home; the door shut behind them. She hated herself for not having the courage to run across the street and rescue her children; she lacked the tenacity of her sister, Marietta. She had always been the timid one of the twins. Today was no different.

Beatrice started her walk back toward St. Peter Street, demoralized, yet feeling a small sense of victory. She had seen her daughters, and she knew where Harriett lived. Her only goal now was to convince her master not to sell her them at the quadroon ball as he had sold the others. So, on the way home, she paid a visit to Marie Laveau.

I will ask Laveau to teach me how to make red syrup and torment him with desire until he tells me everything.

Once she arrived at the hairdresser's home, Marie Laveau readily agreed to teach Beatrice the age-old recipe.

CHAPTER 15

Sherman noticed Ronelle walking in his direction with a sandy ponytail that waved in the noonday breeze and radiant skin that gleamed from a block away. The site of her was pleasurable to his eyes; her denim-wrapped legs and curved hips were an unlimited source of spicy stimulation. *I am not worthy.*

She pranced with the high springy steps of a ballerina, both graceful and urgent. Unlike a ballerina, her arms and legs were better suited for the floor routine in the summer Olympics; thick and full in all the right places. To him, at least; they were all the wrong places for Ronelle. They were areas of her body that she wanted to trim back to her freshmen year in college, but it was those curves that made her the most alluring woman Sherman had ever held.

From about three car lengths away, Ronelle smiled her way back into the passenger seat, bursting with elation.

"Well, what happened? How did it go?" Sherman asked impatiently.

"It went great, baby. I'll tell you about it at dinner tonight," she joked.

"Ronelle . . ."

She giggled. "Well, I was just given a grand tour of 1005 St.

Peter Street."

"Abigail invited you in?"

"Just like that," Ronelle boasted. "Do you know why?"

"Because you're . . . awesome?"

"That's right. I'm awesome!"

"So how much access did she grant you?"

"Full. To the entire house. And even invited me back for a second viewing."

"You-you . . . you really pulled it off?"

"I also found that beam in the attic."

"No kidding?" Sherman leaned across the center console in excitement. "Abigail allowed you to view the attic?"

"*Oh, ye of little faith,*" she said in a Moses voice. "Bam . . . there's the beam." Ronelle handed Sherman her camera.

He enlarged the picture. "Nine notches!"

"Yes, and I think I've made a new friend. Abigail is now invited to our wedding and loved my ring." Ronelle held her ring in a ray of sunlight. "Everything Uncle Clarence said was the truth. Your great-great-great-grandmother left a mark for every child conceived in that house. It's in the attic."

"This is more than I ever expected," Sherman said as he kissed her. "I don't know how to thank you."

"Well . . . later tonight under the covers, I will list the nine ways you can thank me." Ronelle returned the kiss. "Your uncle's theory has been confirmed. You're related to Abigail."

After dropping off Ronelle, Sherman parked in front of his grandmother's house to find his dad and Uncle Clarence shoulder to shoulder on the front porch shooting the breeze and waving at neighbors. The 5600 block of Dauphine Street was one of those New Orleans neighborhoods where all the residences were second or even third generation. They knew every member of each household, treated each other as next of kin, and did life together as one big family.

"Here comes my favorite nephew! I was just talking to your

dad about how proud I am of you for what you're trying to do for the family." Clarence patted Sherman's shoulder once he approached.

"Boy, do I have a surprise for you," Sherman grinned.

"Is it anything like that green surprise you gave me this morning? I like those kinds of surprises." Clarence gave Sherman a hard wink.

"Uncle Kool, it's better than the surprise this morning—a million times better." He returned the wink.

"I would appreciate if you two knock off the silly winking and let me in on this surprise," his dad said impatiently.

"Right after I hug Granny, but you may want to meet me at the kitchen table for this one." Sherman continued through the house in a straight line toward his grandmother.

"Grandma . . . where ya at?" Sherman yelled from the living room

"Who dat at the door? Is that you, Puddin'?"

"Yeah, it's me, Grandma."

"I'm back in the washroom."

Sherman walked to the back of the shotgun home where he found Grandma putting her last load of clothes into the dryer.

"Grandma, why are we paying a Home Health nurse?" Sherman complained.

"Why you think they call her 'nurse?' She ain't no housekeeper. Besides, what else I got to do? Ya ate yet?"

"Yes, Grandma, I had something to eat earlier."

"Puddin', when you gonna graduate? You still working that internet job? You makin' any money with that?"

"I graduate this year, Grandma, and yes, I've still got my internet business. It's doing well, which is a good thing because I'm going to need every cent for the wedding."

"The wedding? What wedding?"

"Grandma, I asked Ronelle to marry me, and she said yes."

"Glory to God! You gonna marry that little Fortier girl? What her people say about that?" Her expression changed from excitement to worry at the thought of her grandson marrying a white girl.

Sherman had no intention of telling his parents or grandmother about what happened at the Fortier's the night he asked Ronelle to marry him. Although his mom was highly educated, she could turn ghetto in a second if someone harmed one of her boys. His mom's most famous saying was from Prateek Jain: *I don't have a short temper; I just have a quick reaction to bullshit.*

"Yes, I plan to marry that Fortier girl. I'll be expecting a big pot of your red beans at the reception, too."

"Well, Puddin', if you can pull that one off, you deserve more than a pot of beans. Lord, looks like we got a wedding to plan."

At that moment, Sherman's dad and Uncle Clarence walked in and joined them at the kitchen table. It proved to be the perfect time for him to show them the photos.

"I'm glad I have the three of you here—you have to see this. Uncle, your suggestion involving Ronelle was brilliant. Going undercover as a photographer, Ronelle was able to document the entire estate, including the attic. Everything was right where you said it would be. We not only found the beam with the nine notches, but we also have photos."

"Wait a minute! What beam? What nine notches?" Melvin asked.

"Dad, Uncle Clarence told me about a story he heard when he was a boy about your great-great grandma—my great-great-great grandma. Well, I did a ton of research and discovered her name was . . ."

Susan Campbell interrupted him. "Great-Grandma Beatrice."

"Yes, Grandma. I have confirmed her name was Beatrice, and she had nine children."

"I knew that boy was smart—smart like Unc! Ain't that right, nephew?" Clarence elbowed Sherman.

"Will you hush so I can hear what my son is saying?" Melvin cut Clarence a look.

"I knew it! I knew I was right! I know what I heard," Clarence continued gleefully. "Just because I drink a beer or two now and then don't mean my hearing's bad. I know what I'm talking about."

"Well, I have never heard the story about notches in an attic," Melvin said. "All of this is news to me."

Sherman loaded up the pictures in his camera, then scrolled through the slideshow. His grandma's hand covered her mouth in awe; her eyes widened as she viewed the photos.

"Look at all the antique furniture in Abigail's house," his grandma said. "I always knew Abigail's side of the family had a lot of money, but this is my first time seeing how she lives in that beautiful house."

The photos of the interior of the house showed that Abigail was clearly a wealthy woman, far wealthier than any of them could have imagined. Next, Sherman showed them the attic pictures.

"Obviously, in the 1800s, Beatrice probably couldn't read or write well, due to the laws at the time. However, she did her best to reveal to the world and record that she gave birth to nine children."

They all leaned in to study the photo. On the beam, from top to bottom, they could see the following:

BB
G
G
G
G
G
GG

"This picture right here is our connection to that house. Here are the marks Beatrice left for each child she conceived during slavery. This beam is our link to Abigail as a blood relative, and also to the slave master who left Big Mama Beatrice that house in his will," Sherman explained.

"See there. I tried to tell y'all for years! See there. I knew I wasn't crazy!" pleaded Uncle Clarence. "For years people thought I was talking out of my head. Nephew, this is irrefutable evidence, on this camera, that proves Big Mama and Abigail were related. I knew it."

"Let's not move so fast, Clarence," Melvin said. "Son, you're telling me these photos are from inside of the attic at Abigail's house?"

"Yes, sir," Sherman answered.

"You took these pictures in front of that beam?" Melvin asked.

"Yeah, well, actually, Ronelle took them."

"Well, Puddin', I hate to say it, but you did a lot of work for nothing," his grandma said.

"Huh? Why do you feel it was all for nothing, Grandma?"

"Abigail can't stand herself. So, you'll never be able to prove it. Back in 1956, I believe, Abigail, whose full name is Abigail Phipps Guillory, tried to sue the State of Louisiana to have the word 'Negro' removed from her birth certificate. She claimed she had always been white and that she married white both times. She said her mother looked white, and her dad had blue eyes, so this made her and her sisters white. She lost that case after spending a whole heap of money. That only made Abigail hate black folk even more," Grandma explained.

"Wait, her real name is Abigail Phipps Guillory?" Melvin asked.

"Yes, that is her full name," Grandma confirmed. "Even when we were fighting to integrate schools, it was Abigail who led the resistance to keep McDonough Nineteen Elementary School segregated. As those *lil-colored* children were getting escorted by the United States Marshals, Abigail was out there screaming, 'One-two-three-four, all niggers got to go. Five-six-seven-eight, we don't want to integrate!' Abigail blended in right with the screaming white folks. She has passed for white all these years. I think she plans on dying as a white woman, so don't count on her for nothing."

"Momma, I remember those angry crowds outside of Mc-Donough Nineteen Elementary School. You mean to tell me Abigail was one of those evil women out there yelling and spitting at us?" Melvin asked incredulously.

"She was! I looked her right in the eye, and she winked at me. Then called me a nigger to my face. As the SCLC taught us, I kept on walking, never turned my head. Yes, it was Abigail."

CHAPTER 16

Sherman set his phone to voice record and started taking notes. Every dusty story his grandmother told about segregation in New Orleans was a precious gift to his dissertation. Like a hidden goldmine, her memory yielded one nugget after the next with vivid details about people and places of yesterday—details that couldn't be found anywhere on Google.

Luckily for Sherman, even though her life was off the grid, all it took was a simple question asked at the perfect time. Then she teleported him to the exact second an event happened during that decade. A series of life events colligated chronologically, gift-wrapped and presented at the table. She remembered it all.

Seated next to Sherman was Melvin, who frantically emailed his paralegal about the *Abigail Phipps Guillory v. Louisiana* case. *I need every detail*, was the subject line of his message. Melvin had been among the first wave of black kids bussed to schools that had been forced to integrate under the *Brown v. Board of Education of Topeka, Kansas* decision in 1954.

"Ma, why have you kept this bottled up for so long?" Melvin asked.

"There was no need to talk about it. Abigail was entitled to her opinion. I got the last laugh, though. Melvin, when you graduated from Tulane Law School, I walked to her house later on that night. I left the newspaper clippings of the segregation protest, along with a copy of your law degree, in her mailbox." Grandma laughed. "I wrote a little note on that law degree that said, *No weapon formed against us shall prosper.*"

"So, Abigail has passed for white all these years?"

"Oh, Lord, yes. One day after I dropped Clarence and Melvin off at school, I strolled down St. Claude Avenue and saw Abigail and two other ladies walking in my direction. The closer they approached, the more their faces frowned, all *bent* with hate."

"Did Abigail acknowledge you?" Sherman asked.

"There was no way in hell she was going to. Not in front of two full-blooded Southern Belles. What she wanted was for me to step aside—off of the sidewalk, into the muddy gutter. As if she were the Queen of England. Well, I refused. So, the four of us just stood there . . . for what felt like a day." Sue Campbell smiled with pride.

"Let me guess; they spat on you?" Sherman feared.

"Lord, no."

"They pushed you into the gutter?" Sherman assumed.

"Who? Abigail? *I wish she would have*; would've ripped her lips off," his grandmother huffed. "Like we say on this side of the Canal: I don't start no trouble, but I damn sure don't run from trouble."

It was then that Sherman's grandmother became distracted by another photo Ronelle had snapped of the formal dining room and four sterling candlestick holders. Eight empty plates waited patiently for eight exclusive guests.

"Look at all that *nice china*, and that silverware! My, my, my."

Sue Campbell was in awe of the floral printed mats on Abigail's dark mahogany table that coordinated with floral printed suede seats of the dining chairs. Each chair had a padded armrest, and the legs of the table featured carved designs by a master craftsman. "Must be nice." Something about the pictures clearly rubbed her the wrong way.

"So, what happened, Grandma?" Sherman tried to reel his

grandmother away from the photos.

"Finally, they parted a little crease, and I walked through. I wasn't five steps past those cows before Abigail called me a *stinky nigger* behind my back. I turned and smiled with all my teeth and said, 'Cousin Abigail, you should know a *stinky nigger* better than anybody . . . because you one, too!' You should have seen her face; it turned red like that bottle of ketchup." Grandma burst into laughter.

Suddenly, Melvin's interest in the house on St. Peter Street piqued. "Momma, I have walked past that house many times. One thing I know for sure . . . it's worth at least five million dollars."

"It's definitely prime real estate," Sherman recalled from earlier. "A few blocks from Bourbon Street, in the heart of the French Quarter."

"Me and Mrs. Lite walked by there the other day," Clarence added.

"Mrs. *Who?*" Grandma asked.

"Mrs. Miller Lite . . . we're engaged," Clarence slapped the table in laughter.

"Well you should be, she takes all your money," Grandma said.

"All I know is, whoever left Abigail that house was filthy rich when they built it," Melvin concluded. "It's time to set the record straight on that property and the entire estate. We may be the black side, but we share the same great-great grandfather."

At that moment, Sue Campbell turned pale—as if she'd seen a ghost. "I think my pressure is high," she whispered.

"Momma, you want to lay down while I get your pressure pills?" Melvin asked.

"I feel so . . . light-headed."

Melvin and Clarence quickly helped her from the table and carried her over to her bed."

"Should I call your doctor?" Melvin asked. "Do you feel like I need to take you to the emergency room?"

"No, it just my pressure," she murmured. "Get my pressure pills on the counter, and that will calm me until my nurse arrives around eight o'clock tonight."

Melvin administered his mother's medication and monitored her until she drifted off to sleep. Then he kissed her on the side of her face and softly closed the door.

With his mother sound asleep, Melvin returned to Clarence and Sherman in the kitchen and signaled for them all to lower their voices.

"Our inheritance was stolen!" he said in a loud whisper.

"You damn right! We come from money just like that prune Abigail!" Clarence fussed.

"I intend to use every legal and political muscle I have to retrieve every dime they stole from us," Melvin said.

Sherman protested. "Dad, this is not about money for me. This is about my dissertation. I'm not interested in lawsuits. Just knowing we're related to her side of the family is enough for me—"

"Son, Abigail's side of the family is our *got-damn* side of the family too."

"Better recognize," Clarence agreed.

"Son, at this point, it's not about you or what you want. It's about the restitution we're owed. They will pay for what they've done to us . . . going all the way back to slavery. So help me God!"

Clarence found his point to jump in. "My mom and dad struggled all their lives—never asked the government for a dime. To have them steal from us like that? And none of them went to jail? And all of them lived high on the hog? That's some bullshit right there!"

". . . and criminal," the attorney for the family established. "In Louisiana, we are under the *Civil des Français*, which is also known as the Napoleonic Code. I have the right to bring this matter before the courts at any given moment, and that moment has just arrived. Abigail is about to pay up!"

"Hay! Hay! Here we come, *bitch*," Clarence cheered.

"Oh no," Sherman whispered under his breath.

CHAPTER 17

L ife at the Fortier residence was quiet and tense. Both Steven and Brandon avoided Brenda as much as possible; she could feel their anger. Over forty-eight hours had passed since Ronelle moved out of the house, and Brenda was sick with worry.

Ronelle was her only daughter, and the longer she stayed away from home, the more Brenda felt like half of her body was in decay. All throughout the past two decades of her life, it was always she and Ronelle together. They were more like girlfriends at times than mother and daughter. Now Ronelle was gone. Most of her clothes were gone. Her car was gone. The background noise of her reality television shows and '90s grunge music was gone.

Brenda couldn't take the silence any longer. She had to ask her husband if he'd heard from Ronelle, or if he knew where she'd slept last night. She saw him walking through the hallway out of the corner of her eye, so she took a deep breath and approached him.

"Steven, have you heard from Ronelle? Has she called you?" Brenda could not hide the desperation in her voice.

He looked through her, then walked away.

"You at least owe me the respect of a reply. I am still your wife, dammit!"

"I owe you the same respect you showed Sherman. None! What I do owe you is silence, Brenda. The difference is I have a reason for not liking you right now. My reason has nothing to do with your skin color, and everything to do with how you act. I owe you the right to treat you like an asshole, but I will not stoop to ground level."

"You're calling me an *asshole?* Really!"

"I said I have every right to treat you like one, because that is how you handled the most memorable day in our daughter's life. You ruined it, Brenda. You fucking ruined it. If things are not how you want them, then you force your will. It's either your way or no way. So now my child is out there somewhere, feeling like it's her against the world, when it's clearly just her against you and your outdated racism."

Normally around this time in the evening, the two of them would be having dinner together at the table. Tonight, however, Steven took his meal back to his office and slammed the door.

A moment later, the front door opened. It was Brandon. He started to walk past his mom without giving her his usual peck on the cheek. He was angry.

"Brandon, have you heard from your sister?"

"No, Mom, I haven't. But if I had to guess, I would say she's at Sherman's."

"Would you be kind enough to confirm that, so at least I know she's safe?"

"No problem."

It had been a week since Ronelle packed her things and moved in with Sherman, but the storm clouds continued to linger in the Fortier home. Brandon was sitting with his long legs sprawled out in front of him on his bed, pecking away at his paper, when his dad walked in and took a seat. Brandon instantly got a bad case of déjà vu. Whenever his father came into his room, it meant he had something important to talk to him about; something gloomy. The last time his father had come into his room and taken a seat was August 27, 2005. That was the day they were deciding whether to evacuate for Hurricane Katrina.

"Son, can you take a few minutes away from your work?"

Brandon closed his laptop and set it on the desk. "What's on your mind, Fonz?"

His dad was a dead ringer for Henry Winkler, except for the added pounds around his midsection. His salt-and-pepper hair was still very full across his entire scalp, which gave Brandon hope that he, too, could escape baldness.

"Things between your mom and I are getting worse, though it didn't begin the other night. It's been deteriorating for some time now. The situation with your sister only caused us to smack rock bottom. I don't think we're going to make it out of this hole. I plan to move out for a while and see if space apart will help us, but right now I am so angry with her. The air in here has become very toxic."

"Are you serious, Dad? The two of you wait until you're in your sixties to talk about splitting up?"

"Sometimes people grow apart," Steven shrugged.

"Dad, I keep saying it over and over, I'm a big boy now. Please, would you spare me the 'we've grown apart' speech? You're pissed off about Mom's hidden racism. Now you're scared to death of the word getting out that you're married to a bigot; it'll damage the relationships you've spent more than forty years building in this community."

"Touché. You're absolutely right. It would be catastrophic."

"Don't worry, Dad, I know Sherman like I know this surgery scar on my knee, and he would never share with anyone what happened here because he cherishes the relationships involved. Nothing's getting out."

"I tried to hide it, but I can't. I'm troubled. Your mother's been hounding me to break up their relationship for years. My failure to follow her orders has turned into resentment. From the moment they started to date, she became very bitter and distant. Well, I didn't see anything wrong with your sister and Sherman's relationship, but Brenda hated how I stood down and allowed them to grow as a couple. She even blamed me when your sister didn't get selected as Queen of Carnival. Somehow, she made it my fault our daughter was tarnished in the eyes of her friends. I like Sherman. I always have."

Brandon let out a deep breath. He had never known—until the other day—how his mom felt about Sherman and Ronelle's relationship. It was a topic no one had ever discussed. "Well, Sherman and Ronelle are engaged to be married. So, I don't know how Mom plans to handle it, but from the looks of it, that show will go on."

"That's great news," his father said.

"Think Mom will go to the wedding?"

"I hope she will. The Campbells are very dear to me. When your mother rejected Sherman, I felt like she also rejected a part of me. Melvin has been closer to me than a brother. Our friendship is forty years old."

After a moment of silence, Brandon spoke. "Dad, Sherman and I have discovered things about our families that neither one of us knew going into this project. It's getting crazy. Then, on top of it all, to discover my very own mother doesn't like African Americans, after all of this time . . . it's way more than I can swallow."

"Son, we're going to get this thing all sorted out, but until we do, I'm going to need you to do me a favor."

"What is it?"

"Can you stay close to home when I'm not here? You know the crime in this city drives me crazy."

"Not a problem, Dad."

"Thank you, son. Your mother makes me angry as hell, but I still wouldn't dream of leaving her in this house all by herself."

"I've got it covered, Dad."

"Thirty years of marriage and this is the first time we've lived apart out of anger," Steven sighed.

Brandon nodded sadly. His parents were at the beginning of the separation process; another long-term marriage was on the brink of failure. He shook hands with his dad, then watched him move from room to room, packing.

My dad is really leaving my mom, and my sister is not speaking to my mom! What has happened to our family?

From his bedroom window, Brandon watched his dad toss a

suitcase into the bed of his truck.

Brenda stood in the front door and watched her husband in disbelief. *He's really going to leave me.* She wanted to stop him, but her pride wouldn't allow it. She wanted to fall to the floor and wrap her body around one of his legs, but her dignity prevented her knees from bending. Like a ceiling fan on a gray winter day, Brenda stood perfectly still, locked in an internal battle that pitted her family against her image. She harbored a vested interest in both, and both were inseparable in her life. Brenda had always thought that she would grow old with Steven; they would die of old age in their bed, together.

I should drag each one of those bags back into this house—he doesn't have the right to leave me.

The more trips Steven made to the driveway, the more her heart shattered. Over the years, Steven had packed for many business trips, but this time he was packing to leave their marriage. Finally, she freed her lips from her pride.

"Steven, you're wrong about me," Brenda said in a shattered voice as he breezed past her. "I just want you to know that. You're so . . . so wrong about me."

He paused mid-stride. "Brenda you're not that difficult to figure out. The fake you could not even handle the humiliation of watching your clone marry a black man."

"Steven that's not true . . . "

"It is, but I wish it weren't." She heard a loud grunt as he hoisted golf clubs into the back of his truck. "Ronelle loves who she loves. I can't stop that, nor would I. And you couldn't stop it, no matter how many brick walls you built. They were just meant to be together."

Steven's words were painful but true. She couldn't stop it, and she had certainly tried. She signed. Sherman just wasn't a *good look*. Brenda was a graduate of the University of Mississippi—Ole Miss—and a beauty pageant veteran with many crowns under her belt. She was a product of traditional Southern etiquette and values. Brenda was paper-thin with supermodel breasts that had been implanted in 1994. People often took her for Oscar-winning actress Helen Mirren; the resemblance was just that striking.

Every item Steven placed in his suitcase shattered her perfect image of her family.

"Steven, I will say this one last time—I am not a racist. Yes, it hurt that Ronelle's relationship with Sherman cost her the title of Queen of Carnival. I worked my ass off to put her in a position to reign. That meant everything to me. To watch twelve years of my best efforts go down the drain due to a boyfriend . . . yes, it pissed me off. They are too young for marriage, and Ronelle is not ready to be a wife!"

"And you were?"

"Steven you know things were different back then. We were different, more mature . . ."

"Cut the shit, Brenda! We were married right around the same age, and you learned on the job. You can't control everything! You've already had your proposal, and you said yes. Your parents gave me their blessing! But you ruin it for my daughter?"

"Steven, what's wrong with wanting more for my daughter? That doesn't make me a bigot!"

"Brenda, what makes you a bigot is that you see Sherman as less! Sherman is perfect for my daughter, and if she loves him, then he is the perfect son-in-law for me. It was you who decided to live her life! You're selfish and controlling! Like Ronelle, I'm tired of being controlled."

With that, her husband slammed his truck door, leaving Brenda standing on the porch. She watched Steven back out of the driveway, then fade to black between the shadows of the streetlights.

THE MASTER'S WIFE DIARY ENTRY SIX

May 23, 1854

Dear Diary,

Why won't he make love to me? Why does he reject me? What have I done to bring this curse of loneliness into my life? I am his wife, not his bookkeeper. All we ever talk about in bed is business and money. If his own wife isn't worthy of his love and affection, then who is? I know I'm still desirable—I see the way men look at me. I see the way Timothy and his brother make every attempt not to look at me, the way Mr. Lafitte's mouth waters like a dog . . . but not my husband.

Oh, no, not my husband. He would prefer long walks alone at night to showing me even a bit of affection. With so much exposure to the night air, it's a wonder he hasn't contracted yellow fever already. Every family in this neighborhood seems to have one affected person, but he doesn't seem worried. It's his routine: he takes a long walk, slithers back into bed, and never bothers me. Not even a kiss on the cheek.

Just the other night, I could have sworn I walked in on him relieving himself! For God's sake! Here I am, in the flesh, willing and able to fulfill his every desire, and he'd rather relieve himself on a rag. What have I done to deserve this? Aren't I deserving of a husband who hungers and thirsts for me? Dear Diary, I am exasperated. I've tried everything I can think of to make him want me. Perhaps God will send him a familiar scent—one that reminds him of the first time he held me. Or, maybe a work of art in a museum will remind him of my breasts, my body, my lips . . .

Dear God, please remind him of much I need his touch, how much I love to kiss him, to feel him. Until then, I will wait. I can do nothing but keep waiting for a tender moment when my husband realizes I am alive and in need of his lips. He must think I'm so pitiful . . . if he thinks of me at all. It's so trite, Diary, that I keep begging and begging for just one night of impetuous passion, but you must agree I am not without justification!

A Damsel in the Desert.

CHAPTER 18

Melvin's Law Office
Monday Morning
9:30 a.m.

Melvin Campbell arrived at his law office escorted by the morning sun, ushered through the door by a great sense of anticipation. The coffee pot was clocked in, as was his paralegal, who pinballed between the printer and her desk. This morning would be the first of many discovery sessions, and his goal was to find more bulletproof evidence that officially linked his mom to Abigail by blood—something in addition to the nine notches in the attic.

Unfortunately, his case was one rooted in a two hundred-year-old grievance. He knew that cases like these were often tossed out of court, but Melvin was undeterred. He had a secret weapon: his ruthless five-star general.

She was a relentless strategist who took every case personally—one who sniffed out every weakness and pounced on enemies with unmerciful violence. And the best part of it all was she was in-house, just on the other side of a glass petition wall. Her name was Chantrell.

Chantrell was a paralegal superhero who couldn't pass the

Bar—she had recently failed a second time. She knew the text-books better than her law professors, but suffered from test-day anxiety that always paralyzed her cognitive processes five minutes into the exam. She was devastated, yet extremely efficient. Internally pissed, yet cordial.

Melvin's favorite part was her fangs.

Razor-sharp daggers that hid behind peppermint-colored lips—undetected until Melvin assigned her another target. The scent of litigation caused the same reaction in Chantrell as a gallon of fresh blood evoked in a nearby shark. She was a master of the surprise attack from dark depths—she relished in watching Melvin's opponents bleed out in front of a jury before sinking her fangs around their jugular, deep and hard, until the case was dead.

"Good morning, Vietnam," Melvin called out to her as he made his way to his office.

"Good morning, Councilman-At-Large. I have a briefing for you when you're ready."

Her voice was the kind of voice you hear on urban radio stations in the morning; the voice that announced the traffic areas to avoid, the sultry voice-over for a new beauty supply store commercial. Her tone was controlled sassiness, filtered through a professional refinery. Polished, yet still very much sassy.

"Thanks Chantrell, give me one second to power up my laptop . . . then let's get it on!"

Secretly, he liked her style in clothes and how she stopped right at the *too sexy for the workplace* line. She had the body of a woman who used to run, used to play basketball, and used to teach yoga, but she gave it all up in the name of love. That far-fetched idea of going to law school, the constant prep for the Bar Exam . . . it was all in the name of love.

The object of her love was an undocumented man from Honduras named Jony Gutierrez, a contractor she had hired to renovate her home after Katrina. Every day that he worked, she found a reason to visit the construction site just to see him, just to have a moment of his time, just to watch him climb down a ladder. After the renovations were complete on her home, Jony renovated her heart. Rehabilitated her trust issues. Repainted her dull, insecure walls with beautiful, warm colors.

For ten years, they were happy and in love.

Then, America changed presidents.

Then, the climate toward immigrants turned cold.

Then, Jony faced deportation.

She remembered that day as if it had happened twenty minutes ago—sitting at the red light on St. Claude and Caffin Avenue, inhaling Gucci Boom from the inside of her wrist, singing "Dangerously in Love 2" dangerously off-key. That's when the call came from the immigration officer. That's when that intersection, that perfume, and that song by Beyoncé became time-stamped on the worst day of her life.

Jony Gutierrez was eventually deported due to a traffic warrant for failure to appear. That was eleven months ago. Since that day, Chantrell's motivation was to save the only man who'd ever loved her as hard as she loved him, who gave more to her than she gave to him. If only she could pass the Bar. So, Melvin had taken her under his wing as a personal project. He was equally committed to helping her pass the Bar and achieving a work visa for Jony.

And yes, the thought of a fling with his lonely paralegal had entered his mind. She was a ripe thirty-eight years old and bodaciously sexy. Smooth Hershey skin. Naturally styled hair. Full, perched lips. Melvin was miserably trapped in the last rodeo of manhood—when married men risked it all to indulge in— to get lost and tangled in—a woman like Chantrell. But Melvin was nearly twice her age, with a lower back that gave out after fifty humps, more nose hair than head hair, bizarre delusions of rapper 50 Cent, and a mustache the color of cigar ash.

Even despite those facts of life, Melvin figured he could go twelve rounds with a woman like Chantrell, if not for his wife of twenty-nine years.

A man can look as long as he doesn't touch.

Right?

In between assignments, Chantrell was serious and silly, sexy and suppressed, divulging and discreet. Melvin sighed to himself. Both his paralegal and his wife were too vital to his life and daily happiness to risk.

But wouldn't it be nice if I could pull it off—a work wife and a wife-wife—hmmm . . .

Melvin grabbed his legal pad and hurried to the conference room. Today, Chantrell wore a 1940s Katherine Hepburn-inspired dress with a classic business V-neckline and four navy buttons up the center. Gray and navy polka-dot fabric with a perfect shoulder design. The dress hugged every curve of her voluptuous body and somehow made her appear as if she'd lost twenty pounds.

She looked amazing. Her scent was tempting.

Focus, Melvin, focus.

"All right, what ya got for me, bay-bay?!" Melvin shouted in his New Orleans accent, which he could conveniently turn on and off depending on the listening audience.

"Well, first of all," Chantrell sipped her coffee in midsentence, "the house at 1005 St. Peter Street is two hundred years old. It was built on the site of what once was a slaughterhouse. The house was a gift from the Governor Jacques Phillippe Villere to his youngest sister. It remained in their family until she died. Then there was the estate will with an attachment mentioned on the cover, but the attachment is no longer attached. It has somehow disappeared."

Melvin loved Chantrell's voice and sought every opportunity to keep her serenading him with legal mumbo-jumbo. "What do you mean, no longer attached?" Melvin reclined. "What happened to that attached will?"

"My question exactly! When I inquired about it, the clerk told me the head of the estate probably sealed it from the public records."

"So, they're admitting that such a will exists, with the attachment?"

"Yes, they at least admit that it did. Then, I researched Governor Jacques Phillippe Villere's younger sister and ran into another dead end."

"I want to know the previous owners of that property before it landed in the hands of Abigail," Melvin said. "Is she a lifelong squatter? Who included her in a will?"

"Get out of my head, Councilman! I took a look at the tax rolls, and there I discovered something you might find interesting."

"What was that?" Melvin asked. Chantrell looked down at her notes; his eyes focused on the natural curls in her hair, the fresh-cut lily, the shine. He wanted to reach across the table and touch her hair, but she looked up at him and the fantasy dissipated. He refocused.

"Abigail started paying the taxes on the property in 1964, but prior to that, an entity called Tureaud Trust paid the taxes," Chantrell continued.

Melvin mulled over it. "Tureaud Trust. Where have I heard that name before?"

"If I can unearth who was on the board of Tureaud Trust, it would give us insight on how Abigail received ownership of that house. I guarantee it," Chantrell asserted.

"Tureaud Trust. That name is so familiar. I wonder if we closed a land deal with them back when all my business was titles and deeds? Maybe I sued them on behalf of a client? I'm telling you, I know that name from somewhere. It'll come to me."

Melvin thanked Chantrell for her hard work, then watched her walk out of the conference room. She made coming to work exciting. Deep down, he feared the day she passed the Bar because of the possibility of her leaving his firm.

I will just have to make her a partner, he resolved as Chantrell returned to her desk.

I should ask Chantrell out this evening for drinks, a few martinis might loosen her up just enough—

Suddenly, his phone buzzed. It was his wife, Yvonne Campbell.

The call was regarding dinner.

After ending the call with his wife, Melvin shifted his attention back to the bullets points from his discovery session with Chantrell. A boom echoed off the walls of his conference room as his fist banged the table.

"Where have I come in contact with Tureaud Trust?" he muttered.

Files flickered through his mind like a blackjack dealer's deck during a shuffle break. Through three decades of clients ranging from child support to capital murder cases, Melvin opened one mental folder after the other in search of Tureaud Trust. Just as he closed in on a possible connection, his cell phone buzzed again.

"Hi, Dad. You busy?" Sherman asked.

"Just sitting here at work, doing some thinking. How are things with you and my future daughter-in-law?"

"I can't complain, Life is good with Ronelle."

"I bet it is, you lucky dog!" Melvin said as Chantrell walked into his office to search for a file. The file was in the last bin of the cabinet, and the search caused her to bend her curvaceous body. On the other end of the phone, Sherman was totally oblivious to the fact that his father was entertaining raunchy fantasies about the paralegal in his office.

"Anyway, the reason I called was to get your legal advice on a strategy concerning Abigail."

"See, if you had followed me into the family business, you wouldn't have to call me for legal advice. Consider this the last piece of advice I will give you for free, young man."

"Whatever, Dad. I was wondering if we could force Abigail, through a court order, to submit to DNA testing."

"DNA testing?"

"Yes, I think it will prove she's directly related to Grandma."

Melvin was quite impressed by his son's strategy. "I have to admit I'm feeling a little twinge of jealousy that I didn't think of it first." It was Melvin's belief that Sherman would have made a high-powered defense attorney. He had one of those minds that could find a needle in a haystack from a block away. If there were any women on the jury, Melvin felt Sherman's appearance alone would make him one of the top defense attorneys in the country. His son had the perfect height, the perfect smile, a military-style haircut he wore at all times, hazel eyes women loved, and a baby face no juror could resist. The only problem for Melvin was that Sherman had no interest in law.

"You know, that could work if I could find one piece of solid proof that our ancestors were fraudulently removed from that original will. If we can prove that one fact, then I can file a motion for discovery seeking to establish paternity on her grandfather. It's called a Family Reconstruction DNA Test, a test performed in cases where the deceased's DNA sample is not available. They are also performed in cases where the alleged father is missing. It's a long shot, but if we find something concrete, I can get a court order in the time it takes to fry a hot sausage sandwich with cheese," Melvin laughed.

"You just made me hungry! But anyway . . . that's exactly what I was thinking. I just didn't know the actual name of the court filings to order the DNA test," Sherman said.

"Well, if you would have gone to law school as I suggested, you would have known," his dad snapped back.

"There you go again with the law school jabs! Dad, I have no desire to roam the hallways at criminal court hunting for clients. I remember how stressed it would make you when your client count dropped, or the child support duckers skipped out on your retainer. Mom got you through those months, but if it weren't for her, you would have jumped off the Claiborne Bridge to escape the pressure, and you know it."

Melvin was silent as his son spoke; every word was true.

"I will stick with my goal to teach at the college level, knowing I always have my brilliant dad should I ever need legal advice. Hey, Dad, I have to go."

Sherman abruptly ended the call with his father, because the focal point of his affection had entered the room wearing his Tulane alumni T-shirt and a pair of green panties.

She was Britney Spears and Janet Jackson, all rolled into one. He loved to watch her move around the house doing whatever. She was the typical busybody. The last of her things were unpacked, and now his bachelor pad was no more. His apartment was now their home, and Sherman couldn't have been happier. She went to the kitchen to get a chair so she could hang her last piece of dance memorabilia on the wall. Then, the transition would be complete.

"Hey, sexy momma, you need some help with that?"

"No, sir, I got this."

That was cool, because he enjoyed the view of the woman he had hand-picked for these moments, when the two of them were alone as one. Forever. Furthermore, to his surprise, Ronelle was quite the little homemaker. She loved to cook different types of dishes inspired by the *Food Network*, replaced his fake flowers with ivories and ferns, and cleaned constantly as if they shared the apartment with three toddlers.

Oh my God, she is so sexy. I am not worthy.

That Tulane T-shirt and green panties pushed him over the edge of composure. *I can't take it anymore.* As she stood on the chair trying to get the picture perfectly centered, he came up behind her and pulled her T-shirt up to the middle of her lower back. He kissed and nibbled through the panties, then turned her around on the chair. Her perky breasts jiggled inches from his lips, so he removed the T-shirt. Now he had full access.

"Hmmm, what are you doing?"

"Hmmm, nothing . . ."

"Then why are you undressing me?"

"Because your body makes my eyes . . . *feel good,*" he said in Barry White's voice. "I'm about to do something nasty to you."

"Oh, really? I dare you!"

Sherman lifted her over his shoulder caveman-style and spanked those green panties all the way to the bedroom.

"Time to make good on my threat," he asserted.

"I double-dare you," she answered.

From a height of six feet-five inches, he gently laid her on the bed. "As much as I love seeing you in these green panties, they have to go." Sherman removed the panties with his teeth. Ronelle licked her lips. He tossed the panties. She growled. He removed his shirt. She purred like Eartha Kitt. He sucked her lower lips. She scratched his back. He slapped her high on her thigh. She bruised. He bruised. They kissed. She ended the kiss with a slap to his face. He bruised again. He bit her shoulder. She bruised. He placed his hand around her neck, as if to choke her.

"I dare you," she tempted.

"Oh, you dare me?" he accepted her dare.

That's who they were, and that's what they liked. The kind of sex found only in clubs on the farthest end of town, the ones with no advertising signs and no windows. Clubs where the men were charged to enter, and everyone was consenting. That was their type of sex, and Ronelle couldn't get enough.

Sherman and Ronelle remained unavailable until lunchtime.

CHAPTER 19

May 24, 1854
8:20 p.m.

Tonight was Marietta's first night leaving Mr. Lafitte's house since Clarice had stolen her baby. Though still in lingering pain, she couldn't stand that room another minute. Her master had left to go drinking. She waited an hour after he departed, then left to pay Beatrice a visit.

Marie Laveau had provided the address to find Beatrice. Marietta endured the four-block walk. She entered Beatrice's living quarters and took a seat on the bed. Beatrice handed her a glass of water.

"My dear sister, your bedroom is beautiful. He treats you so good," Marietta said, looking wide-eyed around the room.

It had been a week since Beatrice followed Clarice to Harriett Green's house, and tonight was her first chance alone with Marietta to share what she'd witnessed.

They two were twins, completely identical in hair, eyes, and complexion. The only distinguishing feature was a long scar on the left side of Marietta's jaw, a scar from the day she had stolen the necklace. When she saw that her necklace was missing, Mrs. de Marigny wanted Marietta to confess to stealing the jewelry, but the girl had repeatedly denied the accusation. As punishment, Mrs. de Marigny forced Marietta to lie on the floor behind her rocking chair with the right side of her face flat against the dry wooden floor.

"Where have you hidden my necklace?" she asked.

"I ain't got it," Marietta answered.

Mrs. de Marigny then leaned back in the chair, repeatedly smashing the left side of Marietta's face under the wooden rocker. The torture went on until Marietta's left top and bottom teeth were knocked out; she swallowed most of them as she screamed. The child could no longer chew on that side of her mouth. The rocker left permanent scarring on her jaw, marks that distinguished the twin's lives in more ways than one. Aside from the scar, Beatrice and Marietta remained mirror reflections.

"I saw two of my daughters the other day," Beatrice said. "I think two of da other ch-children are for you."

"Where, Beatrice?" Marietta grabbed Beatrice by the shoulders. "You think you saw my children?"

"Yes! Clarice had my two, and I know the other two are for you. I just know it."

"And where did you see them?"

"She lives on Royal Street."

"I knew it! I knew my children were somewhere close. I could feel them, Beatrice. I felt them in my spirit. Sometimes, when I am taking a bath, I look down in the water, and I see their faces. Not as little babies. No, no, no! I see their faces as big kids. Then they wave *bye* and disappear. All this time and my kids are on Royal Street!"

"The water between your legs in the tub? I see my children there, too. Those children I saw was our children walkin' with Clarice. I know it in my heart."

"I believe you, Beatrice. That no-good bastard Lafitte has a stack of supply lists on his desk for Royal Street, but I never knew why. I read everything on his desk, and I knew he was partners with your master, but I never thought the *Beatrice* written on his documents was my very own sister. I also read their partnership agreement from many years ago, an agreement for a breeding business, raising girls for a life as quadroon concubines."

"So it's true."

"Yes Beatrice, that's why they're breeding us like cows." Marietta walked over to the window and noticed a young couple walking toward Rampart street in no particular hurry. While still eyeing the lovers in the moonlight, she asked, "what do you think Clarice gets when they sell our babies?"

After a brief silence, Beatrice replied, "My masta owns Clarice like he owns me. She gets that house, and she gets to walk around like she a free nigga, but ain't. I don't think Queenie know nothing 'bout him sellin' our children. She don't take good to sellin' folk."

"You think your master is hiding this from his wife?" Marietta was intrigued.

"Yes, I heard him tell her all of us niggas are free, and that he hired us. But we not free. He lied." Beatrice walked over to her chest to refill Marietta's glass of water.

"I say we go around there right now and kill that bitch, then take our children. I know a place we can run and hide among the Indians in the swamp," Marietta said.

"No, Marietta! You not well for no killin' and runnin'. You talk foolish. If they catch us, they hangin' us. I want to find all my ch-ch-children and that will take time. I thought 'bout killin' Clarice many nights, just like you. But if you put a hand on her, you will neva see none of them babies. We got to wait." Beatrice invited her sister to have a seat on the bed.

"I could sleep on this bed for a week and never wake." Marietta pressed the palms of her hands deep into the cotton-stuffed mattress with thick, quilted bedding.

The sisters sat on the bed in Beatrice's living quarters with their backs against the wall. Marietta gazed at the night through the windows in Beatrice's room, wishing her quarters had windows and fresh air. It didn't take long for fantasies of Beatrice's life, and the affectionate relationship she shared with her master, to enter her mind.

"I can tell he loves you," Marietta said to Beatrice. "He treats you like a wife."

"Husbands don't sell their children," Beatrice said through

clenched teeth. "*I'm no wife.*"

It was then that Marietta removed her shoe and handed Beatrice two folded sheets of paper. On one sheet was the alphabet and six basic sentences. On the other sheet of paper was a clipping from a classified section of the newspaper. Marietta had circled several classified ads pertaining to the sale and capture of fugitive slaves.

"If we are going to find all of our children, then I need you to be my eyes down here—that can't happen if you can't read. We need to get away for lessons three times a week even if it's only for a few minutes. Before I leave tonight we will cover the alphabet and I will read these wanted ads from the slave catchers. You never know, sometimes I read about folk I know who ran away."

Beatrice's eyes became cloudy. "I didn't think I would ever learn to read, thank you."

"No need to thank me, we're sisters. But your master and his wife can't know. If he finds out you can read, they will sell you away."

"But why?"

"Because *niggers* who can read always teach other *niggers*, and they don't want that. I will teach you, but it's our secret," Marietta said as they started to braid their hair together and recite the alphabet. After several passes of the alphabet, Marietta read each sentence on the sheet, while sounding out every word for Beatrice.

> **I am free.**
> **This is my girl.**
> **This is my boy.**
> **I like your dress.**
> **I am not a slave.**
> **This is my house.**

"Well, it's time for me to get back. If he comes home and I'm not there, he will beat me all night. Come see me when you can, and we will continue our lessons. If he comes home and he sees you, don't look him in the face; always at the floor and walk fast by him. He likes you. He told me to fix myself up more like you. Says you're very pretty. Beatrice, don't pay him no mind if he comes around you, grinning like a chess cat. He is the devil. You hear me?"

"Yes, Marietta," Beatrice replied, "but I don't think no man will come grinning around me."

"Why you talk like that, Beatrice? You are very pretty. You don't have any marks on you from beatings as I have. Your skin is like a spool of silk; you have soft hair. Any man would love to have you, so don't talk like that, Beatrice."

"I know men look at me. They think I'm fair and everything, but none gonna look at me for a while and that's for sure."

"Why do you say that, Beatrice?"

"Marietta, I am with child again."

"No, Beatrice! No . . ."

The Birthing Room
February 19, 1855

The sheets that covered the table were the same ones used during her previous six pregnancies and provided no comfort from the deep ridges in the wood. Any other day, the same table held sacks of flour, in a futile attempt to keep the rats from feasting. One such rodent sat in the corner of the room, watching Beatrice like an old friend who had stopped by to pay a visit. Along the wall in front of her were the same three pots of water, carried in by a little old lady who showed no signs of slowing down.

Delia was dressed in her usual eggshell-colored dress that swept the floor as she moved about, humming unfamiliar spirituals from deep within her soul. The aroma of sweat and pralines perfumed her clothes.

Through the window to her left, a stoic Beatrice listened to the sound of roosters clearing their throats. Annoyingly they announced the dawn and enthusiastically they invited the sun.

Through the same window came the sound of wagon wheels commuting across bumpy cobblestone roads. A delivery man walked along with clinking bottles, all filled to the top with fresh milk.

Beatrice wanted a glass of milk. She wanted to be anywhere but in a pantry that doubled as a birthing room. She couldn't suppress her craving for escape.

Congo Square, perhaps?

A dry spot alongside the Mississippi River, perhaps?

Beatrice wanted to be back in Mandeville, because New Orleans was like a nightmare with no awakening and no conclusion. When she was a child, she would often wet the bed and awaken from a deep sleep cold and ashamed. That's how New Orleans made her feel every day. Like all bad dreams, she was frustrated by the helplessness of her condition, and anguished that no one could hear her cry.

Beatrice was pregnant again for the same man and expecting the same outcome. At the end of her labor, Clarice would appear and ride off into the sunset with another one of her beautiful baby girls. Each time was like the last time. The labor pains. The never-ending discomfort. The anxiety. It was all familiar.

Delia's spirituals served as a constant reminder that she was still his slave, and he was still her master. This baby, like the others, was little more than a source of income. Ever-obedient in her role, she was ready to add to his wealth; her baby was ready to enter the cruelty of servitude.

"Beatrice, push real good for me," Delia said.

"Ahhhhhhh!"

"Push some mo', Beatrice, push some mo'!"

"I'm pushin'!"

The top of a wet head slowly appeared, then a half a face, closed eyes . . . then a complete head from the neck up.

"The baby head is out, Beatrice. Push, push, push!"

And so, she pushed with everything she had until her baby rested in Delia's hands like a soft loaf of bread.

Delia cut the cord with a six-inch paring knife. Seconds later came the sound of an infant taking its first breath and letting out a loud scream, followed by heavy grunting as it struggled to catch its breath. Delia placed the baby and the paring knife on a small chest where she wiped and cleaned as the sound of a newborn filled the birthing room.

"What is it, Delia? Is it a boy? Did I have a boy? Please tell me it's a boy!"

Delia answered her in a spiritual:

> *In the days of my youth a dream had I, good Lord.*
> *These times I am growing old, full of dreams am I,*
> *good Lord.*
> *I have dreams of those good times gone by!*
> *When I was a slave, one boss had I, good Lord!*
> *These times when I'm needing rest all hands serve I,*
> *good Lord.*
> *I have dreams.*

"Delia, please! Did I have a boy?" Beatrice yelled through Delia's humming.

> *Yellow girl goes to the ball;*
> *Nigger lights her to the hall.*
> *Fiddler man!*
> *Now, what is that to you?*
> *Say, what is that to you, Fiddler man?*

Delia didn't have to turn around, nor did she have to hand Beatrice the baby. The words of the old Creole spiritual told her everything she needed to know. Like a bad meal rushing up her esophagus, the pain regurgitated from the deepest parts of her soul. Her head turned away from where Delia was cleaning her baby. Her eyes found somewhere else to look. Her heart dug another grave in the cemetery of despair. It never got any easier. Beatrice knew it was a girl.

Delia finally finished cleaning the baby and handed the bundle of screaming joy to Beatrice. She looked into blue eyes, caressed damp, sandy hair, and held little fingers that clutched her thumb.

In an act of defiance, the old midwife told Beatrice, "Before

Clarice come, go on and nurse yo' baby. Put her on the tit."

For the first time, Beatrice nursed one of her daughters; for the first time, she watched one of her girls suckle and feed. Then there was a knock at the door.

"*Who there?*" Delia called out, but there was no answer. "I have work to do with this baby. Come back later."

The person on the other side of the door knocked again.

"I said go away." Delia called, assuming it was one of the other servants in the house.

The door opened.

Beatrice was happy to see Marietta holding a vase with flowers in one hand and a small basket of pecan candy in the other.

"Beatrice, she is beautiful!" Marietta exclaimed as she leaned over to watch the baby girl nurse.

"She is beautiful, Marietta! Yes, she is."

"And look at those fat little legs! Look at that belly on that baby! I see why you was eating so much. She is some greedy. Look at her sucking on you like that!" Marietta started to cry. "She is so beautiful!"

"Ahhhhhhh!" Beatrice screamed! "Ahhhhhhh!"

"What's wrong, Beatrice?" Marietta asked in a panic.

"Take the baby, take the baby!" Beatrice screamed at Marietta. She handed the baby to her sister.

Delia immediately inserted her arm inside of Beatrice to check the placenta; it was normally around this time that the afterbirth would pass. "Beatrice, you're about to pass your sack," Marietta said as she rocked the screaming infant.

"Ahhhhhhh!" Beatrice cried out again as the midwife continued to feel around her womb. That's when Delia felt it.

"Push some mo', Beatrice! Push! Push! Push!"

"Why am I still pushing, Delia?" Her voice was filled with agony.

"It hurts because you have another baby! I felt another head! Now push this baby out."

"What?!" Marietta screamed. "Beatrice, you're having another baby! You carried twins!

"AAAAAAAAAAAAH!"

"Push! Beatrice, push! I see the top of the head! Push hard

one more time!"

"I can't! I can't! Ain't got nothing left to push wit'."

"Yes, you do! Push, Beatrice! And Marietta! You put that baby down and come help me. Press down on her while I fetch this baby," Delia demanded.

Marietta set the screaming baby down on the small chest and did as Delia asked. She pressed down on Beatrice's lower ribcage.

"Push now, Beatrice. You got to push, or you gon' kill it in your womb! Now push!" Delia screamed.

Beatrice found the strength to push. The second baby slowly oozed into Delia's waiting hands. Delia cut the cord with the paring knife. The baby took its first breath.

"Beatrice, it is another girl. You had two beautiful girls," Marietta said. A euphoric breeze of joy filled the room as the three women celebrated the successful delivery of another healthy baby girl. "Here, Beatrice, you nurse this greedy little piglet while I check on the first baby," Marietta instructed.

Beatrice guided her nipple to the baby's mouth and the infant started to feed. To nurse her baby was the greatest gift of all. Beatrice cried. Delia walked over with the other baby and placed her on Beatrice's right breast. The infant girl instinctively latched on. Beatrice looked down at both of her babies as they enjoyed her milk, then looked up at Delia and her sister.

"Thank you, Delia. Thank you with all my heart. If I live ten mo' lives, I will spend every day thanking you," Beatrice said as she cried tears of joy.

Delia cried.

Marietta cried.

Suddenly, the joyful breeze that blew through the window was cut off as a head veered inside.

"She had that baby yet?"

All the oxygen left the room. All the joy left the room. Any particle of humanity evaporated with one simple question asked by a very dark and iniquitous soul.

"She had that baby yet?"

"Yes, Clarice, she had that baby," Delia sighed.

"Well, hand it to me through this window. Hurry!"

"You may have to come on in and fetch them yourself," Delia said.

"No! No! No, Delia! She can't have them! She can't take my babies!" Beatrice wailed.

Moments later, Clarice entered the birthing room. She looked at the two babies. She looked at Delia. She frowned at Marietta, who greeted her with a hiss.

"You had twins?" Clarice asked. Beatrice didn't answer, hoping against hope to hide one of the babies somehow.

"Delia, are those two girls? You better answer me!"

"Yes, *that's two girls*. She had two girls. Just let her nurse 'em a little while longer, Clarice. They both came out mighty hungry, and Beatrice full of milk," the old midwife pleaded. "See no harm in letting them babies feed on her a while. Least until they full. I see no harm in that, Clarice."

"Old maid, hush your mouth! I ain't asked you nothing! Now hand those babies to me, and I will be on my way. Don't go making trouble for Masta."

"Clarice, I can't. If you want dem babies, then you take them off dem tits yourself. I ain't doin' it no mo'. Not much you and Massa can do to me anyway. I done lived a long life. Don't want to answer to sweet Jesus for none of this. My soul gon' see Jesus one day soon, but not like this. You want dem babies, you take em." Delia looked Clarice straight in the eye.

"I said hand me them babies now!"

"And I said I ain't." The old midwife started to sing another spiritual as she applied healing herbs to Beatrice's womb.

The moment Clarice took a step toward Beatrice and the two feeding infants, Marietta grabbed the paring knife off the chest next to Delia and blocked her path, her right arm stiffly extended. Her fist was tight around the handle of the knife, her heart filled with hatred and revenge. Her mind was loaded with all the motivation needed to slash Clarice with more holes than a rice strainer. She dared Clarice to take another step. Clarice didn't.

"You not woman enough to cut me, you yellow whore!" Clarice said with an evil grin. "While you was a house nigga stealin' from Mistress, I was cutting sugar cane with a knife as long as your arm. Now put that knife down before I show you how to use it on your neck," Clarice threatened. "Hand me those babies."

"We ain't handing you a damn thing." Marietta raised the tip of the knife to eye level. "You will not take these babies, Clarice. You have taken plenty already from my sister, and you got my children. Leave us! Leave us now, or they will carry you out of here dead!"

Out in the courtyard, several maids paused and huddled around the door while the confrontation escalated in the birthing room. Clarice was universally hated by all the maids. Each of them had a daughter stolen by her at one point or another. Mr. Lafitte had a thing for dark-complexioned maids.

"Ha, ha!" Clarice appeared unfazed. "Marietta, you put that knife down and move out my way. Not tellin' you again. Dem babies belong to Masta, and I am here to take them. Nothin' you and that whore in that bed gon' do to stop me."

"Clarice, you take one more step, and I will cut your ass end to end. I've been waiting to cut you for a long time."

Clarice took a step toward Beatrice. Marietta stabbed her in the arm, opening a four-inch flesh wound. Clarice's right arm bled onto the floor, but she was undeterred.

"Bitch, you cut me!" Clarice pulled up her black maid's dress and untied a small machete from her thigh—a blade she used to fight off slave smugglers like Mason and his brother. Clarice pointed the machete at Marietta.

"I asked you nice. Not askin' no more." Clarice approached Marietta.

"Oh, Lawdy, they fightin', they fightin'," Delia muttered as she bolted out of the room to get help.

"Stop it! Please stop it!" Beatrice begged. "Put your knives away. You can have my babies. Just put the knives away."

"Beatrice, she will not take these babies. To hell with Clarice! I am killing this bitch!" Marietta jabbed at Clarice a second time but missed. Clarice's counter-swing whistled from right to left, but she also missed, and her blade sawed deep into the wall.

"Stop! Please stop!" Beatrice yelled from the dry, rotted table. "Marietta, hand her the babies. No need for me to lose my babies and my sister. I have no other family other than my boys.

Remember our promise, Marietta."

"No, Beatrice. This ends today." Marietta launched again at Clarice with her knife and missed, which allowed Clarice to grab her by the collar of her dress and body-slam her against the back wall. With the handle of the machete, Clarice hammered Marietta on the wrist, causing her to drop her weapon. Clarice placed the blade of her machete firmly against Marietta's throat, cutting into her skin.

"Say one mo' word, yellow bitch, and you dead," Clarice threatened.

Marietta smiled. "Do it, you black wench. I am already dead. You killed me a long time ago," she spat. "Kill me!"

"Clarice, no! No, Clarice! Here, take the babies! Here, Clarice, you take them!" Beatrice removed the first baby from her right breast, causing a slight popping sound as the nipple was forcefully released from the child's mouth. The baby cried. Then Beatrice removed the second baby from her left breast, causing another popping sound as the suction grip was released. The second baby cried as loudly as her sister. Beatrice kissed both screaming babies as many times as she could, only pausing for a moment to record their little faces in her mind.

"Clarice, let go of my sister. Here are my children. You can take them now. I just wanted to feed them, that's all."

"I will deal with you later, high yellow dog! I owe you a cutting!" Clarice lowered the blade from Marietta's neck.

Marietta never flinched nor blinked an eye. Her anger was apparent in her breath, which reeked of retaliation.

"You know where to find me when you're ready, and next time I will have a bigger knife," Marietta said as Clarice backed away.

Moments later, Clarice vanished into the night with a baby girl in each arm, leaving Beatrice minus two infants. Beatrice's breasts leaked from the fading cries of her two babies, who were still very hungry, still craving their mother's breast.

The following day

Marietta rushed over to her sister's bedside and tried providing comfort to Beatrice, but it was a futile attempt. Both of them had lost children to Clarice and the commodities market of slavery and sex, but this was the first time she had taken twins. Marietta struggled to understand why Beatrice had given up her children so easily without a fight, but deep down she knew the answer.

Whereas Marietta never accepted her role in the economy of slavery, Beatrice unconditionally surrendered. Whereas Marietta never lost hope of freedom from the inhumane treatment of Mr. Lafitte, her sister Beatrice accepted her servitude as a never-ending reality of life. While she often fantasized about freedom, she never truly let herself believe it was possible.

Marietta continued where Delia had left off in applying healing herbs to her sister's womb. Then, she took great care to clean her up and remove her soiled gown. When Delia finally returned to the birthing room, they called for one of the male servants to carry Beatrice back to her living quarters. Once Beatrice was in her bed, Marietta requested everyone to leave.

She shut the door behind them.

She wanted to be alone with her sister.

Marietta wanted to care for Beatrice and provide her with the same care and love she'd shown her a little over a year ago. Love and attention she had never experienced in the back room of the red brick house—not in the aftermath of any of her pregnancies. Beatrice had re-entered her life at a time she had desperately needed her sister.

"I was ready to die for you, Beatrice. I was ready to give my life to keep those babies."

"I know, Marietta, I know."

"I know why you let her take them. If I get in the way of your master's business, he would have Lafitte sell me off. The two of them are close, like two peas in a pod. Long before I knew he held you down here, your master would come over to smoke with that old bastard. I heard him talk about how good you made him feel. He even said one time he thought about moving you to France where he could be seen with you like a wife. He is in love with you. I heard him say it all. I used to place my ear to the wall and listen. Then my master would remind him you is his nigga and don't go falling in love with you. They needed you to make more girls. That's all he saw me as: someone he could lay with to make more girls to sell. But I still say your master really loves you," Marietta said as Beatrice quietly wept into a pillow.

In a defeated voice, Beatrice finally said, "I agree with you that if we cause them any trouble, they will sell us off, but we have to work harder to find our children—"

"Enough of this! I am not making any more girls, and neither will you. The babies Clarice took tonight are the last children we will ever have. I hope they make as much money as they can because our rearing days are over. Get some sleep, and I will be here in the morning to help you, after I meet with Marie." Marietta kissed her sister on top of her head and departed into the night.

The next day, right after Mr. Lafitte headed out to the slave auctions, Marietta hurried next door to the home of Marie Laveau. She knocked on the door; Marie was expecting her visit.

Marie was in the kitchen cooking on a large wood-burning stove. On top of the stove were four medium-sized pots. The pots didn't give off the aroma of boiling chicken, rabbit stew, or soaked red beans, but rather the scent of verbena, catmint, and quassia. On every counter in her kitchen were freshly-pulled roots from her garden, vegetables from passing vendors, and pressed oil from nuts and berries.

Marie's kitchen was more than just a kitchen; it was one of the first pharmacies in the city of New Orleans, and everything was for sale. The majority of Marie's clients were mistresses from as far north as the plantations in Kentucky and as far south as U.S. Barracks. Her clients were loyal, frequent, and believers in her medicinal remedies. One of those remedies was the reason Marietta took a seat at her table.

"Madame Laveau, my sister and I need your help."

"You do? Well, I'm not in the business of helping runaways make it to the promised land. I hope that's not what you're seeking."

"No, that's not it. Not yet at least."

"Then what is it? You need Lafitte to sleep long and hard, so he doesn't touch you? Ha!" Marie laughed out loud. "You want him to sleep for three days? I can help with that for sure. Ha!"

"No, that's not it either, Madame Laveau."

"*Alors qu'est-ce que c'est, Madame? Dites-le moi.*"

"We do not want to have any more children—not like this, not born into slavery. That's all we ask, Madame Laveau. Make us bleed each month. No more children unless we have them for our husbands. A while ago you told me about the soup you took before you were a free woman. I want the same soup. Can you teach me how to make it? That is all we ask."

"So, you want to make the soup?"

"Yes, please teach me, and I will teach Beatrice. This way we never have to see Clarice again."

"Yes, I can teach you, but you must know one thing first."

"Please tell me, Madame Laveau."

"Once you drink the soup more than three times, there is a chance you may never have children again. You must know this first. After the third time, the child you have is your last. Êtes-vous sûr?"

Marietta took a moment to think about the options Marie Laveau had just presented; she wrestled with the finality of it all. She hated having children for Mr. Lafitte, but she dreamed of one day gaining her freedom like Marie and having a family. In her dreams, a tall, dark, chocolate man would appear from nowhere, educated up North in some of the best institutions, active in the cause of freedom for her people. He would sweep her off her feet. She dreamed of having his babies, but not another Creole half-breed for her master.

"Yes, Madame Laveau, I am sure. I understand drinking it could mean I never have another child, even for my husband. That is a risk I am willing to take. Please teach me."

Marie Laveau pointed to a black basket that sat on the floor in the corner of the kitchen. "Very well. First hand me a cup of danshen in the basket over there, and we will get started. It is the least that I can do."

For the next four hours, Marie Laveau taught Marietta how to make a soup she called *dernière soup de bébé,* after which

Marietta went home and prepared a pot for Beatrice. After each sexual encounter, Marietta and Beatrice made a pot of soup, and neither one of the sisters produced another girl for their masters.

The soup made them both sterile.

CHAPTER 20

Tulane University
Office of Professor Davis

Brandon and Sherman arrived at Tulane University in hopes of getting some real work done on their paper. They also had a quick review session scheduled with Professor Davis. In the hall next to his door was a wrought-iron bench with a smooth oak seat. The walls were a few shades off from white, and the building had a ceiling that trapped voices in the upper corners. The two buddies took advantage of the stillness of the corridor and simultaneously booted their laptops.

"So, what's your word count?" Sherman asked Brandon, braced for an answer of five thousand or less.

"No comment."

"B!"

"Fourteen thousand, and you?"

"Twenty-seven thousand!"

"How in *da-fuck* have you written twenty-seven thousand words?"

"If I tell you, then I have to kill you!" Sherman laughed.

"For real, how did you do that?"

"Adderall, it helps me get shit done!"

"So, you're on drugs? That's cheating . . ."

"It's not a drug, like crack or heroin, it's more like . . ."

Brandon cut him off. "Dude, it is a Schedule One narcotic! It's a drug!"

"I don't use it to get high; I use it to focus! It helps me write. It clears my thoughts. It gives me mental energy. Without it, there's no way I would've hit twenty-seven thousand words."

"It's still a drug. But give me some!"

"No!" Sherman laughed. "Get your own prescription, all of these are accounted for."

"Bro. Give me one!"

"Can't do it, ain't gon do it!"

"Sherm, I'm struggling my ass off." Brandon grabbed Sherman's backpack.

"B, *chill out!*" Sherman snatched his bag. "On a serious note, how are things at home?"

Brandon reclined on the bench and blew out a deep sigh. "Separated."

"What? Seriously? Who moved out?"

"Dad."

"Because of that night?"

"Apparently how my mother handled your request that night was the last straw. The following day after you asked for their approval to marry Ronelle, he was out the door and down the street."

Before they could get further down that line of conversation, Brandon was first to notice Professor Irving Davis approaching from the farthest end of the History Hall. They leaped from the bench as if the oak seating had turned into orange heating coils.

"Hello, gentlemen! What a pleasant surprise—it's two of my favorite students. What a beautiful day to discuss American History," Professor Davis greeted them with a handshake and a proud smile. Their professor was a clean-shaven, skinnier version of Sidney Poitier—the *Guess Who's Coming Home for Dinner?* version of Poitier.

Sherman and Brandon followed their professor to his office in hopes of obtaining his take on their research, and to pick his brain for possible pitfalls. They were a continent away from the required word count. They lacked the essential data to deliver on the primary thesis of their research. They were off the pace—and Sherman had made a graduation promise to his grandmother.

When Brandon and Sherman entered Professor Davis's office, they were immediately humbled by his workload. On his large desk were at least forty manuscripts from other doctoral students; all appeared much thicker than what they had managed to gather about the Fortier family and the Campbells.

"Sir, we would like to run something by you if you have a free minute," Brandon began.

"Of course, take a seat."

Dr. Davis was obsessed with historical facts; the clutter in his office was the evidence. Davis had written six books on topics related to slavery throughout the Confederate states, as well as the Reconstruction period in Louisiana. Sherman was beginning to understand why Brandon wanted to stay far away from anything dated from the 1800s.

Behind the professor's desk—from the top of the ceiling down—were all of his advanced degrees and certificates. On his desk was a little sign that read: *I learn something new every day, which makes me less dumb than yesterday.* There was nothing dumb about Dr. Davis. Their final Ph.D. topic was his area of expertise, and they were shaking in their proverbial boots, to put it mildly.

"So, what have the two of you discovered on your journey thus far?" Dr. Davis asked as they settled into the awkward office chairs.

Brandon sighed. "I need a minute to think about that question, because everything I've discovered about my family and race relations thus far was not what I expected."

"Hmm, you expected squeaky clean?"

"Pretty much, but the truth about the Fortier family is far from squeaky or clean."

"For example?"

"Well, sir, in the 1800s, it appears that my family was on the wrong side of history," Brandon said.

"Are you referring to their support of the Confederacy?"

"So, you were aware that my family financed the Confederate cause?"

Professor Davis chuckled as he opened a side drawer. "After all, I am Head of Historical Studies for Tulane and the Director of the New Orleans Historical Museum and Society. It behooves me to be knowledgeable about such events." Professor Davis coughed into a white handkerchief, then placed it back in the drawer. "Go easy on your old grand-pappy; it was to be expected of the leading *Jacksonian* of his time."

"I'm sorry Professor Davis, the what?"

"The Jacksonians. Oh, my. You don't know?"

"I'm afraid I don't know, sir."

Professor Davis went on to recap the early history of Brandon's family, as if everything had happened just yesterday, with every fact and detail intact. "Dear innocent child, I dread being the one to introduce you to this page in the history of your family, but your great-great-great-grandfather was perhaps the leading supporter of Andrew Jackson's racially based legislation of genocide—like the Indian Removal Act of 1830."

"Dude . . . the Trail of Tears." Sherman whispered.

"Wait! What!" Brandon stood.

"Yes, Brandon, your family's involvement in the removal of Native Americans and the mixed-race blacks living amongst them is well documented. Many of the Natives who made their livelihood along the shores became a nuisance to your family's plans to expand their docks throughout the Gulf Coast. Andrew Jackson and your grandfather were not only political allies, but also business partners. Some of the money to finance the round-up and compensate the soldiers was provided by Fortier Shipping Lines."

"We financed the Trail of Tears? The march at gunpoint out of the South that killed thousands? My family?!"

"Brandon I'm sorry you're only discovering this today," Professor Davis said in a remorseful voice.

"So, we financed the Confederacy and the Trail of Tears . . . two of the worst things to happen other than the Civil War?! I think I'm about to puke!"

"Brandon, you must know spin doctors have been around

since the first scandal during biblical times. You can't fault your family for protecting their brand and burying many of these stories. You may need to take some time to strongly consider whether you want to go with this topic."

"It's too late to change the topic," Sherman interjected.

"I'm not changing topics . . . but this is a sack of bricks," Brandon replied softly.

"Brandon . . . companies like Fortier Lines have always maintained someone on staff whose primary job is to protect the image of said company. The fact that you're just learning of these accounts speaks to the success of your grandfather's executives in protecting the legacy of Fortier Lines International."

Dr. Davis's words did little to provide comfort to Brandon's feelings of misplaced guilt. Although he had absolutely nothing to do with the sins of his great-great-great-grandfather, he was riddled with feelings of responsibility for everything that the man had done.

Sherman remained mostly quiet, allowing Brandon to have the floor until it was his turn. When his turn arrived, Sherman shared with Dr. Davis that his dad was ready to track down the estate owner of 1005 St. Peter Street, and informed him about the pending lawsuit for his grandmother's inheritance.

"My father feels that the nine notches in the attic could serve as evidence in the lawsuit he's preparing."

Professor Davis suddenly seemed ill at ease, but he hid it by refilling his pipe. "What do you feel?" Davis asked.

"You know, Dr. Davis, I feel like a toddler trying to walk a very big dog down the street. This research takes me down a different path each day. However, the one thing I know for sure is, I didn't start this journey looking for opportunities to file a lawsuit over events that happened during slavery. I am not one of those reparation junkies—but my dad would sue a toothbrush if it were possible."

Professor Davis laughed. "I've known your dad since we were students at Tulane, your description is one hundred percent accurate. He loves lawsuits. I'm surprised he hasn't filed a wrongful death lawsuit against the Jews for what they did to Jesus." Professor Davis chuckled as he cleaned the lenses of his glasses. "Sherman, most of us in this city are descendants of slaves. There's no surprise there. One great aspect to explore is how your family has recovered from slavery. Another is forgiveness," the professor suggested.

"And then?" Sherman asked.

"When you uncover the slave master who owned your family, that is when your journey will take a sharp turn. And then, well, that's when the fun will begin." The professor stood to signal their meeting was over. "Now, if you gentlemen don't mind, I have a huge stack of papers here to grade before I call it a day."

"Thank you for your time, Dr. Davis," Brandon said as he and Sherman filed out into the hall. Behind them in his office, the professor lit his pipe again and propped his feet on the desk.

"B, Professor Davis just laid some heavy stuff on us. I think we should return to our respective corners immediately and process. I'm now in high pursuit of a slave master."

"I agree," Brandon said. "I don't know who we are anymore, and the part I know is fake."

They parted ways without another word.

On his drive home, Sherman called Ronelle. "Hey, sweetie, what time are you getting back?"

"Classes are running late. I've got to work tonight, babe. Dance recital rehearsals, remember?"

"All right. What do you want to eat tonight? I'll pick it up," he offered.

"How about fried chicken from Dooky Chase Restaurant?"

"That'll work," he said.

"And cobbler, babe. I've got to run. I love you."

Before heading inside, Sherman decided to make one trip to take care of all the errands. So, after parking his car, he walked to the mailbox. It was overflowing now that Ronelle forwarded all her mail from the Fortier home. Awkwardly, he made his way to the door with the takeout bags from Dooky Chase and the mail.

Once inside, Sherman placed everything on the kitchen counter. Sherman's condo was the classic open-concept layout that allowed a broad view of the living room/kitchen area the moment you entered, with one bedroom on the far left and another on the far right.

It didn't take long for the smell of Dooky Chase chicken to escape the bag; the aroma was too enticing to ignore. He stuck his hand in the bag, grabbed a chicken breast, and bit into it hungrily.

"Hot, hot, hot. That's hot and good," he said as he quickly ejected the golden-battered breast from his mouth before it scorched his tongue.

Not one to back down from a fight, Sherman blew on a bite-sized portion until it cooled a few degrees, then re-stuffed it into his mouth. "My goodness, that's good! Thank you, Dooky! You guys never let me down when I'm starving."

Pulling up a kitchen chair to the edge of the counter, Sherman sorted through the mail with one hand while he savagely devoured four pieces of chicken with the other. "Ronelle better hurry home or she'll have to settle for Corn Flakes tonight. This chicken is history." He shuffled through all the bills and junk mail from Domino's Pizza, furniture rental companies, and campaign mailers when a single white envelope fell from the stack.

The envelope was addressed to Ronelle Fortier. The sender was Tureaud Trust. The outside of the envelope read *Statement Enclosed*. He couldn't see what type of statement was enclosed. He wondered if Tureaud Trust was a savings and loan. He searched on Google.

Nothing.

He resisted the urge to open the envelope, but he did hold it up to the fluorescent light. He was surprised to see what appeared to be an ACH payment for 17 million dollars paid to the order of Ronelle Fortier.

Sherman sat at the counter, deep in thought. He could feel his blood pressure rising. He tried to decide what type of anger he would deploy. Scream and yell or play the incredibly hurt role? One thing he was sure of was that when she walked through the door, it was going down. He began to pace from the kitchen to his bedroom like a lawyer delivering closing arguments. His emotions were all over the place; the types of emotions typically reserved for infidelity, not the discovery that your future spouse has secretly hidden 17 million dollars. Nevertheless, Sherman felt betrayed.

Why did she feel the need to hide this from me?

He received a text message from Ronelle. *Hey, babe, I'm leaving now. Should arrive in twenty minutes.* He didn't bother to respond; he was too upset. He intended to make Ronelle pay emotionally for hiding this aspect of her life.

After about twenty minutes had passed, there came the sound of bells and clinging of trinkets on the other side of the front door. That could only mean one thing: Ronelle was home. As soon as she opened the door, Sherman was standing there.

"Why did you keep this from me?"

"What is that?"

Sherman held the letter stiff in his hand. "It's just a little letter from something called Tureaud Trust. From what I can tell, you have 17 million dollars we've never discussed."

Ronelle dropped her dance bag on the ottoman and took the envelope from his hand. "Really? Tell me this isn't about an earnings statement from my trust fund? A fund I've had ever since I was, what . . . a few months old? Our grandfather set up that fund years ago. By the way, so you know, Brandon has one too, and it's worth a lot more than that!"

She tore open the envelope, ripped out the statement letter, and began to read it aloud to the point of yelling each word.

"We are pleased to inform you that your twenty-five-year accumulated interest and earnings totals—"

He interrupted. "So, you think it's cool I'm just finding out like this? We talk about everything. We share everything. Then today I discover you have a secret stash! As if you have to hide it because I hound you for money. What happened to all of the transparency and communication crap you've thrown at me for three years?"

"Sherman, I have been getting those statements for so long, I don't even open them anymore. Money has never meant to me what it means to most people. It doesn't faze me to have a check for this amount. Besides, I can't touch it until I'm thirty or married; and I'm neither thirty nor married. We've been getting those statements with checks like that for years. It's been torture," she sighed.

"Is that right? I know plenty of folks who'd love to feel your pain."

"I was born into the Fortier family. For more than two hundred years we have been in the top ten percent of privately-owned corporations. Sherman, if I thought for one second your interest in me was because of my family, I would not be here, and you would not be in my life. You're wrong on this one. I know how it looks, but you're still wrong. I wasn't hiding anything from you. Now pass the chicken."

Her explanation was sufficient, but Sherman still wanted to milk his yearly opportunity to be pissed off to the fullest. He followed her into the kitchen. "So, Tureaud Trust is a fund set up for you and Brandon? Where does all of the money come from?"

"See, if you had just asked me in that manner from the beginning, we could have skipped all of the drama! The Tureaud Trust is sponsored by Fortier International, and has been in place for more than 130 years. I know you can't tell from only looking at me, but I am an heir. Soon Brandon and I will split the responsibilities of running the entire conglomerate, and the pressure will fall on us to keep the company going."

"You think that's the reason your mom is against us getting married?"

"Now that I think about it, once we're married, you would also be entitled to everything I own. Fortier International is worth more than five billion dollars. I guess it's time for me to find out if that's why she's against us being together."

"I don't think it's that complicated," Sherman said as he handed Ronelle a dinner plate. "I feel it has everything to do with her daughter marrying a black man. Open and shut."

"Could be, but right now I am too hungry to think about Tureaud Trust, that ACH, or Mommy Dearest. Pass the chicken, please! I will deal with my mom in the morning. Let's eat."

"About the chicken . . ."

"You didn't!"

"You see . . . when the Adderall wears off, I—"

"There you go with the Adderall excuse again, *fuckkkk!*" Ronelle stormed to the kitchen counter.

"Baby, I can run to Popeye's right quick."

"I don't want Popeye's! I wanted chicken from Dooky Chase!"

"Well, I did leave you two wings! I was angry, and when I get angry, I eat a lot."

"Sherman, you ate six pieces of chicken by yourself?" Ronelle took the two chicken wings into the bedroom and slammed the door. "I am angry, and when I'm angry, I like to sleep alone. Enjoy the sofa!" she yelled through the door.

THE MASTER'S WIFE DIARY ENTRY SEVEN

April 20, 1855

Dear Diary,

I know it's been a few months since I have written you, but there was so much going on I could hardly see straight. The good news is that Beatrice is back at work for the first time since my husband informed me she lost her babies—twins, at that. I have tried to get pregnant for years and would desperately like to have a son, but I would never want to experience delivering twins into the world deceased.

What kind of cruelty is that?

Mother Nature at times is prone to barbaric tendencies, without compassion or thoughtfulness, I suppose. Nevertheless, I am overjoyed to have Beatrice back, and she seems to have appreciated the time off to heal and recover.

Oh, I almost forgot to mention something. Late last night, my husband pulled me over to his side of the bed. Unfortunately, I was not there for long. He had difficulty becoming erect—he had more of a problem with it than any other time I can recall. It has only been five times this year that he has pulled me to his side of the bed, and here we are in April. If you're wondering how if felt when he eventually got the little thing working properly, well, he never could get it working properly. It felt as if someone were trying to force a small spool of silk inside of me. I'm sure he considered it a generous gesture.

The worst part was, I could tell his mind was somewhere else—or, more likely—with someone else. I was nothing more than a warm body for him to fondle. As soon as he gave up and fell asleep, I started my nightly routine of pleasing myself for hours on end. Lord help me I know it's disgraceful, but what else am I to do? With one hand, I pleasured every deprived area of my body. With the other, I squeezed his buttocks, just to gain some sense of belonging. Such is life in this beautiful house with this ugly marriage. I have a grand second-floor bedroom, and a lovely bed in waiting—nothing more.

Queen of the Unquenchable Fire

CHAPTER 21

ouncilman-at-Large Melvin Campbell presided over a
city budget meeting that was on the verge of turning
into a fistfight. The director of the sanitation department and a councilman had exchanged verbal insults for the past
half an hour, and the exchange was rapidly drifting into personal
attacks and innuendos.

Councilman Kirk Thomas was furious because *The
Times-Picayune* newspaper had voted his district the filthiest
in New Orleans. In a standing-room-only town hall meeting,
Councilman Thomas and Director Mark Green squared off like
heavyweight boxers. To add intensity to their anger, citizens
from his district, who were still upset about a recent property tax
increase, were in attendance and actively demanding his head.

Normally, Melvin maintained more control over his meetings, but his mind was somewhere else. Tureaud Trust and Abigail were distracting him. As he instructed Councilman Thomas and the director to move on in their debate, he noticed that
Chantrell had just entered the room.

She took a seat in the back row, wearing a cream business
suit, slightly fitted pants, and a burgundy floral scarf tied around
her neck. Chantrell always sat in the back row. It was her way
of getting Melvin's attention when she had something important

to say; she held his attention the moment she entered the room. She also provided Melvin with the perfect window to call for a recess.

"Gentlemen! Gentlemen!" Melvin banged his gavel repeatedly, finally taking control of the exchange between the two political enemies. "I'm calling a fifteen-minute recess. We'll continue this discussion on the other side of the break. Ladies and gentlemen, we will reconvene at six-thirty sharp."

Bang! went the gavel.

Melvin exited the room to a cacophony of angry outbursts from the residents of Councilman Thomas's district. Through the crowd, he saw Chantrell heading to his office. His gut was telling him Chantrell had something big. When he reached his office, two other staff members were waiting to discuss the political implications of tonight's meeting. Besmer Collins, his campaign director, was licking his chops because of all the juicy attacks that had been aired out loud in open session. Besmer had been positioning Melvin to run against the mayor in the upcoming election. If what had happened tonight had played out during any other city hall meeting, Melvin and Besmer would have chest-bumped in his office—but not tonight.

"Besmer, Chantrell and I are going to need the room. Ten minutes."

"Not a problem, Mel. I'll grab us some sodas and hot dogs from the concession stand. See you in ten minutes." Besmer and the stenographer left the room. Melvin gestured for Chantrell to take a seat.

"What ya got for me, bay-bay? Your workday ended at three o'clock. Seeing you at a six o'clock city council meeting tells me you have a fish on the hook. A big fish!"

Chantrell reached into her satchel and retrieved a file labeled *Tureaud Trust*. "Here's your big fish. It's called Tureaud Trust!"

"You tracked it down?"

"More than tracked it down. I reeled it into the boat," Chantrell proclaimed.

Melvin leaned back in his chair and rested his feet on the edge of the table. "Do share, do share!"

"Tureaud Trust is a nonprofit subsidiary of Fortier International and Fortier Malaysia, Inc. It operates as an independent private entity, with a separate oversight board located in Amite, Louisiana."

"Run that by me again!"

"That's right, a nonprofit subsidiary of Fortier International. The trust was established in 1873 by Mrs. Anne Boleyn Pishon Fortier, wife of the founder. The Tureaud Trust serves as the philanthropy arm of Fortier International and makes no private investments."

Melvin popped to his feet and leaned across the table to get a closer look at the Fortier file. Chantrell started to read the current board of directors list. As she arrived at the chairman of the board, Melvin finished her sentence.

"Steven Martin Fortier."

"Yes, you're correct, Melvin. Steven Martin Fortier is the chair of that board. I continued to track down every possible lead I could find on Tureaud Trust, and all of it leads back to your friend, Steven Fortier."

It was not the news he was looking for. Steven and Melvin had a friendship that went back more than forty years. Steven donated to just about every cause Melvin supported, including purchasing uniforms for Melvin's little league football team. Every week, they traveled to LSU football games in Steven's luxury RV to watch Melvin's sons play. Steven was one of his closest friends.

Chantrell handed Melvin the folder and walked around the desk to hug him. "Melvin, I wish I had better news. Sorry."

Melvin was shaken. "Thank you, Chantrell. No, that wasn't the news I was looking for, but the facts are the facts. I'll see you in the morning. Nice work, as always. You're my five-star general."

As Chantrell headed out, Besmer came in with drinks and hot dogs. Melvin's appetite left with Chantrell. He could only think of Tureaud Trust belonging to his friend, and his friend's connection to Abigail. Melvin wanted to make Abigail suffer for how she'd treated his mother. She'd robbed his mom and his entire family of their property rights. He intended to make her pay, but not at the expense of Steven.

Besmer was chomping on his hot dog and talking steadily, but Melvin wasn't listening. He nodded and agreed on autopilot. His mind was wrapped around the folder Chantrell had left with him.

The fifteen-minute recess was over, and Besmer had devoured both hot dogs. It was time to get back to the council meeting.

⚜

On his way home from the city council meeting, Melvin remained in a state of shock and disbelief that his buddy Steven Fortier owned Tureaud Trust. That house was a luxury estate that had been passed down for two generations. It had skipped over his mother, and therein lay the problem. While Abigail and her family had lived a luxurious life, his parents had been forced to work two jobs each to keep food on the table and send them to the best schools they could afford. Melvin was committed to making Abigail fork over every dime she had taken from his mom. Nothing was going to change that. He just had to figure out how to work around taking legal action against his friend. In the middle of his thoughts, Sherman called.

"Hi, Dad. Are you on your way home?"

"Yes, I am, but I have some bad news regarding your research."

"Bad news? Like what?" Sherman asked.

"Bad news like Chantrell discovered Tureaud Trust is owned by my friend and your future father-in-law, Steven Fortier."

"Dad, I learned . . ."

Melvin interrupted, lost in thought. "I still need to find the connection between Abigail and Steven Fortier and only then will we will learn how . . ."

"Dad, please!" Sherman yelled.

"What is it, son?"

"Last night I discovered a monthly statement in a batch of mail for Ronelle. The envelope was from Tureaud Trust. When I asked her about it, she shared that her grandfather established the fund for her when she was a baby and that Brandon also receives an inheritance."

"Are you serious? Ronelle receives payments from that Tureaud Trust?"

"Her cut is seventeen million dollars," Sherman said.

"This plot is getting thicker than your grandma's gumbo," Melvin replied.

"Dad, I need to ask you something directly."

"What's that?"

"Will you reconsider this idea of filing a civil suit against Abigail if you discover it would involve also having to file a lawsuit against Ronelle's father?"

Melvin was already wrestling with the same dilemma. It was becoming clear that if he was going to get to the bottom of what happened 150 years ago, he might have to go head to head with his buddy, Steven Martin Fortier.

"Son, I can't give you an answer to that because a wrong has been committed against our family. The one thing I will say . . . wait, hold up one second, Sherman. Your mom is calling on the other end. She's called me three times in a row now. Hold on."

After three minutes of being on hold, Sherman was just about to hang up when his dad clicked back over.

"Sherman, get to your grandma's house, now!" Melvin hung up the phone.

Sherman was just minutes away from his grandmother's house. Once he arrived on her street, he could see first responders parked directly in front of her home. A New Orleans Police car was posted behind the EMS vehicle, and its patrol lights were on. Sherman was forced to park at the end of the block. His heart raced. He recognized some of the faces that had gathered in the middle of the street.

His grandmother had lived in her house for over sixty years, and everybody knew her because she was also the Frozen Cup Lady. In New Orleans, just about every neighborhood had one little old lady who sold all sorts of sweets like sweet potato pies, Now & Later candy, pickles, potato chips, and a New Orleans favorite, frozen cups. A frozen cup was a cup of sweetened Kool-Aid placed in the freezer and frozen solid.

Sherman watched as the coroner rolled a body out of Grandma's house on a gurney, covered by a sheet. From a block away, he ran as fast as he could to the house. He could see his father walking alongside the gurney, talking to someone through the sheet.

"Just let me see her before you take her. Just let me see her one more time. That's all I ask," Melvin cried. The first responders continued to roll the body to the truck.

Grandma was dead.

Clarence tried with all his might to hold Melvin back so the ambulance workers could load her body for transport to the morgue, but he couldn't. Ms. Vera attempted to give everyone a sense of calm with a song.

"I'll fly away, oh Glory, I'll fly away," she sang.

By this time, the word was spreading. Other family members started to arrive. The scene turned into massive public grief. One by one they arrived, and one by one they fell to the ground and into the arms of others, crying uncontrollably.

"I'll fly away, oh Glory, I'll fly away!" Ms. Vera bellowed.

Sherman was equally destroyed but fought through the crowd to get to his dad, who had lost all composure. Sherman had never seen his father cry like this. It was as if he'd reverted to a three-year-old state.

"Momma, I hope I made you proud. Momma? I hope you're proud of me, Momma! I only wanted to make you proud of me, Momma! Lord God, why? Why take my momma? Lord, why take her from me?" Melvin cried. "You could have left her a little while longer, Lord! Why did you have to take her before I could say goodbye? Momma . . ."

The coroner loaded his mother into the back of the van; Melvin collapsed. Clarence and Sherman lifted him and walked Melvin to the porch. They say a man is born twice in his lifetime: the first time is at birth and the second time is when his mother dies. The entire family soon received the news that their matriarch was gone at the age of ninety-five. The air filled with loud screams of grief and sweet comfort in song. Ms. Vera serenaded her best friend and neighbor:

Some bright morning when this life is over
I'll fly away
To that home on God's celestial shore
I'll fly away
I'll fly away, oh glory,
I'll fly away in the morning
When I die, Hallelujah by and by
I'll fly away.

The next day
The funeral arrangement gathering

Cars were parked for two blocks in both directions as family and friends migrated to Grandma's house, even though she was no longer there. She had enjoyed a personal relationship with all her grandkids, though she had many. Uniquely, she had touched them all.

Sherman finally found a parking space in the middle of the next block and grabbed the cases of soft drinks he'd purchased—he knew there would be at least one hundred people at the house. As he walked past the neighbors toward Grandma's house, Mrs. Sharon came out and stacked a pan of baked macaroni on top of the soft drinks.

"Here you go, baby, take this on down there with you and let them know we will send more food for the repast. Your grandmother was one of my oldest friends. Sue, Vera, and I were *Young & the Restless* buddies. There was no other like Sue, and there never will be."

Sherman thanked Mrs. Sharon and prayed he would make it to the door without dropping the macaroni. About halfway to the house, Uncle Clarence spotted him struggling with the cases of drinks and the food on top and ran to help.

"Boy, I done ran all the way down here to help you, and you

don't have one case of beer? Don't you love your uncle even a little bit?"

"There are two cases of beer in my car, but I had to park a block past Mrs. Sharon's house. There was no place to park any closer."

"Give me your keys. I'll get you closer."

Handing him the keys, Sherman said, "Please don't get a DUI while trying to park my car."

Sherman knew far in advance that he better not show up at Grandma's house with soft drinks but no beer for Clarence. His uncle guilt-tripped the entire family into enablers, and all of them, whether they were aware of it or not, contributed to keeping him drunk.

The moment Sherman stepped through the door, all he could see were family and friends. Some had a place to sit, and some made a place to sit, but none of them sat on Grandma's plastic-wrapped sofa. Someone had placed a framed picture of her in the middle of the sofa, and it instantly became a shrine. Not long after he entered, someone took notice of Sherman standing in the door with the drinks and food, and a loud cheer erupted.

"Hey, Melvin's boy is here!" they cried.

"You mean the professor?" Aunt Camille yelled.

Then his cousin Jynika, who was usually present whenever he would come over to see his grandmother, yelled out to him, "Boy, you ain't graduated yet?"

Everyone got a kick out of it because Jynika performed the perfect impression of their grandma. Sherman laughed along with them, but deep down he ached. It finally hit him that he would never hear his grandma ask that same question again.

Boy, you ain't graduated yet?

Several family members came to relieve him of the drinks and food. Moments later, he was calmed to see Uncle Clarence come through the door with the two cases of beer. The arrangement gathering was in full swing. In the rear of the house, Melvin was meeting with the funeral home director, organizing the order of service.

Sherman only wanted to speak to his mom and dad, then quickly leave. Funeral homes and funeral planning just weren't his thing. As soon as he tried to sneak away, however, his dad called him to the table. His mom was also at the table—taking notes, selecting flower arrangements, basically taking charge because his dad could barely speak. His grief had engulfed him.

"Sherman, we're mapping out the order of service. Would you like to say a few words over your grandma?"

Sherman knew he would be asked to speak, which was the other reason he had tried to sneak out so quickly. "I don't think I can do it."

The funeral home director got to the part of the obituary where it was time to name the people that had preceded Grandma in death. This was the moment Melvin made eye contact with Sherman.

"Well, I know Momma had another sister, Aunt Sheryl, but she died in the forties. I never had the chance to meet her. I don't think she had any kids. Now my grandmother, Momma's momma, was named Annette. I'll have to look up her full name," Melvin said.

Clarence made his way to the kitchen. He wanted to make sure he was on the program. Melvin didn't have any patience for Clarence today, and the expression on his face said it loudly and clearly. Sherman's mom, sensing an argument was about to break out, did a wonderful job of redirecting Uncle Clarence with one question—something she had a knack for.

"Clarence, you're just the person to help me with this part. What was the name of that gospel song your momma loved to sing in church?"

"Oh, you talking about, *I Won't Complain!* I can hear her singing it right now. "*I have some good days; I've had some hills to climb . . .*"

"That's it, Clarence, that's the song. I'm trying to get someone to sing it for us at the funeral. What about you? Can I put you on the program to sing it?"

"Hell, yeah, I'll sing it. Put me down for it."

Yvonne added Clarence's name to the program, then crooked her perfectly-manicured index finger toward Clarence, beckoning him to come closer. "Now, Kool, you know you can't come in those people's church all tipsy, right? So, promise me you will hold off on drinking until after the service, and I promise I will have the biggest bottle of Crown Royal you've ever seen waiting for you. Deal?"

"Doctor-in-Law, that's a deal!"

Clarence always called Yvonne "Doctor-in-Law," and she very rarely called him Clarence; it was always "Kool."

The funeral home director asked for the burial policies to complete the arrangements. To Melvin's surprise, Grandma's policy only covered five thousand dollars of the cost.

"Wait a minute, wait a minute," Melvin said, slamming his palm on the table. All the papers Yvonne had so neatly arranged scattered everywhere. "My mother paid on this policy for as long as I can remember, at least thirty years. You telling me it's only good for five thousand dollars? That can't be right; she paid thirty-five dollars a month on that policy. Hell, I have a policy that I pay sixty-five dollars a month for 150,000 dollars of coverage!"

It wasn't just the issue of the money; Melvin began to realize that a life insurance company had taken advantage of his mother all those years, having her pay on a funeral policy that barely even covered the cost of a casket.

His mother had taken funerals very seriously. The oldest joke in the family was how she would go to funerals of random people just to see how they were "laid out." There were certain funeral details that had to live up to the Susan Campbell expectations of excellence. For this reason, she always kept a calendar from Rhodes Funeral Home on the refrigerator. She would always say:

If God calls me home today, then you make sure Rhodes Funeral Home comes to get me. That way I know I'm laid out right.

Sherman and his mother—and, surprisingly, even Uncle Clarence—tried to calm Melvin down. Melvin hopped up from his chair, sending it crashing against the washer and dryer. He screamed at the top of his lungs. "I bet that bitch Abigail don't have a five-thousand-dollar burial policy!" Like a gavel, he slammed his fist on the table. "Momma, I promise you I will get everything they stole from you."

Most of the house fell silent at this point. Suddenly, piercing the silence, Melvin began to cry hot, angry tears. His emotions were all over the place.

"What is the final total?" he asked the director.

"The total cost of the funeral comes to 11,550 dollars, minus the policy benefits, leaving the balance at 7,500 dollars. How did you wish to pay the balance, Mr. Campbell?"

"We will pay in cash," Melvin replied.

"We have all these people here. You want me to let them know what the cost is and collect some of this money?" Clarence suggested.

"Kool, I'm not holding a collection plate to bury my momma! Do I look like I need to go begging for donations to bury my momma?" Melvin yelled.

"I wasn't saying nothing like that! Shit, she's my momma too, *motherfucka!* I was just asking in case some of them in the living room wanted to give something toward the cost, that's all. You *hoggin* all the plans and shit like you was the only child." Clarence's chair flipped to the floor as he stood. "This is how bullshit pops off at funerals . . . leaving other people out like they ain't mean shit to momma! You ain't the only one hurtin . . . all of us hurtin! The-fuck wrong with you?"

Melvin's chair slammed into the sink cabinet as he moved toward Clarence.

The funeral director grabbed her binder and took cover behind Yvonne.

"Please, you guys. Please!" Yvonne yelled. "You know it would break your mother's heart to see you two at each other's throats. She raised you two better than this! Melvin have a seat! Clarence have a seat! Both of you . . . calm down!"

"Let me just leave because Melvin on some straight bullshit, bro, and I ain't 'bout to be fussing over Momma's grave." Clarence walked out of the room.

"Kool! Kool! Don't leave, man, I'm sorry," Melvin called after him. "It hurts so bad."

Clarence sighed, walked back into the room, and wrapped his arm around Melvin. "I know, all of us are hurting."

Once everyone regained composure, Yvonne finished the proof for the newspaper obituary, and the arrangements were finalized. Susan Campbell's funeral services were set for Saturday morning. Sherman's grandma was gone.

CHAPTER 22

April 12, 1858

Today was her birthday. Beatrice was thirty-eight years old, but didn't look a day past twenty-eight. He couldn't keep his hands off her. Long before there was a concept called Stockholm Syndrome, there was Beatrice, but she managed to keep her feelings on a short leash.

In the French Quarter, the relationship that existed between the master and the enslaved took on a different meaning from what was common on the traditional plantations in Hammond. On plantations, slaves lived in rotted shacks near the fields where they worked. In the French Quarter, slaves like Beatrice lived in rear slave quarters, or in cases like Marietta's, in the rear quarters of the master's home. In fact, when you travel through the French Quarter today, you're actually strolling through a living, breathing plantation—one which survived the trauma of time to tell a solemn tale.

With the proximity between master and slave also came closer bonds, and slaves in this particular neighborhood enjoyed more freedom than most. They wore better clothing, and one meal was commonly shared between slave and owner. Despite this, Beatrice fought the good fight against falling in love with her master—the scar tissue on her heart from the sale of her daughters never healed. But she cared for him. After all, she had lived with him for twenty-three years, and he had never raised his hand to her, not even one time. However, she never allowed herself to visit a town called love. Not for her master.

To his credit, her master was still the same kind-faced man who had rescued her from getting sold up the river to Natchez, or chained to the back of a wagon headed upstate to Virginia. *I would have died the moment the straps slapped the hides of those horses.* That's how she felt about that three-week trip north.

"But that was then and today is Easter Sunday!" Beatrice said to herself as she freed herself from her bedding. "I am going to the Methodist church with Queenie. And then later, I think I will visit Congo Square—I should think on those things."

Beatrice was up at the break of dawn. She skipped over to her window and welcomed the endless possibilities of the day. A cool breeze accepted her invitation. Then she loped to her vanity and with the grace of a harpist, brushed her hair with long, rhythmic strokes. She peered at the woman in the mirror with squinted blue eyes. They held a gaze that asked, *Have we met before?* This was the woman she'd evolved into during her captivity, and for the first time, she felt beautiful.

In a canary kind of way.

On Easter, several Methodist churches in New Orleans would permit slaves to attend in a designated area. This was the only time that slaves were allowed inside. Every Easter, Beatrice looked forward to church with Queenie, and every year, she made Queenie a stunning dress to show her gratitude.

Timothy and Lawrence stood out front, dressed in Brooks Brothers-inspired suits, shoes gleaming in the early morning sun. The mule and buggy were pulled around to the front of the house, tied and waiting.

Beatrice and Marietta were twins; so too were Timothy and Lawrence. Unlike Timothy, Lawrence had a carbon copy-like resemblance to an Anglo-Saxon man, which is why he traveled with his master as a personal assistant. Lawrence resembled his father—the master.

Lawrence was a trained concierge, a fancy boy, a biracial slave with very little African features. His hair was straight and light brown. Timothy's hair was wavy, his lips were fuller, and his nose was wider. Lawrence followed the master around everywhere, always two paces behind, attentive to his every need like the military adjutant for a general. Nevertheless, the brothers loved each other unconditionally, despite their slight difference in occupation. They cherished their time together in the late evenings.

Beatrice stepped out of her living quarters wearing a full-length yellow dress with matching yellow head wrap. On her hands, she wore white gloves. On her arm hung a yellow and white purse she had made just for the occasion. Above her head perched a yellow umbrella. Moments later, Queenie walked down the stairs that led to the courtyard wearing a full-length white dress with yellow trimming and yellow ruffles around the collar. Queenie held a yellow-and-white custom umbrella to match her silk purse. Beatrice had designed both gowns to complement each other, but arranged the colors so that Queenie's dress would attract more attention.

"Well, don't you look like a beautiful flower this morning," Queenie said to Beatrice.

"If I was only as pretty as you," Beatrice replied.

Queenie smiled at Beatrice. The four of them enjoyed Easter mass. Beatrice enjoyed the sermon; she also enjoyed having her sons seated next to her in the pews. She prayed for all her daughters and asked God to make it so that one day, they could all attend Easter service together.

After church, Queenie lounged, spending the rest of the day reading in her room. Her husband was on a ninety-day visit to India; he'd offered to let her come, but she'd declined.

Beatrice and her sons decided to walk the few blocks to Congo Square instead of taking the buggy. The outside temperature was an idyllic sixty-eight degrees. The atmosphere throughout their neighborhood was festive.

Beatrice wanted to invite Marietta to join them at the Congo Square worship service; she hoped Mr. Lafitte would grant her permission. Beatrice arrived at Marietta's house and knocked on the door. No one answered. Knowing Marietta was always in the rear of the house, she knocked again, but still, no one answered. Figuring Marietta had her own Easter Sunday plans—because most servants were typically given Easter Sunday off—Beatrice and her sons continued to Congo Square.

Right before Beatrice, Timothy, and Lawrence reached the corner, a voice called out.

"Beatrice, come back! Come back!"

They walked back to Mr. Lafitte's house, where Marietta invited them into the living room. "I will be right back," she said.

"I just wanted to ask you to join us in the park," Beatrice said to Marietta.

"Beatrice, just stay right there. I'll be right back," Marietta said.

After about ten minutes, Marietta returned to the living room with a teenage girl who trailed behind her a few paces. Beatrice and her sons were mesmerized.

"Oh, my Lawd! Sweet Jesus!" Beatrice screamed.

April 5, 1858
One week earlier
Home of Mr. Lafitte

"Marietta, you get your ass in here right now!" Mr. Lafitte ordered from the living room.

Marietta had just finished cleaning up from breakfast. She ran as fast as she could to the front of the house to see what he wanted. Standing at his side was a teenage girl. The girl held her stomach. Her face was red from raw emotion, soaked with fresh tears. Lafitte's hand was on her neck as if he had shoved her down St. Ann Street. Marietta wondered if Mr. Lafitte had to shove the girl because she refused to walk, or because she refused to leave a place she called home. The teenage mulatto girl had blonde hair that was combed to the back, full breasts like she had just given birth, and full, reddish-blue eyes. The girl was crying; no matter how much he yelled, the girl couldn't stop crying.

"I need you to take her in the back and make a place. Her name is Eva."

"Yes, suh," Marietta replied, changing her voice to one he found appropriate. "I willz do it right nah, sir, yes-suh I willz do as you ask!"

"You two may have to sleep in the same bed, unless I need her for the night. She needs a few more clothes. Fetch a few things for her to wear!" her master yelled.

"Yes, sir," Marietta replied.

"I am headed to the market to grab a few more supplies. When I come back, I expect you to have Eva settled in and taught a few chores. You understand me?"

"Yes, sir!" Marietta answered.

Lafitte left the house and slammed the door. The girl kneeled on the floor and cried, holding her lower abdomen the entire time. Marietta hurried to her and helped her stand. The girl continued to sob and never raised her head.

"You don't have to cry. Dry your eyes. I know he is mean as a hound dog, but I will help you with him," Marietta said. "Come on back with me and let's find a place for you."

Marietta sat the girl on her bed, then dug through a chest of old dresses. It wasn't long before Marietta found four dresses she felt would fit Eva.

"How do you like this one?" Marietta held the dress against her body. Eva never raised her head. "What about this dark purple one with ruffles in the collar? I always thought this one was very pretty."

Eva never raised her head. Marietta sat the dresses next to her while she took a seat on the other side.

"I would like to help you, but I can't if you don't talk to me. Did Lafitte buy you at the auction?" Marietta asked, but Eva didn't reply. "I see you don't feel like talking much, but if we don't work together when that devil comes back, he will beat you good. I don't want that to happen to you. I don't want him beating on you. Lord knows he damn near killed me many nights. You have to talk to me. That is the only way I can help you. Did he buy you today?"

Eva shook her head from left to right.

"Okay, so he didn't buy you. Did someone loan you out to him for pleasure?"

Eva shook her head from left to right.

"So, you are not a loan. So, who cared for you?"

Eva still didn't reply to Marietta.

"Eva, I know how it feels to be scared of them. I still am scared. Every day. If it weren't for my sister Beatrice, I would have lost my mind by now. We take care of each other. She lives down the street on St. Peter Street. If you let me help you, I can. But if you don't, then he will have no mercy on you. Do you hear me?"

Eva nodded her head up and down.

"So, who cared for you before he brought you here?" Marietta asked again.

"My nanny," Eva said.

"Does your nanny live around here, or did you come here on horse and buggy?"

"She lives here. Not too far from here, but he put me in the back of a buggy."

"Why did he take you from your nanny? Did he tell you?"

"No, he did not, but my nanny told me to prepare for the ball, so I got dressed for the ball. I did as she said. I walked how she taught me to walk. We even had a school where we learned to read, count, and write. She taught me how to bake and cook. She was the only mother I've ever known. She was kind to me. Taught me good manners and how to be a lady. She took me to the Get Ready House, and I met Miss Harriet Green. At the Get Ready House, Miss Green taught me more manners and how to carry myself at the ball and how to make a man happy. More satisfied than a mistress could make him. I did everything they asked me to do. I lived with Miss Green for two months getting ready for the ball. I was happy there. One night in our dorm by Miss Green's, her boy came crawling into the room, pulling on my leg to wake me. When I woke up, he was pulling me out the room with his hand over my mouth. Ended up in a little house out back where he . . . where . . ."

"You wasn't a virgin no more after that," Marietta said.

Eva sobbed off the bed, crumpled herself into a ball on the floor, and covered her face in shame. "He wouldn't get off me."

Marietta lifted Eva off the floor again and sat her back on the bed. She wrapped her arms around her, squeezing tightly.

"He forced himself on you. I know how it feels to have a man push himself in you. It happens two days a week to me in this house," Marietta said.

"I was a virgin. If I weren't a virgin, no one would pick me at the ball. When Miss Green's son finished forcing himself in me, when he got off me, I wasn't a virgin no more. He then dragged me out of that little room and left me in the courtyard. I knew then I wasn't going to the ball. I knew they were going to send me back. I told Miss Green what happened, and she started beating me, said I tempted her boy. Then she sent me back to my nanny. My nanny, she treated me so mean. My nanny never talked to me like that before."

"Eva, when did this happen?"

"Nine months ago, and then I got pregnant. Yesterday I had my baby."

"Was it a boy or a girl?" Marietta asked.

"It was a girl! A beautiful little girl. She died," Eva sobbed into the palms of her hands.

Marietta pulled Eva's dress up to the middle of her thigh and saw that she was still bleeding. Her body was only a day past childbirth. "Eva, you just had a baby?"

"Yes, ma'am."

"Eva, what is your nanny's name?"

"Clarice!"

CHAPTER 23

Easter Sunday Miracle

Every step Eva drew nearer to Beatrice, the weaker her legs became. Both Timothy and Lawrence helped her to stand. Eva slowly approached Beatrice with her eyes, her mouth, her brow, the same color hair, the same shoulders and neckline, the same hands . . .

"Beatrice I would like for you to meet Eva," Marietta said. "Eva, I would like you to meet your mother."

Beatrice's hands covered her mouth. "My Lawd! My Lawd!"

"My mother?" Eva questioned.

"Beatrice, this is one of the girls you saw that day outside of Harriett Green's house. Clarice has named her Eva, but . . ."

"I named you Delicia, after Momma Delia, the midwife who saved you during birth," Beatrice said to Eva.

"You are my mother? But I thought my mother died in childbirth. That's what my nanny told me."

"Eva, we will explain more to you later, but this is your real mother. Alive and well," Marietta said.

At first sight, Beatrice knew Eva was one of her babies Clarice had stolen in the middle of the night. Eva needed no introduction. Beatrice would not and could not let Delicia go.

"Lawd, thank you! Thank you, Lawd, for bringing one of my daughters back to me. I knew it would be on Easter. Thank you, Lawd!" Beatrice cried.

"Delicia, this is Timothy and Lawrence, your older brothers," Marietta introduced.

Beatrice released Delicia long enough that her sons could hug their sister; then she pulled her daughter back to her bosom. Beatrice held Delicia as tight as she could until Marietta pried them apart.

"Beatrice, follow me. Delicia, you talk to your brothers, we'll be right back," Marietta said as she pulled Beatrice into her bedroom.

"Beatrice, we can't let master know that we know who Eva is. If they find out, they could sell her—or one of us—and we will never see her again."

"But I can ask my master to let her live with us. Even you said he was kind."

"Beatrice, no! Lafitte is mad because he can't sell her as a virgin. Harriett Green's son, Ulrich, stole her virginity!"

Beatrice's fist clutched. "He did what?"

"Don't waste a thought on Ulrich. Lafitte brought her here to make babies. I am not with child because of the soup, and you're not with child because of the soup. By this time of year, one of us would have been with child. I have seven daughters— no sons—and Lafitte took all seven. The only reason he brought Eva here is to make babies. The moment she makes more, and I don't, my ass will hit that auction block. We can't let them know that we know. Do you hear me, Beatrice?"

"So, I can't see her?"

"Yes, you can see her, but her name is Eva."

"That's not her name," Beatrice said as the tears soaked her face.

"Remember our promise, I taught you how to read, and you taught me patience. Now I need you to have patience and trust me. Do you trust me?"

". . . Yes."

"Then you are not her mother, but you can see her as much as you like. Leave her with me, and I will protect Delicia from

Lafitte."

The sisters agreed that no one else would ever know Beatrice was Eva's birth mother, and Marietta would do her best to protect her from Mr. Lafitte. In the living room, Timothy and Lawrence also agreed to keep matters concerning Delicia very private, and to refer to her as Eva. The group hugs continued. Beatrice's joy continued. Marietta continued to watch the front door.

"Lafitte will come home soon. He has been out all night drinking. Beatrice, I will ask Lafitte if you can train her as an apprentice. That way she can earn money for him. He will like that idea, and you can spend all the time you like with your daughter."

Beatrice released Delicia and threw her arms around Marietta. "Thank you! You always take good care of me. I love you!"

"I love you too, and I will bring Delicia to you again, hopefully before the week is out."

Three weeks later

Marietta knew who he was and where to find him; Eva made sure of it. His name was Ulrich Green, and he was a free man of color. He was also Harriett Green's only son. Ulrich was born free in New Orleans; his back never felt the cutting leather of a whip, his hands were soft as silk with no callouses, and his bare feet never touched the grimy French Quarter streets, because his mother was very resourceful. She knew how to make merchandise of women, and she knew how to profit off the fantasies of white men. One of the perks that came with a mom who owned brothels was his freedom to sample all the goods.

The one thing Ulrich loved to do more than anything else was indulge in his mother's collection of sex slaves. It is safe to say that if it hadn't been for the family business of selling teenage girls to wealthy men, Ulrich would have never experienced a woman's touch. He felt entitled to the women who worked for his mother and harbored a perverted lust for the virginity of the debutantes. Without his mother granting him access to her girls, Ulrich would never have gotten up the nerve to say hello to a woman, let alone ask her for sex.

He was shy, barely five feet tall, with pus-filled acne no doctor could cure. Most men in their early twenties from his social class in the black community would have had their choice of potential mates, but not Ulrich—not even close.

His mother had desperately tried to marry him off several times, if for no other reason than to end the constant complaints she received from her workers about how he harassed them for sex. He battered them during the process. If only Ulrich were a little taller, a little slimmer, and perhaps a little less obnoxious, Harriett would have stood a chance of getting him out of her house, but as it was, she was stuck with Ulrich.

Harriett Green had four cream-colored daughters; all of them contributed in some way to her goal of presiding at the very top of the Social & Pleasure Society in New Orleans. She had paired off all her daughters with the wealthiest men who visited her balls; the youngest one she accepted payment for was twelve years old. Whereas Beatrice grieved over losing her daughters to the quadroon life, Harriett Green relished in it. In her girls, she saw opportunities to profit financially and politically.

Harriett had presented her third-oldest daughter to the mayor as a gift; he had graciously accepted. In return, Harriett became the only black woman who could request a meeting with him in his office. Once her daughters were married off, she continued to control them, strategically positioning them as heirs in the event their common-law husbands died. Then there was Ulrich, who she couldn't give away.

He was too much of a coward to fight, so Harriett still had to hire strong men to protect her brothels. He was impulsive, so Harriett still had to hire managers. Ulrich was also lazy, never waking up before noon, and never lifting a hand to clean his living quarters. The house slaves hated him, the brothel workers hated him, and though she would never admit it, deep down, Harriett hated him. The only thing Ulrich every truly excelled at was raping debutantes during the sixty-day period they lived with Harriett in the final prep for the quadroon balls. Many of the girls he raped kept the experience entirely to themselves, knowing they would never get selected if word leaked regarding their lost virginity. Eva, however, had no choice.

Ulrich had not only raped Eva, he had also impregnated her—something that enraged his mother. Harriett was a broker for several other slave owners, like Beatrice's master and Mr. Lafitte. Each time Ulrich raped a debutante, Harriett had to compensate the owner in full and return the girl. It was a total loss for Harriett; even the baby belonged to the original master. Upon discovering that Ulrich had raped Eva, Harriett Green became so infuriated that she evicted him out of her main house and forced him to sleep in one of the slave quarters. He was not allowed to enter any of her whore houses, and, if he wanted money, he had to find a job.

With no trade or skills other than living off his mother, day in and day out, he quarantined himself in the slave quarters of her home, eating leftovers from the kitchen, reading, and sleeping all day. Like a wolf howling at a full moon, his arousal always spiked at midnight; that was his preferred time to create new victims. To molest. Ulrich preferred the debutantes because they were virgins, as compared to the more experienced brothel workers who could hardly feel his fingertip-sized manhood.

It was 11:50 p.m., and the moon was full in the sky.

A few paces from his front door, Ulrich gazed at the third-floor dorm room. All the lights were off. On the third floor, his mother housed fourteen girls who were all scheduled to make their debut on the first of May. One of the girls in particular caught his eye. She was a redhead with matching freckles, tall as a grandfather clock, with a beautiful smile, slender body, and no facial evidence of her African mother. She was also deaf.

Ulrich had stalked the girl's every move from the day she arrived. Harriett Green owned the red-haired girl; she was the child of one of her brothel workers. The brothels were a steady source of little girls to train as quadroons. Harriett Green's brothels were also a great source of virgins for Ulrich to sample, and the tall, redheaded, deaf girl would be his next tasty treat.

Ulrich about-faced into his apartment, removed his boots,

and swept the dirty clothes that littered his floor to a side wall. He planned to wake the girl and quietly force her to come to his room. All the debutantes knew he was Harriett's son, and they all knew of his reputation for midnight perversion. They never challenged his authority; through coercion, he wore down their resistance and stole their cherished virginity. Once his apartment was half-decent—meaning enough space on the bed to have sex—he left and headed for his mother's house. As he walked, Ulrich suddenly spotted what appeared to be a female seated in one of the lawn chairs in the courtyard, eating an apple.

The courtyard area was pitch black, but he could see that the girl looked like a Caucasian woman, though she wore a hooded overcoat and never looked at him directly.

"What are you doing out here?" Ulrich asked the girl, who was busily taking large bites of the apple. "You girls are not allowed out here after dark. If my mother finds out you disobeyed her, she will send you away."

"Waiting on you," the girl said. "I wanted to meet you and know you. I've heard so many wonderful things about you."

"You heard wonderful things about me? Like what things?"

"Like how you please a woman like no other man. I wanted to see for myself, so I came here to wait for you."

"That's what you heard about me?"

"Yes, and that is what I have come to feel."

"Follow me. Right this way."

The girl followed Ulrich into his apartment. Once inside, she seductively drew Ulrich toward her, then pushed him back onto the bed.

"I like you already," he said. "Please remove your hood for me so I can see your face."

"My face is not important," she said. Pushing Ulrich flat on the bed, she climbed on top of him and opened the bottom portion of her overcoat to reveal her naked body. "Do you like?"

"Oh, yes. I like you. I like you."

She moved seductively on top of Ulrich, taking both of his hands and placing them on her hips as she rotated her waist.

"I need to remove my clothes," he said. "I would like to feel you."

"You would?"

"Yes, I would like to feel you now. Just allow me to pull down my . . ."

"So, you would like to push inside of me?" the hooded girl whispered in his ear as she leaned down and began kissing his neck.

"Yes, please don't tease me like this," Ulrich urged.

"Would you like to slide inside of me the same way you pushed inside that innocent girl?" she whispered.

"Innocent girl?" he asked as he tried to shove her away to see her face, but he lacked the strength. "What innocent girl?"

Not budging from his ear, she whispered, "Yes, that innocent little girl, my innocent niece, Eva." At that moment she lifted herself up, pulled the hood back from her face, and looked Ulrich in his terrified eyes.

"My name is Marietta, and you raped my niece, Eva, and got her pregnant. You treated her like a whore. She was a virgin. Tonight, I have come to collect payment."

From her garter belt, Marietta pulled a knife. With a swift swipe of her wrist, she slit Ulrich's throat. She slapped Ulrich in the face as he clasped his throat with both hands. He tried to stop the stream of blood that sprayed through his fingers, but he couldn't. With the handle of the knife, she punched down on his face and shattered his nose. She watched the expression of horror on his face as he bled out.

"Eva! Eva! Eva! Eva!" she whispered as Ulrich choked in blood.

Marietta left the gray three-story house on the corner of Burgundy and Barracks Street and returned home. After a quick bath to remove all traces of her romantic visit, Marietta crawled into bed with Eva just as Mr. Lafitte stumbled through the front door. She took Eva in her arms and whispered in her ear.

"Aunt Marietta took care of that problem for you. Sleep well, Eva."

CHAPTER 24

Uptown New Orleans
Commander's Palace Restaurant

Ronelle was attempting to put her differences with her mother aside for the sake of Sherman and his family, so she had asked her mom to meet her at Commander's Palace Restaurant. Ronelle arrived first, and the waiter escorted her to their normal table.

She was consumed with thoughts of Sherman and the loss of his grandmother. *I was looking forward to having Mrs. Campbell at my wedding. I think I will mail the invitation anyway. Even in spirit, she's invited.*

From her window seat, Ronelle watched her mom come to a rolling stop in front of the valet, then whisk into the dining area. The waiter greeted her mother, then guided her over to their table.

It wasn't like her mother to be late. She was never late for anything. On top of that, Brenda appeared disheveled, like she'd thrown something on and walked out the door. No makeup, no matching accessories, no rings—not even her wedding ring. Her hair was pulled back and held in place with a cheap ribbon. Ronelle even noticed that she was carrying the wrong purse for the outfit. That was the most definitive sign something was seriously wrong with her mother. Ronelle could tell Brenda was dying inside.

Brenda Fortier was a one-man woman who had lost her man. Her life no longer felt like a song worth singing. Her appearance was an analogy of how she felt inside: depressed!

"Mom, I've already ordered our drinks and crawfish bisque with sides of potato soup. The waiter will return with them shortly. Thank you for coming today," Ronelle began.

"You're welcome, sweetheart. How is Sherman holding up? I was so sorry to hear about his grandmother. I'm sure they were very close."

"He's as well as can be expected—spending a lot of time in the bathroom. He hates for me to see him crying, but I can still hear him . . . crying. I feel so helpless."

"I know, darling, I went through it with your dad when his parents died. The best you can do is to give him space when he needs it. Just as one day you will need someone to be there for you."

"Mom, don't go there!"

"Death is a part of life, sweetheart. You will have to accept that I will not always be here, and yes, one day the man in your life will have to comfort you in your time of grief. It's the circle of life."

"I know, but it's still too hard. Speaking of hard to deal with, have you and Dad worked things out yet?"

"No, he no longer takes my calls. I stopped calling more than a week ago. I know your father. It will not be long before I receive papers in the mail. Every day, I look for the carrier."

Brenda's downcast facial lines gave the impression she was about to cry, but her tear ducts were empty.

"I don't believe that will happen. Our family will remain intact. Mom, you can help all of us out, including Sherman, by sharing with me why you rejected him. I never knew you had a problem with African Americans."

Brenda banged her fist on the table. "I don't have an issue with black people!" Her neck and face were hot as a furnace. A glass once filled to the brim with ice water rolled toward the edge of the table. Ronelle secured the empty glass before it hit the floor. The waiter moved the items on the table and proceeded to clean the spill. Brenda apologized to the waiter, then her eyes left the room through the window.

Once the waiter was at a discreet distance, she looked back at her daughter and continued. "It rips at my soul to hear members of my family accuse me of something so despicable."

"But your actions and attitude lend that impression."

"Well, I wouldn't feel that way if you . . ."

Ronelle cut in. "Allowed you to live my life and yours? Is that it, Mommy?"

"Years from now, you will understand. You are a queen. It's too soon for you to settle for the first joker with a shiny diamond and miss out on a king." Brenda's voice was heavy with disappointment.

"Too soon? I'm twenty-five years old."

"And you haven't even lived. You haven't accomplished any of your post-college goals, and once you're married, the next thing to come will be a baby, and then it's over."

"Excuse me, Mother, but, over? You're speaking as if I will fall into a black hole after the wedding and you will never see me again—or my imaginary baby."

"This thing with you and Sherman will hit a wall, and he will grow tired of you after the fascination is over—"

"Mother!" Another hard bang on the table, and another glass of spilled water. "Fascination? As in the fascination that he has a white girl? So, he doesn't love me? And you say you're not racist?"

The waiter returned to clean another spill.

"Ronelle, you're making a huge mistake . . ."

"Well I invited you here today with the intention of hearing you out and getting past this, but it doesn't seem possible. It's his skin color that bothers you."

Outside of their window, directly across the street, was a white two-story French townhouse with four columns that supported a balcony, and four that held a beveled roof on the second floor. Brenda looked transfixed, as if the nineteenth-century home were a city lot with new construction, but Ronelle knew this was just her mother's way of escaping the tension at the table.

Brenda's gaze slowly returned to the table. "I refuse to allow the three of you to turn this into an issue of race. I have not rejected Sherman. I told him I could not give him my blessing to marry you."

"If you tell him he can't have your blessing, that's rejecting him."

"No, rejecting him would equate to not allowing him to step foot into my home! That's rejection!"

Ronelle leaned in. "Why didn't you, Mommy? Why pretend all this time all while quietly hating my boyfriend? I'd rather you had slammed the door in his face than fool us with fake hospitality."

"You listen here!" Brenda's teeth bit into her bottom lip. "I have never disrespected Sherman or treated him any differently than the rest of your friends."

"How about you listen to me? Sherman is more than just my friend; he's my future husband. He will be your son-in-law whether you like it or not."

"But not for long, because you're his practice wife. And before you remind me of the decisions I made in my youth, yes, I was married young—but damn me to hell for wanting a better life for you. If you make it five years, I'll be surprised."

"Mother, I believe if Jared had asked you the same question with the same engagement ring, you would have gladly given him your approval, because he's white."

Swiftly, Brenda threw her purse strap over her shoulder. "I didn't come here to listen to you insult me over and over again."

"And I invited you here because I wanted to work this out. I miss you. I miss our family. This is crazy." Ronelle freed her utensils from the thick white cloth and dabbed beneath her eyes.

"Ronelle, I don't approve of this marriage, but I have my reasons. Many of which I can't discuss. I will continue to support you as my daughter and be there for you, as I've always been there for you." Brenda turned to leave.

Ronelle reached across the table and took hold of her mother's arm. "Then this is about Fortier International?"

"What!" Brenda exclaimed. "How did you arrive at such an idea?"

"The other day Sherman and I had a little misunderstanding when one of my earnings statements from Tureaud Trust arrived in the mail. So now he feels my inheritance is the reason you're against this wedding."

"That's ridiculous!" Brenda growled. "Your inheritance is irrelevant to my position. But since you brought it up, have you considered having Sherman sign a prenuptial agreement?"

"No, and don't plan to. Did Dad have you sign one?"

"He did. Your grandfather demanded that I do so. Your father was their only child, and they were concerned that if he died before me, I would come into full ownership of the company and remarry. So, I signed it. However, once Brandon was born, your dad canceled the prenup. In all honesty, honey, I never even entertained the thought of Sherman getting half of your inheritance."

"Mom, how you feel about Sherman matters to me. It hurts that these are not the wedding moments we used to joke about when I was a teenager. I wanted to do this with you."

The tears started to fall faster than Ronelle could dry them. Her mom was first and foremost her best friend in the entire world. She missed her friend. Brenda and Ronelle shopped together and vacationed all around the world at the drop of a hat.

"Sweetheart, I am here for you, and I will do this with you. I just need you to respect that I have my reasons when it comes to you marrying Sherman. Can we leave it at that?"

Brenda looked toward the hostess station and saw her husband. "There's your father. Did you invite him to lunch with us?"

Ronelle smiled. "Yes, I did."

"Why?"

"Because it's time for you two to talk, face to face. Today is that day!"

"So, you made that decision for us?"

As the waiter escorted Steven to the table, he quickly noticed that his wife was seated with Ronelle. Ronelle positioned the seating in a way that placed her parents across from each other.

Her seat was now on the outside middle, the same area where waiters normally placed a child's booster seat. All three of them sat in silence for the first time in a month. Ronelle took a deep breath.

"I invited both of you here today because I'm trying to save your marriage. I don't want to get married only to have my parents file for a divorce. Dad, Mom has agreed to support me at the wedding, even though she disagrees with my decision to marry Sherman. I'm okay with that, and I'll soon be ready to set my date and start making plans. Dad, as you know, Sherman is dealing with the loss of his grandmother right now, so we have put some things off for a while. My question is, can you two at least agree to talk?"

Her dad was a master at avoiding direct questions, and Ronelle had given him the little opening he needed to escape.

"Melvin told me about his mother this morning. I remember when Melvin and I were doing those demonstrations at Woolworth back in the sixties. His mother worked in the Woolworth's cafeteria. When Mrs. Campbell peeked out and saw her son, her face was filled with pride and fear. Boy, you're talking about an intense moment, and she couldn't let her boss know her son was involved in the protest. So, she watched through the order takeout window of the kitchen as angry white customers spat on us and poured milk over the top of our heads."

Brenda and Ronelle had heard this story at least ten times each, but they suffered through it again.

"The next day, photos of us at that demonstration made the national news, and Woolworth's Department Store was so embarrassed by the incident that they integrated their cafeteria counters. So, you see, Brenda, when you rejected Sherman, you rejected me and everything I have stood for."

When the waiter returned to the table with their food, Ronelle excused herself to the restroom. She knew that if she could just get them together, they would at least talk and begin to work through their issues.

As Ronelle made her way to the restroom, she noticed a jazz band setting up for the afternoon brunch. Ronelle handed the band director a very generous tip and asked him to play "A Kiss to Build a Dream On" by Louis Armstrong. The director opened his hand to view the tip and cued the band. Every year on her parents' anniversary, they would end the evening with that timeless ballad and a kiss.

The lead singer made his way over to her parents' table. Steven and Brenda were caught completely off guard.

Suddenly, the singer reached for her mother's hand and asked if he could have this dance. After what seemed like an eternity of hesitation, and with encouragement from the patrons, Brenda accepted. After a minute or so of watching the singer dance with his wife, Steven asked to cut in. So, they danced. Mission accomplished.

While sitting in the parking lot of Commander's Palace, Ronelle sent them both a text: *I miss my Mommy & Daddy.*

Susan Campbell's House
In New Orleans, you are guaranteed at least three major parties in your honor: your first birthday party, the day after you die, and two hours after you're buried. A strange fact of death is it attracts people, whether you want them there or not. In New Orleans, people always appear. The good news is they never come empty-handed; the bad news is they always leave with plates of food.

Family giveth, and family taketh away.

Brandon drove well below the speed limit on his way to one such party. The gathering at Susan Campbell's house had swelled by the time he arrived. Out of the front door and windows of the house flowed the sounds of the family talking way above nostalgic tunes like Earth Wind & Fire's "Shining Star," mixed in with the soulful voice of Al Green's "Love & Happiness." Those who knew the words to every song serenaded the neighborhood. On every porch, people embraced and inquired about old friends.

"When was the last time you saw Pootie?" a man asked his old friend, who had parked in the middle of the street to acknowledge him.

"Just the other day at traffic court. He's working at Avondale Shipyard now," the other friend yelled back at him. Their conversation continued as the backdrop of a two-block family reunion among neighbors. They had all come together at the spur of a moment for the Frozen Cup Lady.

Sue Campbell had nicknamed Brandon her white grandson, a nickname he loved and cherished. Whereas Sherman danced like a hippie at Woodstock, Brandon had *soul*. He would camel walk for her like James Brown. Sue Campbell would then ask Sherman to camel walk, but he couldn't. Grandma would fall out of her chair laughing. Brandon loved making her laugh until she coughed with tears in her eyes.

As he approached the house from down the street, Brandon spotted Sherman's cousin, Jynika, standing outside talking to some friends from the neighborhood. He was not going to miss an opportunity to say hi to her.

"Here comes my husband!" Jynika Campbell joked as he drew closer and they hugged. Brandon had a huge crush on Jynika. Brandon only dated black women, and he would always end relationships when girlfriends tried to emulate what they thought his mom would like. He wanted someone who was comfortable being black, all the time. Jynika was just that—comfortable being Jynika—and Brandon was crazy about her. Jynika was also naturally New Orleans.

Brandon had asked Sherman to set him up with Jynika more than nineteen times, but Sherman never gave her the messages—on purpose. Jynika was tall like a runway model, with a complexion even lighter than Sherman's. Soft, shoulder-length hair, hazel eyes, and lips that begged for a kiss. She wore glasses, but the kind that expressed her sexy-nerd style. She was an honors graduate of Xavier University and had plans to open her own pharmacy. Super-smart and very down to earth at the same time. Brandon was in love.

"What's up, Nika? Where's my boy at?"

"Inside with Uncle Melvin and Aunt Yvonne. Go on inside and head to the kitchen. Just a heads up: it may take an hour to get back there!"

"Can I get another one of those hugs? Just in case you decide to leave before I come back?"

As she hugged him, he whispered in her ear, "Don't leave without letting me know."

"Okay," she smiled.

Brandon made his way through the house, hugging and shaking hands as he went to the back. What was normally a fifteen-second walk from the living room to the back of the shotgun house took Brandon almost fifteen minutes. There was no pathway, just shoulder-to-shoulder family members. He greeted and embraced all of Sherman's relatives. All of them knew him. Finally, he made it to the kitchen to hug Melvin and Yvonne. Keeping with a New Orleans custom, Brandon handed Melvin an envelope from his dad.

Melvin pushed it away. "Man, I can't take this."

"Uncle Melvin, if you don't take it, then my dad will think I stole it. He doesn't trust me. Aunt Yvonne, you are my witness that I gave it to him. My dad will press charges against me if he thinks I didn't deliver this envelope! I don't think Jynika will come visit me in jail and kiss the glass."

"Yes, Brandon, I'm your eyewitness, and you're right. Nika will not step one foot around that jail."

They all burst into laughter. Brandon had a way of making everybody laugh and be happy; it was his gift to the world. Melvin opened the envelope; it was a check for ten thousand dollars made out to him. He put his head down on the table and started crying again.

"Dude, do you have any more of those envelopes, because I want to cry too," Sherman said as his mom joined him in laughter.

"You know your daddy. That man will cry at the drop of a hat," Clarence said.

"Y'all are just beautiful people. I am at a loss for words," Melvin said. He hooked Brandon around the neck and hugged him again. "Tell your dad I'll see him later on."

"Okay, Uncle Melvin," Brandon said.

Melvin thanked the funeral home director who'd packed all his mother's things and was ready to leave. He now had more than he needed to bury his mother. However, he had been prepared to pay the entire bill out of his own pocket if needed.

Clarence pulled Sherman to the side and whispered in his ear, "I need to speak with you right now!"

"Okay, let's go on the front porch."

The sound of The Staple Singers' "I'll Take You There" blasted, and the voices of fifty-plus people made it impossible to hear. Sherman and Clarence decided to take their conversation to the backyard.

⚜

In Clarence's hand was a timeworn Bible, so old the glue that held the pages to the cover had lost all adhesiveness. Long before ancestry websites, African Americans recorded the births and deaths of their loved ones on the first five or so pages of their Bibles. This way, every time they grabbed their Bibles, they also grabbed the memories of those they lost over the years. Susan Campbell had recorded every birth and death in the family in her Bible. She had also made a few entries about people who died before her, like her mother. On the third page, she maintained a family tree that started off with her great-grandmother Beatrice, but no last name was mentioned.

Uncle Clarence's index finger marked the next entry on the tree—*Annette Fortier*! Sherman couldn't believe what he was seeing. His great-great-grandmother's maiden name was Fortier.

"Whoa! Get out of here!" Sherman said. "Was this the reason Grandma never wanted to talk about her grandmother? Was it because of my friendship with Brandon that she tried to conceal the fact that we are also members of the Fortier family? Is that the reason many people in my family are lighter in complexion as compared to the average African American? Could this be a sheer coincidence?" he thought out loud.

Just about every member of Sherman's family was extremely light-skinned, and some of them could even pass for white or Latino. He had African American cousins who had freckles and blue eyes. Some even had blond hair that appeared in every generation—a feature none of them could explain. Clarence didn't say a word; he only pointed at the name Fortier with his index finger. Then he discreetly pointed in Brandon's direction.

"We're related to them people!" Uncle Clarence said.

"Let's not put the cart before the horse, Uncle. Just because we share the same last name doesn't mean we're related. Fortier is a common name. Many people share the same last name but are not blood-related."

"Nephew, I'm telling you we are related to those people, and this proves it."

"Uncle Kool, let's do this. Let me hold onto this Bible until after the funeral, and then we'll research it more in detail. Our secret. Okay?"

"Okay, that's a deal, nephew. We'll wait until after the funeral, but I'm telling you, on my momma's grave, we're related to Steven Fortier. I know my momma, and she didn't like to kick up no bullshit, so she tried to take this secret with her to heaven."

Clarence handed Sherman the Bible, and they left the back-yard with an agreement not to say a thing to anyone about it until after the funeral. Sherman felt a little anxiety coming on because he knew Clarence could not hold his liquor. Clarence could spill it all in one drunken rant.

Once Sherman made it out to the front yard, he saw Brandon and Jynika out near the street, talking alone in what appeared to be the start of something intimate. Sherman wanted Jynika and Brandon to meet without any assistance on his part, and it seemed like his plan was working.

Jynika was Uncle Clarence's only daughter. His pride and joy. No man—not even a rich man—was good enough for his daughter. Not even Brandon.

"Nika, you know if Uncle Clarence catches you talking to a boy he will beat yo' ass," Sherman joked.

"Child, please! You and my daddy better go sit down some-where," Jynika said to Sherman. "I'm a grown-ass woman. My daddy wasn't this worried about my love life when I was sixteen years old. All in my business asking, '*Who that dude is?*'" Jynika chuckled.

They all laughed for a moment. Then, Brandon noticed Sherman holding the Bible. Brandon placed his right hand on the Bible, then turned to Jynika.

"I, Brandon, do take Jynika as my wife to have and to hold until death do us . . ."

"*Brandon!* Stop it!" Jynika yelled, laughing and blushing at the same time.

"What? Did I say something funny? I'm serious! We have a preacher standing here with a Bible. I think this is a good time to get it done. I'm not getting any younger. Fuck the formalities! Let's do it right here. She's single, I'm single!"

"Dude, I'm no preacher." Sherman corrected.

Jynika was in love. Her red cheeks and full smile made it plain as day. For the first time, a real man wanted her so much he didn't mind doing something silly to prove it. For most of her life, she had unintentionally intimidated men. She felt their eyes on the back of her neck, but they never approached.

Every time she heard someone say, "I can't believe you're single," she felt like going to Popeye's and jumping in the chicken grease. For Jynika, light skin equated to *Dateless in New Orleans* on Saturday nights and attending weddings alone, hoping to meet the right one. It didn't take her long to realize not many black men attended weddings alone.

Light skin for her came with a ton of failed relationships with darker-skinned men who treated her like a conquest, like the next best thing to having a white woman, without the pissed-off glares from other black women.

Brandon had asked Jynika to his prom, but she had a boyfriend at the time, a guy who got her best friend pregnant shortly after prom night. She regretted declining the invitation. Nevertheless, Brandon chased her, and Jynika loved it. With every flirt, she wanted to jump into his arms and fly away. Like Sheriff Rosco P. Coltrane, Brandon was in high pursuit of Jynika, and she found it irresistible. Intoxicating. Addictive.

They both had a hoop dream.

She and Brandon were both tall.

They were both basketball junkies.

They both played in high school and college. They both blew out their knees, which ended their dreams of professional basketball careers.

"Bruh, let me see your Bible. It looks really old," Brandon said as he extended his hand.

Sherman quickly pulled the Bible away from Brandon out of fear that he would see the first page with Annette Fortier's name.

"Now you know if Grandma saw you with that Bible she would beat you down," Jynika said.

"That's why I'm taking it home before one of our relatives steals it. Grandma is not even in the ground yet and some of them in there talking about what furniture they would like to take." He held the Bible close. "This baby is going home with me, so I can have it restored."

Sherman started back-pedaling to his car. "Well, I will leave you two lovebirds to finish sucking face. B, thank you, brother."

"Sherm, you know we love you. We're family and don't you ever forget that!"

"I will call you later," Sherman said.

Once he made to his car, he set his grandmother's Bible on the passenger seat. "Brandon, I am getting the feeling we're more family than you realize, bro!"

CHAPTER 25

Going Home Celebration for Susan Campbell

E veryone was dressed and decked in their Sunday best. Those who didn't attend church on a regular basis purchased a quick suit for the special occasion: a funeral. Facial expressions were unanimous across the crowd—*I hope I can make it through this one.*

Planned for today was not only a funeral, but also a second line procession with a seven-member walking jazz band. Today, Sherman wrestled with the guilt of not wanting to be there. He did not want to attend, nor did he want to see her in a flower-draped coffin. *That's not my grandmother in there*, he tried to convince himself. But it was.

Sherman wanted to cherish the memory of his grandmother dotting around her kitchen, or sitting in her favorite chair watching *Jeopardy*—not in a coffin, not on a table in the front of the church engraved with *Do this in remembrance of me.* Like Lenny Kravitz, he wanted to get away and fly away, but he was grounded, outside of the funeral, where he accidentally became the unofficial greeter. The first to arrive of his grandmother's lifelong friends were Ms. Vera Branch and Mrs. Sharon Morgan.

"Good morning, Mrs. Morgan," Sherman said with a voice of honor and respect.

"Good morning, sweet boy. What a time in the Lord we will have this morning. It will be a celebration like no other. Sue was a very special lady, and closer to me than a sister."

Trailing Mrs. Morgan was Ms. Vera. "Hold on, Sharon, let's walk in together like we do every week."

Brandon also arrived around the same time. He took Ms. Vera's hand as he helped her up the steps.

"Good morning, Ms. Vera, and thank you for all the food you sent over last week," Sherman said.

"Boy, you don't need to thank me. Lord knows I miss her. I miss her more than I can tell you."

Once inside the church, Ms. Vera held Sharon's hand, and they walked in together to say their goodbyes to a member of their Church Mother Sisterhood.

"Lord, this happened too fast. It was just last week Sue was in the first pew with us, now she's gone to be with the Lord." Sharon Morgan clasped her hands on the Bible that sat on her lap.

"What a time we had last week!" Ms. Vera took her seat next to Sharon. "If I would have known. If only I would have known last Sunday was the last Sunday." Vera's voice filled with sorrow.

"But we're going to send her home right today. Amen?"

"Amen, Sharon, it's down to two of us! Let's send her home with a shout."

One after another, group after group, more people started to congregate directly in front of the door. Sherman was the greeter, whether he wanted the gig or not.

"Is that Melvin's boy? Yes, that is his boy! *Lil' Whippersnapper!* Haha! I haven't seen you since you were knee-high to a doorknob," one of his grandfather's fishing buddies called out.

Sherman cordially greeted the gentleman, but couldn't recall his name. Most of the people called him Melvin's boy, nothing more. The bottleneck grew in front of the church as people waited for a copy of the obituary. He decided this was as good a time as any to get away from the door, but it was too late.

"Good morning, *Mr. and Mrs. Fortier*. Thank you so much for being here."

"Good morning, future *son-in-law*," Brenda Fortier said. Brenda leaned forward to hug and embrace. Her greeting was the highlight of Sherman's morning.

Steven Fortier shook his hand. "Hey Sherman, we're so sorry for your loss. Is my buddy Mel in there?"

"Yes, sir."

"When you get a chance, please let him know we're here."

"I sure will, Mr. Fortier, and thank you so much for coming."

Directly behind them was Ronelle, who had ridden with her parents. "So, how are you holding up Mr. Campbell?" She wrapped her arms around his waist. "You want to be anywhere but here," she said, looking up into his eyes.

"Is it that obvious?"

"It's written all over your face."

"I'm just ready to get it over. Today will be one of those funerals where church ushers will carry my family members outside screaming, starting with Jynika. That's how it was for Grandpa's funeral, and I expect far worse today. Welcome to the black funeral experience."

"The *black funeral experience*? Please explain."

"I don't have to; you'll see it today in full color."

"How different could it be, it's a funeral . . . right?"

"Just buckle up, okay." Sherman shot Ronelle a look of cautious humor. "Everything will roll along smoothly during the reading of the obituary, and expressions from family and friends."

He opened the program and pointed: *Solo by: Clarence Campbell*. "Right before the pastor delivers the eulogy, Kool is going to sing."

A glow appeared in Ronelle's eyes. "Uncle Clarence can sing?"

"Yes, he can . . . and that's the problem."

Ronelle shot him a confused look ". . . and why is that a bad thing?"

"Long before the heavy drinking, my uncle was a member of a community choir called the Gospel Soul Children. The director was Albert Hadley. The choir was comprised of the most talented singers from churches all across New Orleans, and at one point Uncle Kool was the featured singer."

"Are you serious." Ronelle was astonished.

"Before his brief career in the NBA, all of his youth was spent in that choir." It was then that Sherman guided Ronelle's eyes down the sidewalk, where a choir dressed in crimson and white robes was exiting three church vans.

"The Gospel Soul Children came to perform for my grandmother because she was their first organist. Don't let the Miller Lite fool you when my uncle is sober; he's all five Temptations rolled into one."

More family members waved and slowly made their way into the church. Sherman greeted them all. Some wanted a hug.

"Wow, I'm honored to be here and experience this part of your life." Her head rested on his chest.

"I just want to go home."

"We'll get through this day, babe, and before you know it, this will be a memory, a treasured memory of Grandma Sue. That's what funerals are for . . . the living. When we mourn as a family."

"And you're right, let's get it over."

When Sherman and Ronelle finally made their way into the church, just about all the available seats were taken. Many of Melvin's political friends from City Hall where in attendance, as well as political enemies, who came as a show of respect and diplomacy. It was Clarence who made space on the first pew for Sherman and Ronelle.

"Psst . . . Puddin', you sit next to me. You too, Ronelle, you're family too."

Word of Expressions

One by one, the members of the Campbell family, friends, and Melvin's colleagues from City Hall (including the Mayor of

New Orleans) all shared words of encouragement and memories of Sherman's grandmother. Some shared scriptures, a few of the speakers even managed to generate smiles and laughter from the grieving family.

Last in the line of those who wanted to share comforting words during the period of Expressions was Steven Fortier. Ronelle watched as her dad made his way to the pulpit of the church, shaking hands with old friends from City Hall along the way. At the podium, he leaned into the mic a bit and cleared his throat, then he greeted the church with a warm smile. The church smiled back.

"Many of you may not know me, but Sue Campbell had a third son. Melvin and I are twins, and for those of you struggling to tell us apart, if you look real close you'll see a noticeable difference." Steven pulled out a comb and slowly groomed his hair to the back. "Momma give me a head full of hair, but Melvin . . . pooooor Melvin." Steven shook his head in pity as the church bent over in laughter.

"He's bald as an egg!" Clarence yelled from the pew.

"Yes, Clarence, I've seen beach balls with more hair, poor fella." A lighthearted moment the congregation appreciated.

"For those of you I've haven't had the pleasure of meeting, my name is Steven Fortier. It was on a basketball court at Tulane where Melvin and I became brothers many years ago—we've remained close all throughout life. If Melvin were up here, and thank God he's not, he would share the stories of how we protested everything under the sun. His mom worried about us. She once told me:

That Klan ain't going to treat you no different when they catch up to you protesting with colored folk. They will treat you like one of us.

I will never forget that day; I said Momma Sue, *I am one of you.* Then she hugged me and said, *Yes, you are.*"

It was then that Steven's voice started to crack. "Melvin and Clarence, your mother was loved—she touched many lives—and I'm so happy she touched my life. Rest in Heaven, Mrs. Susan Campbell." Steven exited the pulpit to the sound of roaring applause as he walked into the arms of Ronelle and Brenda.

A Song Selection

The first difference Ronelle noticed was the serious facial expressions of the choir members, and how they stood as one with a lift of the director's hands. Then the musicians keyed up a song that was upbeat from the first thump of the bass drum. The choir clapped on that upbeat, and before she knew it, Ronelle was swept away by the rhythm.

It was then that Clarence left the first pew and joined the baritone section. Though he was the only one without a robe, it didn't matter. After about eight measures, Ronelle watched the choir director slap his hands together as if he were trying to swat a giant fly, and that's when she felt the power in their voices.

> *Can't stop . . . praising his name*
> *I just can't stop . . . praising his name*
> *Can't stop . . . praising his nammmmme!*
> *Je . . . sus!*
> *Je . . . sus!*
> *Can't stop . . . praising his name*
> *I just can't stop . . . praising his name*
> *Can't stop . . . praising his nammmmme!*

It was power and passion, hope and heaven all in one song. At the peak of the song, Ronelle noticed that the entire soprano section of the choir froze stiff like mannequins, while the baritones and the altos continued with the music. Then the altos froze in motion, leaving just the baritones for one single measure. Suddenly, the entire choir froze stiff, including the choir director and the band. Ronelle heard the song continue in the pews of the church, with no music, only the clapping of hands and the stomping of feet. The congregation became the music.

On a silent count only they knew, the choir awakened from their block of ice and burst into a joyous praise Ronelle had never experienced.

Can't stop . . . praising his name
I just can't stop . . . praising his name
Can't stop . . . praising his nammmmme!
Je . . . sus!
Je . . . sus!
Je . . . sus!
Je . . . sus!

Then the song was over—but the organist would not allow the church to calm or catch their breaths before he zipped them into another high praise, high tempo gospel song.

Oh my God, this is amazing, Ronelle thought.

"Why were you so concerned? This is awesome!" Ronelle whispered in Sherman's ear.

"You will see in two minutes, just sit tight," he warned.

Without an announcement, the organ morphed from high praise to an extended hum that calmed the entire sanctuary. Clarence made his way to the microphone. Stoic. Heavy. Stricken with grief. The mood changed like a cold front, and Clarence was three days sober. Yvonne smiled at him and blew a kiss. The musicians played the instrumental to Grandma's favorite song.

Before he performed, Clarence took the opportunity to share a few words with the church.

"I want to thank all of you who came out this morning to say goodbye to my momma. It means a lot to me. She was good to me, a loving momma that never asked me to leave her house when life didn't go my way. She was my best friend."

I've had some good days
I've had some hills to climb
I've had some weary days
And some sleepless nights
But when I look around
And I think things over

All of my good days
Out-weigh my bad days
I won't complain.

Ronelle felt the pain of the song in the spaces between each rib in her chest, where every lyric jolted her soul, making it difficult to sit still, and impossible to look away. The sniffles were as loud as the organ.

Because God has been good to me
He's been so good to me
More than this world would ever be
So I say thank you, Lord! Thank you, Lord! Thank you!
People talked about me but thank you, Lord
People laughed at me, but I say thank you, Lord
I've been lied on, but thank you, Lord!
I won't complain.

Clarence's voice came from a place of pain Ronelle never knew existed. His grief wouldn't allow him to continue.

Clarence handed the microphone to the choir director, who started the song over from the top. "I Won't Complain" continued for another ten minutes, three of which were vocals only.

Sherman leaned left and whispered, "Welcome to a black funeral."

As Sherman had predicted, on cue, funeral staff escorted grief-stricken family members outside the church, one by one. From directly behind Ronelle came a scream that sounded like someone was having a tooth pulled with a pair of pliers, with no injections to numb the pain. To her left, she watched another woman scream out in grief to the point that she slid off the pew and wallowed on the floor until the ushers arrived.

The ushers and staff from the funeral home became overwhelmed with one grief-stricken mourner after the other. Out the corner of her eye, Ronelle could see Melvin unraveling along with the rest of the family. Melvin left his seat and started in the direction of the casket, but Clarence and Sherman corralled him back to the pew.

Once the choir finally stopped, everyone in attendance applauded Clarence's heartfelt tribute to his mother. Especially Ronelle.

"Uncle Clarence's voice was amazing—that reminded me of Broadway performer Norm Lewis," Ronelle whispered as she joined in the applause.

Following the tribute, the pastor was able to lift the spirits of the family by sharing memories and funny stories about Grandma and how she loved to dance in church.

"You see, your grandmother wasn't just a praise dancer in the church. We called her *The Praise*. No matter if she was in the last pew, by the time that organ clicked on, she would have moonwalked all the way up here to the front of the church, and then it was buck jump time!"

The church congregation laughed and hugged each other as the pastor shared one funny story after the other about Grandma Sue and her famous praise dancing. Then the mood changed again.

Final Viewing

"It's time for the final viewing before the closing of the casket; I need those in the back to file into the aisle and then around the sides. We will meet you all at the cemetery," the pastor instructed.

Pew by pew, friends and family mournfully strolled past the coffin. Some walked away on their own, others were carried away. And then there was the first pew of the church, which was reserved for the mourners—the pew where Sue Campbell had sat with her friends.

Ms. Vera and Mrs. Sharon locked hands as they led the final viewers. As expected, it was a very emotional goodbye. They had shared a lifetime of *secret* recipes for gumbo and other local favorites, home remedies for ailments, bingo strategies, and neighborhood gossip. They had also often boasted about their

grandkids. For about a minute, they stood there silently and examined their lifelong friend with damp eyes of approval.

"Well, Sue, they sure did lay you out nice," Ms. Vera said as
she leaned over the casket.

"They surely did," Mrs. Sharon chimed in. "Cherries Jubilee
lipstick, the color you loved. Ain't that a Revlon lipstick, Vera?"

"I think it is. It sure looks like it. You look real pretty, Sue.
They got your bangs fixed real pretty."

"Looks just like First Lady Michelle Obama, don't it, Vera?"

"It sure does. They got flowers all over you. It looks like
you're sleeping. They laid you out nice today. Real nice. We'll
see you again soon, Sue."

Vera and Sharon kissed their fingers and laid them softly on
Susan Campbell's cheek; a final goodbye.

It was time for the family to say their farewells. The grandchildren took it the hardest; all of them needed consoling. Especially Jynika.

"Grandma! Grandma!" Jynika screamed. Brandon and the
funeral director tried their best to guide her away from the coffin. "Just one more kiss. Let me go! I just want one more kiss."

Ronelle reached for Sherman's hand and squeezed. She
needed his strength after watching the pain in Jynika's face.
She'd always known Jynika to have the biggest smile, and she
always roasted Sherman with a brutal barrage of jokes—but not
today. Jynika's screams were carried out with her all the way to
the waiting limo.

Ronelle felt the magnitude of their loss. She lowered her
head and wept.

Just as it was Sherman's turn to say goodbye, a group he
didn't recognize walked up to the casket. Two white women, who
appeared to be in their mid-fifties, accompanied a senior woman,
escorting her by her fragile arms. Once in front of the casket, the
two younger women stood at either side and supported the elderly
woman, who appeared to be their mother.

"Liddy-Pop, I'm sorry, I am so sorry, and I never had a
chance to tell you. Liddy-Pop, please forgive me."

When the trio turned to head back down the center aisle,
Ronelle took a gasp of air and began to pound on Sherman's

leg, hard. She whispered without turning her head, "That's Ms. Abigail and her daughters, Sandra and Stephanie."

Melvin, Clarence, and Yvonne all heard Ronelle, and the three of them turned to look at Abigail again. Ronelle nodded her head in confirmation.

Clarence whispered back, "Only the older generation called Momma Liddy-Pop. That's Abigail, all right."

The three women disappeared just as quickly as they had arrived. The Campbells were dumbfounded.

It was now Melvin and Clarence's turn to say goodbye to their mother. Both kissed her on the head, then turned and hugged each other in front of her coffin. She had raised them to always care for each other in times of need, and today they needed each other.

"We will keep your grandkids together, and still have Red Bean Mondays in your honor. Thank you for giving us all you had to give, we love you, Momma."

Last but not least, Sherman walked up to his grandmother's coffin right before the ushers closed it.

"Mondays will never be the same. Grandma, I wanted to make you proud. After I graduate for the last time, I'm coming see you—and I'm bringing my degree—to prove I finally graduated. See you soon, Grandma."

The funeral director closed the coffin, rolled Susan Campbell out of the church, and paused behind a waiting hearse. The jazz band played the traditional New Orleans funeral song, "I'll Fly Away," as Susan Campbell was rolled into the hearse. Then, the procession made its way to the cemetery.

The repast and block party were over. The DJ crew loaded the last speaker into the rear of the van. All the guests waved goodbye with one hand and held foil-covered plates in the other. Sherman, Ronelle, and Clarence held a moment of reflection on the porch.

"I still can't believe that was Abigail," Sherman said.

"You can't believe it? Hell, I almost pissed my pants," Clarence confessed.

"Well, it was definitely her, and her daughters. They welcomed me in and gave me a grand tour. And I was so excited to get the pictures in the attic that I forgot we took a selfie together." Ronelle scrolled through the pictures in her cell phone. "Here it is, the one on the left is Sandra, and the one on the right is Stephanie. They were so welcoming—but Sandra was the one who provided the historical details of the home."

"So, Stephanie and Sandra are twins?" Sherman noticed.

"I believe so."

"Let me see that." Clarence leaned over Ronelle's phone to view the photo of Stephanie and Sandra. "They're twins, all right. But how you come to a funeral and speak to nobody? You couldn't miss us . . . on the first pew. Some people have no manners!" Clarence was still annoyed.

"Based on my last interview with Grandma, it's clear that the only reason Abigail came was to apologize," Sherman suggested.

"Well, my momma would have appreciated that when she was living; it would have meant something. Could've healed some old wounds, but it is what it is. She still should've spoke to us . . . that's all I'm saying."

Clarence finally got around to opening that thirty-two-ounce bottle of Crown Royal Yvonne had awarded him for remaining sober until after the funeral. He took his first gulp in three days.

"I'll tell you why Abigail was here today . . . guilt. She feels so guilty that it's eating her ass up. They know they did my momma like a dog, but we will get to the bottom of it all. But for now, I just wanted to bury my momma."

Sherman realized in that moment that Ronelle did not yet know that he had already connected her to Abigail, and now, Clarence was getting full of liquor. Once Clarence hit the point of complete drunkenness, he couldn't help but be brutally honest. Today was not the day for the uncut truth.

"Uncle, we're about to head home. I'm dead tired, but I'll pass back through tomorrow to check on you. Will you be okay in this house by yourself tonight?"

"I appreciate that Puddin'," Clarence took another sip. "I guess I am alone. Never been alone. She was always here. Yeah . . . I'll be just fine."

"Kool, are you sure? It's no problem for me to spend the night here," Sherman suggested.

"I'm sure, and I won't be alone. I have this beautiful bottle of Crown that will give me all the company I need. I'll see you later, nephew."

Sherman and Clarence hugged. Ronelle stood behind Sherman, waiting for her turn.

"Uncle Clarence, I want to be your manager. That voice you have is amazing."

"You like that, huh? Didn't know Uncle Kool could blow like that, huh? Haha!"

"You should be on Broadway with that voice."

"Like George Benson? *Bi-di-doot diddy dit-do-doooo . . . on Broadwayyyy.*"

"Yes! Like George Benson on Broadway. And I have a stage play coming up. We could use that powerful voice, so please consider it."

"Will you pay me a lil' something-something?"

"Yes, we'll pay you, and you can travel with us."

"Then I don't have to consider it, cousin. You have yourself a singer!"

Ronelle and Clarence sealed their deal with a hug, then she buckled into the passenger seat.

Back at their apartment, Sherman and Ronelle shared a romantic shower, then quickly tucked under the comforter for the night. Sherman was glad to have this day behind him and planned to start fresh on his research in the morning, after breakfast at Anita's Grill.

"Did you hear Uncle Clarence refer to me as a cousin?"

"Yes, I heard it, and it was probably just the Crown Royal."

"Hmm, that was strange."

"It was nothing, Ronelle. Goodnight, babe. Kiss, kiss!"

"Goodnight, my love."

THE MASTER'S WIFE DIARY ENTRY EIGHT

July 30, 1858
Breakfast Entry

Dear Diary,

Today is my birthday, and I received the greatest gift ever. Lust came to me in the most masculine form, risqué in all his ways. So powerful. Not in the flesh with arms full of roses, but in my dreams. My dream lover slid under my sheets, and then between my thighs. He loved me until I fainted. This morning when my eyes opened for the first time, he was gone. Only the evidence of how much I enjoyed him remained with me. To my bedding, I offer my heartfelt apology. I could not help it.

For so long, I wondered what it would be like to be in the clutches of a man who has pledged his heart to my heart. It was just last night I received a glimpse into my romantic destiny—a pleasurable peek.

On the side of my bed this morning was a small jewelry box; the same as last year, and from the same person. Kindness out of forced habit lacks sincerity, regardless of the value of the gift. I did not even bother to open it. I'm a stranger to my husband. What I desire is not so easily purchased, but must derive from a deeper place within his soul. A place of longing, a place only suitable for me, a place only I could satisfy. I held it last night—

just for a moment—above a cloud in my dreams.

Why can't I have him in the daylight like the lovers who stroll along the banks of the river? Why must I drift into a state of unconsciousness to find my true love?

In my dream, he was mine to have and to hold—but only in my dream. Oh, how I wish I could return to him and kiss him deeply, but God has awakened me against my will, and the realities of life would not permit such pleasures. Therefore, I dream with open eyes. I relish thoughts of his skin, the fine hairs on his forearms, the broadness of his shoulders, and his hands, as thick as leather. All of him is perfect to me; the color of his skin is but a vanity. All of him is perfect to me.

My breakfast is done, but thoughts of him consume me. I am desperate to see him again. Dear Diary, I plead for your wisdom! Give me clarity of thought, damn you! Should I indulge in a quick nap? Perhaps he would return to me. If not, then I hope to see him tonight. The best birthday gift ever has been the anticipation of pleasure, even if just for a night.

Though it may surprise you to hear it, Diary, I harbor not even an ounce of guilt.

The Happy Dreamer

CHAPTER 26

December 15, 1858

It was a perfect overcast morning to say goodbye. The sky revealed the kind of day that seemed unfair to a hopeless romantic; no sunlight to glimmer the water, no torrential downpours, just the dullness of empty-handed clouds. *What A pitiful sky to match my pitiful marriage*, she thought.

Queenie knew he was excited to leave this morning, and she was overjoyed to wave goodbye. Her face was a fraud, and her displayed emotions were a façade that convinced her husband that this business trip was too long. The truth was the duration didn't bother her at all. She needed the distance and privacy to explore every inch of the man she made love to in her dreams and fantasized about during the day.

The longer my husband is away, the longer I can savor him, she anticipated.

Step by step, her husband squeezed the space between her fingers as they approached a port that buzzed like a beehive, with riverboats as far as the eyes could see. The wood that curved around the ships reminded her of that dry, rotted table in her storage pantry. The table was tacked together by a few nails and a ton of hope, yet the boats floated effortlessly like hungry seagulls.

To her left, barely clad men with tea-colored skin carried huge sacks on their heads and lifted them up to workers on the ship. Queenie could tell the white men who waited on the sacks were only a nickel up from the slaves—some but a penny—and some were slaves to debt. Next to the nearby ship was a shiny new passenger riverboat that docked patiently for her husband and a few other couples. She watched as a wife held her husband by the collar of his top coat.

"I will not breathe until you return," the wife said, consumed by the anxiety of separation.

But not Queenie. Her husband couldn't board that boat fast enough.

She kissed him on the dock because he kissed her first, and it was wonderful. Not because she craved his thin lips or the flavor of his tongue, but because it was a farewell kiss. Better yet, it was a don't-hurry-back kiss.

Lawrence trailed her husband with a handcart of luggage, then they departed on his voyage aboard a new steamboat vessel called the *Natchez II*. His first destination was the Gulf of Mexico, where they would board another vessel to St. Dominique. Her husband's other destinations included a voyage to Porte de Versailles, and then onto India to establish new shipping ports. All in all, his travels would take him away from her for a total of ten months, bypassing New Year and ending in late autumn.

She waved in character every time he glanced her way. Then he blew her a long kiss. Queenie blew one back.

She yelled, "I love you!" but her words were muted by deck bells and the thrust of a violent paddlewheel, threatening horns, heartbroken damsels, and pelican flocks that scattered to the west bank of the river.

The *Natchez II* slowly backed away from the Port of New Orleans. Like a giant slug who had discovered the secrets of buoyancy, it snailed south to the Gulf.

In the center of the boat stood two giant red stacks that puffed black smog into the air like cigars for the gods. Every detail added to the gloom of the morning. Slowly, the riverboat crawled with the wind to its bow, while its stern tossed muddy water to and fro.

Queenie watched and waved until the river bent and the boat disappeared beyond the cypress trees that hugged the banks. Her husband was officially away for a long while. There was a time when his departure would have brought debilitating sadness, but not anymore. Queenie was far too familiar with being alone.

She was fifteen years younger than her husband—in age, in energy, and in zeal for life. Queenie possessed the kind of optimism for life that annoyed her husband at times, but it was to be expected, because she'd hardly lived any of her life the way she had envisioned. Her dream was to sing in the best opera house in France and then descend from the stage onto plush Iranian carpets. She had enjoyed the opportunity to formally train with French composer Hector Berlioz, only to have her father marry her off to her current husband. Her dreams were trampled before they could materialize.

In her father's house, he had controlled all matters concerning her future; then she had married into another form of control. If she'd had a say in the matter, 1005 St. Peter Street would have been the furthest place from her mind.

Queenie belonged in Paris—not a bootleg version like New Orleans, but embedded in the cultural dynasty of France. After all, she looked the part with her high cheekbones, caramel brown eyes, flowing black hair, and youthful face. She had the breasts of a woman with six kids, and a waist that appeared too small for childbirth. Her husband had not been her first choice—not even her fifth—but his face was kind, and he had those deep blue eyes.

During their courtship, people often assumed she was his daughter, and she prayed the day would never come when she didn't look the part.

After a score of deep sighs and a short walk, Queenie made it back to her driver: Beatrice's oldest child, Timothy. He assisted her to her seat by lifting her, and he didn't leave her side until she was safely seated. Timothy had Caucasian skin with matching freckles; even his ears and nose were freckled. Above his nose were eyes as blue as the sky with no clouds, blue as the shores of St. Dominique with no vessels, blue as a field of cornflower promenading in the wind.

His body was muscular from the strenuous days he was leased out to load bales of cotton on the shipyard. Some thought he was an Irishman who was down on his luck. The slaves knew he was one of them; some even called him Buck.

His shoulders, chest, and arms were well-defined and bulging. His mind and speech, not so much. Timothy spoke slightly better than the other slaves, with just enough elocution and clarity to hold stimulating conversations with Queenie on her long rides. Timothy collected old newspapers she left in his buggy or at the breakfast table, and late at night, he stuttered through the articles as Beatrice taught him to read.

When Timothy wasn't leased out to Mr. Lafitte, he drove Queenie everywhere she wanted to go. Although they spoke often, she never knew his real story. Her husband told her he had rescued Beatrice from slavery and that all of them were hired servants, minus room and board. Queenie thought that was a good deal, considering the cruelties of slavery. She prided herself in belonging to the abolitionist arm of the Methodist Church, and a crusader of her status would never condone slave traders. Timothy was a hired hand just like any hired hand, and she never inquired any further.

In less than ten minutes, they arrived back at 1005 St. Peter Street. Queenie sat perfectly still as Timothy tied the mule, then helped her step down off the buggy.

"Ma'am, will you need anything else before I return to the dock?" he asked.

She let out a helpless sigh. "Only to refill the lighting in my room and the bathroom. It is terribly dark up there with only a few candles. It feels even dimmer up there alone."

"Ma'am, will twelve do?"

"Yes, Timothy, twelve is more than enough."

"Yes, ma'am. I will have it done before dark."

Later that day, Timothy returned from the docks with Mr.

NINE NOTCHES / 259

Lafitte, tired, dusty, but not worn out. He headed straight for the pantry to gather the supplies needed to fix the lighting in the master bedroom and bath. Before climbing the flight of stairs that led to the second floor, Timothy decided to take a quick bath to wash the sweat and cotton debris off his body. All fresh and clean, he trotted up the courtyard to say hello to his mother, who lived directly above his room.

"Ma, dear, how are you today?"

His mother was finishing up the last of her alterations for the day on a full-body mannequin, a Christmas gift from Queenie. The mannequin was custom designed to Queenie's exact dress size, which resulted in perfectly altered gowns for her mistress in fit and design. Beatrice looked over her shoulder, saw her son, and smiled.

"There's my handsome boy! I hope they didn't work you too hard today. I heard that Mr. Lafitte is terrible to work for!" They hugged just inside the doorway.

"No, Momma, not too hard. He promoted me to watch the others. But I still hope one day to work in the factory and not the shipyard. Too many of us get snatched upriver working out there."

A look of worry covered his mother's face. "I never trusted those captains and deckhands. They have stolen us for years, it's what they do best. Well, be careful, you hear me?"

"Yes, Momma," Timothy replied. "One day I will earn enough from labor to buy you free."

"Don't worry about buyin' me free. I want you free long before me."

"Don't forget you have reading lessons tonight." Beatrice returned to her replica of Queenie.

"I won't, and I have today's newspaper." Timothy kissed his mother on the cheek. "Love you! If you need me, I will be across the courtyard. I've got work to do for Queenie."

Timothy left Beatrice's living quarters, walked across the outdoor balcony, and entered the main house. He knocked on the door that led to the master bedroom.

A voice called out, "Is that you, Timothy?"

"Yes, ma'am. I come to fix the lighting."

"I'm in the bathroom, so start by the bookshelf and on the side of my bed. I will just be a moment," Queenie replied.

"Yes, ma'am, right away."

Timothy immediately began the task of replacing candles throughout the bedroom and refilled the two oil lamps beside her bed. When it came to things broken or needing replacement around the house, Timothy had emerged as the resident serviceman. When he wasn't traveling with the master, his brother Lawrence polished everything in the mansion while Timothy fixed everything that was broken or needed replacing, including the lighting throughout the estate.

Today he was just in time; the sun was rapidly setting. Carefully, he attended to each candleholder and flambeau in the room until the entire bedroom was illuminated.

"Ma'am, I'm all done with the bedroom. Would you like me to come back later for the bathroom?" Timothy asked.

"Please close all the drapes."

"Yes, ma'am." Timothy closed the drapes on all four bedroom windows, causing the room to depend solely on the candlelight.

"All done now, Mrs. . . . ."

Queenie entered the room wearing only a thin, sheer nightgown with white rose petal embroidery: a gown Beatrice had stitched to ignite passion. However, her husband was halfway to St. Dominique; too far away to see it, too in love with Beatrice to care. When Queenie wore the same nightgown for her husband, he had fallen asleep before she'd stepped out of the tub. But Timothy noticed. In great fear, he turned to face the wall.

"So sorry! So, so sorry! Would you like me to come back another time?" Timothy's face pressed against the velvet-covered wall.

"No, I want you to stay," Queenie said as she walked over to where he stood. "It's okay; it's okay, Timothy," she said as she touched him on the shoulder. "Turn around, please."

Timothy slowly turned. The moment he faced her, she tiptoed to his lips and kissed him. He didn't kiss her back. Queenie smiled.

"No need to be afraid. You're not in trouble, and my husband will never know. But I have wanted to kiss you for a very long time. I wanted to kiss you this morning when you took my hand and helped me out of the carriage. I have dreamed of you. I've touched myself thinking of you," Queenie confessed as she tried to calm his fear.

"I heard stories of Negroes who lay with white women. Bad things. Bad, bad things. I must leave now," Timothy said as he tried to step around Queenie.

She blocked his path of escape. "Didn't my husband leave you here to take care of this house?"

"Yes, ma'am."

"Didn't my husband leave you here to fix things that are broken?"

"Yes, ma'am."

"Didn't my husband tell you to always tend to my needs?"

"Yes, ma'am, he did tell me that, but . . ."

"Well, I need this." Queenie grabbed between his legs. "Oh, my, you are much larger than my husband," she said in a voice filled with awe.

Queenie took Timothy by the hand as she backed across the room to the bed. She then sat down on the bed and pulled the string that held his trousers. He grabbed her hand in a last-ditch effort to stop her, but she slapped his hand out of the way. As Timothy's linen trousers fell to the floor, Queenie lay back with open legs. He followed her. He entered her.

Down the hall, back across the exterior balcony walkway on the other side, Beatrice was just dozing off to sleep after a hard day's work. Suddenly, she caught a chill. She sat up in her bed and started to hyperventilate. She started to panic. Beatrice covered herself in a large coat and ran down the stairs toward Timothy's quarters. She opened the door; he was not in his room.

Love you, I've got work to do for Queenie, replayed in her mind. She stepped out of Timothy's room into the courtyard and looked up toward her master's bedroom.

"Timothy, no! No, Timothy," Beatrice whispered.

Beatrice ran back up the stairs and down the balcony walkway that led to her master's room, only stopping once she reached the bedroom door. She silenced her breathing, placed her ear to the wall, and used one of her greatest survival skills—eavesdropping. Beatrice heard the sounds of two adults making illegal love, but neither sounded coerced or entrapped. She heard her son Timothy pleasing Queenie, taking huge bites out of a forbidden fruit. He knew it was forbidden, but the woman had made him do it, so he took a bite.

Timothy, no! I warned him over and over.

Don't touch white women.

Don't look at white women.

Don't think about white women.

How could you, Timothy?! Queenie, how could you? Beatrice thought to herself, but the question was rhetorical. She knew how, and she knew why. Her son was doing what he was told to do, and like her, no wasn't an option.

Beatrice walked back to her room, fearful for her son, shattered that he'd disobeyed her greatest warning.

If a white woman tries to lay with you, run as fast as you can, run for your life.

It continued every other night around the same time, with the same excuses.

I need to do something for Queenie.

Timothy no longer reported to work at the shipyard. Queenie saw to it that there were enough chores around the house to keep him within view at all times. When he wasn't around her, she was her usual self, busy managing her husband's shipping company in his absence. But when Timothy entered the room, she changed.

Like a seventh-grader with a crush on a senior, Queenie had long thought Timothy was the most irresistible man in the country. She got away with spending time with him because she knew her husband's schedule. She routed his business travel, therefore it took very little effort for her to increase his days away and create more time to spend alone with Timothy. Over time, she formulated a plan: a plan she had hatched one night five years prior after getting humped and dumped on her side of the bed, followed by her husband taking another walk to clear his mind.

Around ten o'clock that particular night, Queenie heard a disturbance in the courtyard area. She hurried to the window to see if it was her husband returning to finish making love, but no such luck. It was then that she spotted Timothy and some of his friends in the back corner of the yard, engaged in a cockfight. Timothy wasn't wearing a shirt. She pressed her body against the glass. Timothy never noticed her watching him in the window that night, but she did watch him, like a woman who'd just spent five years in prison. Every thirty seconds, she wiped the fog from the window so her eyes could continue to stalk him— the man from her dreams.

The following morning when Timothy greeted her at the breakfast table with her morning paper, Queenie had a brief moment of shame and guilt over the way she had lusted from the window. However, her guilt was quickly overruled by more lecherous thoughts, one after the other. Those naked thoughts of Timothy became the reason for her long buggy rides with no particular place to go. Each was another opportunity to be alone with him.

It is said that the opportunity of a lifetime must be seized during the lifetime of that opportunity. For five years, Queenie hid her real feelings for Timothy, until her husband informed her of his long prospecting expedition to India. The opportunity to make love to Timothy was presented to her when her husband waved at her from the deck of the *Natchez II* riverboat.

Queenie seized that opportunity like a lioness.

Timothy was more than just sex to her. She could have accomplished that anywhere. For Queenie, it was about taking back control of her life. For the first time, she made a life-altering decision free from her father's demands and free from her husband's expectations. Timothy was something just for her—as gratifying as a day of pampering with Marie Laveau. As empowering as managing payroll for their employees. Each encounter resulted in another encounter, sometimes on the side of the road in the back of the buggy, or ten steamy minutes in a hallway closet.

It was her ego that wanted more. Whereas sex with her husband was her duty, sex with Timothy was liberating. It happened when she wanted it; it happened how she wanted it. Adding to the deliciousness of it all was Timothy's total loyalty, confidentiality, and his expressions of love. The feelings were mutual.

⚜

Today marked the ninetieth day of the affair; it was the seventeenth day of February, Wednesday, to be exact. Around ten o'clock at night, they always connected. Beatrice blew out a reading candle and dragged her rocking chair over to the window that faced the balcony walkway. Besides Beatrice, no one knew about the affair.

Outside the window, frozen precipitation blew in the wind. It was unseasonably cold, but not cold enough for a snowstorm. Earlier that day, Timothy had covered all the temperate flowers to protect them from a winter that was unrelenting and cruel for those who had to labor outdoors. Timothy covered just about every section of the courtyard that was dear to Queenie. She oversaw the entire project from her bedroom window while Beatrice spied.

Her protective nature would not allow Beatrice to inform Timothy that she knew about his late nights with Queenie. Her fear was setting off a chain reaction of scandal, auction sales, and new masters. Every night, her son kept his salacious appointment with her master's wife. For that reason, her thoughts were exclusive to the ramifications of Queenie and Timothy getting caught in the act, her son getting dragged through the streets of New Orleans by a mule, and later being burned alive as an example for other Negroes.

Timothy was becoming predictable. The possibility of them raising suspicion was a fatal probability. Beatrice was deeply troubled. Suddenly, she spotted a shadowy figure rushing through the sleet toward the stairs that led up to Queenie's side of the balcony.

Once he entered the master bedroom, the room would dim.

Once the room dimmed, Beatrice would walk across the balcony and lock the door to the main house. This was a fool-proof way of ensuring no one entered the house from that door—not even the master should he arrive unannounced. Beatrice was the only one who had a key to that door. She wanted to buy her son time to hide should he ever need time to hide. The room dimmed, so it was time to lock the door behind him.

The next day Beatrice took her laundry to a section of the house where two maids scrubbed the clothes by hand. She glanced around the washroom for Queenie's dirty clothes, especially the bedding. Beatrice wondered if there was any evidence of the affair on the sheets. Surely the housemaids knew the master was away, so who would have the pleasure of his wife? Her paranoia was getting the best of her, but this was her firstborn twin, and Timothy had managed to get himself into the worst possible predicament for a black man in the South.

When she was about to leave the washroom area, Beatrice overheard one of the maids say, "Queenie must be wit' child. She ain't bleed in a while."

Lord, please protect my son. Please, Lord! Beatrice prayed.

THE MASTER'S WIFE DIARY ENTRY NINE

December 28, 1858
Breakfast Entry

Dear Diary,

A powerful current is pulling at my spirit day and night, even in my thoughts. I am at a loss. I suspect that I'm with child, but joy is absent, and only dread remains. I never anticipated the day when the latter would accompany my firstborn into the world. Joy is not present, not for this child. How sad! If it were not for the uncertainty, I suppose I would feel more elated, but dire consequences loom should my child enter the world with a resemblance to his father. I hold firm to the slight possibility that my husband is the father, but every morsel of my body points to Timothy.

In my lust, I was so foolish!

Just last night, I had a dream of being in the heat of my labor, wailing and suffering in pain. I gave birth to a baby that had skin dark as a stallion; it scared me so. I awoke in a fright, panting for air, drenched from the horror of it all. The dream was very strange to me. Timothy is just as white as I am, except for that wooly hair. So why was the baby so black in my dream? Such horror!

Though I love Timothy, this marriage is where I ought to be, and regrettably, where I should be. But the selfish side of my being refuses to remain silent because I must have both—my husband and my prince. Timothy is beautiful to me in every way, like a ripe apple hanging from the highest branch. Fulfilling and sweet. I can't have him as a husband, but I want to taste him more and more every day. Maybe on some distant island, we could live as husband and wife and raise this child? There I go fantasizing again! How silly am I?

If this baby resembles Timothy, then my husband will question whether a black man raped me during his travels. How I answer that question will decide if Timothy lives or dies, but living through such a confession is very unlikely. I also have the option of shipping the baby away. Most women in my predicament simply sell the child they conceived with a black man into the same system of slavery. I would not dare sell my baby into servitude; the thought alone is quite savage and disgusting. It is still my child, after all.

Maybe I'm just overreacting, panicking about what could be instead of focusing on what is. My husband could very well be the father of this baby. At the same time, I pray my child has Timothy's eyes—those deep blue eyes that pull me into a sea of pleasure every time I'm with him. My child with Timothy's eyes would truly be divine.

Dear Diary, I have gone mad; a perfect fit for any asylum. To even think these thoughts with all the rumors of war with the North reveals my total detachment from reality. Nevertheless, our lives hang in the balance should this child appear as a Negro. In acting on my innermost desires, I may have sentenced Timothy to death. He is the greatest love I have ever known, and I have placed his life and the life of my unborn child in the greatest peril. Nevertheless, we have a perfect love.

The insanity of lust is unrivaled.

The Queen of the Mad

CHAPTER 27

September 22, 1859

A t a certain time of night, the cobblestone roads in the French Quarter take on a unique characteristic of newness. They appear both polished and cleansed of all imperfections, as if little angelic hands had wiped away the sins of the previous day—but it's not celestial, it's just the dew. It was that time of night when it happened. That awkward time when those in their right minds are unconscious, and very few are conscious of their whereabouts. Only the restless.

Only those who rambled.

Only those who sold forbidden pleasures.

Only those who were frightened out of a dream.

Only those whose water broke in the middle of the night.

Through the thick fog, they raced against time, tormented by "what if this?" and "what if that?"—anguished by urgency. Marietta banged on the door as hard as she could, but the doctor was sound asleep.

"Timothy, go knock on the side of the house, under every window until someone opens the door—I must hurry back in case your mother needs me," Marietta called to him.

Frantically, Timothy tried to wake the doctor. There were

few options left, and he was second to last. Queenie was in full-blown labor and having complications; all hands were on deck.

The birthing room was the master's bedroom. All the windows were open, and two of the housemaids actively fanned Queenie to keep her cool. A total of two midwives were there to assist. At the foot of the bed, a small breakfast table was covered with a shiny satin sheet. On top of the table was a small bucket of warm water, washcloths, and a silk blanket. In each corner of the room was a large vase stuffed with twenty-four red roses. On the dresser was a heated candle tray of frankincense oil; the pleasant, therapeutic aroma wafted throughout the bedroom and down the hall.

Queenie was in intense pain.

All night.

Without cease.

Without pause.

The amount of time she suffered was longer than any of them had ever experienced or known any mother to survive. They found no comfort for Queenie, and the September heat only made matters worse. Her water had broken twenty-five hours ago, around the same time on the previous night, but there were no signs of the baby. Clarice was in charge of the delivery, with Delia providing support.

"Where is Beatrice? I want Beatrice!" Queenie cried out.

Beatrice made her way through the few who had labored for as long as Queenie had been in labor, attending to her needs from the moment her water broke.

"I'm here, ma'am, I'm here. Take hold of my hand. We'll get through this together."

The mistress was thirty-nine years old and about to give birth to her first child. The midwives were getting concerned because of the amount of time it was taking for her to deliver, and unfortunately, none of their methods to speed things along had worked.

"This has gone on too long," Beatrice said to Clarice. "Time to force the baby out."

"You ain't never delivered no baby—not one—I don't need your help," Clarice snapped.

"Your way ain't working."

"Since you know everything about midwifin', what would you have me do?" Clarice asked.

"We have to stand her up and lean her on the bed. That is the only way. Delia saved my baby that way, and it will work for this baby," Beatrice argued.

"That ain't gon' work!" Clarice screamed at Beatrice.

"You! I don't know who you are, but you will not speak to Beatrice in that rude manner. Leave. Now! Get out," Queenie ordered. "Ahhhhhhh! I can't take this anymore!"

Today was the first time Clarice and Queenie stood in the same room. Queenie knew Clarice's name because of the entries in her husband's logbook under the *supplies* category, but she was oblivious to her true duties. What she was fully aware of was that twice a week, he sent goods to a house on Royal Street, but she had never inquired any further.

Clarice stood up and walked over to the doorway to watch. "I hope that baby die in her belly," Clarice whispered near Beatrice. "That way they blame you . . . *high yellow heifer.*"

"*Go to hell,*" Beatrice whispered back. "Momma Delia, please help me stand her up."

"Come on sweetheart, let's get you on up so we can deliver this child. Beatrice is telling you right. I tried to tell Clarice the same thing, but she shoo me like a fly," Delia said as they helped Queenie to stand.

"Ma'am, imma need you to trust me now. We gonna have this baby, but you need to trust me. Lean across this bed. We have to get this baby out right now!" Beatrice instructed.

Queenie pressed her body weight on the side of the bed and widened her stance as Beatrice instructed her. At the same time, Beatrice positioned herself behind Queenie on the floor and placed both of her hands inside of her thighs like a quarterback.

"All right now, I will catch this baby, but I need you to trust me and push! Come on and push! You can do it. Give me another push!"

"Ahhhhhhh!" Queenie screamed.

Delia who could only provide support because of her age, started to sing.

> Hail, oh hail, ye happy spirits,
> Death no more shall make you fear,
> Grief nor sorrow, pain nor anguish,
> Shall no more distress you there.
> Around Him are ten thousand angels,
> Always ready to obey command;
> They are always hovering round you,
> Till you reach the heavenly land.

"Push this baby out!" Beatrice coached.

"Ahhhhhhh!" Queenie yelled.

"That was a good one, but I need another just like that. Now push," Beatrice demanded.

"Beatrice, I have nothing else left to push with. I can't!"

"You will, I say. Now push!" Beatrice demanded.

POW, POW! Beatrice slapped Queenie in the center of her back so hard it startled her and caused just the reaction needed to aid in pushing the baby out. Slowly and steadily, the baby dropped down into Beatrice's waiting hands.

"You did it. I knew you could do it!" Queenie exclaimed.

The baby cried for the first time. Beatrice gave the child to Delia so she could cut the cord and clean the infant.

"What did I have?" Queenie asked as she tried to catch her breath.

"It's a fat little boy, ma'am," Delia said as she wiped the child. Beatrice walked over to the cleaning table at the foot of the bed. She needed to see him.

Does the baby look at all like my Timothy?

Did the baby have my son's wavy hair?

Delia wiped the baby's face slowly and thoroughly—far too slowly for Beatrice, who was on the verge of having a panic attack. But the child resembled any other child conceived by a Caucasian father. In that short, drama-filled moment, Beatrice

forgot her son Timothy and Queenie's baby shared the same father. That is, if her master was the father. If so, then the infant
child was as much Timothy's brother as Eva was his sister. In
that moment, Beatrice prayed away all African features like full
lips, a wide nose, and wavy hair. She even prayed away those fa-
ther-identifying traits that could appear as the child grew—like
freckles. Such was the case with Timothy.

Delia handed the baby to Beatrice, and Beatrice cautiously
handed him to Queenie. "It is a boy, a precious little boy. Here
you go."

"Oh, my dear Lord," she panted. "He looks just like his father!" Queenie was elated as she began to nurse. "When my husband arrives, he will be so happy. I gave him an heir. Finally, he
has an heir. His firstborn son."

Marietta made eye contact with Beatrice, who released a depressed sigh. Standing in the room watching Queenie feed was
far harder than Beatrice had anticipated. Marietta waved for Beatrice to join her in the hallway, so she followed.

"Are you okay? I am worried about you," Marietta said, putting an arm around her twin's shoulders.

"It's not fair. It's just not fair. The Lord is not fair."

The *Natchez II* pulled into the Port of New Orleans around
eight o'clock in the morning. Timothy was there to greet his
master.

"Did she have the baby yet?" he asked Timothy. Queenie's
letters had provided an estimated delivery date, so he had rushed
back to New Orleans as fast as he could.

"Did you say something, sir? I couldn't hear you," Timothy
replied.

"Did my wife have the baby?"

"I'm sorry, sir. Hard of hearing out here with all this noise.
Getting deaf in my old age. Haha," Timothy laughed.

"Haha," His master joined him in laughter.

A few minutes later, Timothy pulled the buggy in front of
1005 St. Peter Street. His master leaped out before they could

come to a complete stop. Less than ten seconds later, he entered the bedroom to see Beatrice standing next to his wife as she nursed.

"Our son came today!" Queenie smile was wide and joyous.

He walked over and held his son for the first time.

"I wanted Beatrice to be here when you walked through the door because if it weren't for her, both of us would have died," Queenie told him.

"Is that so, Beatrice?"

"Yes, we are only alive and well right now because of what she did to save our baby." Queenie turned toward Beatrice, who stood on the other side of her bed. "Beatrice, I will find a way to repay you double for what you've done for my family. I owe you, and my husband owes you. We will reward you for saving our son. I give you my word and promise on my child."

He watched as his wife kissed Beatrice on the hand.

"It appears I missed all the excitement, and it was probably best I wasn't here. I would have made a mess of everything. But Beatrice, thank you."

"I waited until you arrived to give him a name. I wanted you to have the honor," Queenie said.

His heart swelled with pride. *What a gift from God*, he thought, to be able to name the first child born to his wife.

"A child that we thought we would never have," he said as he walked over to the window with the baby in his arms. "A child we only dreamed of. We tried so many times. I lost hope, but thank God it happened. Thank you, Anne."

"Well, Bernard, what will you name him? I've sent word to my family, so my mother is en route here from Amite. Therefore, it would be a fantastic idea to have him named before she arrives. I know you wouldn't want my dear old mother selecting some French name like Pascal."

The two of them shared a laugh out loud.

"I have the perfect name for our boy," he beamed.

"All right, we're waiting! What is it?" she asked.

"We shall name him Steven Martin de Fortier."

"I love it! It's an excellent name," his wife said, "one I was also considering. I will send out the announcement later today that Bernard and Anne Boleyn Fortier welcome their firstborn, Steven Martin Fortier."

Bernard Fortier handed the baby back to Anne, and she immediately placed the child back on her breast. While Anne was distracted, Bernard Fortier blew Beatrice a kiss, but received no reaction. Beatrice left the room fighting back tears, and he followed.

Bernard caught up to her on the balcony. "Beatrice, wait, don't go."

"I can't watch another minute of it."

He looked confused. "Beatrice, what's wrong?"

"Timothy is your firstborn son, then Lawrence, and seven girls you sold away like mules. I pray every day you look at this baby you're reminded of our children!" Beatrice pulled free of his grip and wept loudly across the balcony to her room.

CHAPTER 28

S herman and Ronelle arrived at Anita's Grill on Tulane Avenue for breakfast around nine o'clock, and were delighted to find their favorite table available. Anita's Grill was one of the last traditional eateries in New Orleans that remained open twenty-four hours a day. On the left side of Anita's was a traditional full-length service counter with bolted swivel seats. The walls of the eatery were plastered with celebrity pictures. Anita's served all walks of life.

Sherman and Ronelle took their seats at a booth directly in the middle of the row. They were greeted by a heavyset waitress who rested her large breast on the counter. To make things easier on her, they both ordered pancakes, scrambled eggs, bacon, orange juice, and coffee.

"Thank you, sugar, I will have your coffee over to you in a minute."

Sherman turned from the waitress. "Ronelle, I want to thank you for your support this past week. Not sure if I would have made it through yesterday without you."

"You don't have to thank me. I know you would do the same for me."

The waitress brought out their coffees and informed them their food would be out shortly. Then she looked at Sherman.

"Young man, who *your people?*"

"Ma'am, I am Councilman Campbell's oldest son."

Her entire demeanor changed. A huge smile appeared across her face. "I knew it from the moment you hit the door—I'm old friends with your dad."

Sherman was accustomed to everyone knowing him as 'Melvin's boy.'

"Boy, your daddy was just in here last week with his big-time friends, making all that noise. I told them as long as they keep tipping me, they could make all the noise they want to. Your daddy is all right with me, he cares about the working man in this city. I'll be right out with your order."

Before she could make good on that promise, two men entered the diner. One was wearing a black hoodie, and the other—a really short guy—had a red bandana over his face. They both drew guns. The one with the black hoodie aimed at the waitress, and the other pointed his trembling gun at Sherman and Ronelle.

We'll give them what they ask for, Sherman's eyes said to Ronelle. After getting a closer look at the two men, Sherman noticed that neither could have been more than sixteen years old, and both seemed very nervous.

"Give me all the money, put it in this bag, and no one will get hurt! Anybody jump stupid, I will blow your fucking head off!" the hoodie-wearing robber demanded.

The second gunman with the red bandana moved in closer to Sherman and demanded his money. He brandished a smaller weapon, a .22-caliber pistol that shook like Tourette's syndrome. The last thing Sherman wanted was for the rookie to prove himself today.

"Giv-giv-give me your wallet," the little robber demanded.

Sherman's wallet contained 975 dollars, and he didn't hesitate handing it over in hopes that they would consider it a score and leave. The robber quickly snatched the wallet from Sherman, then aimed his weapon at Ronelle.

"And you, give m-me your purse."

That's when Sherman confronted the man by jumping in front of the gun and Ronelle.

"Look, there is more than nine hundred dollars in my wallet. You can have it. Please, don't point that gun at my wife."

"*Mu-muda-fucka,* did I ask you?" The robber reached for Ronelle's purse. Out of impulse she held onto it, a move that caused her to fall on the floor. Sherman threw himself in front of Ronelle, and that's when the shaky-handed robber with the red bandana fired one shot.

Sherman was shot in the chest.

The scuffle happened so quickly that the young thugs never got the chance to get the money from the waitress. They ran out the door with Sherman's wallet and Ronelle's purse, leaving Sherman bleeding on the floor.

"Call 911!" Ronelle screamed.

Sherman was losing a lot of blood. The waitress dialed 911 while Ronelle fought to tear open Sherman's button-down shirt. There it was—a bullet hole right below his collarbone. She removed Sherman's shoes and socks, remembering a scene from one of her theater performances. She did her best to stuff the socks into the bullet hole.

"Sherman! Baby! Baby! Stay with me please, stay with me!" she yelled at Sherman, who was losing consciousness. LSU Medical Center was only a few blocks away. Ronelle was in the process of dragging Sherman to the car when the first police officers finally arrived at the scene.

"Ma'am, are you injured as well?"

"No, sir. Please, can we put him in your car and rush him to the hospital?"

"No, ma'am. The ambulance will be here within the next five minutes. They've already been dispatched."

"We don't have five minutes, he will bleed to death!"

Ronelle struggled to lift Sherman's unconscious body off the floor, but she slipped in his blood. The officer pulled Ronelle away from his body. She became frantic and began to lose all composure, fighting against the officer's best effort to gain control of the crime scene. The NOPD officer knew he needed to redirect her, so he asked for Sherman's full name.

"This is Councilman's Campbell son . . . Sherman!"

"What? I worked a few details for Councilman Campbell at

City Hall a few years ago. I thought he looked familiar. Call his dad while I locate the ambulance. Tell Councilmen Campbell we're taking him to LSU Medical."

In all the commotion, Ronelle could not find her cell phone. It had slid under the booth and out of sight.

"I can't find my phone!" she screamed in agony. Then she heard the ringtone that was assigned to her mother; "Do-Re-Mi" from *The Sound of Music*. After locating her phone under the booth, she answered it right before the call hung up, screaming into the phone.

"Mom, Sherman's been shot! They shot him!"

"What? Shot Sherman? Ronelle, what did you just say?"

"We were having breakfast when these two guys stormed in and robbed the diner! When one of the men threw me on the floor, Sherman jumped in the middle, and he shot him! Sherman gave him the money, and he still shot him! He's still lying on the floor of the diner right now! I'm trying to get him to LSU Medical! He will not die on this floor! Wait, the ambulance is here now! Please call Miss Yvonne right away and let her know!"

The first responders made their way inside. They immediately administered CPR. They rapidly placed Sherman on a gurney, then removed the bloody socks from his wound.

"Ma'am, are you riding with us?"

"Yes." Ronelle reached for her purse, but it was gone. She followed the police officer out of the diner and climbed in the back of the ambulance. In what felt like an out-of-body experience, Ronelle watched helplessly as the medical technicians worked to save Sherman's life.

"Ma'am, do you know if your husband is allergic to any medications?"

"No, he isn't that I know of, but his mother will meet us at the hospital."

"The police said he's Councilman Campbell's son. Is that true?" The technician worked and asked questions at the same time without missing a single detail. He worked in the area of the bullet entry point and prepped Sherman for surgery. Sherman never said a word, never flinched, and never moved during the entire ride to the hospital. Lifeless.

"Yes, he's Councilman Campbell's son. We were having breakfast when the diner was robbed. The guy shot him. Is he going to make it? Please tell me he is going to make it!"

"Well, ma'am, we'll do our best to give him every chance to make it."

Ronelle's cell phone blared again. This time it was Mr. Campbell.

"Sweetheart, please tell me my son is alive!"

"Mr. Campbell, we're in the ambulance now, headed to LSU Medical. He's been shot in the chest, and they're working on him. Oh God, help us!" Ronelle screamed.

"We're on the interstate right now and headed to you. Is Sherman still responding?

"No, sir. He's not. Please hurry!"

She could hear Melvin scream, "Lord, no! No! No!" as he hung up the phone.

Less than twenty-four hours ago, they had buried his grandmother, and now she was in the back of an ambulance watching the life bleed out of Sherman. When they arrived at the hospital, a team had already been notified that they were en route with the son of Councilmen Campbell.

Melvin Campbell was loved throughout the city. When the hospital staff discovered his son had been shot, the entire surgical team wanted to join in the life-saving effort. Sherman was quickly removed from the back of the ambulance and rushed into an operating room, where surgeons were waiting for him.

Though she had been allowed to ride in the ambulance, the medical staff prohibited Ronelle from follow them into the operating room, though she did try. Alone, she sobbed in the waiting room for what seemed like an eternity until the first person arrived. It was her brother, Brandon.

"Ronelle, tell me he'll live!" Brandon insisted.

Ronelle fell into his arms and began to cry. The love of her life had been willing to make the ultimate sacrifice. It had all happened so fast, she couldn't even remember what the young man who pulled the trigger looked like. All she knew for sure was that Sherman, without a second of hesitation, had jumped in front of the bullet to save her life.

Now, his life dangled in the wind.

Moments later, Yvonne and Melvin arrived at the hospital and immediately went to the nurses' station. Yvonne introduced herself not only as Sherman's mother but also as a doctor, and asked if she could sit in on the surgery. The medical supervisor declined her request as a matter of medical ethics. She assured Yvonne that Sherman was in the hands of the two best surgeons on staff and that she would personally provide her with updates on his status. So, Yvonne provided Sherman's medical history and took her seat.

Shortly after, Brenda and Steven Fortier arrived. Steven found Melvin speaking with an investigator as they tried to piece together the robbery at Anita's Grill. Brenda wrapped her arms around Yvonne and tried to comfort her as best she could.

Minutes turned into hours as more and more family members arrived at the hospital upon receiving the news. A lot of the family was still in town for Susan Campbell's funeral, so there were more people in the waiting room than would normally have come. Sherman was loved. He was smart. He was handsome. He was driven. No one was ready to remember him that way. They all prayed for a miracle.

Off in the corner of the waiting room, Jynika and Brandon sat holding each other up, fighting off the emerging grief. Down the hall in the operating room was Brandon's best friend, childhood buddy, and soon-to-be brother-in-law—if Sherman survived the shooting. As the hours ticked by and morning gave way to afternoon, Yvonne turned to Melvin and tried to comfort him as best she could, but nothing worked. She finally found the words that gave him some hope.

"Melvin, based on my experience, no news is good news."

After what seemed like an eternity, the lead surgeon emerged with the first update for the forty-five family members and friends who had waited all day for information on Sherman's condition. The doctor pulled his parents off to the side and began to explain what Sherman was up against. The news was grim.

"Your son was shot in the upper right side of his chest, and the bullet is still in his shoulder. When he arrived, he was hemorrhaging internally from the entry area, and he has a collapsed right lung. We have stabilized him, but he will need as much blood as we can locate, which is proving difficult because of his rare blood type, AB-negative. It appears you have a lot of family members present. Can you ask them for blood donations?"

"Yes, I'll get right on it," Melvin said.

"So, will he live?" Yvonne asked.

"The good news is, we have stopped the bleeding. The not-so-good news is it will take another thirty-six hours to monitor the impact of this trauma on his brain."

Later that afternoon, Melvin and Yvonne visited Sherman's room. Yvonne walked over to the front of Sherman's bed and started flipping through the medical charts that were maintained by the attending physicians. As she read, she cried, "My baby is showing signs of being brain dead!"

Sherman was breathing with the use of a ventilator. The monitors and beeping sounds in his room spoke to the severity of his condition. The attending nurse peeked in the door and told them their time was up. Yvonne agreed to leave within five minutes. On her way out, she picked up Sherman's chart again and viewed his list of medications. That's when she noticed a ray of hope. *Pentobarbital.*

Pentobarbital is a drug used to induce a coma-like state, especially when the attending physicians are trying to limit a patient's brain activity.

"Come on Melvin. We have to get out of their way now. I feel reassured about the treatment he's receiving, and if it's bad news, then just know bad news is never delayed."

Melvin walked around to the front of the bed and kissed Sherman on the forehead before leaving the room. Yvonne's arms wrapped around Melvin's waist; Melvin's arms wrapped around Yvonne's shoulders. Step by step, they left the room, but not their son. A nurse closed the door behind them.

The entire waiting room fell silent except for the sounds of *Maury Povich* playing in the background. Only the nurses seem interested in the TV. Still hung over from last night, Uncle Clarence slept on the floor along the back wall of the waiting room.

In the far corner, an NOPD detective notified Councilmen Campbell and Ronelle that the robbery suspects were in custody. The security video from Anita's Grill had been instrumental in helping the police identify the getaway car. The only thing remaining was for Ronelle to identify them after she left the hospital; she agreed. Melvin thanked the detective for quickly apprehending the criminals.

Later that day, around five o'clock in the evening, one of the physicians returned and asked to speak with Dr. Yvonne Campbell in private. They knew each other from their days in med school, so she was relieved to discover he had performed the surgery on her son. Yvonne braced for the update.

"Dr. Campbell, let me start by saying we're doing everything possible to help your son. At the moment, he's in an induced coma state until we're sure he's out of the critical zone. We have stopped all internal bleeding, but now our concern remains his right lung."

"Excuse me, and I hate to interrupt you, but what about his blood level? Were you able to restore it?"

"Yes, we found two perfect matches, one was his father and another came from someone named Steven Fortier III. Just to be sure our donors were an exact match, I ordered DNA tests on the specimen from donor Fortier. It was the same as Melvin Campbell's. Both were exact matches, and both donors will need to make two more contributions. At that time, I believe we will be home free."

"Did you just say Steven Fortier was an exact match to my son?" asked Yvonne.

"Yes, that's correct. Steven Fortier, your husband, Brandon Fortier, and your twins, Chase and Chance Campbell, were all good matches, but none were closer matches than the first two. If not for those socks his fiancée stuffed into the bullet hole and the pressure she applied, this conversation could have gone a lot differently. We still have a lung issue that will require additional surgery, but I have put his chance of recovery at seventy percent, for sure."

Yvonne Campbell was very excited and could not wait to tell her husband the good news. She walked into the waiting room and made the announcement - news that many of them had waited most of the morning to receive.

"Guys, Sherman will live! My son will live!"

The room erupted in a cheer as the family began to give praise and thanks for Sherman's survival. Melvin was consoling Ronelle at the time they heard the announcement. Yvonne walked over to where they were standing and told her the exact words the doctor had shared in the conference room.

"The doctor said your quick thinking with those socks helped in saving my son's life. From the bottom of my heart, thank you."

"Miss Yvonne, I love him. You don't have to thank me. That bullet was for me, and Sherman pushed me out of the way. He was willing to give his life for me."

Yvonne's eyes filled with tears as she wrapped Ronelle in a warm hug.

Once the crowd began to disperse, Yvonne and Melvin took a short stroll across the street from the emergency entrance to the hospital.

"Sweetheart, why are we out here?" Melvin asked.

"Because the doctor shared something that has me puzzled. You, Sherman, the twins, and Steven share the same blood."

"What? Yvonne, what are you talking about?"

"They ran tests on all the people who donated blood today, and it seems they made four matches. Clarence didn't give blood because of obvious reasons. You and Steven have the same blood that's flowing through Sherman's veins."

"So, Clarence was right. We're related to the Fortier family. This is too much to deal with right now," he sighed. Melvin had shared some of Clarence's suspicions with Yvonne, though he hadn't yet told her all the details of what he had discovered so far.

"I know it is, Melvin, but I wanted to let you know because Steven's blood helped save our son's life, and we will need more. We'll pick this up later. Here comes Steven and Brenda's family."

Once Brenda and Steven Fortier exited the emergency room, both couples hugged.

"Well, Mel, old buddy, we came real close to losing our children today," Steven sighed.

"Man, tell me about it. Just like that, our lives could have changed."

"That young man stepped in front of a loaded pistol to protect my daughter. I am at a loss for words to express how I feel right now. You have a special young man. He is very special indeed."

"Well, your baby girl's quick action saved my son's life."

Ronelle was standing a few steps behind her parents. Melvin pulled her into the group hug with them.

"Thank God you thought of those socks . . . you saved my son's life! The doctors said he is in an induced coma, and they expect him to make a full recovery, thanks to you, Ronelle," Melvin told her. She managed an exhausted smile.

"I'm overjoyed to hear Sherman is going to pull through! Mel, I'm standing by should you need anything at all. Do not hesitate to call me," Steven said.

"I know you are. Thank you."

An hour later, the waiting room crowd had dwindled out. Except for Uncle Clarence still finishing his nap in the corner, no one was left except Melvin, Yvonne, and Ronelle. As long as Sherman was in the hospital, they planned to sleep at the hospital.

"Hey, where did everybody go?" Clarence asked with a yawn. "What did I miss?"

Yvonne smiled. "Kool, you missed a lot, but it's all good."

CHAPTER 29

May 1, 1862
5:50 p.m.

For the mother and daughter team of seamstresses, the day would always start around seven in the morning and end after dusk. Right after breakfast, Beatrice gently pulled the material while Eva cut along the pattern. She made each cut effortlessly and precisely. Eva had evolved into a master seamstress just like her mom. During their time together, with Eva serving as Beatrice's apprentice, her mother taught Eva everything she knew about the art of making a dress. Eva could design and sew a full wedding dress with a veil in less than three days.

The same dress would now take Beatrice six days to complete, due to a chronic arthritis condition that was making it difficult for her to hand-stitch anything. Beatrice worried about the pains in her hands, but she never mentioned them to her master. She still feared being sold away for failure to perform. Now in her mid-forties, Beatrice was well beyond childbearing age. She earned her keep by making dresses, but her hands could only stitch for one minute and then rest for two.

Her beautiful daughter stood on the other side of the cutting table with strong hands and keen eyesight—the two most important qualities seamstress Beatrice had lost over the years, somewhere in the rolls of fabrics. On the days Beatrice and Eva would finish early, they spent the rest of the day talking and researching how to find her siblings.

Whenever her master and his wife were away together, Beatrice and Eva would snoop through his files in search of evidence regarding her kids, but they never found anything that provided transaction history. They never stopped searching, nor did Marietta.

"Momma Bee, before I leave for the day, I need to talk to you. I am bothered. Troubled in my spirit," Eva said as she packed to leave. It was getting close to dinner, and she was due home to help Marietta.

"Well, you did most of the work all day, so the least I could do is the listening. What is it, Eva?" Beatrice asked.

"I don't think what we're looking for is here. Why would my father keep it here if Anne never knew all of these years that he owns us?"

"Eva, you make sense—a lot of sense—but if not here, then where?"

"Clarice raised us for Harriett Green, so she would know where to find my sisters. Clarice and Harriett knew those men who paid for Cecille, knew them like old friends. Harriett and Clarice are just as guilty as Master Fortier and Mr. Lafitte for what they did to you and Aunt Marietta. They will get theirs in the end," her daughter said.

"Don't let no one hear you talk like that. It could cause a lot of trouble. You hear me?"

"But it's the truth."

"I know it's true, but we made it this far by keeping secrets. We don't need no more trouble," Beatrice warned.

"So, my husband owns you? Is that what you're saying?" Anne Fortier asked.

They never saw her standing in the doorway. Anne had heard their entire conversation. Startled, Beatrice and Eva dropped the dress they had been holding and faced Anne.

"Lawd, no! Ma'am, we don't mean to start any trouble with

you and Masta," Beatrice tried to assure her.

"So, it's true," Anne said softly. "Beatrice, all these years, you have never called my husband 'master' in my presence. Eva, on the day you started here as an apprentice three years ago, I could not ignore the strong resemblance you have to my husband. Your face is his face, but as a woman. I've wondered about it every day since, but I held my peace. Beatrice, I remember a day not so long ago. It was a beautiful, sunny morning, and my husband and I decided to have breakfast in the courtyard. On this particular morning, you were sitting in that window over there. My back was to you. I was reading a newspaper, but I saw my husband blow you a kiss. It all makes sense now."

Her husband called out from down the hall. "Anne, could you come help me with a few bank matters?"

"I will be right there," Anne Fortier replied. "Beatrice, is my husband the father of Eva?"

Beatrice hesitated.

"You are not in trouble, but I need the truth, Beatrice. Is my husband the father of Eva?"

"Yes, Mrs. Fortier," Beatrice replied.

"Very well, I appreciate your honesty. I will inquire with him further about this matter," Anne said as she started to leave the room.

Fear overcame Beatrice. Her breath caught in her throat.

"But I am not the only one," Eva said firmly.

"Eva, no!" Beatrice tried to silence her, but it was too late.

Anne was four steps down the hall when she heard Eva's words. She stopped dead in her tracks. After a brief moment, she turned and stepped back into the room. The blood had left her face.

"I am not the only one," Eva said again.

"Beatrice, is this correct?"

"Yes, it's true. I gave birth to seven girls, and your husband sold all of them at the ball but Eva."

"You have seven daughters?!" Anne walked over to a chair and took a seat.

"Yes, Mrs. Fortier, seven were taken. All made with your husband; some made while you slept." Beatrice looked up at

Anne, her eyes brimming with years of pain. "I couldn't stop him. It's funny how they treat you when you're property. It's not rape when they own you."

"Oh, dear Beatrice, I never knew . . ."

"Guess I could have said something, but Timothy and Lawrence were no taller than a cutting table. Couldn't risk losing them to the auction or losing myself to the same. All my girls were sold at the ball, not the auction."

"*Sold at what ball*, Beatrice?"

"The quadroon ball, where they pair girls with rich men," Eva said. "Clarice raised us all for Master at the house on Royal; then we sold like cows."

"Oh, my! Oh, dear!" Anne said as she got to her feet. In the background, her husband called again. "I will be right down," Anne shouted back. "Well, now, I must inquire about these other matters with my husband, as well."

Eva wrapped her arms around her mother as Beatrice wept in fear of the impending storm. Before Anne could make a half-turn out the door, Eva shared more. "I'm one of seven girls who was fathered by Master, but it was a total of nine of us."

"Wait. There were nine of you? Who are the other two?"

"My brothers, Lawrence and Timothy."

"Timothy? Timothy! Did you say, *Timothy*?" Anne Fortier asked. "My husband is also the father of Timothy?"

"Yes, ma'am. My mother gave birth to nine children; your husband is the father of all nine. Timothy is the oldest," Eva clarified.

With her hand covering her mouth, Anne stormed across the balcony walkway that led to the main house—down the same balcony walkway Beatrice traveled every time her master rang his bell. Down the same walkway Timothy traveled on his way to make love to her whenever her husband was away.

Anne stumbled into the master bedroom holding her lower abdomen with one hand and bracing herself against the wall with the other. Moments later, her husband entered the room and saw her nearly doubled over.

"My love, are you feeling labor pains this early?" he asked. She was five months pregnant.

"No, I'm feeling something far worse."

"Far worse, my dear?"

"Like I want to kill you!"

Bernard locked the bedroom door behind him and stood there.

"Anne, I can explain . . ."

"You can explain? Please do. When were you going to tell me about your daughters?"

"What daughters?" Bernard attempted to lie.

"I know the truth!"

"Who told you?"

"Does it matter?" through tight lips, she rebuked him. "For years, I died inside because I could not give you a son. Then I was overjoyed when I finally gave you an heir, only to discover that my son is not your firstborn. Timothy is!"

"Anne, it doesn't work that way—not in this world—and you know it."

"*There's only one world!*" her voice boiled over. "Here's what I know; my husband is the father of nine, plus one. All this time, I've been surrounded by your mistress and your children."

"Beatrice is not my mistress . . ."

"Then what is she?" Anne's face was a portrait of bewilderment. "Bernard, do you take me for a fool?"

He paced in a small circle. "Anne, I'm sorry . . ."

"That's it? That's all you have to offer after twenty years of lies?"

"Anne, there were so many times I—"

"Do you love her?"

"I, I . . . never wanted to hurt you. Please believe me."

"*Do you love her?*" Anne screamed.

"I own her!" He screamed back in anger. "Beatrice is my property! All of them are my property! The same as my cattle and my boats and this house. All of it, I own. We own! I own her!"

Anne Fortier's legs became weak as twigs. She staggered a

few steps to an upholstered wingback chair that was just on the other side of the window seal. It was the chair where she curled up and read novels at dawn. The chair where she sat and watched nameless faces wander up St. Peter Street, wanting to wander with them, if only for a night. The chair where she waited for her husband to return after late evening walks. She realized in that moment that she'd never caught a single glance of him entering the courtyard door, and had never thought to look anywhere else in the house.

"Anne, I know you're disappointed in me, but what choice did I have?"

"The truth was a choice, Bernard. You chose to lie!" Anne snapped. "All this time! When I thought the help was paid labor, *my husband* was in the business of slaves! The entire time? The allowances?"

"Anne your outrage is not without justification. As your husband, the least you could do is allow me to explain . . . please! When the British formed the blockade, selling Negresses was the only way I kept food on the table and our business afloat. We needed the money."

"So, you and that miserable goat Lafitte sold your daughters into slavery?"

"They're not my daughters, Anne! They're slaves! And the law of the land says they have no rights."

"Humans, Bernard. They're not slaves, but people! Human beings with feelings and rights under God. *How could you?*"

"I don't expect you to understand. I mainly ask for your forgiveness. But with God as my witness, I treated them better than anyone else could have under the circumstances," Bernard said.

In that one outburst, her husband destroyed everything Anne had once believed. Bernard had promised his wife he would never venture into the slave trade. Bernard Fortier knew how much his wife hated slavery and how hard she worked in the Abolitionist movement from their summer home in Amite. With the help of a local Methodist congregation, Anne Fortier's financial backing had played a vital role in transporting thirty-seven slaves to freedom. Anne wanted no part of her husband's business dealings.

"You treated them better? That makes you less of a monster because you treated them better? You sold people! All the efforts I've made to end the buying and selling of human beings! Tonight, it's been revealed that you alone are the owner of this slave depot." Her voice gargled with sorrow. "Out of seven girls, did you hold any of them as infants?" she asked rhetorically. The room fell silent.

After ten minutes in their respective corners, Bernard approached his wife with caution and lowered to one knee.

"For so long, I wanted to tell you the truth. For over twenty years, this haunted me. The truth is, every man I know owned slaves. It was something we all did together. To not own slaves took me out of a certain circle that was essential to many of my business relationships. I don't expect you to understand. Yes, I am their father, and I denied every one of them. Yes, I sold them as quadroons, but only to men who could afford to provide them with the best life could offer."

"And that's how you justified your filth—the fact that they went to the highest bidder? They were your daughters! Tell me, what was the cost of purchase for a *Fortier quadroon?*" Anne yelled in disgust.

Bernard avoided her question because it exposed an ugly side of a secret life he had kept well hidden. If he responded, she would know the depth of his descent into the slave trade, and the true source of their wealth.

"I can't take back what I've done, but the pain of this night was not in vain. I no longer have to lie." He stood and moseyed back to the bed.

Her anger said *leave and never speak to him again.*

Her hurt said *ask more questions to try to make sense of it all.*

Her abolitionist's heart said *you are Beatrice's only hope of finding her daughters.*

Anne spoke in a broken voice. "You have destroyed us tonight. The only question that remains is, do you love Beatrice as you love me?"

He lounged on the edge of the bed. "Yes, I do. I love Beatrice, the same as I love you. From the day I saw her shivering, half-naked in the cold, standing on top of shipping carts, I've loved her." Bernard appeared pale and relieved.

The words slithered off his tongue, snaked across the room, and bit her in the heart. But she needed to hear him say it. Like the benediction at the end of a funeral, she needed to hear it, even though it would bruise her like a backhand slap. After years of soothing lies, she needed to hear the ear-piercing truth. He loved her. He loved Beatrice. He was in love with Beatrice.

My husband loves his slave and his wife the same.

Anne became enraptured in an epiphany. *All the nights he needed a long walk because something was bothering him, he was with Beatrice. All the nights he slept next to me but was distant, he was with Beatrice. All the nights I was startled out of sleep, he must have been calling her name passionately . . .*

Anne Fortier realized at that moment that she shared something in common with Beatrice—she was also nothing more than one of his concubines.

"Then, in that case, there is a sin that I need to confess, as well," Anne began. "You are not the only one who has a secret. I have one too, and this is the perfect night to tell you. Timothy and . . ."

Before she could finish her sentence, there was a great commotion outside her window—so loud that Bernard ran to her side. Together, they stood shoulder to shoulder in total shock at the scene just below their windowsill. Life as they knew it had changed in the blink of an eye.

Just as Anne was about to confess her love for Timothy and the possibility that he was the father of their son, as well as their unborn child, their collective worlds changed forever!

MAY 1, 1862
NEW ORLEANS, LOUISIANA
9:25 P.M.

Hear ye, hear ye! I, Major General for the Union Army, under the order of the President of the United States, at this moment issue the following order. All Negroes under the sound of my voice are hereby free from slavery if you agree not to take up arms against us. This expedition was ordered by the President of the United States to notify all captive people that you are forever free. You are now free men and women of color, meaning free from forced labor without wages, free from deeds and titles, free to travel as you please. Slavery in this region has expired without renewal. Welcome to the United States of America.

The Union soldiers erupted in a loud roar!

New Orleans was now under the control of the North. Conquered without having to fire one shot. Strangely, it was the slaves and former slave masters who struggled most to process what General Benjamin Butler had declared.

Slavery officially ended in New Orleans that day at 9:27 p.m.

CHAPTER 30

May 1, 1862
9:30 p.m.

T he former slaves rejoiced: "We's free! We is free! Don't have to work no mo'! We is free!"

Marietta had been nearly finished with the dishes when she heard the cheering through a narrow kitchen window. She froze stiff as a block of ice. In the next room, her master was still seated at the dinner table when he heard the announcement by the Union soldiers. He walked over to the front window on the left side of the door while Marietta stood in the right window. She had a full view of the street and sidewalk.

Slaves poured out of homes as far as Marietta could see. They stepped out of their slave quarters as free people. Mr. Lafitte stepped out of his house to confirm the announcement. Directly outside of the door were rows of Union troops marching in formation. It was confirmed. New Orleans was no longer a stronghold of the Confederacy for every enslaved person of African descent. New Orleans had been liberated.

"Where are the records of who bought my daughters?" Marietta demanded, turning to look her former master in the eye.

"Nigger girl, what did you just ask me?"

"Somewhere in this house, you have a record of my daughters. You sold them all and I demand to know where! I'm free. All I want is my children."

It was over. It had ended without bloodshed. That night, in that living room, nearly 150 years of servitude to French, Spanish, and European Americans ceased. There they stood, face to face in the living room of the red brick house on St. Ann Street—the former slave and the old slave master. To his rear was a wall; on it hung a coat rack. To her rear, up against the wall, a wooden stool held a candle lantern. On the adjacent wall, a seven-foot-tall mahogany grandfather clock with a brass bell and swinging pendulum showed the time: 9:30 p.m.

Only six feet of space separated them, but Marietta had demanded the location of her daughters, so that distance quickly closed. She was free from her master and the only retribution—the only compensation she felt she was owed for services rendered—was the whereabouts of her children.

"Where are my children?" she yelled. "All I want is to know where I can find my children. The least you can do is help find them!"

Mr. Lafitte stepped forward and backhand-slapped Marietta. His hand connected with the same side of her face that Mrs. de Marigny had crushed with the rocker of her chair. He slapped her so hard she crashed into the lamp stand. He hurried to his gun rack to retrieve a pistol and load his rifle. With blood dripping from the side of her mouth, Marietta picked herself up off the floor, walked past Lafitte as he loaded his guns, and retreated to the kitchen.

"Now you listen to me, nigger girl," he called out. "I'm going out to investigate these matters, but when I return, you can expect another beating for back-talking me. Whatever is going on out there don't have anything to do with you. You are my nigger, and you will remain my nigger. Do you hear me, gal?"

"Yes, sir!" Marietta answered from the kitchen.

With both guns loaded, Lafitte returned to the window to assess the situation. Outside his door, more liberated Africans flooded the streets. Many were heading to Congo Square to celebrate, while others searched for nearby loved ones. At an hour of evening when hardly any slaves would have roamed the French Quarter, black people of all complexions took to the streets. Jubilant. Elated. A few, however, were full of rage and revenge.

Lafitte slowly opened the door. "Never seen so many niggers in the street in all my life. This is horrible, absolutely horrible."

Before he could fully open the front door, he heard Marietta say, "Masta, you can't leave without your hat, sir."

When he turned, she was standing behind him with his hat in her right hand. He reached for the hat. Marietta was left handed, and in that hand was a wide-bladed knife. While he perfectly positioned the hat, she plunged the knife deep into his chest, all the way to the handle.

Mr. Lafitte slowly slid down the front door to the floor. She lowered with him, steadily pushing the knife deeper into his chest. He clung to life, the pace of his breathing cut in half, eyes begging for mercy, barely able to whisper. A whisper was all Marietta wanted.

"I cared for you all of these years, even cared for your wife until she died in my arms. I loved your wife. She was my friend; she was kind to me. I never told her you were selling our children. I let her die thinking you were breeding me out to other slaves. You owe me peace in knowing who bought my children. Do one good deed before you meet your maker, and I will forgive you," Marietta said, inches from his face. "When I take this knife out of your chest, you will quickly die, so I will ask you again. Where are my children?"

Lafitte's lips moved, but she could barely hear him. Marietta screamed again, "Where in this house are those records? Who bought my daughters?"

A faint voice replied, "Clock."

Marietta could barely hear him, so she leaned in. "Say it again."

"*Clock*," Lafitte gasped.

Marietta looked down at his hand and noticed he was trying to point. In the corner was the large clock. It was then she remembered that late at night, whenever he returned home, he always visited the grandfather clock in the living room. Still holding the knife in Lafitte's chest, Marietta looked over her shoulder at the bottom of the clock. The lower part was a chest with a brass handle. Only then did Marietta release her grip on the knife and walk over to the clock.

She opened the chest and revealed a stack of ledgers. The books on top were mainly bills of landing from the shipping yard, but the very last item in the chest was a black binder. Marietta opened the binder, and there on the first page she read:

The Lafitte & Fortier Quadroon Company

Name	DOB	Mother	Father	Housed	Highest Bidder	Return
Cecille	1837	Beatrice	Fortier	Royal	See Bernard Fortier	$1500
Ruth	1836	Heif	Laffite	St Ann	Preston Farra	$1850
Tempie	1838	Beatrice	Fortier	Royal	See Bernard Fortier	$1832
Faye	1839	Heif	Laffite	Royal	William Claiborne	$1990
Emma	1840	Beatrice	Fortier	Royal	See Bernard Fortier	$2100
Grace	1840	Fannie	Laffite	Royal	Joseph Walker	$2265
Cora	1841	Heif	Laffite	Royal	Charles Derbigny	$2475
Chloe	1841	Fannie	Laffite	Royal	Warren Moise	$2220
Eva	1842	Beatrice	Fortier	Royal	*Harriett Green	$2950
Amelia	1842	Heif	Lafitte	Royal	John Sandidge	$2300
Mattie	1842	Beatrice	Fortier	Royal	See Bernard Fortier	$2525
Lena	1842	Fannie	Lafitte	Royal	Henry K L Dupre	$2230
Bertha	1843	Fannie	Lafitte	Royal	See Bernard Fortier	$2680
Eunice	1843	Heif	Lafitte	Rampart	Ducan M Kage	$2800
Emma	1844	Heif	Lafitte	Rampart	LC Michaels	$2700
Bella	1844	Heif	Lafitte	Rampart	LC Michaels	$2700
Louise	1845	Beatrice	Fortier	Royal	No Sale	
Annette	1845	Beatrice	Fortier	Royal	No Sale	
Clara	1852	Fannie	Lafitte	Royal	No Sale	
Helena	1854	Fannie	Lafitte	Royal	No Sale	
Delphine	1858	Eva	U. Green	Royal	No Sale	

All her daughters were listed, as were all Beatrice's girls,

Eva's girl—who seemed to be alive, despite what Eva had been told—and the offspring of another woman Marietta didn't recognize. The well-kept record also revealed that Pierre Lafitte and Bernard Fortier maintained another nursery on Rampart Street. At that location, they held eight more underage girls until it was time for them to make their debuts at the quadroon ball. Lafitte also owned a brothel—a partnership he had with Harriett Green.

Marietta saw the word *'Heif'* listed as the mother of the children born on St. Ann Street. That's when her fist clenched, and her anger erupted again. Seated on the floor with his back against the front door was the person who had omitted her name as their mother.

His chest was dark burgundy from where the knife had entered down to waist level. His life dripped away, but Mr. Lafitte was still alive. Marietta knelt down in front of Lafitte, who still struggled to speak. He pleaded for mercy as best he could. With his ledger in her hand, Marietta's rage honed in on him.

"You called me 'Heif' in this little book here. 'Heifer' is what you thought of me. Here is what I think of you. Hope you burn in hell."

Marietta slowly pulled the knife out of his chest and watched him take his last breath. She stood over his body feeling no remorse. She regretted she hadn't killed him after he took her first child. All the nights he came home drunk and raped her replayed in her head like a bad movie on fast forward. If she could have killed him again, she would not hesitate at that moment to do so.

"I think I will burn his body in this house!" Marietta said to herself. Looking down at him didn't give her the sense of satisfaction she had expected—only more anger. Barely hidden rage that was long overdue.

Suddenly there was a knock at the door. Only then did she come to terms with the realization. *I just killed my master.*

Another knock convinced her she should run and hide. Running made more sense, so that's what she decided to do. A louder knock shook the door. Then came a voice she recognized.

"Marietta . . . it's Beatrice!"

10:15 p.m.

Marietta kicked Lafitte's body to the side. With hands still moist with his blood, she opened the door. Beatrice and Eva stepped over his legs as they entered the house. Lafitte first appeared as if he were taking a nap on the floor with his eyes open, but once Beatrice saw the front of his shirt, she knew his rest was eternal. For as far back as she could remember, her sister had been prone to violence. Seeing Mr. Lafitte's corpse with a gaping hole in the middle of his chest came as no surprise.

Beatrice remembered when they were seven years old on the Marigny Plantation. Marietta had climbed a tree and waited all day for a particular boy to walk by alone, and he did. From nearly twenty feet up, Marietta dropped a huge brick that hit the boy on the head. She killed him—all because he'd his hand under Beatrice's dress.

Beatrice was always the peacemaker of the two, but her sister was born a short-tempered warrior who couldn't keep the last lick. It all held true about Marietta. Her master kept the last lick. He had no choice.

Beatrice and Eva couldn't take their eyes off the deceased Mr. Lafitte as he lay in a fetal position, nor did either of them have to guess who had killed him. They knew Marietta had done it. No one said a word; the only sounds heard came from the freed slaves celebrating down St. Ann Street to Congo Square, en route to give God praise.

"I should have killed him a long time ago," Marietta broke her silence. "Many nights I thought about killing him in his sleep, but I didn't. I knew the right time would come to kill him. Tonight, it was time for him to die."

Beatrice took Marietta by the arm and led her to the kitchen, where she quickly washed the blood off her sister's hands and arms. Eva ran into the bedroom and returned with another dress to replace the one Marietta wore, the one splattered with the blood of her former master. Marietta stood still while they washed and dressed her. She was emotionally numb, murmuring, "I should have stabbed him in the ass."

Marietta handed Beatrice the black ledger. "All of our children are in this book—all of them and more. The girls they haven't sold are somewhere between Clarice and Harriett Green. It's all there. We don't have to look too hard. He kept good records, even of the men who paid for our daughters. It's all there in that book."

Beatrice opened the book and read it. Eva looked over her shoulder. "Aunt Marietta, all of your daughters were sold, it's right here, and we have their names. Momma, there's a chance the twins are between Clarice and Harriett's houses."

Only then did Eva realize that Clarice also had her baby—her only child, conceived by the man who had raped her. Ulrich Green.

"My Lord! My Lord, Momma! Aunt Marietta! Clarice has my daughter that was taken from me. She has her in the house on Royal. They told me my baby died in her sleep. When I woke up, my baby was gone. Clarice has hid my child all this time! Clarice will pay for every night I cried."

Eva ran out of the house and down St. Ann Street, leaving her aunt and mother still standing in the kitchen.

"Time to pay Clarice a visit," Marietta said.

"Bring that knife," Beatrice replied.

11:35 p.m.

Marietta and Beatrice eventually caught up to Eva, thanks to Timothy, who had been driving around looking for his mother. The buggy came to a stop in front of the home where Clarice held their kids. The front door was open, but no one guarded it, nor was Clarice anywhere in sight. With the door open, they could hear the sound of children crying. The crying caused Eva to leap from the back of the wagon and run into the house. Marietta and Beatrice quickly followed.

Once they were inside, they saw a woman neither of them recognized, seated with three girls on the sofa. One after the other, the woman inspected the children. It became apparent to Beatrice that the woman was trying to identify which two out of the three frightened children were her kids. The woman wore a red scarf tied around her hair, and her dress was black with white trimming, like the kind worn by housemaids. She appeared to be in her late forties, with a very thin body frame and dark brown eyes. Once Eva walked over to the sofa, the woman examined her face and knew which two were her kids.

"That one ova' there must be yours," the lady said. The woman's skin was a mocha tone, but not as light as Eva's; maybe a few skin tones darker. Unlike Eva, she had jet black hair. Both of the little girls on the sofa had jet black hair that proved to be a perfect match. The one remaining girl on the sofa blinked dark blue eyes—the same eyes as Beatrice, as Eva, as Marietta. The other two girls had dark brown eyes, the same as the lady who had come for them.

"I can say for sure those are for you and that little girl is my granddaughter," Beatrice said. Beatrice opened the ledger book, which was still splattered with Mr. Lafitte's blood on the cover. She asked the woman her name.

"My name is Fannie," the woman replied.

In Lafitte's ledger, Fannie's name was recorded six times for having six daughters—all fathered by Lafitte. The two remaining girls were her last two held by Clarice.

"I feel you right," Fannie said. "Masta done took all my gals. I knew that bitch Clarice had my last two. Been following her for a long time, knew I would catch up to her one day." She grabbed the two girls by the arms and tried to leave the house, but the more she tried to get them to leave, the more they resisted. Clarice was the only mother they knew.

All three girls hugged and clung to each other on the sofa, calling out for Clarice and the other midwives. The more Fannie tried to separate the girls, the tighter they held onto each other.

Eva walked over to her daughter, who was just as hysterical as Fannie's daughters, and tried to sooth each of them by asking their names.

"Delphine," her four-year-old daughter said.

"Clara," said Fannie's oldest daughter, who was ten years old.

"Helena," Fannie's eight-year-old daughter said.

Eva sat down with the girls and gently told them she once lived in the same house with their nanny Clarice. It was only then did the crying cease. Eva explained that she too was taken from her mother as a baby. She then pointed to Beatrice. "This is my momma, and I look just like her."

Eva then asked Fannie to come over and sit down on the couch. Once Fannie was seated, Eva pointed out her full, jet black hair; the same texture as the two little girls.

"Look at that pretty hair! It's just like your hair, isn't it?" Eva asked. The little girls agreed. Fannie invited both of them to touch her hair, and they obliged. Eva continued, "Nanny Clarice is not your mother. This is your mother, and she has come to take you home." The crying stopped, and Fannie allowed her daughters to say goodbye to Delphine.

"We gon' be leavin'. My masta done took off runnin' to Hammond," Fannie said.

"I hope to see you around," Beatrice said.

"I hope to see you too, but in the morning we goin' Nort', up where they don't beat niggas. Where niggas been free."

"Where is that?" Eva asked.

"We going to a place called New Yorkah." With her two daughters hand in hand, Fannie walked out of the house on Royal.

"Fannie, where did Clarice go? Do you know when she'll return? I still need to ask her about my other children," Marietta called after Fannie.

"Oh, Clarice? She in da back of da house the last time I saw her. She should still be back there, I reckon," Fannie called as she continued down Royal Street with her two little girls.

Marietta said, "Eva, please take Delphine out to your brother in the wagon. We need to speak with Clarice before we leave."

Eva nodded and took Delphine by the hand. Delphine looked up at her mother with wide eyes. She still looked apprehensive, but did not protest as Eva led her out to the wagon.

Beatrice and Marietta headed to the back of the home on Royal in search of Clarice, one wanting answers, the other wanting blood. Marietta followed Beatrice through the house, passing the many beds that filled each room. There were no portraits on the walls, like there would be in a typical home, and very few toys. One of the rooms served as a classroom with a chalkboard.

The Royal Street home functioned as an orphanage, with the only difference being that all the girls housed inside were for sale at the quadroon ball. Handed over to the highest bidder. When they got to the very back of the house, Beatrice unlocked the rear door; that's when they saw Clarice and two of her assistants in the backyard.

All three of them hung from a tree, beaten and bloody, but none worse than Clarice. Her face looked like fresh ground beef from a butcher. Though she was barely recognizable, Marietta and Beatrice both positively identified Clarice. Her hands and arms had taken so many of their children that they knew every scar on Clarice, from her shoulders to her fingertips. It was her. It was her calloused hands. Her thick, leather skin, her scrapes and bruises that could only come from years in the sugarcane fields. It was definitely Clarice.

The backyard of the house was silent. The only sounds were those of the cracking ropes that hung the bodies. Other than that, it was peaceful. Clarice was finally peaceful.

"Looks like someone beat us to her," Beatrice said.

"Good thing for Clarice," Mariette said.

"Well, that still leaves Harriett Green," Beatrice replied.

"Yes, it does," Marietta said as she hid the knife under her dress.

⚜

May 1, 1862
11:58 p.m.

Danger and death polluted the air as some of the freed slaves took revenge on abusive masters. One block away from Harriett's house, directly on the corner, four black men were beating a white man unmercifully. The white man appeared in his late sixties. As they hit him, he called out for help, but no one stopped to aid him. One man held the elderly man up from behind with his arm around his neck while the other three men took turns punching him in the face.

As Beatrice and Marietta's buggy approached the scene, the man called out, "Help, please, help me, somebody!" It was then that Beatrice recognized the elderly white man. She asked Timothy to slow down just a little as she looked into the eyes of Mason, the slave trader. His beard was much lighter than the face she saw all-too-often in her dreams, but it was him.

"*Don't grow tired, boys,*" Beatrice called as she encouraged Timothy to continue to Burgundy and Barracks Street. "Take your time with him."

"Even if it takes all night. We owe Mason a good-ass whipping!" one of the men yelled back, causing the other three men to laugh out loud.

Once they arrived at Harriett Green's house, Beatrice and her family saw that a crowd had already gathered out front. The street was completely blocked in both directions with buggies and outraged parents; all had come for their children. On the porch stood Harriett Green. She aimed a shotgun at the angry crowd, spewing insults, blocking the door to her house, not allowing anyone in, and not allowing any of the girls to leave. The crowd was closing in on her.

"You don't have enough bullets to shoot all of us," a voice from the crowd yelled at Harriett. It was Beatrice.

The parents parted like the Red Sea as she and Marietta made their way through sixty people to Harriett's porch. Harriett aimed her gun directly at them. Every parent that stood in the street in front of Harriett's house had the same complexion. Some even looked purely European, but all of them were descendants of African mothers.

Out of all the people who convened in front of Harriett's house, few had suffered more than Marietta and Beatrice. Combined, they'd lost a total of fourteen girls to Harriet's enterprise, and two of Beatrice's daughters was still upstairs on the third floor, where all the debutantes were trained.

"Don't you two take another step on my property. Just turn around and go back where you came from," Harriett said.

"Harriett, I think you know I am not leaving here without my daughters Annette and Louise!" Beatrice said.

"Your daughters were sold!"

"Lies! You have both of my daughters on the third floor of this house, and I am not leaving here without them. My daughter Eva was also raped in your house, raped by your son Ulrich. She became pregnant for your son."

"I paid your master for that rape! After my son was viciously murdered, I received that baby as a gift. We do a lot of good business together, and he hated to see me pay so much while I was in a time of mourning. I intend to recoup my money off Delphine and the money I lost on Eva when I get my cut off Annette and Louise. I ain't letting none of these girls leave this house until I get my money. *All of it!*"

"Slavery ended tonight. I have come for my girls, and you have to answer to all of these people about their daughters. Only you can make this right, Harriett. Send out my daughters," Beatrice said.

"Beatrice, I suggest you step away from my porch before I send for Clarice. She has wanted a piece of you for a very long time. Now get on away from my door and take the rest of these niggers with you."

"Harriett, you can send for Clarice all you want to. She will never come."

"If I send for her, she will be here before you can step back in the street," Harriett said.

"I don't think so!" Marietta laughed. "Clarice and all her help are dead, hanging from a tree as we speak. That's where we found them, and that's where we left them. If you don't want to face the same death, I suggest you release those girls."

"Clarice is not dead! She is not! I talked to her around dinnertime. She sent food over here."

"Harriett, it's true. No need to lie to you. Clarice is dead, so drop the gun and release my daughters with the other girls you have upstairs," Beatrice urged.

It was only then that Harriett showed any fear or lost any confidence. Clarice was a vital part of her enterprise, and the commissions off the girls she raised made Harriett very wealthy. Together the two dominated a little niche market within the slave trade, a niche few people even knew existed.

"I will believe Clarice is dead when I see her dead body with my own two eyes."

"Stop pointing that gun at us and go see for yourself. Clarice is dead! Either you send out Annette and Louise, or I'm going in that house to get them," Marietta said.

"Over my dead body!"

"I am just fine with that," Marietta replied with a glint in her eye.

"I'm here for my daughters, Harriett, so either you shoot me or get out of the way. But I'm walking in that house," Beatrice said.

Suddenly, behind Harriett, the front door opened and out walked Annette and Louise, who'd heard every word from their dorm window. Harriett turned and pointed the gun at the girls. "Get y'all asses back in that house."

While her back was turned, Beatrice and Marietta rushed Harriett and grabbed her gun. It fired up into the air. Marietta took the knife she'd saved for Clarice and stabbed Harriett in the right thigh. Harriett fell to the ground in pain. Only then did she release her grip on the gun. Marietta pulled the knife from Harriett's leg and pressed it against her throat.

"We asked you nicely to release those girls. It didn't have to come to this. Now we're leaving with Annette and Louise, and those other girls inside are leaving with their families. That still leaves all these folks out here who also came for their daughters. Just remember we asked you in a nice way," Marietta said.

After Beatrice recovered Annette and Louise, they hurried to the wagon where Timothy was waiting to take them home. All but two of the debutantes were paired with their original birth mothers that night, and the two unclaimed debutantes went home with a mother who agreed to take them home with her daughter.

The crowd that remained started to converge on Harriett. All of them wanted information about their daughters, but Harriett refused to talk. Some of the angry parents began beating Harriett, while others searched her house for additional purchase ledgers, but none were found.

The beating on the porch continued until Harriett fell silent. She never spoke again after May 1, 1862, nor did she ever breathe again. By the time the crowd dispersed with most of her precious antiques and jewelry, the only thing that remained was her mutilated body, balled up on the front porch like a bloody sheet of paper.

In less than ten minutes, Timothy got them all home and tied the buggy. All the girls followed Beatrice and Marietta up the stairs to her living quarters. Later that evening Timothy and Lawrence joined them, and the rest of the night was filled with hugs and laughter!

Across the courtyard, from her second-floor window, Anne Fortier watched the blissful scene with joy. "Beatrice, I am so happy for you—I really am. You deserve this night after all you have gone through."

On the night the slaves of New Orleans were granted their freedom, Beatrice wrapped her arms around three of the seven daughters she had lost to slavery.

Annette.

Louise.

Eva.

And Delphine—her granddaughter!

CHAPTER 31

B randon camped out in Sherman's room and worked on their dissertation. A little over three weeks ago, his best buddy had been shot in the chest during the armed robbery, and the miracle that he had survived wasn't lost on Brandon. His recovery was going well minus a few setbacks associated with the collapsed lung. Also complicating his recovery was a recurring respiratory infection, shortness of breath, and spikes in his heart rate.

Nevertheless, Brandon was there every single day, all day. He relieved the nursing staff by helping Sherman into the shower and engaging in as much conversation as he could handle. It was hard for Brandon to see his buddy so weak and frail, but there was nowhere else he wanted to be.

The good news was he was dating Sherman's beautiful cousin, Jynika. Since Grandma Sue's funeral, they had been inseparable. Outside of the dissertation, she was all he could think about every hour of the day.

On one of those teal green hospital sofas that converted into a sleeper, Jynika sat with her laptop, researching footnotes for Brandon. She'd volunteered to help with Sherman's end of the research and writing until he recovered, an offer Brandon accepted without hesitation. Brandon found having a fresh set of eyes to line edit just as sexy as her tight jeans and Christian Louboutin heels. Jynika was just about through proofing Sherman's research on the Campbells when Brandon made a discovery.

"Hmmm, that's interesting."

"What's interesting?" Jynika asked.

"Just out of curiosity, I created a profile on Sherman's ancestry site for the Fortier family. What's interesting is most of the names that populated I recognized, but not this one—not at all."

"But wait, I thought the website Sherman developed was a genealogy database of African American families? Why are the Fortiers even mentioned?"

"I thought the same until this mutual name appeared."

"What's the name?"

"Annette Fortier," Brandon said. "When I searched our family tree from the certified record of our estate, I swiped from my dad, but her name was not mentioned in the category of blood relatives, nor do I see her listed as a descendant. What's even more peculiar is this website says there's a ninety-five percent chance Annette Fortier is directly related to Bernard Fortier, my great-great-great-grandfather. I get the feeling there's a story connected to this woman."

"Does the site say how she's related?"

"No, it doesn't, but I bet my father knows," Brandon said.

A nurse entered the room to administer Sherman's last batch of meds for the night.

"Excuse me, Brandon and Jynika, our visiting hours have ended." It was the same nurse who evicted them from Sherman's room every night around the same time.

Brandon and Jynika packed away their laptops and hugged Sherman before leaving. Sherman was sound asleep, still under the influence of a previous dose of meds. Brandon watched for a few more moments as the nurse attended to Sherman. He didn't want to leave his best friend, not even for a night, but in the intensive care unit, only Melvin and Yvonne were allowed to stay overnight.

Jynika nudged him by the arm out of the room. Sadly, they made their nightly hike back to the parking garage. Ever the gentlemen, Brandon carried Jynika's bags as they walked to her car.

"Still can't believe how close we came to losing him," he said. "If Sherman wouldn't have pulled through, it would have been a second funeral, back to back. I wouldn't have survived the grief. That's my roll-dog-for-life."

"I totally understand. We just buried my grandmother the day before, not even an hour to mourn her, when I received news about Sherman. My grandma would always say, '*The Lord never puts more on you than you can bear,*' but the jump from her funeral to the ER was too much for me. Way too much!" Jynika shuddered.

"I don't know how I would have made it through these three weeks without you by my side. And you jumped right in to help with Sherman's side of the paper. I'm so impressed with you."

"Sherman would have done the same for me, without a second thought. That's my cuz, and I love him," Jynika said.

"Well, what about me?"

"What about you?"

"Can I get some of that love too?"

"In time, in time. You're still on sixty-day boyfriend probation."

"Probation!"

"Yes, I said probation," Jynika laughed. "At the end of your probation, I might consider making you full time."

"Is that full time with benefits?"

"I guess I could throw in a few. Until then, I could fire you at any time," she giggled as they entered the parking garage.

His arm gently across her shoulders, her arm hugging him around the waist, they arrived at her car. The parking garage was empty; only a few cars enjoyed the spacious accommodations. Walking toward them was a lot attendant who collected trash left behind by hospital visitors. He was completely enthralled in a hands-free phone conversation, something regarding his mix tape that was soon to release. He nodded at Brandon as they walked by, then returned to his ear-bud discussion.

With her back pressed against the driver's side door, Brandon kissed Jynika.

"Happy anniversary," he said.

"*Anniversary?* What are you talking about?" Her neck rolled.

"We have been a loving couple for thirty consecutive days. Today is our one-month anniversary," Brandon laughed.

"Boy, bye," Jynika said as she opened her car door and started the engine. "Please let me know when you arrive home safely. I wouldn't want anything to happen to my thirty-day king."

As she drove off, she saw Brandon in her rear-view mirror, dancing like a ballerina while blowing kisses at her car.

Jynika smiled to herself. "He is so silly. Just one of the reasons I love him so."

CHAPTER 32

May 2, 1862
6:30 a.m.

A ll her kids, as well as her granddaughter and Marietta, were still sound asleep on blankets stretched out
across the floor. In the far corner of the room, Beatrice could see Marietta slowly waking up to greet the day, her
eyes opening like window shades, adjusting to the intruding sun.

"Good morning, Marietta," she said.

"Good morning, Beatrice."

"I see they finally ran out of things to talk about?"

"I think Eva and Annette just dozed off about an hour ago. I
just listened as they went on and on about any and everything.
Hearing their voices is more than I ever dreamed."

Today was the morning after liberation, a morning that formally introduced them to a new world and all the uncertainties
therein. Even her spirit struggled with this new concept called
freedom and all it entailed. Only yesterday, the room where she
slept was known as a *slave quarters,* but today, there were no
slaves in her quarters. Beatrice was free, with no clue as to what
it meant to be free. She was bewildered.

How do I act free?

How do I live free?

How do I look free?

Where do I go as a free woman of color?

But she was free. Indeed, the Union general had proclaimed it, and she was ready to embrace her new existence. All the former slaves shared the same struggles with this new word: *freedom*. Many of them were the descendants of three generations of chains, and knew no other life outside of servitude. Freedom was a word so unfamiliar, so unrecognizable, so foreign that it caused many of the former slaves to feel like refugees, even in a city they called home. Life in the French Quarter was known to flow effortlessly with the synchronization of a marching platoon—on the beat, in step—but not this morning. The right foot was before the left.

Yesterday, the natural sounds of the city were just as reliable as Beatrice's daily alarm clock. Consistent. Predictable. The conversations of black men who strolled past her window en route to their jobs on the shipyards, the resonance of their camaraderie, the *eau de toilette* of testosterone that trailed them; a damp, raunchy musk she deeply inhaled like oxygen. The clattering of milk bottles delivered on the other side of the courtyard, carefully placed to the left of the kitchen door by shaky hands . . . All of this was a guarantee, but not this morning.

The slaves who were forced to work the shipyard docks, carrying bales of cotton on their shoulders for no pay, were free. So too was the little old man who delivered milk every morning. A slave for more than seventy years, he was free.

The only consistent sound outside was the shuffling of a mass evacuation. People were leaving as fast as they could in hopes of following the Union Army to the North. They left in every available direction, by any and all means, totally oblivious that their newfound freedom was only limited to the extent of Orleans Parish and other occupied Union cities. Unfortunately for the former slaves, hundreds of Confederate townships were still plentiful in between New Orleans and the Promised Land.

Nevertheless, they left. Some left as couples, others in groups of six to fourteen, all interacting with approaching groups, sharing information, inquiring about lost loved ones.

A chorus of crying toddlers also filled the air. Discombobulated teens were forced to walk in unknown directions, their lives suddenly disrupted without explanation. Then there was another group; a horde of confused and frightened servants who found themselves homeless, all because their masters had fled in fear of the Union Army. The former servants were left to fend for themselves, without even a loaf of bread as a severance package.

It was this group in particular that didn't welcome freedom with the same enthusiasm as the others. Like standing in the aftermath of a tornado, their faces were filled with despair, world-ending horror, and debilitating uncertainty.

As was Beatrice.

From the kitchen came the sounds of pots, pans, and utensils settling into the bottom of large garlic sacks, followed by a raid of the chicken coop for fresh eggs. One after the other, the cooks and maids who had so faithfully maintained the Fortier home loaded as much as they could carry and prepared to leave. Just below Beatrice's window was Timothy, who stood right outside their door, not sure what to make of it all.

"Where y'all going?" Beatrice called out to one of the cooks who hurried towards the courtyard gate.

"You ain't heard that souljah man last night? We is free! Free to leave here and free to find work wit' *dem souljah men.* You now have ya master all to ya self, because we now free of him," one of the cooks replied, carrying a sack of pots.

"We goin' to dah *Promised Land,*" another maid yelled out with no fear of chastisement.

It wasn't that Beatrice loved Bernard Fortier more than her freedom, but four of her daughters were unaccounted for, and he was the only one alive who knew their whereabouts. Marietta stood beside Beatrice and held her hand as they watched the servants of 1005 St. Peter Street loot the kitchen and leave. In every corner of the Fortier home was a valuable piece of furniture or a painting, but the former servants only took the tools of their trades, and nothing more.

A maid and mops.

A cook and pots.

A nanny and diaper cloths.

Beatrice turned to her sister. "Marietta, you don't have to stay here with me. You now have your freedom as well. I do want you to stay with me because you're all I have, outside of my children, but I can't leave here until I know what happened to my daughters—all of them."

"And go where? I have nowhere to go and wouldn't dare step foot in that house with Lafitte. He will be stinking pretty soon. It's only a matter of time," Marietta said. "Beatrice, I'd rather stay with you and the kids if I can. I only have the rags on my back, but you can let Mr. Fortier know I'm willing to cook and clean for him if he would bless me with room and board. I also have to piece together as much of my family as I can. Have to find my children as well, and your master has all the answers."

"Marietta, he is not my master anymore," Beatrice said in a soft voice. "I have never been free. Gonna take a lot to get used to it. But he's none of our masters anymore," Beatrice replied.

From the rear, they heard footsteps walking across the balcony toward Beatrice's room. It was Anne Fortier. She stuck her head in the door.

"Good morning. Beatrice, may I speak with you for a moment?" Anne asked.

Beatrice agreed and followed Anne back to the main house, where they took a seat in the living room.

"Beatrice, all of this happened so fast. There hasn't been an opportunity to grasp it all. It was only last night that my husband confessed to being a slave trader, knowing full well how I feel about buying and selling people. Nevertheless, I pray God will forgive him of his sins. I also ask for your forgiveness on behalf of my family, because I was kept in the dark about his dealings."

"I know, and all is forgiven," Beatrice said.

"All of the servants have left the house. Some left last night, while the few that remained departed this morning. I have no nanny because Tullis has also departed with the cooks. We have no one to help keep the house. I saw that you were still here. I wanted to know your plans. Are you . . . planning to leave me as well?" Anne asked with her fingers interlocked, pressing down into her lap.

Beatrice took a moment to answer. She was at a loss for

words. This was her first time sitting in the formal living room, though she had lived in the house for twenty years. At one point or another, she had polished every piece of furniture in the house, but was never invited to sit on any of the four French settees in the living room. Imported in 1842 from France, the settees were covered in rich jacquard upholstery, with radiant hand-carved chestnut frames and glittery brass nail heads. Only the rarest fabrics from the most exclusive textiles factories in France were cut for the four settees in the living room, and Beatrice's hands could not resist the softness. Once her two-decade-old curiosity was satisfied, only then did she reply.

"Mrs. Fortier, I didn't plan to leave. I have nowhere to go; this is the only home I know. My sister is here, too. She has nowhere to go. Mr. Lafitte threw her outside last night when the soldiers from the North came. Quite a ruckus down there. Just awful, she told me. As for my kids, my sister, and me, we would like to stay here, if you would have us. Marietta can cook really good, and there are enough of us to keep this house. We don't ask for much."

"Oh, thank you, Beatrice, thank you so much. When they all left in haste, I didn't know how I was going to maintain this place. Yes, we would love to have you all, and I will compensate you for all services rendered."

They both stood. Anne immediately pulled Beatrice to her; they hugged. Suddenly, their embrace was joined by a third person as Anne's son Steven, who was now three years old, wrapped his arms around their legs. Beatrice hadn't seen little Steven in six months because Anne frequently took him to Amite to visit her mom. When they were home, his nanny Tullis usually kept him tucked away in the nursery.

Beatrice stared at the child. Only then did it become apparent why she hadn't seen much of little Steven.

His hair.

ANNE FORTIER
DIARY ENTRY TEN

May 2, 1862
4:30 a.m.

Dear Diary,

Hello, old friend, it's been a while since I've written you. Lord knows there was plenty I could have shared, but in the time it takes to thread a needle, my life has changed. The evil institution of slavery that was belched from Hell has come to an end, and only God is worthy of the praise.

Even though the stench of slavery is gone, it has left a great stain on my family. It is with great sorrow that I inform you this morning of the sins of my husband, sins I am not sure can be forgiven or atoned. Though all have fallen short of the glory of our Lord, including my own shortcomings, my husband has committed an enormity of offenses well beyond anything mentioned in the Holy Scriptures. Even if Bernard were forgiven for half of his transgressions, I'm afraid he would still enter Hell with little additional effort. Secretly, my husband was a slave merchant, an auction bidder of the worst kind, and a breeder of females. I'm still disgusted to learn of this, but there is no hole large enough to hide from these atrocities.

Moments before the Union Army declared their occupation of Orleans Parish, I discovered that my husband purchased Beatrice in the winter of 1835 and has since fathered all of her children—seven daughters and two sons, including Timothy. Yes, including Timothy.

To add more horror to my grief, all his daughters were sold as concubines at the quadroon ball. His own daughters! How could my husband—or any man, for that matter—sell his own daughters without a second thought? Bernard confessed that he entered the slave trade after the War of 1812. He claims he had to because the British closed all his trading routes. Along with Mr. Lafitte, he created an enterprise of quadroons and something commonly referred to as fancy boys—young black men with little African resemblance, sex servants by trade. Those were his products. I am mortified, absolutely mortified.

By the grace of God, one of his daughters was recovered prior to the quadroon ball, but it was only because Eva/Delicia was raped, which destroyed her value. My husband was reimbursed 2,800 dollars for his troubles. Imagine that! The poor child, a virgin, was raped by a monster, and Bernard was compensated.

His troubles?

What troubles?

How atrocious and vile! How demonic and devilish of him!

Still, he remains my husband: Bernard Fortier. If I could leave him right now, I would. If there was ever a just cause for divorce, I should think this is it. But this current crisis has pressed us tightly together like the orange bricks in the walls that surround the courtyard. I am enslaved in this marriage, with a life of lies that tread upon my head, over and over again.

There was a time I wanted to know everything about him; I wanted complete and total honesty. I wanted every door in his world fully accessible to me exclusively. Now that the curtain has been drawn, I would rather have the life of a street vendor, selling pecan candy to the whores who walk the streets at night, rather than pretend I have the greatest husband in the world. The truth is, I am married to the embodiment of the South and everything I detest about it.

Another revelation!

Dear Diary, I now know the reason for all of the long walks he took in the late evenings, rarely kissing me on the way out the door, and never kissing me when we made love—at least what I thought was love. The reason for the long walks was that my husband loves Beatrice. He has always loved her, and though she was his slave, she is his second wife, or perhaps my equal. Am I without fault or blame? Not at all, but it was his neglect and rejection that pushed me into the arms of another. My sins most certainly pale in comparison.

I always felt there was something about me he didn't find attractive—and then I took one good look at Beatrice. I should have stood firm in my objection. Then there would have been no competing lover right under my roof, but I also love Beatrice. In the end, I obeyed the advice of my mother and adhered to the laws of submission. My mother advised me to allow it.

How wrong was she? And how beautiful is Beatrice? How could any man resist Beatrice? Whether I care to admit it or not, Beatrice is the perfect assemblage of all God has created. And so, he loves her—but not the children he conceived with her. My husband may very well be the devil; which makes me Satan's wife, I presume?

He deserves my wrath.

Mistress Lucifer

CHAPTER 33

When Brandon arrived home, he could see his mom and dad talking in the living room through the large window in the front of their house. His mom held a cup of coffee, while his father held the remote. Because of his sister's efforts, Steven and Brenda were making a determined effort to heal their marriage. Growing up, Brandon could remember more peaceful days than arguments, more family vacations than door-slamming fights between his parents. He had no point of reference for the distance that had formed between them aside from recent events surrounding Sherman and Ronelle's engagement.

Brandon was convinced that had Ronelle not forced them to reconcile, his parents' marriage would be over. For that reason, he was truly grateful. Lately, there were more walks in the park, more charity events together, and more nights like tonight during which they just seemed to enjoy each other's company. To his delight, Steven Fortier was no longer sleeping at the condo—but Brandon was making full use of it with Jynika.

The outdoor security lighting and chimes notified his parents that someone was outside. Moments later, his dad stuck his head out the door to confirm it was one of his kids. Steven left the door slightly ajar so Brandon could come in, which he did, following right behind his father. He walked over to where his mom was seated in the living room and kissed her on the cheek. After giving his parents their daily update on Sherman, he decided not to waste another second with small talk. It was time to dig in.

"Dad, Annette Fortier! Why no mention of her . . . at all?

As Brandon waited for his father to respond, his mother excused herself from the room.

"Mom, please stay because I have questions for you as well."

"No, I'd rather your father deal with this one. Besides, it's his side of the family you're investigating." Brenda said.

Steven walked over to his cherished wine cabinet and grabbed the bottle of 1978 Montrachet he'd won in a bidding war hosted at an auction at Sotheby's of New York. When his dad popped the cork on the 28,000 dollar bottle of wine, Brandon knew he was about to hear something of significant importance. His dad frequently joked that if he were ever to lose everything, his wine collection would be all he needed to bounce back.

"Well, son, I found out about her the same way you did. My father never spoke of her or the rest of them, and he never allowed their names to be mentioned, either. However, I have known for some time that they existed."

Walking over from the kitchen area where he had poured a glass of his prized possession, he took a seat in his leather recliner. He had saved two bottles of Montrachet—one for the night he toasted the man Ronelle would decide to marry and the other for the day when one of his children would stumble upon Annette Fortier. Tonight, his coveted wine would age no more, and the truth would finally pour out, as well.

"Son, it was always a secret, and it remains a secret. Not only a secret kept solely by the Fortier family, but by the descendants of Annette Fortier as well. All I know is Annette Fortier had two daughters, Glenda and Gladys. One daughter was able to pass for white, while the other wasn't. The sisters were the products of an illicit affair, so when my grandfather died in 1941, a fight ensued over inheritance, and the one that passed for white formulated a side deal that blocked the other sister."

"Dad, who did Gladys strike a deal with? Who made the deal that blocked out Glenda?" Brandon wanted to know.

"Brandon, we remained on the sideline and allowed our trust fund to handle it."

"The Tureaud Trust? She made a deal with the trust to eliminate the other sister?" Brandon asked.

"Yes, The Tureaud Trust. As I said, that fight was not our fight. You should also know that I was not an eyewitness to these events. I was not yet born during this time. I was briefed on it by my father, the same way I'm briefing you. That scandal is still casting a very dark cloud over our family, but my dad made me promise to stay out of it."

"So, you never asked another question? Did you go along to get along, totally cool with sweeping it all under the rug? Dad, that's ridiculous! It was criminal what they did Glenda, and you know it!"

"Brandon, my father didn't give me the luxury to question his decisions. You should consider yourself lucky," Steven said in a stern voice. "I did as I was told and did not question my father's intentions or motives! I knew then that whatever offense we committed, it was in our best interests to let it collect dust."

Steven Fortier poured himself another glass of his treasured wine. He downed that glass, then poured another. "And that is all I know—and all I was privileged to know regarding Annette Fortier. Sadly, that was all my father felt I could handle. He trusted me enough to pass down a 150-year-old inheritance but didn't trust me with many of the family secrets. Legacy was everything to my dad, and to his dad, and so on," Steven said as he walked over to a five-foot oil painting of his father that hung on the dining room wall.

"Dad, the same thing Grandpa did to you—why are you doing it to me? You of all people know how it feels to get spoon-fed vital information, or to feel as if your dad doesn't think you're mature enough to handle the truth. Why?"

"Brandon, your grandfather wasn't the type of man you could push into the corner, and I knew not to cross any of his lines. I left it in the hands of the Tureaud Trust. Indefinitely. That one little office is the keeper of many secrets. You just happen to have stumbled upon one. Your grandfather gave the director of the trust his specific instructions; it was sealed. He took all details to his grave."

"Okay, Dad. I accept that much, but have you ever reached out to any of Annette Fortier' children?"

"No, because my father and his attorneys advised me against it. But it didn't take a scientist to figure out why. Opening that can of worms could lead to a succession battle that could tie up the assets of our entire company for decades. It's something I've always wondered about, but I just figured some secrets are better left secret. Brandon, listen to me. To find out the truth behind Annette Fortier could end up connecting additional people back to Bernard Fortier, which would eventually cost us more in the end. That's just not worth it."

"But, Dad, it would explain who we are! Who are we to hide what happened in the past as if it never happened? I'm sorry, Dad, but I can't support your position of just letting things lie. I want to know these people. I want to fix this!"

"Brandon, I am asking you as nicely as I can. Don't go down that road. Soon you'll replace me as CEO. Think about the future of this company—and this family."

"Is it because the children of Annette Fortier are African American?" Brandon asked. He walked over to the painting and stood behind his father. "Please don't lie to me!" Brandon yelled.

Steven did an about-face, bringing him nose-to-nose and toes-to-toes with Brandon, but he didn't answer.

"Is it because Annette Fortier leads to a black side of the family we never acknowledged? I demand you tell me!" Brandon exclaimed again, but his father sidestepped him and returned to the kitchen, where he refilled his glass of wine.

Brandon stared at the painting of his grandfather, who was immortalized standing on the side of his executive desk, arms stiff, fists clenched and pressed against the surface edge. Brandon recognized the desk; it was the same desk in his dad's office. The eyes of his grandfather made contact with his eyes. Their souls interacted for the first time as men in front of that painting on the wall, the one Brandon never acknowledged. Steven Fortier, Jr. cried out from his grave, cautioning his curiosity, but Brandon spoke back to his grandfather. *Grandpa Fortier, who is*

Annette Fortier, and why are you hiding her from me?

His dad, with his fourth glass of wine in hand, slouched on the red leather chesterfield sofa in the living room. In the next room over, Brandon continued to stare at the painting.

"Have you ever wondered why I never said anything about Sherman and Ronelle, or about you and Jynika?" Steven called to Brandon. "You think I don't know how hitched you two have become? You think I don't know you two have practically moved into my condo? Well, I don't have a problem with it, nor do I have a problem with two people of different races finding love. I believe . . ."

"Finding love?" Brenda said as she hurried back into the room, making it clear she had heard their conversation. "So now you and Jynika are dating?" she hissed. "What in the hell is going on, Steven? Why didn't you tell me about this? Don't I have a right to know about these things?"

Steven leaned back into the sofa and found a section of the ceiling to study. "Brenda, I didn't tell you because it's none of our business who Brandon dates!"

"The hell it isn't!" she yelled.

"Here we go again! You didn't learn a damn thing from the night you ruined Ronelle's engagement, did you?" Steven yelled back.

Brandon left the dining room painting and returned to the living room. To the left of Steven Fortier, Brenda. To the right of Steven Fortier, Brandon.

"Mom! Dad is right. It isn't any of your business who I date, and I'm not going through what you put Ronelle through. That's not happening!"

"Oh, my God, Brandon. Please don't tell me you're already having thoughts of marrying Jynika?" Brenda covered her mouth.

His silence spoke volumes.

Brenda stomped on the cherry wood floor. "Brandon, you are the first in line to everything this family has built, and I think it's time you start thinking like an heir!"

"You know what, Mom? Ronelle let you off the hook too easily when your hidden hatred for black people was uncovered, but I won't be so tolerant. If the fact that she's black is the only reason you dislike Jynika, then you and I have a major problem. I couldn't care less how you feel!"

Brenda pumped her fist into the air. "Brandon, I never said one damn thing about her race! Not one single word!"

"Then give me one reason why you don't like Sherman. Give me one reason why you don't like Jynika."

"Brandon, I'll do one better than that!" Brenda stormed out of the living room and down the hall to a utility closet. In that closet, behind a fake wall she had installed thirty years earlier when her husband was away on business, was a dusty safe. Inside that that dusty safe was one very precious item. Steven and Brandon were both standing shoulder-to-shoulder when she returned. She stormed over to the island in the center of the kitchen.

"I didn't want to do this . . . not now, not ever, but I am sick and tired of being attacked by the three of you and called something I am not, something I consider vulgar and disgusting!" With her index finger pointed at the center of her chest, she continued. "Racist! The nerve of all of you, to call me . . . a racist!" Her eyes watered with tears that never had the chance to fall, tears that were quickly absorbed by anger. "I would have my daughter—and both of you—know I am not a racist, not now, nor have I ever been. You asked me for one reason I'm against you marrying Jynika or Sherman marrying Ronelle. I will give you nine!"

From behind her back, she slammed a book on the counter—a timeworn book with loose-fitting covers and cream-colored pages. A book none of them, including her husband and the Tureaud Trust, previously knew existed.

ANNE FORTIER
DIARY ENTRY ELEVEN

May 2, 1862
8:10 a.m.

Dear Diary,

My old friend, I know I have written you once today, but in all my pain and tears, I forgot to inform you that all of our house servants abandoned us at the crack of dawn. Some took things that didn't belong to them; there was little I could do to stop them. Deep down, I didn't want to stop them from leaving.

My husband and Lawrence (his son) left in the middle of the night to secure our loading docks and prevent them from getting commandeered by the Union Army. They seem to take what they want without permission. A huge section of my soul is convinced that my husband ran off in fear of retribution by the Northern Army, especially since he received the news of what a soldier did to Mr. Lafitte. At least he died defending his home. Like a coward, my husband has yet to return. This one particular time, I pray my gut is wrong, but he still has yet to come back to his family.

Though there was not a single shot fired, the consequences of war are still equally unbearable. Timothy came to me this morning and asked for permission to stop the looting of our home, but I asked him not to interfere. Allow them to leave with something in hand, it was the least I could do. At the moment of my deepest despair, Timothy vowed he would never leave our son. That gives me great comfort. Timothy is my real protector, not my husband. He also suggested that I ask his mother if she would consider staying on and helping with the house, so I left him and Steven alone in my room and ran across the balcony as fast as I could.

It is with great joy that I report to you I have just spoken with Beatrice. She has agreed to stay, along with all her children—or shall I say, all our children. A new ray of hope came in the form of Marietta, a cook by trade; she too has agreed to stay and take over the duties in the kitchen.

Dear Diary, before I go, it would be remiss of me to not report the following life event. After all the slaves departed, Beatrice and I went room by room taking inventory of the possessions in the house. That's when we discovered one servant who remained. Delia was still in bed when we entered her room, peaceful as a dove. I've become aware that my lack of exposure to the realities of life has left me in a state of naivety I pray one day to overcome. Beatrice knew from the moment she opened the door.

Just last night, I saw Delia from my bedroom window, standing in the courtyard after General Benjamin Butler's declaration that honorably discharged her from service. I thank my Lord she lived to hear those liberating words. I watched Delia rejoice with the others. She danced, shouted, and lifted her hands. With great sadness, I report that the little old midwife, *Big Momma* to us all, went home to be with the Lord this morning. After eighty-two years of service, and many pans of pralines and calas, she died a free woman.

God bless the memory of my dear friend.

Momma Delia
Sun rose: May 2, 1780—Sun set: May 2, 1862

CHAPTER 34

July 30, 1866

The noon sun settled directly above the city and refused to move, baking everything that dared step foot outdoors. The heat was relentless and punishing, even in the shade. Beatrice and Timothy exited the courtyard gate on their way to the market to restock the pantry when they spotted a black man in the street. He was battered and bleeding from chest to waist. The man walked with a full tilt down Orleans Street, relying on a wall to keep him upright. Beatrice rushed to help.

"My Lord! Sir, you're bleeding! Let us help you."

They were just in the nick of time because the man was weakened, possessing only the strength for a few more steps before he collapsed on the sidewalk. Propping his arms across their shoulders, Beatrice and Timothy carried him the short distance to one of the vacant rooms once occupied by the cooks. They gently laid him on the bed. Beatrice unbuttoned the man's shirt to expose the area where the blood was coming from. It was then she realized the man had been viciously stabbed several times in his upper left shoulder. If she did not find a way to stop the bleeding, he would surely die. Timothy watched as his mother cleaned the stab wounds and applied a bandage, to no avail. The blood continued to pour. The bandage quickly turned a deep, dark burgundy, as did the mattress where he lay.

"Sir, I am Beatrice, and this is my boy, Timothy. You just lay right here, and we will do our best to stop this bleeding." Beatrice turned to Timothy, who stood behind her, helplessly watching the man die. "Timothy, go find a doctor or midwife. Go now. Hurry!"

Timothy took off to find help before his mother could finish speaking. The man continued to drift in and out of consciousness, and every time he regained consciousness, he'd ask, "Are you an angel?"

"No, I'm not an angel," she replied each time, only to watch him drift away again, slowly dying by the minute. While using all her strength to apply pressure to his injury, Beatrice couldn't help but notice the man stretched out before her. He was a very tall, dark-skinned man with a smooth, clean-shaven face. Beatrice could tell he had once been a slave from the iron brand on the right side of his chest. The brand *Rob Boy 38* meant someone named Robert had purchased him in 1838. Other than the scar tissue from the brand, his skin was flawless. When she grabbed his hands, she noticed how soft they were—like the hands of a baby.

Thirty minutes later, Timothy returned with a young medical student from Tulane who had just been leaving a delivery next door. The young student immediately joined Beatrice in her efforts to save the man's life. After what seemed like an eternity, the young medical student was finally able to stitch the lacerations and stop the bleeding.

The man was going to live.

Beatrice turned to the young doctor. "Sir, thank you so much for helping us. He would not have made it without you. Thank you!" She opened her purse to pay the young student out of the little money she had, but he declined.

"Ma'am, I can't take your money. I'm only a student, but thank you anyway. Your husband will need to stay in that position for the next forty-eight hours, getting up only if necessary. I can come back in a couple of days to check on him if you like."

Beatrice nodded, thanked the doctor again, and stood off to the side, staring at the man. Even though the physician was completely wrong in his assumption about her and this handsome gentleman, she liked the sound of *your husband.* Late into the evening, the doctor's voice echoed.

Your husband!

Ma'am, your husband!

That incorrect affiliation, that one mistaken association, caused her to realize that in her entire life, she had never considered being a man's wife. Beatrice had never harbored one single thought of having a husband. Like becoming President of the United States, the concept was just as far-fetched.

Today was as close as she'd ever been to any man other than Bernard. She sat in a chair across from the man and watched him sleep. She noticed that his shoulder bag was stuffed with books and papers. *This mighty fine black man can read,* she thought to herself. Beatrice badly wanted him to wake up, so she could hear him speak. She noticed a pair of reading glasses in the vest pocket of his suit. His clothes were made of the finest material, just like Bernard Fortier' suits. His shoes gleamed with a wet shine.

"He's beautiful. I have never seen a black man look so clean. He must be one of those men from up North that Marietta always talks about," she whispered to herself.

Oh, how she wished he would wake up—if only for a moment—for no other reason than to hear him speak. Beatrice decided to give her patient space to rest as she prepared a bed in the living quarters next door to him, just in case he should wake.

Around noon the next day, the man woke up!

When she heard the man tossing in the bed, Beatrice quickly returned to her chair—the same chair she'd sat in for hours, watching him late into the night, waiting for him to wake. She wanted her face to be the very first face he saw when he opened his eyes, and it was.

He smiled. "It's . . . the angel again."

She blushed "No, just me."

"I died yesterday, and God sent you down here to carry me

away from this hell. But I'm still here. If I have to be here, then at least I am in the company of a beautiful angel . . . an angel on earth, refusing to fly away."

Beatrice smiled. "Thank you, sir, but I'm no angel."

That voice! She'd waited twenty-four hours to hear that voice again. He spoke in a deep baritone, the same as a seasoned Methodist minister. She had never heard any black man speak with such clarity and perfection. As he struggled to pull himself to an upright position, Beatrice was in complete awe of his strength.

"Sir, please don't move. The doctor said you should remain still if you can."

But he continued to rise until his back rested against the headboard of the bed. He sat in full view of Beatrice, shirtless. She could see all of him, and she loved it. Beatrice could tell that his hair and beard had been maintained in a salon parlor. *But where?* she wondered. Where could a black man go to receive the same services as a white man? She had to know what part of the world produced such a god of a man.

"How do you do, sir? My name is Beatrice."

"Hello, Beatrice. My name is Thaddeus Calvin Hooks."

"You have three names, sir? Most of us around here only have one. Why do you have three names?"

"I'm not from around here; at least, not lately. I'm here for the Republican Convention, and we were attacked by a mob of angry white men. Every black man in my delegation was murdered, slaughtered like hogs. Thank you for saving my life."

"You're welcome, but . . . what is a Republican Convention?" Beatrice asked.

"Well, Beatrice, it's a gathering of the only group in this country crazy enough to stand up for us. I thank God for them every time I pray, and you should as well. Just when I was ready to call on God to kill every white man on Earth, a group of white men—Republican men—risked their lives for a bunch of slaves. Out of the turmoil and bloodshed of the Civil War emerged a victor. Tensions remain high throughout the Southern states, and especially among politicians—you know, those who make laws for the country."

Beatrice nodded her head as if she understood entirely, but many of the words he used were foreign to her. She wanted him to continue. She loved his voice.

"It is a bad situation down here. The white community is seeking revenge, while the black community is seeking rights. There is no middle-of-the-road. But I thank God for the Radical Republicans and their efforts to rid us of these black codes of segregation. After what I experienced yesterday, I doubt if I will see real change in my lifetime, but I don't regret joining the fight."

Thaddeus had been an organizer at the convention and was a member of the Black Delegation of Greater New Orleans. He had escaped from slavery in 1850 and made his way to Boston, where he was formally educated and worked as a teacher. Now fifty-two years old, he wanted to come back to New Orleans and help educate many of the former slaves in the city, believing education was the best way to improve their quality of life. His mission was needed, honorable, and essential to the transition of the black community, but there was just one thing standing in his way—Southern residents who blamed former slaves for their financial hardships.

"I saw your hot brand. When did you get set free?"

"I was not set free. I ran to freedom. I was not too far from these parts in a town called Amite, Louisiana, which is right above Hammond. A Methodist congregation helped me escape. They shipped me all the way up to Boston, and I have been free ever since. That was sixteen years ago."

"Did you have a wife and kids in Amite?"

"No, ma'am, I've never been married. Nor did I want my master to pair me up with someone. I wanted to love on my own, not because Master needed more babies."

Thaddeus had just described her entire world in one statement. Every word he spoke sounded like the music she enjoyed in Congo Square. Thaddeus was well educated, and a former slave. He knew what it was like to be in bondage. Most importantly, he knew what it was like to experience freedom. Thaddeus was one of those black men Marietta had told her about after she accompanied Mr. Lafitte up North to attend his mother's funeral. Beatrice thought Marietta had fabricated the tale until Thaddeus spoke. She knew from the moment she heard his voice there was a whole new world out there—a world she had never experienced.

He cleared his throat. "Let's talk about you. Who lives here with you in this breathtaking mansion?"

"I live here with the man who was once my master, his wife, five of my children, one granddaughter, and my twin sister. Her name is Marietta."

"You have five children, but you said you have no husband. Did he die in the war?"

"My master is the father of my children."

Thaddeus nodded as her situation became clear to him. She was a New Orleans mulatto woman, the sex product of a white man and a woman of color. This gene pool experiment had produced a multitude of skin tones and biracial offspring. Now that slavery was over, the evidence of rape was everywhere. Very few slaves born with skin as pale as their masters were involved in consenting relationships. Most pregnancies were the result of rape by a white man of an enslaved woman.

"May I ask you another question?"

Beatrice didn't mind his questions. He was the first man to show genuine interest in her outside of her master, because she was too white for the slaves in her area. None of the available black men in the neighborhood would have dared approach her out of fear of getting lynched. Not to mention, her former master still tried to dominate her life, although he no longer pulled the string over her bed for sex. His wife had ripped down the bell a few days after Beatrice was set free.

"Ask me whatever you like," Beatrice replied.

"Why have you remained with your former master? Slavery has ended; you're free. Why stay? You are free to leave. Help me to understand why you've decided to stay."

"Well, sir, my master sold most of my children. His wife has agreed to help me find them because she didn't know he was a slave owner. Mrs. Fortier is a good woman and a woman of her word. Now that we are free, we get paid for our work around the house, more than most Negroes make around here. They're real good to us, real good!"

At that moment, Beatrice heard Timothy's voice as he halted the buggy. Bernard Fortier was his passenger. Beatrice hurried to put distance between herself and Thaddeus. Deep down, she still felt like she belonged to Bernard. Even in the presence of a single, available man, Beatrice displayed the mannerisms of a hitched woman, as if she were someone's property, another man's woman.

Timothy was first through the door, then her former master, Bernard Fortier, entered the room.

"Greetings. I'm Thaddeus Calvin Hooks of Boston," he winced in pain as he tried to stand up.

"Don't bother standing. Timothy has shared with me the extent of your injuries," Bernard said.

"Thank you kindly, sir. I am a schoolteacher here to establish schools for former slaves. I come to spread good will and the gift of learning."

"Nice to meet you, Mr. Hooks."

There was no formal handshake between Bernard Fortier and Thaddeus Hooks—just the traditional nodding of the head, which was customary in the meeting of two gentlemen. This event was historical in itself because this was the first time Bernard Fortier ever acknowledged a former slave as a gentleman.

"I pray you have found your accommodations comfortable as you recover?" Bernard asked.

"Yes, sir, and I'm most appreciative to you and your household for saving my life. I have no money to repay you, but I'm a skilled carpenter and teacher. Therefore, I hope you will give me the opportunity to return this good will."

Beatrice could tell Bernard Fortier was just as impressed with Thaddeus as she was.

"Indeed, your offer comes at a time of great need for skilled craftsmen. I have an active construction project that's falling way behind schedule. I could use more manpower—that is, once you're healthy enough to contribute," Bernard said.

"Thank you kindly, Mr. Fortier. I look forward to joining your crews."

"Very well. Continue to make yourself comfortable and enjoy the food prepared by my excellent cook, Marietta. You are now a guest in my home," Bernard Fortier said.

Bernard Fortier and Timothy nodded "good day" to Thaddeus and headed into the kitchen by way of the courtyard. Once inside, he notified the rest of the family that Mr. Thaddeus Hooks was his guest, and to make him feel welcome. Little did Bernard Fortier know, Beatrice intended on making Thaddeus feel more than welcome.

February 13, 1867

Seven months had passed since Beatrice discovered Thaddeus stumbling down Orleans Street, and six months since he signed onto Bernard Fortier's construction project. The project was on track to finish ahead of schedule. Thaddeus had downplayed his skill set but over-delivered once he arrived on the job site. When he was a slave in Amite, Thaddeus had supervised work crews of builders for his master, who was one of the wealthiest plantation builders in the state. When Thaddeus escaped to freedom, it devastated his company because the slave master could not read architectural designs; Thaddeus was an expert at reading designs. Bernard Fortier quickly recognized Thaddeus as someone unique, because his most experienced supervisor was learning a thing or two from the new addition.

Even Timothy was learning how to read designs from Thaddeus, as well as the art of framing a house. Whereas his brother, Lawrence, was the understudy for Bernard Fortier, Timothy became the understudy for Thaddeus. Timothy began to emulate everything about Thaddeus, from his pattern of speech to the clothes he wore on Sundays . . . even the sweet flavor of tobacco he smoked in his pipe. On Sundays, Timothy also smoked a pipe as he walked the streets with Thaddeus, learning about life in the North.

Beatrice loved every minute of it. Every day, she watched Thaddeus return from the job site, leading a group of men who followed him to the doorstep just to hear more of his stories and lectures. Thaddeus had become their leader on and off the job. In the evenings, Beatrice always made sure his room was spotless when he returned; a task she reserved for herself. She made sure all his work clothes were washed and pressed. Beatrice also made Thaddeus three Brooks Brothers-style suits to wear on Sundays. Each morning, she delivered his breakfast to his room, and in the evening, she returned with a full meal. She grew deeper in love with Thaddeus with each passing day.

As did Marietta.

Beatrice didn't see it coming, but Marietta did, and she set a plan in motion to win his heart. Beatrice felt like Thaddeus was her man. She had seen him first, she'd saved his life, and to her, that settled it. Marietta couldn't care less who saw him first, as long as her face was the last one he saw at night for the rest of his life. The battle was on.

The following day around noon, Beatrice noticed that Marietta was missing. Marietta and Beatrice discussed everything, so it was unlike her twin to leave without informing Beatrice of her plans. On a hunch, Beatrice went down to the job site, and there was Marietta with a lunch basket, waiting for Thaddeus.

"That heifer!" Beatrice took several deep breaths to calm her rage, but it didn't work. "I cannot believe her. Marietta is trying to steal Thaddeus away from me."

She watched from a distance as Marietta handed Thaddeus the basket of food. She saw the way Marietta pranced around him and giggled like a thirteen-year-old girl. Marietta was a master of seduction; her body language, the way she whipped her sandy blonde hair from side to side, the batting of her deep blue eyes, and the way she leaned into Thaddeus and spoke with a weak, airy voice.

To Marietta, Thaddeus was her dream man. Beatrice, from the moment she cleaned his stab wounds, wanted him for herself.

Suddenly the site horn sounded, and all the men returned to work. Beatrice continued to stalk her sister, knowing what city blocks she would turn down en route back to St. Peter Street. One block from their house, they collided face-to-face, like two ships trying to anchor in the same dock.

"How dare you try to steal my man?!" Beatrice snapped.

"Your man? Mr. Fortier is your man!" Marietta snapped back.

"Marietta, you know damn well Bernard doesn't touch me, hasn't in six years. How could you go behind my back like that and take food to him? How could you be so low?"

"Beatrice, you never said one word about Thaddeus being your man! You spent all of your time making sure you didn't hurt old Massa Fortier's feelings by standing too close to Thaddeus. Now, all of a sudden, you're mad at me because I can be with him. He likes me, Beatrice. Why can't you be happy for me? Be happy that I found the perfect man."

"Lies! He doesn't like you! You threw yourself at him, that's all! You did not find a damn thing. I found him! I saved his life! All you have done since he's been here is flaunt yourself," Beatrice yelled.

"And you don't? I watch you run across the court every morning with food! You never lifted one pot in this house until Thaddeus moved in! In the evening, you serve him dinner I cook in the hot kitchen all day. Never once told him I cooked it. But he knows now. I made sure of it."

The two sisters continued down the street, engaged in an argument that became so heated it echoed off the buildings on St. Peter Street as they approached their house. A full-blown catfight. Beatrice grabbed Marietta by the sleeve of her thick, quilted dress so hard it ripped from the collar down across her chest, leaving her right breast exposed. Marietta was unfazed. By the neck, Marietta slammed Beatrice against the brick wall alongside their house, only feet away from the courtyard gate.

"Beatrice, don't make me hurt you!"

"How, Marietta? How would you hurt me? By cutting my throat like Mr. Lafitte and Ulrich? Bitch, you have already cut my throat!"

Anne Fortier, upon seeing the exchange, handed her son to Eva and ran to the gate to stop the fight.

"Ladies, get in here right now," she ordered. Both sisters sighed and followed her into the dining room.

"Please tell me this fight between two sisters—two women I love—is not about the attention of Thaddeus. How dare you allow a man to come between you?" Anne Fortier scolded. "Ladies, you know very little about Thaddeus! Why do you fight like this? He's here today, but tomorrow he could very well stumble into another town and another heart. The two of you are sisters forever. Forever! I will not have you two fighting over this man. I don't know what has to take place for this nonsense to cease, but it will cease today. We are family!"

Beatrice and Marietta just stood there like two heavyweight boxers waiting for the next bell to ring, never making eye contact with Anne. They remained silent, but were determined to continue the fight. Anne was already too late. Beatrice had claimed Thaddeus in her heart. In Thaddeus, she saw her first chance at real love—the opportunity to have her very own husband for the first time in her life.

Marietta had also claimed Thaddeus in her heart. Over the years, she had slowly given up on finding any of her daughters. It had been too long, and none had appeared. Every lead Mrs. Fortier had followed to try to find them turned out to be a dead end. The men who had bought them, as named on the ledger, had apparently fled the city, because Anne had no leads. Marietta decided to stop dreaming and focus on what was in front of her: Thaddeus. He was her ticket out of New Orleans; an opportunity to live the second half of her life up North.

Neither of the sisters responded to Mrs. Fortier, because Thaddeus had already come between them.

CHAPTER 35

February 14, 1867
11:45 p.m.

It was around midnight, and the entire house had long since shut down for the evening. Thaddeus was awakened by the silhouette of a woman standing at the foot of his bed. Her perfume had completely transformed his room from the natural aroma of testosterone to the luxurious fragrance of a flower garden in spring.

"Beatrice, is that you?" he called out to her as she drew closer to him.

Crouching on the side of his bed, she kissed him on his neck with a gentle press of her lips and a few naughty nibbles from her teeth. His hands surveyed her breasts. The heat from her body transformed his drafty living quarters to a cozy hub. She wanted him. She made use of the full moon to admire his face and body. All the years of hard work had chiseled Thaddeus like a Roman sculpture; not an inch of blubber to pinch, the arms of a god still attached, and the neck of prized oxen. His face reminded her of the photos she'd seen of Frederick Douglass, but Thaddeus was much darker than the influential lobbyist.

She stood for a brief moment, allowing him to appreciate a

full view of her, as much as the moonlight would allow. Curiosity had gotten the best of her body, so she mounted him like a stallion, slowly and gracefully. Not a second later, she welcomed him inside, gasping from the sudden pressure. He was much larger than her former master, so she struggled to adjust. He felt good. The way he filled her up inside felt good, so she continued her ride. She wanted to scream in ecstasy, but wouldn't. She wanted to moan until the walls shook, but couldn't risk the noise.

Then came the poetry, her passionate lyrics, sung in whispers in between gasps of air. Thaddeus was under the influence of a serum she had purchased from Marie Laveau and placed into his wine at dinner.

"Oh, Thad. Oh, Thad. Oh, Thad. Will you have me, Thaddeus? Will you have me, Thaddeus? Can I feel this every night, Thaddeus? I want to be your wife if you would have me. Can I please be your wife?"

She continued to stroke him with her body until she heard him say the words she wanted to hear. "Yes, I will have you! Beatrice, I stayed here just for you. I am not leaving here without you."

Then she felt it, like a blast of warm wax; she had conquered his body. In the aftermath of intense pleasure, she rested on his chest. After five minutes passed, the serum recharged him. He wanted more.

"Beatrice, break time is over. Let's do that again."

As soon as Thaddeus sat up to flip her over, the door to his room blew open.

"Marietta, you bitch!"

Beatrice entered, holding a lantern that illuminated the entire room. Thaddeus rose up and looked Marietta in the face. He saw the scar.

"Wait, Marietta, you let me think you were Beatrice?! I even called you Beatrice, and you never said a word. Why would you do that?"

Marietta stood up and slid on her nightgown. Angrily, she stared at Beatrice, totally unapologetic. "Beatrice, I see you still enjoy listening to the walls. Did you like what you heard?"

"Marietta, I see you still like stealing. Maybe if Mrs. de Marigny had smashed the other side of your mouth under that rocking chair, you would have learned your lesson. Then again, once a thief, always a thief," Beatrice growled.

Marietta walked across the room to where Beatrice held the lantern. "Steal? What did I steal? He's not your man."

"Marietta, you know how I feel about Thaddeus! How could you trick him into thinking . . ."

"Thaddeus is a grown man! How about we ask him to decide right now, tonight?!" Marietta stood at the foot of the bed, while Beatrice stood a few feet inside the door in the far-right corner of the room. Marietta shifted her focus back to Thaddeus. "Mr. Handsome, you can only have one. Which one of us will you have as your wife?"

"Thaddeus, you don't have to answer her. I know she tricked you," Beatrice said.

"She's right. I allowed you to think I was Beatrice because she was chasing after you like a hound dog, knowing full well she can't be your wife. Thaddeus, you just made love to me, not Beatrice. I pleased you, not Beatrice. We are twins, but I would make a better woman for you, and you know it. So, which one will it be, Thaddeus? You have to decide this tonight. If it's Beatrice, I'll leave in the morning."

One leg at a time, Thaddeus put on a pair of tailor-fitted slacks, adding a white business shirt that was buttoned halfway—all of which Beatrice had sewn for him. "I never wanted to come between sisters. It's not fair to put me in this position."

"Marietta, you know damn sure well Thaddeus did not make love to you. He made love to me, thinking you were me! I never thought I would see the day you would stoop so low as to steal a man like this!"

Marietta slowly walked toward Beatrice with her fists clenched. "Beatrice, I'm going to say this one last time. I did not steal Thaddeus from you, because he does not belong to you."

Standing face to face with Beatrice, Marietta's frown quickly transformed into a smile, then laughter.

"Beatrice, you could never have a man like Thaddeus. All you have known all your life is one man, the father of your children, Anne Fortier's husband. The man standing behind you! *Ha!*"

Directly behind Beatrice stood Bernard, who had secretly followed Beatrice through the night as she raced to Thaddeus. Beatrice turned to face him. "What are you doing here?"

"Beatrice, I love you. I have always loved you."

"Bernard, don't do this! I don't owe you anything. I have given you all I have to give."

"Beatrice, I love you, you know I do."

"When you paid for me all those years ago, I thought your face was the kindest face, but I was fifteen years old, and didn't know no better. Your face is just as dark and evil as your heart. You don't love me. You loved what I gave you, and the money I made you with every one of my girls you sold away. The only reason you down here is to keep me from loving this man. But I know you, I know your ways, and this doesn't have anything to do with love. This is about your property. I've been free seven years now, master of my own body, master of my own heart. Your wife called me 'sister' yesterday, and she's right—we are family. All of us, including that backstabbing cow over there."

Thaddeus interrupted. "Mr. Fortier, I did not touch Beatrice in any way, sir, and I apologize for all of this confusion this evening."

"Thaddeus, there is no need to apologize. You have done nothing wrong," Bernard said. "Beatrice, I do love you, and many nights I thought about marrying you, but I couldn't."

It was then that Thaddeus walked over to Marietta and got on one knee. "I'm taking you out of this equation tonight, Marietta. Will you marry me and be my wife?"

"Yes, Thaddeus, I would love to be your wife!" Marietta emphatically replied.

Beatrice turned back to Bernard Fortier. "I hate you, and I will hate you until I die!" She blew out her lantern and sobbed out of the room.

The room faded to black except for the light of the moon. Thaddeus quickly lit another lantern that was beside his bed, and there standing behind Bernard was Anne Fortier. She had followed her husband across the courtyard as he had followed

Beatrice—just as it had been throughout her entire marriage. Anne had heard it all and knew it all. Bernard walked past his wife without saying a word and headed back to his bedroom.

"I will give you two weeks to find another place to live. Two weeks and not a day longer," Anne Fortier told Thaddeus and Marietta as she left the room and slammed the door.

The following morning after breakfast, Anne Fortier found Beatrice with her granddaughter, Delphine, and her daughters Eva, Louise, and Annette. A sewing class was underway in Beatrice's living quarters; the passing down of her trade and as many life lessons as she could squeeze in. Anne stuck her head in the door.

"Beatrice, I am sorry to interrupt. May I have a quick word with you, please?"

Beatrice excused herself from the class on following patterns, leaving Eva to continue in her place. Anne looked beyond Beatrice's back into her living quarters.

"Look at those beautiful girls. It must make your heart full to see them interacting like that," Anne complimented. "It amazes me how quickly they have all bonded—almost as if there were never any separation at all."

"Mrs. Fortier, I thank God for . . ."

"*Anne*. Beatrice, please called me Anne."

"I'm sorry, it's just an old habit, but I thank God for you every day, Anne. I do. You made it so we can all live here, under one roof, not from pillar to post."

Anne could feel her sadness. It was typical for Beatrice to smile through her pain, but few women could smile after watching their sister walk away with the man they loved. Anne held Beatrice by the shoulders.

"Beatrice, if I could have shielded you from the pain of last night, I would have. I am so disappointed with Marietta for allowing Thaddeus to come between you. I said it yesterday, and I will say it again. Men come and go, but a sister is forever."

"Thank you so much, Mrs. Fortier. It does hurt a lot, but that's Marietta. When she wants something, she takes it—no matter who she steps over to get it. Marietta was just being Marietta. That's all."

"I know, Beatrice, but I still don't like it. My husband being there only made matters worse for all parties involved."

"I'm sorry you had to see that."

"Beatrice, you don't have to apologize. I know what my husband did to you all those years. Everything you said to him was true. He doesn't love you like he thinks he does. It was the thought of you being with Thaddeus that drove him mad. And mark my words: Marietta will one day realize what she lost in a sister. If not for you keeping all of this together, we would not have made it. We are all here today because of you. Thank you, Beatrice."

"No need to, Mrs. Fortier. You have done more than enough for my family and me."

Anne grabbed Beatrice by the shoulders again and playfully shook her. "Beatrice, for the hundredth time, just call me Anne." Beatrice smiled and nodded her head. "Beatrice, I almost forgot why I came down here. I need to ask a little favor of you."

"Sure, what do you need? I will get it done."

"I would like for you to prepare a very special Sunday dinner today, a dinner we will eat as a family in the formal dining room. Please have everyone dressed in their Sunday best when I return around noon."

Before Beatrice could ask any questions, Anne gave her a hug and a kiss on the cheek, then headed out the front gate where Timothy was waiting for her in the buggy.

Beatrice headed to the kitchen to prepare the Sunday dinner, but the task proved very difficult. Across the courtyard, Beatrice could hear Marietta laughing and giggling with Thaddeus. A lifetime of eavesdropping came to an end that morning. The courtship of Thaddeus and Marietta was just that painful. If felt like Thaddeus's voice vibrated everything in the kitchen; that voice she loved so much yesterday backed her up against the wall and punched her in the gut, repeatedly. The more stories he told, the more Marietta poured it on.

The more Beatrice tried to prepare the food, the louder Marietta laughed. To Beatrice, her sister was laughing at her as she took a victory lap around her broken heart. Eva could hear it too.

If it were meant for me to have, then I would have it, Beatrice consoled herself.

Several times, Eva walked over to her mother and consoled her.

"Momma, don't worry about them. They will be gone soon."

Only then did Beatrice refocus. Eva and Delphine joined in the preparation of the meal and tried to get Beatrice to redirect her mind. Over the next three hours, they prepared a meal fit for Thanksgiving, with garlic roasted chicken, fresh-baked bread, stuffed baked potatoes, buttered corn, a side of Spanish rice, and vanilla cream cake. The cooking was finally done. They all headed back to their rooms to change.

When Timothy arrived, Beatrice was waiting in the dining room, Bernard Fortier was upstairs, looking out of his bedroom window. No sooner did Timothy tie up the buggy did Annette come running through the courtyard, yelling, "They're back! They're back!"

Anne called out from the kitchen area. "Beatrice, where are you, my dear?"

"I'm in the dining room, Mrs. Fortier . . . I mean, Anne!"

Seconds later, Anne entered the dining room, followed by a young lady with two little girls. Eva was standing next to her momma when the young lady entered the room.

"Oh, my Lord," Beatrice said.

Her knees gave out, but she did not faint. Timothy and Lawrence rushed over to help Beatrice into a chair. Moments later, Beatrice regained her faculties just enough to stand.

"It's you. It's my baby, my beautiful baby they took from me!" Beatrice said as she reached for Rose.

For twenty minutes, Beatrice held Rose, cried, kissed her face, then pulled her back to her bosom. Beatrice released Rose long enough to hug the person who had made the reunion possible—the one who had kept her promise.

"Anne, thank you! Thank you so much! My God, thank you! You have brought me back a piece of my heart today!"

When Beatrice released Anne, she returned to Rose.

"You look exactly as you appeared in the water. Your face has never left my heart since the day you were born, and I knew exactly who you were the day I saw you at that ball," Beatrice said.

Rose wiped the tears from her mother's face. "I felt something when I saw you, all those years ago. You looked so familiar. I think in my heart I knew. Mrs. Fortier contacted me last week, and I could not believe how close I lived to you. I live on St. Roch and St. Claude Street, a few short blocks away, and here you are on St. Peter Street. I give God praise for this day. They told us you were dead, but you're alive!"

"I am alive, in my right mind, and I have never stopped looking for you. And who are these two little angels with you?"

"These are your granddaughters, Sarah and Scarlet. They're eight years old."

"My Lord, are they twins?"

"Yes, Momma, they are twins."

It was Rose who had borrowed the most from her mother. Only she was taller, with darker blue eyes than Beatrice. She had the neck of a swan in late spring, graceful and elegant. A perfect carbon copy she was, a living, breathing embodiment of a New Orleans mulatto woman, with all of the French etiquette to match. The only distinguishing difference was in their upbringing. Beatrice was never formally indoctrinated into the protocols of the quadroon. Unlike Rose, Beatrice had learned on her back how to conform and comply with all that her master preferred. She was the mold for the perfect concubine.

Beatrice took her seat in the chair and pulled both of her granddaughters to her side. Eva ran over to Rose, and they hugged. They hadn't seen each other since their days on the third floor of Harriett Green's house.

The thunderous sounds of joy that blared from the dining room drowned out Thaddeus and Marietta. Once the dinner and all the dishes were put away, Beatrice and her kids headed upstairs to her room. In a single file, they walked up the stairs, with Marietta watching from below.

Beatrice enjoyed a wonderful dinner with four of the seven

daughters Clarice had stolen from her, daughters she thought she would never see again. Only Alaina, Sophie, and Phyllis—who Clarice had named Mattie, Tempie, and Emma—were unaccounted for, but her determination to find them was now stronger than ever. Unfortunately for Marietta, she had burned her only potential bridge to her daughters just the previous night.

While walking up the stairs, Beatrice made eye contact with Marietta, blew a kiss to her, and waved goodbye. The sisters who were separated at age eleven when Marietta was sold to Mr. Lafitte were separated again of their own free will. Marietta and Thaddeus moved into Mr. Lafiette's old place the following week, and he was allowed to keep his job with Bernard Fortier.

Beatrice and Marietta never spoke again.

CHAPTER 36

S he couldn't stand to sleep at the apartment anymore without Sherman. As she packed an overnight bag, she decided to sleep at her parents' house tonight. After a short drive down St. Charles Avenue, Ronelle entered the front door utterly oblivious to the huge fight in progress, but she immediately sensed that the tension was thick. Her dad was sweating profusely. Brandon's hand covered his mouth. Her mother's face was red as a jar of cherries.

"What's going on here?" Ronelle asked. Then she noticed all three of them staring at a book on the counter. Reading the cover of the book, she asked, "Who is Anne Boleyn Fortier?"

"Anne Boleyn Fortier was married to Bernard Fortier. She was my great-great-grandmother," Steven replied.

Ronelle raised her eyebrows. "Okay."

"Brenda, I can't believe you've kept this from me all this time," Steven said.

"Steven, once you read the pages of this diary, you will understand why I tried to bury it."

Steven finally picked the diary up off the counter. "Brenda, how did you get this?"

Brenda took a deep breath and revealed her deepest secret. "Steven, you may not remember this because it was a while ago, but in 1983, you once asked me to facilitate the donation of some antique furniture to the New Orleans Museum of Art."

"Yes, I remember the museum from an exhibition that ran for about seven years."

"Correct, from '83 to '94, to be exact. Well, before making the donation, I hired a furniture restorer to make sure all the pieces were in the best condition possible, and he was the one who found the diary hidden in the bottom of a chest. A chest that belonged to none other than Anne Boleyn Fortier."

"Wow! You have got to be kidding me, Mom," Brandon said.

Brenda continued. "I couldn't make this up if I tried. I took it upon myself to confirm the authenticity of the diary, and the first entry was November 19, 1835, the day your great-great-great-grandfather purchased a little slave girl named *Beatrice*."

"Oh, my God!" Brandon said.

"Steven, there are passages in this diary that will change everything you think you know about this family. If any of this were to fall into the wrong hands, it would severely damage the legacy of the Fortier name. I have not read these pages in more than thirty years, and I can still remember every entry. It is just that riveting, sad, and life-altering for us. From the first page, all the way through!"

Steven opened the diary, and the inside page was titled *Personal Expressions by Anne Fortier.* Her signature appeared on the bottom of the page, as well. He flipped to a page in the diary and began to read. Ronelle stood next to Brandon. Brenda sat on the edge of her chair.

Steven Fortier read the diary of Anne Boleyn Fortier aloud:

Well, he lied to me. Everything I thought I knew was a lie. All the people who work in this house, people who I thought were paid servants, were all his slaves. People that he purchased at the French Market. All of them were his slaves. I make no excuses for Bernard, none at all. My husband is the sole proprietor of this evil. I have also spoken with Beatrice, and she has confirmed that he is her master. Not only is he her master, he has fathered children by her—nine in total. Dear Diary, this is too much for me to bear. I'm not sure if I want to continue in this marriage.

Brandon and Ronelle both listened in complete horror. Now they knew why their mother had hidden the diary from them for so long. It contained information that their great-great-great-grandfather was not only a slave master, but also the father of children with his slaves.

Steven continued to read.

My husband was also a breeder of slaves. He forced Beatrice to have his children, then sold the girls into the life of quadroon concubines. Attached is a ledger of all the wealthy men who were willing to pay him top dollar for half-white teenage mistresses. What a horrible sin he has committed! Even as I record these events, I repent on his behalf before our Lord . . .

After Steven read the ledger of slaves, he excused himself from the kitchen. From the guest bathroom down the hall came the sound of regurgitation. When Steven returned to the living room ten minutes later, Brandon and Ronelle helped their father to his recliner.

"I can't believe I puked up all of that perfectly-aged wine," Steven said as Brenda handed him a glass of water.

"Would you like to wait until your stomach settles down before you find out more? It gets worse," Brenda told her husband.

"No, lay it on me. I have nothing left in my stomach to puke up," Steven said.

"The slave woman Beatrice continued to live with the Fortier family after slavery, she and some of her children. According to Anne Fortier's diary, her son, Steven Fortier Sr., was involved in love affair with one of Beatrice's daughters. Out of that relation came two daughters, a Glenda and a Gladys Fortier. Even though Steven Fortier Sr. did not marry Beatrice's daughter, after Bernard Fortier died, Anne Fortier acknowledged the children by establishing what we now know today as the Tureaud Trust."

"Wait! What? What are you saying?" Ronelle asked. "I thought that trust fund was something Grandpa established for us."

"That is a half-truth. Your grandpa established an interest-bearing account for you and your brother, but the fund was created long before your daddy was a thought," Brenda said.

"Well, who is the mother of Glenda and Gladys Fortier?" Brandon asked.

"Anne Fortier spared no detail in her diary. The mother of Glenda and Gladys was none other than Annette," Brenda confirmed.

"Annette Fortier?" Brandon asked.

"Yes, she never married, but she took on the last name of her mother, which was the last name of her slave master—who was also her father—which made her officially Annette Fortier. She was the mother of Glenda Fortier, who was the mother of . . ."

"*Susan Campbell!*" Steven exclaimed.

Brandon jumped up off the sofa and ran down the hall to the bathroom. Then came the sound of regurgitation. Steven leaned back into the sofa and found another area on the ceiling to focus on. Ronelle sat motionless with her mouth wide open, fighting to suppress the feeling of nausea, those sudden urges to heave. She eventually conquered it. Over in the kitchen, Brenda poured the last of the wine and took a seat on the side of her husband.

"Mom, are you saying I am blood-related to Sherman? Please tell me this is not true. Please, Mother!" Ronelle said in a dreadful voice.

"Sweetheart, I wish it wasn't," Brenda said as Brandon returned from the bathroom. "Ronelle, you and Sherman share Bernard Fortier and Steven Fortier Sr. Now I hope you understand why I was so opposed to my children dating anyone from the Campbell family. I am not a racist, as all three of you have wrongfully accused me of being. I've been trying to keep this time bomb hidden." Brenda took a long sip of her wine.

"So, I am related to Jynika? This is too much!"

"Well, since we're revealing secrets, there is no better time than this to tell you guys," Ronelle said as she stood. "I don't know how to say this."

"Just take your time and say whatever it is. It can't be anything worse than what I've already shared," Brenda said.

"I think I'm about to have a panic attack, but here goes. I'm two months pregnant."

Immediately, Brenda leaped from her seat and ran down that hall toward the bathroom, but she didn't make it in time. From an area right past the kitchen came the sound of regurgitation—a familiar sound that night.

His mom and Ronelle mopped up the hallway before returning to the living room. His dad continued to gaze at the ceiling as if something interesting was playing out above his head. Brandon stared out the living room window into the night, looking at nothing, lost in thought. The mystery of Annette was no more, and in his mind, there was only one way to proceed. Brandon turned from the window and addressed his father.

"Dad, how are you going to make this right?"

"I don't know, son. Can you give me a minute to process all of this? Our relationship with the Campbell family could go north or south, depending on how I decide to manage this information. As of right now, I'm not completely sure how to proceed."

Brenda interrupted her husband. "Steven, before you start handing out bags of money, as your wife I think your next conversation should involve the attorneys at the Tureaud Trust. After all, you didn't make this mess."

Brandon took offense. "Mom, I understand we didn't make this mess, but what we do from this point forward is an opportunity to clean our hands and display some integrity here. I know that money can't heal any wounds, but I believe it can ease some of the pain."

It hadn't been an hour since his mom placed had the diary on the kitchen counter, and there was already a new disagreement brewing.

"My purpose in sharing the details of this diary wasn't for the Campbell family. I'd rather what was discussed here tonight remain within these walls," Brenda countered.

"Really, Mom? That diary changes life as we know it and life as they know it. No matter how you feel, we have to do what's right," Brandon said. "About a month ago you attended a funeral for one of the grandchildren of Annette Fortier. These are people we have relationships with, talk to every single day, and, according to the news Ronelle just shared, are now pregnant by!"

"Brandon, I understand your position. Trust me, I do. But the moment people get wind of this diary, money-hungry cousins will come from everywhere. There will be a run on our company and our estate! I am not going to allow that to happen. What happened more than 160 years ago has nothing to do with us, and I will fight like hell to make sure it never will."

Brenda left the living room and returned to the kitchen to load the dishwasher. Brandon followed her. When he picked up the diary, Brenda snatched it out of his hands.

"Don't even think about it, Brandon!" Brenda said as she hurried to the utility room and locked the diary back in her safe.

CHAPTER 37

Room 306. The number didn't change and wasn't going to. He had to walk through that door and reveal an unknown fact, an ancient secret. On the other side of the door was his best friend in the entire world, his soon-to-be brother-in-law, and—following the Fortier family revelation last night – his African American cousin. Just as Brandon reached for the door, it swung open.

"Oh, good morning, Brandon," a nurse said.

"Good morning, Karen," he replied while stepping to the side. "I see you're racing off to the next one as usual."

"Lord help me, I have ten more to go. The seven p.m. to seven a.m. shift doesn't get any easier on your body or your marriage. All I know is, my relief better walk down that hall in the next ten minutes, or I'm out of here! I'm dead tired." Nurse Karen had been caring for Sherman since he left the intensive care unit.

"How's this cry-baby doing? Is he ready to get discharged yet?" Brandon asked as Karen continued down the hall to her next patient.

"From what I understand, he's getting discharged today. Wish they all were like Sherman. I wouldn't mind working these nights."

Brandon entered the room and closed the door behind him. From the far corner, in a space no larger than a closet, he heard the rushing sound of water, followed by the type of singing a person does when they think no one is listening.

"I just want your extra time and your . . . *dah dah dah dah dah dah . . . kiss!*"

A few seconds later, Sherman emerged with a handful of paper towels. "What's up, B! I didn't hear you come in."

"If you weren't so busy destroying that Prince song, you would have."

"Haha. Whatever, B! I am so ready to get out of this room, even walking to that bathroom feels like I've gone somewhere!" Sherman crawled back into bed. "Isn't this a little early for you? You generally don't wake up until after lunch!"

"Dude, I'll have you know I have leaped out of bed every day at six-thirty a.m. I'm on my laptop banging out this dissertation, while you play sick in this luxury condo!"

Sherman untied his do-rag and started to brush his hair.

"Well, I'm ready to get the hell out of this condo today! I just called my mom and Ronelle to let them know today is the day I am finally out of here. When I heard the nurse talking, I thought she was greeting your sister, who happens to be on her way up, according to her text a few moments ago."

"I figured she would be. That's why I tried to beat her here."

"Well, I think something is bothering Ronelle, but I'm not sure what it is. She's been so sensitive about everything lately. When I woke up, there was this message saying *we need to talk ASAP* and that she was on her way. I've been calling her repeatedly, and she hasn't responded. Any idea what's going on?"

Brandon placed his backpack on the green recliner and took a seat on the side of it. He searched for the right words to break the news to Sherman about the diary, but there was no way to sugarcoat it.

"Dude, yesterday my half of the dissertation took a dramatic turn. A head-on collision, it may have jumped off the tracks!"

"Whoa! Like what?"

"Sherman, there's something I want to make you aware of, and I'd rather you hear it from me than from my sister."

Sherman extended both arms in Brandon's direction. "Wait! Hold up! Don't do it! Not now! Please don't come out the *gay closet*, Brandon! Save it for Mardi Gras or Southern Decadence like the others. Haha!" Sherman joked.

"Seriously, no bullshit. I wish it were something that simple," Brandon sighed. "I have worked on this project harder than any assignment in my academic career, and it feels like I may have asked one too many questions about my ancestors."

"Well, at least you were able to get some work done. I completed the last regimen of those respiratory drugs yesterday. That shit made me so loopy I could barely hold my head up, let alone type." Sherman continued to brush his hair on the sides. "All jokes aside, I'm proud of how you stepped up. Now about these questions you unearthed?'"

"Well . . . from your ancestry site, I continued to come across the name Annette Fortier, and last night when I pressed my dad for information about her, it turned into a major shouting match."

"What about?"

"About our black side of our family."

"The black side of your . . . what?"

"You heard me correctly, the . . . African American side of our family. Sherman, I'm just going to say it the best way I know how. *Dude, we're related.*"

There was no reaction from Sherman, at least not the reaction Brandon had expected. Sherman looked forward at the wall as if he could stare through it with x-ray vision, at something far more interesting than Brandon.

"Sherman, we are related through my grandfather, Bernard Fortier. He fathered children with his slave, your grandmother Beatrice. One of those children was Annette Fortier, who then got together with Steven Fortier Sr. From those two came Glenda and Gladys. And from Glenda came..."

"My grandmother, Susan Campbell!"

"Yes, and so forth and so on. We're not just related, but at almost every generational tier, we share a common link. Your ancestry site also revealed Abigail as the daughter of Gladys. Sherm, what started out as just a writing project to gain our doctorates has brought to light that we are, in fact, blood-related cousins."

"Which also means I am dating my cousin, your sister. So that's what she wanted to talk about."

"I'm not sure if it's third or fourth, but you're correct," Brandon said as he stood and approached Sherman's bed. "It also means I'm dating my cousin as well, Jynika. We're just as related as you and Ronelle."

"Man! I knew it. Uncle Clarence said it, but part of me didn't want to believe it. When you put it like that, that we are blood-related, something about the relationship I have with Ronelle now feels dirty. I think I have to throw up . . ."

"I felt the same way after my mom confirmed it. That's what started the argument. My mom knew the entire time, since 1983. That's why she . . ."

"Was opposed to us getting married."

"Yes. At first, we thought it was because of the black thing, but that was far from the truth. She knew all this time about Bernard Fortier and Beatrice. The good news is, your idea of researching the lineage of our families has concluded with us being blood relatives. If that is not a winning dissertation, then I don't know what is."

"The good news? You call that good news? Brandon, I am engaged to Ronelle. I asked her to marry me! This has further-reaching implications than just getting a passing grade on a fucking paper!"

"Sherman, bro, you need to calm the fuck down!"

"Calm down, my ass! Since you have all the answers, what do I do now? Tell me! Do I break up with my cousin, or do I marry her?" Sherman stood on the opposite side of his bed. "You might think all of this bullshit is a joke, but my grandma died with this in her heart and mind! She knew what your mom knew long before she discovered it, but never said a word. My dear grandmother probably felt like no one would ever believe we were related to the Fortier family. That's why she never wanted to talk about it, no matter how much we tried. It was still just too painful."

"Sherm, you think this was easy for me? Dude, I found this out last night in a heated argument, a fight in which I was defending your side of the family, trying to convince my mother to do the right thing!"

"The right thing? What's the right thing, Brandon?"

"Again, you need to calm down."

"Brandon, you stop telling me to calm down. The more you say it, the more pissed I'm getting."

"Well, you're pissed off with the wrong person," Brandon yelled back. Down the hall at the nurses' station, Karen and several other nurses leaned over the counter, listening.

"Yes, you need to calm the fuck down, bro, because I cannot un-own you. I had nothing to do with it. I told my mom we need to make this right as it relates to what happened to your grandmother Glenda in 1941, in the days after their father died."

"Brandon, I can't think about that right now, or this dissertation. A better question is, why didn't your mom just come out and say all of this from the start? Why did she allow us to fall in love and then bust out with this diary?"

"Because my mother is also concerned about a run on the Fortier estate."

"*Money . . .*"

"Yes, money! That is the one thing that matters to my mother more than the color of your skin. She concealed all of this because of money!"

"Dude, your mom has fucked my life. She has, for real, Brandon." Sherman looked upward and screamed in the direction of God. "What did I do to deserve this bad luck?" Angrily he grabbed a plastic water pitcher on his food tray and threw it against the bathroom wall. The pitcher was full, and so it cracked open on impact, leaving the drapes and the floor soaked.

"I remember freshmen year, sitting in class with all of these rich, snotty white kids from up North who came down here prepackaged with every stereotype in the book. I mean, those kids really believed that all of us black folk were on welfare, and all Southern whites married their cousins. Here I am, eight years later, a stereotype. How do you think that makes me feel, Brandon? Huh? How do you think that feels to be the one thing you thought you were better than?"

Suddenly, there were three knocks on Sherman's door; it

was Ronelle. "Good morning," she said softly, as if not to wake someone. Neither Sherman nor Brandon turned to acknowledge her when she entered. On one side of the bed stood Sherman, on the other side Brandon. In between, them was hot, contentious air.

"Well, good morning to you too, cousin. How are you, cousin? Now I know why you have avoided all my calls. It's because we are cousins," Sherman said.

Brandon picked up his bag. "I'll leave you two to talk, Sherman. I will get with you later."

"Oh no, you don't have to leave. Let's make this a little family reunion!" Sherman yelled.

"I'll catch you later, once you drop the drama!" Brandon said as he left the room.

"Leaving just like that, huh? All right, then. I will catch you later, *Cuz*. And tell my Aunt Brenda I said we don't need her fucking money!"

Brandon slammed the door on his way out.

Clutched under her arm was a bag of sausage biscuits from McDonald's, two for her and two for Sherman. In her hands she held two cups of coffee, all of which she set on the serving tray that once held the pitcher of water. Her appetite, like the water that once filled the Styrofoam container, was gone. The tail end of her brother's argument with Sherman evaporated any thought she had of a peaceful breakfast with the love of her life.

Ronelle could tell Sherman still wanted to fight. His face was flushed red; his ears looked as if he had survived the losing end on a backhanded slap. He paced from his bed to the window; his wet socks mopped the floor. Seconds later, a nurse entered to take his blood pressure.

"Oh, my," she said as she listened to his heart rate. "You may want to take a minute to calm yourself down before you have a heart attack."

"Ma'am, I'm fine—I am. I just need a minute, that's all."

"Well, your heart rate says otherwise! I'll be back in thirty minutes to check your vitals again, so please try to calm down. With a reading like this, these signs could be mistaken for something serious." The morning shift nurse left the room.

"Sherman, I can tell you're upset, but all of us are just as shocked and taken aback by this. My mom dropped this on our heads last night like a ton of bricks."

"Is that why you didn't call me back? You were under a ton of bricks? How convenient."

"There is more to it, Sherman, and if you stop being a condescending jerk for just a moment, I can explain."

On the side of his neck was a vein—thick and throbbing. Sweat covered his forehead. His eyes were stuck somewhere between rage and tears. Ronelle has never seen him display such anger; she had never given him a reason to.

"Ronelle, everything there is to explain, I already know. Our dissertation is about a slave master who is your great-great-great-grandfather and a slave who is my great-great-great-grandmother. The rest is simple to figure out. The hard part is the ring on your finger. What do we do about that?" Sherman said in anger.

Ronelle took a seat on the side of his bed. She watched him turn his head away from her and fold his arms, but still, she touched him.

"So, you no longer want to marry me because of this?"

"Ronelle, that's not what I'm saying. I'm trying to figure this out. I should just shut up because I'm thinking out loud and don't have an explanation for my every thought."

"Sherman, the crisis is greater than the pages of that diary."

"And how do you figure that?"

"Because I'm . . . *pregnant.*"

"You're what?" Sherman said as he leaned forward to hear it again.

"Sherman, *I am pregnant.* I was going to tell you that morning at Anita's Grill, but . . ."

"I was shot in the chest."

"Yes, so I held it until you recovered. But there's more."

"More?"

"My first ultrasound showed I'm pregnant with twins."

Laughter filled the room, and not the type of laughter that comes after a funny joke.

"I can't fucking believe this! I can't! This seems like a nightmare, like a cruel prank! I got my cousin pregnant, like a typical Southern stereotype. I can't believe this shit. I can't handle this!"

Ronelle tried to hold back the tears, but they broke through. Never in a million years did she think he would greet the news of her pregnancy with an argument. "So, this is all my fault?"

"Ronelle, I'm not saying it's your fault. It's a lot to process, okay? First, I find out from your brother that we're cousins, and then you tell me we're expecting twins. That's a lot to throw on a man in one morning."

"Then ask for a minute! Say you need time to process it! I announce we're expecting twins, and you treat me like I'm trying to destroy you. I'm a victim of this news too—the same as you are. This is not solely about you! So, allow me to say this again. I am pregnant with your babies!"

"Okay. I'm sorry. I didn't mean to snap at you."

"Sherman, this is the only time I'm going to say this, because I will *not* allow you to hold me accountable for something that happened more than 150 years ago. The Fortier family who are still alive today—me, my parents and my brother—have nothing to do with this. We are innocent. When my mother presented us with that diary, it crushed our entire world—both Brandon's world and my world."

Sherman picked up the brush from the serving tray. "Ronelle, you have no idea how messy this will get once Uncle Clarence and my father find out. My dad plans to launch an epic legal war against Abigail over that house. The problem is, he cannot go after Abigail without going after your family. Do you see the pending storm that's about to erupt? Ronelle, this will turn very ugly—fast."

"I know, but I need you to realize this is not our fault. You want someone to fight, someone to blame. But all those people are dead," Ronelle said as she walked around the bed to his side. "I don't want to fight. I came here hoping we would talk about our babies and our plans that were interrupted, but . . ."

"So, we're going through with this . . . *pregnancy?*" Sherman asked.

Ronelle stepped back from him about three feet. "Are you suggesting . . . *an abortion?*"

"I mean, I'm trying to see how this would work being that . . ."

"What kind of question is that? I am ten weeks pregnant, and you ask a question like that? You insensitive fucker! Why do you think I didn't call you back last night? I was up, trying to figure this out, and all you can think about is how you feel and how bad it looks! Well, I didn't set out to fuck my cousin, nor get pregnant with him, so fuck you too! I'll figure it out on my own!"

Ronelle grabbed her purse and keys and headed for the door. As soon as she reached for the doorknob, in walked Melvin and Yvonne. Ronelle greeted his parents as quickly as she could, then hurried to the elevator.

"Do I sense a little spat with you two lovebirds?" his mother asked.

"Yes, Mom, a lot of tension, and it's very complicated."

"All I know is, whatever is going on with you two, I expect you to fix it immediately!" Melvin said.

"I don't think I can fix this one because I didn't break it."

"Then whoever broke it, I expect that person to fix it because we have to get back to our wedding plans," his mother said as she walked to the closest side of his bed. His father approached from the other side.

"About those wedding plans," Sherman said as he turned toward his dad. "What is the Louisiana state law regarding marrying your blood relative . . . you know . . . like a cousin? I may need to know just in case it comes with jail time."

"Boy, what the hell are you talking about?" his father asked.

"Mom, Dad, I think you both need to take a seat.

CHAPTER 38

Since 1882, the Tureaud Trust had functioned out of the same building on St. Charles Avenue. Their primary responsibilities were charitable giving and endowment management. Steven hardly ever interacted with the staff at the trust fund unless it was to make an appearance at the scholarship banquet, but today was different. Steven hadn't stepped foot in the Tureaud Trust building in more than five years, and when the staff greeted him at the door, he remembered why. They worshipped and served him in a way that made him feel extremely uncomfortable, like royalty. Steven never liked the royal treatment. He always longed to be just another guy in the office.

"Good morning, Norman. I'll meet with you privately, and then you may bring the staff on into the back," Steven instructed.

Norman Moret was the manager of the Tureaud Trust, a position he'd held since old man Perkins handed it over to him in 1988. Norman was now in his sixties, and the reason Steven never made any follow-up trips to the Trust. Norman managed the charity trust with precision and efficiency, always passing internal audits, and he had built a great staff that genuinely cared about the community. The Tureaud Trust received its funding from an annual donation from Fortier Lines International, which it used to support their charitable initiatives in smaller donations. This morning, it was time for the trust to cut a check for the largest award ever, with interest.

As soon as the door closed to his office, Steven turned to Norman. "Please bring me the file on Gladys Fortier."

Norman left the room and came back immediately with a file that was about two inches thick. The file looked every bit of seventy years old. Attached were all the payouts Gladys had received from the trust, and subsequent tax payments on the house at 1005 St. Peter Street. Once Steven separated the trust payouts from the tax payouts on the property, the meeting started at one o'clock on the nose.

"Norman, I requested this session with you today in an attempt to right a wrong that was committed in 1941 when your old boss, Mr. Perkins, managed this trust on behalf of my father. Apparently, there was a claim denied for Glenda Fortier. What is that payout in today's value, with interest?"

"Well, sir, that is an amount that requires little math on my end. Over the years I've become very intrigued with the case involving Glenda and Gladys. Mr. Perkins once told me I should always be prepared for this conversation, because one day it was coming. I took his advice seriously. In anticipation of such an inquiry, my staff and I devised a contingency plan, should it ever come to light that Glenda was entitled to a part of the inheritance she was never allowed to claim. I even created a family tree of heirs for both Glenda and Gladys," Norman said.

"So, when you created the family tree, what source did you use?" Steven asked.

Norman directed Steven's attention to a website that was already front and center on his browser. "We used an ancestry website to keep track of the recent heirs."

Steven knew in that instant that it was Norman who'd inadvertently linked the Fortier family to Glenda on the ancestry website—the same site Brandon utilized.

"Sir, if we were to pay out the descendants of Glenda Fortier today, based on the original award at the time Steven Fortier, Sr. died, with interest, that would come to roughly 230 million dollars," Norman said.

"I see," Steven said as he continued to scroll through the list of Glenda's heirs. "And the house at St. Peter Street. Who is the rightful owner of that property, and who is occupying that property today?" Steven asked.

"Sir, that property still belongs to the Tureaud Trust. The property has remained deeded to the Tureaud Trust and prohibited from sale as ordered by Mrs. Anne Fortier's will. The property is currently occupied by the daughter of Gladys Fortier, Abigail Guillory."

"I see," Steven said as he stood and walked over to a portrait that displayed cargo vessels his grandfather commissioned in 1940, one year before he passed. "Norman, I need you to prepare a check for 230 million dollars, leaving the addressee blank. That will conclude everything I need for today. Thank you."

"Not a problem, sir."

On the desk, Steven's cell phone began to ring; it was Brenda. He chuckled to himself. *Funny how you call at the exact moment Norman is in the next room cutting the check.* Nevertheless, he decided to answer it.

"Hello, Brenda," he answered right before the last ring.

"Steven, where are you?"

"And a good afternoon to you too, Brenda."

"Steven, I hope you're not at the trust doing what I advised you not to do."

"Brenda, I'm in the middle of a meeting and will speak with you when I get home."

"Steven, I'm asking you to . . ."

He ended the call.

After printing the check, Norman placed it in a partially sealed envelope and handed it to Steven. "Before you leave, Mr. Fortier, I have to mention that I did receive an inquiry from a gentleman who said he was representing a Cheryl Gullage, but I have no record of her, and she doesn't appear to be an heir of Glenda or Gladys. Maybe it's nothing, but I at least wanted to make you aware of it," Norman said.

"Just keep me abreast should anything come of it. Could be an overseas request for a donation. I've been getting a ton of those lately."

Steven thanked Norman and the entire staff at the Tureaud Trust for all their hard work and headed back to his truck. Before he backed out of his parking space, Steven made a phone call to Melvin and asked if he could come over for dinner tonight. Melvin agreed. He also requested Clarence dine with them if he was available, and Melvin agreed to make sure he would join them.

Standing at the door watching Steven drive away stood Norman and his staff. Some waved goodbye to Steven, while others are high-fived and celebrated.

"I didn't think this day would ever come," Norman said as he watched Steven Fortier drive away. "After all these years, Ms. Glenda Fortier's children are finally recognized as heirs of the Fortier fortune. Glory to God."

Leaving the Tureaud Trust, Steven Fortier continued to ignore Brenda's phone calls, which grew in frequency. All her calls ended with a voice message. He resolved to allow Brenda to sit in the dark for most of the day, the equivalent of a slap on the wrist compared to her thirty-year-old secret about the diary. *The least she could do is wait until I make it home to have this fight*, he thought to himself.

After a short drive down to St. Charles Avenue, Steven arrived at his destination and was surprised to find a parking place directly in front. He exited his grandfather's 1949 Chevrolet 3100 pickup truck—which was in garage-kept condition—and within a few short steps was at the front door of 1005 St. Peter Street. And so, he knocked.

The noonday sun was pleasant. Unlike the dreaded summer days, today was not warm enough for short sleeves, not cold enough for a jacket. A woman opened the door. She was much younger than he had expected, appearing no older than fifty. She was dressed in a peach pantsuit with pearl earrings and a matching necklace. At first glance, she reminded him of former First Lady Laura Bush, with lighter hair color.

"May I help you?" the lady said.

"Yes, I'm looking for a Mrs. Abigail Guillory. Is she home?"

"Yes, she is, but may I ask what this is regarding?"

"It's a private matter, ma'am. I promise not to take too much of her time."

"My mother is resting. Unless you share the reason for your visit, I'm afraid you will have to reach her by phone and schedule an appointment," the lady said as she slowly began to close the door.

"Could you please let her know Steven Fortier is here—I'm sure she's been expecting me for some time now."

When the door opened again, Abigail welcomed Steven into her home for the first time. The scent of freshly-baked cinnamon rolls greeted his nose; the kitchen was only a few feet away. Standing in the home of Bernard and Anne Fortier was like walking back in time all the way through to the antebellum years in the French Quarter.

Abigail quickly took a seat, seemingly overwhelmed by the sight of Steven. "Nice to finally meet you after so many years. This is my oldest daughter, Sandra. Her sister Stephanie will join us shortly. Would you like a cup of coffee? Water, perhaps?"

"I welcome that cup of coffee and one of those cinnamon rolls. Thank you."

Sandra immediately left the room to get a cup of coffee and the baked rolls.

"Nice to finally meet both of you, and sorry to drop in like this. I wouldn't have without an urgent reason," Steven said.

"Oh, it's not a bother at all. Please have a seat," Abigail replied. "And why do I have this pleasure? What brings you by?"

Right before Steven could answer, Sandra returned with the coffee and cream cheese-covered cinnamon rolls. The melted sugary topping nearly caused him to lose his train of thought.

"Mr. Fortier, you'll need these napkins. The rolls are really hot," Sandra warned.

"Thank you so much, Sandra," Steven said as he took a bite and sipped his coffee. Then he took another bite, followed by finger licking until all the sugar was gone. He didn't need the napkins.

"The Bible says a man cannot live by bread alone, but this

cinnamon roll could definitely hold me over for a while," Steven joked.

After Sandra placed a cup of coffee in front of her mother and left the room, he figured it was the best time to explain the reason for his visit.

"Mrs. Guillory, I'm going to cut straight to the chase because I think you know why I'm here."

"To exercise your rights to this house and throw us out on the street?"

"What would make you say that?"

"My mother—she told me one day you would come and stake claim to this property I have lived in all my life, and there was nothing I could do to stop it. For years I have waited for you, and here you are."

"That's not the reason I'm here, Abigail. The last thing I need is another piece of real estate to manage."

Abigail was a formally-dressed, frail-looking woman; her hair was powder white, her bony shoulders were in perfect alignment with her thin arms and waist. Her posture was that of an old church organist who refused to retire; slouched slightly forward, but stern. On her lips, a trace of red lipstick. Time had dimmed her dark blue eyes. Steven noticed the difference in her family photos that hung on the walls. On this day, her eyes were closer to gray than sapphire.

Over the years, Steven had made frequent visits to Susan Campbell's home, and the difference couldn't have been more obvious. From the inheritance Gladys received in 1941, Abigail enjoyed a very grand life in the upper tiers of New Orleans society, as did her daughters Sandra and Stephanie.

"Then why are you here? I can think of no other reason."

"You know as well as I do there is an age-old reason that has little to do with this house and everything to do with the people who once called this house home. Abigail, I may be a little late to the party, but I have arrived, and I know everything that happened to your mother as well as your aunt."

"Aunt? What aunt do you speak of?" Abigail asked, her right hand pressed against her heart, her mouth open, her expression confused.

"You know very well which aunt I'm referring to. Your aunt Glenda, your African American aunt, the one your mother eliminated from the estate."

"So, you have heard the same rumors. I found no truth to it. I have no black aunt."

"Abigail, with all due respect, I didn't come here to argue. Like I said, I know the truth. Your mother and Glenda were sisters, and your grandmother Annette was black. I can show you this in writing, or we can skip the formalities and get to the reason for my visit."

"Carry on."

"What happened to Glenda was wrong, and I'm here to make it right as best as I can. It's time to bring this family together, and that starts with both of us acknowledging her descendants. It's time to recognize them as the Fortier family, with all benefits due and withheld. The same as was done for your mother, I plan to do for Glenda's heirs."

Abigail took a sip of her coffee; her hand trembled, spilling some of her coffee on the saucers. "So, how does this involve me? You have made up your mind, so why come here?"

"I wanted you to accompany me tonight when I meet with the Campbells."

Abigail placed her cup on the coffee table and stood. "I appreciate your visit to ask my support, but I will do no such thing. I don't have a black aunt name Glenda, nor a black grandmother named Annette. These people may have existed, but I do not recognize them. I am a white woman, born white. My children are white, as well as my grandkids. I plan to die as I lived—as a white woman."

"And pretend as if these people are not part of this family? That's ridiculous, and you know it. You can deny Glenda until your last day on Earth, but she is as much part of your story as she's part of mine. I will not live this lie with you," Steven said.

"I enjoyed our little chat today. I hope we can meet again under more pleasant circumstances." She opened the front door.

"Abigail, one day you will see that we are more than a color, a box checked on a birth certificate, and you will have missed the opportunity to know some beautiful people. I'm honored to welcome the Campbells into the Fortier family. I only wish this was something we could have partaken in together, as the first step in healing old wounds. Unfortunately, you treasure living as white more than you cherish the truth."

"And what is the truth, Mr. Fortier?" Sandra asked as she stepped into the living room with her sister Stephanie.

"Sandra! Go back into the kitchen now! Mr. Fortier was just leaving," Abigail yelled.

"Mother, I would like to hear what he has to say!" Stephanie yelled back. "Now please, sir, before you leave this house, share with us the truth!"

"Mr. Fortier, I'm asking you now to leave—as politely as I can. Please respect my wishes," Abigail said.

"The truth, ladies, is you are very much African American, whether your mother chooses to admit it or not. Should you convince your mother to change her mind, take this, please," Steven said as he handed Sandra a card with Melvin's address and the arrival time for dinner.

Defeated in his quest to unite the Fortier family, Steven stepped out of the house on St. Peter Street to the booming sound of a slammed door. Any idea of a reunion with Gladys's side of the family was also slammed shut. Right before Steven put his truck into drive, the front door swung open again. Abigail was pissed. In a straight line, she rushed in his direction, floating on a storm cloud of anger.

"How dare you! You son of a bitch!" Her finger reached inside his truck. "How dare you come here and disturb the peace of my family! Long before you discovered these *so-called facts,* I already knew it, but I never knocked on your door. I never disturbed your home; I never aired out any of the things my mother told me. Some family secrets are better left a secret—tucked away in the darkest places of our minds. Before you drive off, I would be remiss if I didn't reveal a little-known fact about you—a tightly guarded scandal my mother once shared with me."

As she spoke, Steven could see Stephanie and Sandra running out of the house to get their mother, but Abigail refused to budge. The scolding continued.

Abigail gritted her teeth. "Your grandfather was my uncle Timothy, the son of Bernard and Beatrice. Anne Fortier was sleeping with the help; she fornicated with Timothy—her stepson—for nearly twenty years until he died. Timothy was the father of Steven Fortier, Sr. Your dad was Steven Fortier, Jr, and you, my dear cousin, are Steven Fortier the Third. To expose me means you will also have to expose yourself and your children!"

Sandra and Stephanie took their mother by the arms and walked her back into the house. Before the door closed, Abigail looked over her shoulder at Steven and said, "*Welcome to your first day as a nigger!*"

The door slammed.

CHAPTER 39

The drive home was a blur. Steven felt as though Scotty from *Star Trek* had dematerialized him and then beamed him up. *How did I get back to Audubon Place? Did I drive through or over the community gates?* Steven couldn't remember. After teleporting he wondered if he'd engaged in the usual small talk with his neighbor, Tom Benson, the owner of the New Orleans Saints, or if Scotty, from his comfortable chair on the *Starship Enterprise*, had decided to skip that part altogether.

Nonetheless, Steven was home, and each step he took was carefully placed because all the walls leaned slightly left. Because of Abigail, his world tilted slightly to the right. Her voice continued to echo as if she walked directly behind him, like a correctional officer following an inmate to the death chamber. Her voice was relentless.

Welcome to your first day as a nigger.

His wobbly legs took him to the rear of his home, to the place where he would always find his wife whenever she was livid—the sunroom. There she was seated in a lounge chair, fingers interlocked, staring at nothing, which happened to be an oriental rug. He wanted to speak, but a sudden case of aphasia glued his teeth. Steven saw her, but a divergent boundary of *I told you so* prevented Brenda from greeting him with the usual soft kiss on the lips. For some strange reason, he needed that kiss; he needed something that felt like yesterday when everything was normal.

Sitting next to Brenda like a dear old friend—a drinking buddy at happy hour—was the Anne Fortier diary. The diary was opened to the page most relevant to him. It was in full view, ready to reveal more, but he couldn't handle another page. He took a seat on the other side of the diary; like an acrophobic, he never looked down.

Brenda did not acknowledge his presence, ask about his visit to the Tureaud Trust, or inquire about the itinerary of his day. She knew. Couples married for as long as Steven and Brenda communicate on a frequency only they can detect. And so, she continued to admire the oriental rug she'd purchased in India fifteen years ago, while Steven drifted back 145 years beyond that.

After ten minutes of complete silence, Brenda cleared her throat. "One day you will learn to trust me. I'm not sure when, but I pray one day soon."

Outside the sunroom, a blue jay took a bath in the oval-shaped swimming pool, splashing about without care or concern. On the other side of the pool, squirrels chased each other from the ground level up to the highest branches of the trees. Just outside the sunroom, in the flowerbed, bumblebees dove in and out of sweet clovers and dandelions. In the area where the lawn met the pool's cement deck sat ten bags of potting soil and mulch, patiently waiting on Brenda. Her spring rejuvenation would have to wait.

"I just hung up the phone with Norman. He informed me you departed around lunch. Where to, he wasn't sure, but there was no need to ask. After leaving the Tureaud Trust, you paid a visit to Abigail. If all went well, then your next stop was Melvin Campbell, where you planned to knock on the door like Publishers Clearinghouse, but all didn't go well. So here you are, like a child who has just discovered Santa isn't real. Abigail robbed you of your innocence."

Brenda walked over to the glass door of the sunroom, opened it, and took a seat on the first step. "I feel sorry for you because I love you, and I don't like to see you hurting. But you deserve to feel the way you do. I begged you."

Steven's gaze finally veered down at the diary; he picked it up and read several pages. The timeworn pages of the journal left no doubt that Bernard Fortier wasn't the father of Steven Fortier, Sr. The same pages shattered every wholesome image he had of Anne Boleyn Fortier.

There always comes a day when everything you stand for and believe is tested. That dreadful day had arrived for Steven Fortier like a slow-moving hurricane, bringing biblical destruction. He had always prided himself on treating all people the same, regardless of their race, but now he battled negative thoughts regarding the blood that flowed through his veins—part European and part African. The truth was, Steven didn't know how to feel about the pages of the diary. The one thing that was certain was he couldn't deny the facts about his family. Anne Fortier had made it impossible.

"So, you've known about my grandfather all of this time?"

"Are you referring to the male slave, Timothy? Who was seduced by Anne Fortier? Got her pregnant and was the father of Steven Fortier, Sr.? Ha! Yes."

"Brenda, this is painful enough without twisting the knife, so lay off the facetious bullshit, please!"

"So, the fact that you have a black grandfather is painful? Oh, how the table of racism has turned."

"Racism! That's nonsense! Am I not allowed a moment of astonishment?"

"So, it doesn't feel good to have someone attack you as a racist? Welcome to my world," Brenda said with a tone of victory in her voice. "The evidence of this historic scandal is still alive and well in our children. You just never took the time to notice! DNA is a powerful thing," Brenda said as she soaked in the sun's rays.

She continued, "I have also done a ton of research on quadroons and mulattos, and the circumstances surrounding the Fortier family are more common in New Orleans than you may know. Families that started black in the 1800s became white households in the 1900s. And if it hadn't been for a diary to connect all the dots, we wouldn't have known."

"Answer this one question for me. How did you sleep peacefully all of these years knowing this? That part of this is equally disturbing to me. And cruel!"

"Because I wanted to protect this family, you call me cruel?"

"Brenda, I never asked you to protect me. I don't need your type of protection, the kind that makes decisions for me!"

"*I did what I did because I love my family!*" Brenda screamed.

"Brenda that's not how I define love; that's control. This diary gave you power because somewhere in your sick mind you appointed yourself as gatekeeper over every material thing we own. But I never asked for your protection."

Steven closed the diary and tucked it under his arm. "I'm taking control of this ordeal from this point forward. If there are any other unknown things you'd like to divulge, then here is your opportunity. But I better not walk into another ambush and later discover you knew who, what, where, when, and how."

"Steven, everything I know, you now know. I have no other secrets," Brenda said as her husband turned to walk back down the hall. "And Steven, throwing money at this situation is not going to do anything but pacify your misplaced guilt. Once you start handing out money, it will never stop. A line will form at our door. Please don't give the Campbell family that check."

"Since all you care about is money, maybe you should divorce me and take your half. That way, your fortune is protected from my black relatives."

There was no answer from Brenda.

It was time for Scotty to beam him up again. Next stop was the home of Melvin and Yvonne Campbell.

In the kitchen, Yvonne and Clarence put the finishing touches on the dinner for their special guest. Clarence turned off the burners under the simmering crawfish stew, a recipe borrowed from Sue Campbell, while Yvonne opened the oven door to release the heat on the baked redfish.

The dining room table was prepped and waiting for a very special guest, a lifelong buddy—Steven Fortier III. On the radio, Anita Baker was singing "Sweet Love." In the living room, Melvin flipped through all the channels of the evening news, commentating on each segment. "When I'm mayor next year, all of these city-wide problems will end."

"You ain't gon do shit. With your crooked-ass friends the next thing we know is Mayor Campbell will get indicted. And when you call from that jail phone I will be right here to answer it, and I will tell you the same thing you told me." Clarence mocked his brother's deep raspy voice. "*Just sit in there a little while and get you some rest.*" Clarence tapped Yvonne on the shoulder. "Imma hang up the phone and let your ass sit in jail and get some rest . . . click." Clarence danced at the thought of Melvin spending a night in jail.

Suddenly the doorbell interrupted the laughter. Melvin stiff-legged to the door; it was their dinner guest. Steven and Melvin greeted as if they hadn't seen each other in years. Yvonne stood directly behind Melvin and waited for her turn. Clarence stood behind Yvonne.

"And where is Brenda?" Yvonne asked.

"Yvonne, it's complicated . . . very," Steven replied. "My goodness, that smells delicious!"

Clarence stepped forward to hug Steven. "I hope you're hungry because we gonna eat tonight. Believe that!" Steven and Clarence hugged and laughed.

After dinner and in-depth discussions about their kids, Steven decided the time was perfect to hand Melvin the envelope. As soon as he reached into the pocket of his suit jacket, someone rang the doorbell. Yvonne excused herself from the table to answer the door, and Steven slid the envelope back into his pocket.

"What is this I'm hearing about your boy dating my daughter? Nobody told me nothing 'bout them two hookin' up."

"Clarence, I was just as taken aback by it as you were, and it appears those two are very serious," Steven said.

"Wait, hold up! Jynika and Brandon are dating?" Melvin asked. "Since when?"

"Apparently it started a few months back, around the time

Sherman proposed to Ronelle," Steven replied as he sipped his wine.

"All I know is, if your son is going to date my daughter, then I expect fifty-two cows, thirty-nine goats, and twenty-four chickens, or there will be no wedding," Clarence said. Melvin and Steven burst into laughter. Melvin nearly spat out his wine.

"Ain't that how they use to do it back in Africa? Is Brandon trying to court my daughter? Then I want . . . *my cows!*" Clarence joked. The laughter grew louder.

Moments later, Yvonne returned to the dining room accompanied by Sandra, Stephanie, and Abigail. The laughter stopped as Steven, Melvin, and Clarence stood from the table.

"Steven, I would introduce you, but I believe you recently had the pleasure of meeting these three beautiful ladies," Yvonne said. "This is my husband, Melvin, and his brother, Clarence."

Steven was first to step forward and greet them. "What a wonderful surprise this is, Abigail. Thank you for coming. Sandra and Stephanie, thank you."

As they embraced, Clarence made eye contact with his brother. Melvin shrugged his shoulders.

"Well, let's all have a seat," Melvin said as Yvonne offered each guest food and wine.

"Yvonne, what a beautiful home you have," Abigail said as Yvonne hurried to the kitchen.

"Thank you so much! It is a lot easier to keep clean now that all the boys have flown the nest."

"Thank God. I will drink to that!" Melvin gulped his glass of wine.

After the small talk . . . two minutes of total silence. Like leaders at a G8 Summit, they sat, patiently waiting for someone to call the meeting into session. Clarence couldn't believe Abigail was sitting only a few chairs away, being pleasant, charming, and friendly. Then he flashed back to being eight years old, eavesdropping on his mother's conversations with Ms. Vera.

"Girl, that Abigail was putting on out there like she hates blacks so much, knowing all the while her momma was black," Susan Campbell would say.

Then Ms. Vera would reply, *"They did your momma some*

dirty. But God don't sleep; he don't sleep, and he don't like ugly."

Clarence snapped back to reality to find Abigail a lot older and less threatening than she was in her protest days outside his elementary school. Her daughter Sandra was first to break the silence as she addressed Steven.

"As you can imagine, Mr. Fortier, after you left my mother's home today, our worlds halted. I can speak for my sister as well. After you drove off, we were confronted with the fact that everything we thought we knew was not exact. It was like discovering we were adopted. Since that conversation in our living room, the three of us have engaged in non-stop discussions about our ancestry." Yvonne made her way around the table with glasses of water and wine as Sandra continued. "Eventually we arrived at a unanimous agreement. My mother has something she would like to say."

Abigail took a sip of water. With both of her hands flat on the table, Abigail took a deep breath and addressed Steven first. "Steven, I wanted to apologize for the things I said to you today. I should have never spoken out of so much anger. Please, forgive me."

"Abigail, all is forgiven. I'm really happy you decided to join us this evening," Steven replied.

"Melvin and Clarence, I came here tonight to say I am sorry for the way my mother and I treated your family. Your grandmother Glenda was just as much a Fortier as my mother, Gladys. I am now eighty-eight years old, and all my life I have passed for white. Unlike my aunt Glenda, we had that option. Today I confessed to my daughters everything my mother confided in me before her passing, every detail of how she led the effort to deny her sister's inheritance. In the aftermath of it all, my mother regretted it, but the damage appeared irreversible.

To admit she had a black sister was also to confess that I was black. Then my first cousin, Liddy Pop, died, and I never had the chance to tell her how much I wanted to know her. We were close as children. Grandmother Annette made sure of it. Then, when I was around eleven years old or so, we were torn apart by race."

Sandra handed her mother a napkin.

"The day I prayed would never come arrived around lunchtime today. My daughters discovered they are descendants of a black woman. To be honest with you, I don't feel any less now that they know, but I don't want to leave this earth the way my mother did, with so much regret. Melvin and Clarence, on behalf of your aunt Glenda, I wanted to say what a joy it is to meet you finally." Abigail exhaled.

"There is one more thing," Abigail said as she reached down into her purse. "The home where I reside belongs to all of us. Those were the instructions from my mother." Abigail handed Melvin and Clarence two keys wrapped in a bow. "The house on 1005 St. Peter Street is a family house, and it is your house just as much as it is mine."

Melvin immediately stood and walked around the table to Abigail, and they hugged. In that one hug, the children of Glenda and Gladys reached across decades of bitterness to embrace each other as family.

Clarence was next to hug Abigail. "I'm so sorry for all that mean shit I said. You all right for a white woman."

Abigail laughed. "Well . . . you're not so bad yourself." The room erupted in laughter.

Steven stood up once again and asked everyone to join him in a toast. "When I stopped by your home today, I knew I was taking a chance, but it's a risk I'm glad I took. This night has been more than I could have asked for."

Clarence interrupted Steven. "Man, let me tell you. To get these two families together, you something like an angel—a liquor drinking angel. This is a miracle." Clarence was amazed.

"Yes, sir, it is. To Abigail, Sandra, Stephanie, and the Campbells." They all clinked their glasses.

"The other reason I wanted you to be here was to witness something that was long overdue." Steven reached into his pocket and handed Melvin the envelope. "In this envelope is not a loan or a monetary gift, but the inheritance rightfully owed to Glenda Fortier, with interest."

After all the dinner guests were gone, Yvonne, Melvin, and Clarence sat on the sofa in the living room, side by side, gazing at the 230 million-dollar check in the center of the coffee table, afraid to hold it.

"If this is a dream, don't wake me. Even if I've pissed in the bed, don't wake me," Clarence said.

"It's not a dream, and I think I have already pissed myself," Melvin replied.

"Well, aren't you going to pick it up?" Yvonne asked Melvin.

"Nope. I just want to look at it for a little while longer," Melvin said.

"Clarence, aren't you going to pick it up?"

"Hell, nah! With my luck, it would turn into a two-hundred-dollar check the moment it touched my fingers! Mel, hold my share of it in your account because tomorrow I am going check myself into rehab to deal with this drinking. When I get out, I will deposit my portion then."

"Kool, I'm so happy to hear you say that," Yvonne said. "Your mother would be so proud of you right now."

"Sista'-in-law, with this kind of money, I don't need habits I can't control! Momma up in heaven looking out for us, and I will not screw this up."

"I am proud you're taking this step, and I will be there waiting for you when you get out," Melvin said.

"Steven made this right!" Clarence said. "I feel like running out of this house buck-ass naked, but too many police live around here!" Clarence stood and headed for the door.

"Kool, you're leaving? Hold up for a second. I want to pack you at least a plate. No way we can eat all of this food."

"Sista'-in-law, I'm good for the night. I need to take a long ride and figure out how I'm going to get my wife back," Clarence said as he walked out of the house and hopped on his bike.

Yvonne and Melvin watched as Clarence pedaled away into the night, and it was only then that they realized Jynika's mother and Clarence had never officially filed for divorce. Jackie Campbell, a fifth-grade teacher, had just become a millionaire.

CHAPTER 40

Seven weeks had passed since Brandon and Sherman delivered their presentation to a packed room of professors at Tulane, but there was still no word as to whether their dissertation, titled "The Nine Notches of Beatrice Fortier," had been rejected or approved for post-doctorate completion. Professor Davis had mentioned at the close of the presentation that a reply on their grade could take up to eight weeks, and with each passing day, Sherman began to feel like the project had been a failure. The only good to come out of the constant waiting was that his friendship with Brandon was back to normal, especially since he decided to drop his anger issues with the Fortier family.

His life didn't change much after the inheritance check cleared. His mother continued her OB-GYN practice; his dad formed a trust for the Campbells that focused on enrichment projects and charities. Sherman had little interest in either. The only things that mattered to him were getting his doctorate in American History, and the possibility of their dissertation becoming a television series on HBO. While Sherman obsessed over the potential of getting a series deal, Brandon did not.

On the fourth day of the seventh week of waiting for a reply from Professor Davis, Sherman rested in bed with Ronelle, watching *Baby Boom* starring Diane Keaton. Today marked her eighteenth week of pregnancy, and their ultrasound appointment at four o'clock would reveal the sex of their babies. His nerves were all over the place, and he didn't share her excitement—though he would never say those words aloud.

"So, are we going to continue to ignore this giant elephant in the room?" Ronelle asked.

"Huh? Oh, I get it. You're having another one of those internal arguments and finally tagged me in." Her head tilted to the right as she brushed her hair, then to the left with the same motion. "Ronelle, what are you talking about, an elephant?"

With every week their babies grew inside of her, Ronelle wanted the security of knowing Sherman was going to be there as her husband, but he never took the initiative to make her feel secure. Sherman knew this conversation was headed somewhere he didn't want it to go, but he was helpless to stop it. She wanted to talk about something he had avoided for weeks. Therefore, he'd developed a way of working around the elephant.

Outside the window, a midday thunderstorm provided temporary relief from the grip of late spring. Suddenly, a flash of lightning knocked out the power. The sound of thunder vibrated the walls. In between the atmospheric grumblings was the voice of Ronelle. Sherman sat on the bed looking at the television with no power—just a blank screen—while she stood beside the bed looking at a man with no answers, only time-released excuses. One after the other.

"Are we still getting married? I know you want the babies, but do you still want me as your wife, or am I just your cousin/baby momma? I need to know."

"Ronelle, I asked for time to process this, that's all."

"You do realize my brother proposed to Jynika, right?"

"Yes, I was there."

"You do realize Jynika is pregnant, right?"

"I see where you're going with this . . ."

"And you still need time to process! Everyone else has processed it already! Adding to my humiliation is Brandon and Jynika have set a wedding date for just after the birth of their baby. They haven't even dated for six months. We have been together for nearly four freaking years! What else is there to process? Please tell me!" she yelled.

"Ronelle, come on now. How do we go from a pleasant afternoon to an argument? Why do you constantly do this to us? I just want one week during which we don't fight over this topic!"

"Topic? Have you reduced my concerns and feelings to just another topic? Why do I even bother?!"

Ronelle grabbed her keys from the nightstand—her keychain that sounded like a jingling Christmas tree.

"You know what, Sherman? Fuck it! I am not going to beg you to marry me. I refuse to! After you rejected my pregnancy in the hospital, I have tried every day to forgive you, when I really feel like punching you in the face. But I'm done, Sherman. If you don't want to marry me, then don't! I'm not begging you. I can raise my children by myself. It's going to look awful to my mother and her stuck-up friends, but I can't make you want something you don't want. Don't bother coming to the appointment today because I might as well start preparing myself for a life without you."

Sherman never got a word in after that. Ronelle pulled her sweatpants up to the middle of her belly, grabbed her purse, and stormed out of the room. The front door slammed.

"Ronelle, I want to come to the appointment," he yelled to an empty room.

He was alone for the first time in two months, with the same uncertainty and indecisiveness regarding her pregnancy and their engagement. Post-diary, it all felt different to him, and he couldn't deny it. It wasn't their fault. Sherman knew that, but something about his relationship with Ronelle still felt awkward. In his hospital bed, all he thought about was marrying Ronelle. Once he was discharged, all the enthusiasm was gone. However, Sherman planned to attend that ultrasound appointment no matter what. After all, his mother was Ronelle's OB-GYN.

His cell phone rang. It was Brandon.

"What's up, B?"

"That's what I'm trying to figure out!"

"Don't tell me they rejected our dissertation. Please don't say it."

"No, not even close. This is something completely unrelated.

A guy just left our house after serving my dad with court papers," Brandon said.

"Court papers! What kind of court papers?"

"Well, my dad was pretty shaken by it and immediately went into his office and called his lawyers. From what I can tell, someone is suing us for their entitlement in Fortier International."

"What! You mean the inheritance?"

"Yeah, man. This is bad. Atrocious!"

"Who would do this?" Sherman asked.

"That's why I'm calling you. Do you think your dad or Clarence is behind this?"

"Hell, no! My dad hung a picture of your dad on his living room wall last week. All he talks about is how much he loves your father! Clarence is still in rehab until next month, but he would never do something like this."

"Dude, I hear you, but the timing of this seems rather odd, coming after the check has cleared."

"Brandon, I don't like the tone of your voice. It sounds like you're convinced my family is behind this, and that is pissing me off!"

"Pissing you off? My dad nearly caught a fucking heart attack on the porch, and you think I give a fuck if you're pissed off? All I know is your family better not be behind this. That's all I'm saying."

The call ended on a threat.

Professor Davis made it home around 6:45 p.m. As soon as he entered the house, he rushed over to kiss his wife. So many evenings, he repeated the same routine and wondered what he'd done to deserve such a beautiful woman. His buddies would always joke that she was his trophy wife, the luxury fishing boat that he'd always wanted, his Little Red Corvette. Mrs. Davis never took offense at their jokes; she never objected to being his trophy.

Irving Davis had just turned 56 years old, but he still felt like he was in his forties. Mrs. Davis was six years younger than the professor, and no matter how hard he tried, there was no concealing the obvious: he looked old enough to be her father.

They'd fallen in love at Tulane when she was a new math professor and the chancellor seated them next to each other at the new staff banquet. It was love at first sight for Irving Davis. She was what people in New Orleans referred to as a high yellow woman, with beautiful, long, light-brown hair. Sometimes she resembled Caucasian, and other times she appeared African American. It just depended on the season and the angle. She was a Creole beauty in every sense of the word, but when she spoke, you could hear her New Orleans accent loud and clear. After about nine months of dating, they were married in the courtyard just outside of his classroom.

Other than a few issues with his blood pressure and a recurring cough, Professor Davis was in perfect health. His wife was not. Life had dealt Mrs. Davis an awful hand. A little less than three years earlier, she'd fallen to the ground while jogging and couldn't stand for hours. What Mrs. Davis assumed were simply bad leg cramps turned out to be far worse. After she made repeated trips to the doctor and underwent countless medical tests, her physicians' worse fears were confirmed: Amyotrophic Lateral Sclerosis (ALS), commonly known as Lou Gehrig's disease. Professor Davis's dream marriage became a haunting nightmare. Mrs. Davis once jogged three miles a day before seven in the morning. Now she sat in one spot, unable to move a limb.

Irving's anger with God grew out of control. This was the second wife to be taken from him; the first had succumbed to breast cancer. Once again, he had become the caretaker of a dying woman. At a time when he could have retired from Tulane, Professor Davis prepared to work well into his sixties, using every dime from his salary to cover the skyrocketing cost of insurance just to keep his wife alive. Mrs. Davis's treatments pushed their insurance to the limits. For reasons they could not understand, her claims for disability were continuously rejected. He had never pictured life this way, but this was his reality.

To add more misery to his marriage, his beautiful wife had lost her ability to speak. It had been two years since he'd last heard her say goodnight. The best part of hearing her voice was the stories she would tell. Mrs. Davis was very animated; a talent she developed in the theater. He could sit and listen for hours as she shared stories about her great-grandmother and all the complex rules of her Creole family lifestyle.

There was a time, right before she lost her voice, when she'd shared something with him, something he'd never forgotten. The story had been passed down for three generations. It dated back to slavery and involved a famous shipping tycoon in New Orleans. Her grandmother had never given the name of the tycoon. She took his name to her grave. It was family folklore that would soon consume his life in his quest to prove the validity of the tale. No sooner had he started the research, he hit a roadblock. At one point, they had both tried to piece together the story with the use of the University of New Orleans archives, but the bits and pieces Mrs. Davis had were simply not enough. Then sickness paid them a visit and refused to leave.

Across the room, the home health nurse sorted her medications for the long night to come, a regimen he administered around eight p.m. Each night after her last dose of meds, he would make sure she was as comfortable as possible in her hospital bed before crawling under the covers in his cold and lonely king-sized bed. Some nights he would sleep on the sofa because he missed having her in bed with him. His bed started to feel like punishment, taunting him through the evening.

The nurse attending to his wife packed up her things and prepared to leave. Professor Davis gave the nurse a twenty-five-dollar tip just to show her how much he appreciated the care she provided his wife throughout the day. The nurse headed out the door. After he locked up behind her, the professor slid a chair next to his wife and turned her head so she could make full eye contact with him. It was then that he revealed something he had held onto for almost a year.

"Sweetheart, about this time last year, two students in my Advanced American History course came into my office to announce the topic they had selected for their dissertation work. I didn't give it much thought at first because there was little difference between their project plan and those of all the other students, but then something jumped out at me as their research developed. It became clear that these two students—one white and one extremely light-skinned—were telling the same story, but from two different sides of the family. I continued to pay close attention to this story when a familiar name surfaced—a name that was the same as your great-grandmother's. That name was *Eva Fortier.*"

Professor Davis paused to wipe her mouth and adjust her head before continuing.

"Early last month, the same two students presented their final dissertation to the board of professors, and since then I've studied it page by page, sentence by sentence, every day, all day. One slave mentioned in their story is your grandmother, Eva Fortier—daughter of Bernard Fortier, as in Fortier International Shipping Company. Cheryl Gullage Davis, I have found the tycoon your great-grandmother spoke of in wise tales. And the good news is Sherman Campbell and Brandon Fortier, the grandson of Steven Fortier, Jr., did all the work for you. I used this dissertation as evidence in a civil lawsuit our attorney filed last Friday with the Clerk of Court in New Orleans. Sweetheart, I intend to sue them on your behalf for millions. If I die today or tomorrow, I only want the best care for you, and the Fortier fortune is enough to guarantee it."

Out of the corner of her eye, a tear swelled and then fell slowly down her cheek. The story her grandmother had told her was true, but she came from a very proud family, one that believed in acquiring their wealth the old-fashioned way. Cheryl had lost her voice before she could tell her husband the other half of the story—regarding a promise she once made to her mother. *If she ever found the story to be true, she would never make it public.*

Anne Fortier's diary mentioned a covenant between Anne and Beatrice; an agreement to never make the scandals of the family public. The dissertation and the lawsuit Professor Davis had just filed broke that agreement. Cheryl's husband never made the promise that she did, and he desperately needed that money. With her lack of mobility and inability to speak, there was nothing Cheryl could do to stop the epic legal battle that was about to ensue. She couldn't even utter the word *no!*

ANNE FORTIER
DIARY ENTRY TWELVE

December 15, 1878

Dear Diary,

Today I had a meeting with my old friend, Marie Laveau. It was delightful to see how popular she has become. A line of patrons forms outside her door nearly a block long. My belief in her kind has grown over the years; I'm living proof of the power of her herbs and spices. Today there was no need for passion serums or potions, but a greater urgency for her spiritual knowledge—her binding covenants. The binding power of Laveau's covenant is something Beatrice has firm confidence in, and I have total faith in Beatrice.

I tried everything in my power to keep the relationship between my son and Annette from developing. I even sent him away to Harvard College. But I failed. Out of their courtship, two children were conceived at our residence. Both Glenda and Gladys currently reside in living quarters with Beatrice and their mother. Though my son has taken the advice of his father and married another, the honorable duty of Steven Fortier is to recognize and provide for the children he has fathered, as ordered under the Napoleonic Code. It is the just thing to do. I have created the Tureaud Trust for this noble cause.

Earlier today, Marie Laveau pricked each of our tongues and

collected all the blood on a large spoon. She then placed the spoon over a flame until the blood simmered. Once it dried, she touched each one of us with the hot spoon on the back of our necks. The screams of Beatrice's grandkids were terrible to endure. Only during childbirth have I felt such pain, but my minor suffering was worth it. The Fortier legacy must stand beyond reproach. Marie explained that the agreement was a bond sealed with blood

If any of us violates the bond, blood is the payment. Death is certain and will come quickly upon the next-born male, even in the womb.

The Fortier family has agreed to acknowledge and financially care for Beatrice and all of her descendants through our trust. Beatrice and her descendants are in agreement to never publicly associate my husband with the atrocities of slavery, or connect my son with a forbidden union. This covenant will become a death curse the moment any member of Beatrice's bloodline violates this bond, so help them God. On this day, our agreement has been consummated by our family, as recorded in my diary.

Our name is all we have, and it is equally divided between us. The Fortier family must stand the decades to come without spot or blemish.

Anne Boleyn Fortier

CHAPTER 41

S teven Fortier arrived at his office bright and early to find his entire legal team, along with the company's Chief Operations Officer, Mrs. Jacques, already in the Situation Room. The day before, a motion for discovery was delivered to their corporate office on Poydras Street, and to Tureaud Trust on St. Charles Avenue. It was evident to Steven and his staff attorneys that whoever had filed the motion was determined to battle it out for partial ownership of their company or demand a huge settlement, but Steven was in no mood to negotiate with the plaintiff. He saw the motion as a declaration of war.

Though Fortier Lines was one of only a few privately-owned international shipping companies, the activity around his large conference table resembled a group of Wall Street traders in a race against the closing bell. It was, in fact, Black Monday for his company, and the attorneys representing Cheryl Gullage had just launched the first-ever attempt to gain ownership of Fortier Lines by a hostile takeover. In his hand were ten pages of legal paper that read:

CHERYL GULLAGE, Plaintiff v. STEVEN FORTIER III, TUREAUD TRUST, AND FORTIER INTERNATIONAL, Defendants.

Steven took the threat seriously and prepared to go on the attack. Like the New England Patriots with two minutes left in the fourth quarter of the Super Bowl, his legal team broke the huddle and sprang into action. His lead attorney left the room to call the lawyer representing Ms. Gullage, while Mrs. Jacques placed a call to the best private investigator she knew. Fresh-roasted beans permeated the air as the coffee pots shifted into war mode. Even the interns showed no interest in their iPhones. All hands were on deck. Steven, a Rambo fanatic, titled the name of his legal response "Operation Stallone," because plaintiff Gullage had drawn *First Blood.*

Suddenly, a boom echoed through the Situation Room!

The sound came from the rubber doorstop as it tried to redirect an unstoppable force—to no avail. Guitar riffs of Led Zeppelin's "Kashmir" were first to enter the room, followed closely by a fuming Brenda Fortier. As she forced her way in, all the oxygen in the room diminished. With the brute force of the Drug Enforcement Agency, she entered, and no one dared say a word. Several staff attorneys ran for cover, while others backed against the wall as if she'd brandished a pistol in a convenience store. There she stood, huffing and puffing heat, immediately raising the temperature of the room like a furnace, adding to the doomsday feeling of the morning.

To Steven, it felt like she had stared him down for an eternity, but only a minute had elapsed. Then as quickly as she came, she about-faced like a platoon with one Marine and headed directly to his office. Without any choice in the matter, Steven was on the losing end of a hook as his wife reeled him into an inevitable confrontation.

From one side of his office to the other, in the plush area in front of his desk, Brenda marched from left to right like a North Korean soldier.

"This morning, I was having a patio breakfast at La Richelieu Restaurant with some of my friends from the Krewe of Caesar and Rex when some asshole rolls up on a bike and serves me with a lawsuit. In front of all my friends! Never in my life have I been so embarrassed. Are you listening to me?" she screamed.

"Who in the fuck is Cheryl Gullage, and why is she dragging me to court?"

"She served you, too? Oh, my."

Brenda retrieved the legal forms from her purse and pitched them at her husband.

CHERYL GULLAGE, Plaintiff v. BRENDA FORTIER, Defendant.

It was the same motion for discovery, with the same threat of a pending court order to freeze all assets. Steven made no attempts to calm his wife down. Her tightly-clenched fists were only symptoms of far greater anger, the sort of rage commonly associated with Dr. David Banner. Steven feared she was only seconds away from turning green and flipping his desk.

"Brenda, I'm sorry that happened this morning. You have every right to be angry. The truth is, I have no earthly idea who Cheryl Gullage is, or why she filed these lawsuits."

"Really? You have no idea."

"Brenda, you have my word. I'll get to the bottom of this by the end of the day," Steven tried to reassure his wife, but it wasn't working. "I have my entire legal team on it, plus two more attorneys flying in from New York. I will deal with this. Just relax and let me handle it."

Suddenly, Steven found himself in one of those dangerous moments, watching his wife search for an object to throw. He followed her eyes as she spotted a coffee mug—a gift from Ronelle. She pitched it; he ducked just in time. The *World's Greatest Dad* mug shattered on the floor behind his desk.

Brenda pumped her fist into the air. "Relax? You want me to relax?" Her high-pitched voice traveled around his desk like a curveball. "I was just embarrassed in a crowded restaurant! That insensitive jerk even yelled, 'YOU GOT SERVED' over and over again! There wasn't a hole big enough to crawl into! Oh, how I wish I could have found just one hole, then I would have buried myself in it—alive." Boiling tears raced down the sides of Brenda's face, but her voice was a flamethrower. "I cried all the way to the car, chased by laughter, and you tell me to relax?"

Then she paused, but not for long—only long enough to survey his desk. Above her head, Steven could see the volume meter turning up even higher.

"Did you have an affair with that Cheryl Gullage woman?"

"Brenda, are you serious? An affair?"

"Yes. Have you slept with this woman? Do you have other children with this woman you haven't told me about?"

"Brenda, I know you're upset, but that's ridiculous! I have never heard of Cheryl Gullage in my life." Then it dawned on him. "That's where I recall hearing that name. They contacted the Tureaud Trust about two months ago. Norman and I thought it was just another request for donations."

"Steven, do I look stupid to you? The only reason you would say something that asinine is you figure I'm dumb enough to fall for it."

"Brenda, you have to believe me! I'm not lying to you. It's God's honest truth. I have not had an affair. I was served with the same papers yesterday but didn't tell you. I'm prepared to go broke fighting this woman."

Brenda leaned across his desk and pointed her finger like a machete. "I know you come from a long line of adulterous affairs, but Steven, *I swear to God,* if I discover this woman is your mistress, you will never see the inside of a courtroom. I will kill you first, then choke the life out of your gold-digging whore!"

"Brenda, that was low!"

"You wait until I find that bitch. I'll show you low!"

With the force of a high-powered vacuum, Brenda exited his office, leaving a path of destruction like a tornado to the elevator. As soon as she departed, Steven's cell phone rang. It was Melvin.

"Yes, Melvin, buddy. I can only hope your morning is going better than mine."

"Hey, Steve, I can imagine it's pretty tense over there! Sherman just told me about you getting served with a lawsuit."

"Tense is the understatement of the year! Brenda just left from here believing I'm having an affair. Imagine that? Having an affair is the furthest thing from my mind on a good day. But anyway, I have a major situation over here, to say the least."

"And that's what I'm calling about—that situation. I'm offering my entire law firm to help you fight this woman. I know you have a team over there, but my staff can help by beating the pavement. I have a real hound dog in this office!"

"Buddy, thank you so much. We're scratching our heads over here. I'll have Mrs. Jacques email you the summons. Let me know what resources you need as we hunt down this Gullage woman."

"There's no charge at all. This fight is our fight! We're family. I'll connect with you later today with an update. Let's go!"

CHAPTER 42

Campbell Law Firm
9:30 a.m.

Melvin ended his call with Steven Fortier and immediately enlisted his entire firm in "Operation Stallone." Just across from him, Chantrell anxiously waited for the email with the legal filings attached from Mrs. Jacques. Like an angel who needed a seat after a long commute from heaven, Chantrell sat directly in front of Melvin on his champagne chesterfield, the one pressed against the wall under all his academic accomplishments and legal conquests.

Though he had never laid one finger on her romantically, he was able to retain her presence and her keen knowledge of state laws. He kept Chantrell co-dependent financially. Every day she walked around his office felt like a win. Like he had a new wife without divorcing Yvonne. Like he'd skipped the formalities of new nuptials. Chantrell was more than just his adjutant during legal battles; she added a type of progressive style to his professional image. She protected him from a life of retro vernacular, paneled walls, and an expired persona. Though Sherman sat on the other side of his desk, Melvin's gaze kept drifting to Chantrell; her lemon-yellow dress controlled his eyes. Her dress was slightly fitted and only revealed a morsel of curvature. The hem settled three inches above her knee, and her shoulders were covered with a black blazer. Her hair was an Afro-centric bouquet of loosely twisted curls, parted on the left side of her head, with a yellow daisy that flirted with him; playing peek-a-boo throughout the morning.

He could tell Chantrell's mother had invested a considerable amount of time instilling the etiquette of how to sit like a lady, because her thoroughly oiled knees never gifted him one glimpse of her panties. Her cell phone chirped; the email had arrived. His eyes left the room with Chantrell. Below her black blazer, her hips swayed with the motion of an experienced hula dancer, only slower, with no bongos required. When she returned with the copies, she handed one set to Sherman, then slowly walked around Melvin's desk.

Chantrell leaned over him just a little as she placed the legal forms on his desk; not enough for him to view inside her cleavage, but just close enough for him to inhale her Chanel perfume.

She enjoys teasing me, and I wouldn't have it any other way, he thought.

Chantrell carried his eyes with her again as she returned to the same spot on the chesterfield and glanced over the copies.

"Chantrell, your assignment on this one is to . . ."

She interrupted him. "To find out everything I can about this Cheryl Gullage woman and her motivation."

"And I mean everything! Even her favorite soap, and whether she prefers beans or onion rings with her spicy chicken. I need to know that too!" Melvin said as Chantrell hurried from his room. "And let's build a display board on this one, like the Feds do when they profile a crime family. I get the feeling more people are behind this, and we need to track all parties involved. At the top of the pyramid—Cheryl Gullage!"

"I'm on it."

"I know you are. Do that thing you do."

Only then did Sherman raise his head. "No. Way!"

"What, son?"

"Get out of here!" Sherman leaned over his father's desk and pointed to a name on the motion for discovery in the section designated for the attorney representing the plaintiffs.

"I can't believe this. It's the same guy!" Sherman continued to point at the photocopy. "The attorney representing Cheryl
Gullage. This dude sat in on our dissertation."

To gain confirmation, Melvin pointed to the same section.
"This guy right here? You sure?"

"Dad, when we presented our research, he sat on the Board
of Deans. I remember him more than any other because he is an
associate dean of the law school, so I found it interesting that
he was sitting in on our presentation. Our project has zero to do
with law, but this professor was the most attentive, and drilled
Brandon the hardest."

"When you presented your half of the presentation, did this
professor drill you with questions?"

"Not at all. It was night and day. Professor Davis and this
guy asked Brandon a million questions, especially when Brandon arrived at the part about the diary."

It was then that Melvin stood and folded his arms in thought.
"Did they ask to see the diary?"

"Yes, but Brandon told them his parents locked it away. He
allowed them to view a picture of the first-page entry."

"Son, what's the name of your professor again?"

Chantrell re-entered the room and answered Melvin's question. "His name is Professor Irving Davis, husband of the plaintiff, Cheryl Gullage Davis!" With the grace of Queen Elizabeth
II, Chantrell returned to her seat on the sofa. "Her official title
at Tulane is Professor Cheryl Gullage! She is currently on sick
leave, and I know this for sure because seven years ago before I
transferred to Southern University, she was my math teacher in
my freshman year. Their wedding ceremony was held in one of
the flower courts. The only thing I'm trying to confirm right now
is the date they were married—my cousin at the Clerk of Court
is looking into it for me."

"Are you kidding me? Our professor is married to the lady
who filed this lawsuit?"

"Son, it looks that way."

"Melvin, did you see the other thorn?"

"Yes, I saw it. Sherman just pointed it out."

Chantrell's elbows rested on her thoroughly oiled knees. Her face fell into the palms of her hands. Her fingers disappeared into her bouquet of curls. "Melvin, I can't go another twelve rounds with him. I cannot do it. It was too hard picking you up off the floor the last time we lost."

Confused, Sherman asked, "What thorn? Twelve rounds with who?"

Slowly, Chantrell lifted her head and shot Melvin a look of defeat. "Are you going to explain this scheme, or do you want me to?"

"What scheme?"

"Son, they used you and Brandon like a pair of Jordan tennis shoes. From where I'm sitting, this Gullage lady is closely related to Steven Fortier. At some point during your review sessions leading up to the main presentation, that Professor Davis pieced it all together. Chantrell can finish explaining the rest, while I pop about three Advils."

With her arms folded across her stomach, Chantrell explained. "My best guess is, after one of those review sessions, your history professor took a little stroll over to see his buddy at the law school, who just happens to be one of the top civil attorneys in the country. A guy who teaches at Tulane for the joy of teaching. He doesn't need the money after winning so many lawsuits against everybody from GM to Johnson & Johnson— who hired our firm, by the way. We lost that case, and now this fat, juicy steak has landed on his plate. All thanks to his good buddy, Professor Davis."

"The professor who sat in on our dissertation review?"

"Yes, none other than *Attorney Gabriel Raegan*!"

"And we did all the work for them."

"I hate to admit it, Sherman, but you're right."

After washing down the Advil, Melvin said, "Well, *I'll be damned*. Mr. Raegan, we meet again."

Melvin occupied the tiny area behind his desk, pacing only as far as the walls would allow. "Son, this is bad, and I need to tell Steven it will take everything we've got to beat this guy. He is the only attorney living in Louisiana who has won every case he's ever argued at the Supreme Court level."

"Looks like I found the first picture for your board." Sherman held his phone up so his dad could see a wedding picture of Professor Davis and Cheryl Gullage.

"Well, there's your motive for why Attorney Raegan took this case. Thanks to the brilliant research of Brandon and Sherman, this lawsuit is a slam dunk. That dude makes me sick; he is so freakin' good!" Chantrell sighed.

"How do I break the news to Steven that Cheryl Gullage is somehow related to Beatrice, and they've come to collect?" Melvin agonized.

"Dad, how about I do it? After all, I'm responsible for this."

"Sherman, I will not let you take the blame on this one. There was no way you and Brandon could have known about this scheme," Chantrell said.

"Sherman, she's right. It was a trap, and I plan to file a formal complaint with the Bar Association and the Board of Tulane by this time tomorrow. I will break the news to Steven," Melvin said. "Can you two please excuse me for a second while I place this call?"

Once Sherman and Chantrell stepped out of the office, Melvin pressed re-dial.

"Hey, buddy, it's me again. We've got big trouble."

CHAPTER 43

Attorney Raegan's Office
11:30 a.m.

In several ways, he felt guilty for allowing the boys to present their dissertation, then commandeering that information and using it for the lawsuit. But in the unfairness of life, Irving Davis found justification for it all.

Attorney Raegan was on a conference call, so Davis took a seat in the waiting area and enjoyed a fresh cup of coffee. Just from a glance at the walls and expensive furniture that decorated the waiting room, he could tell Gabriel Raegan enjoyed a very successful career in the courtroom. The photos on his wall captured images of all his successful triumphs on court battlefields across the country, and he made zero effort to hide his masonic affiliations and emblems. On the wall behind his receptionist's desk hung a picture of him in his masonic apron, clinching a hammer and spike.

All the plants in the room were real and healthy, not like the plastic flower arrangements he typically saw whenever he accompanied Cheryl to the doctor. Every plant appeared to be cared for by a personal botanist, with moist, dark potting soil and deep emerald-green leaves. The Aztec artwork gave a clue that all the flowerpots were custom designed somewhere in South America, as was the wooden center table that held *Time* magazines.

In his office were three secretaries who worked in close proximity, but surprisingly, they never spoke to each other. The entire time Professor Davis sat in the waiting area, he gazed at them through a sliding receptionist's window that never closed. The three secretaries appeared so busy that they never raised their heads to confirm whether he was still in the room, or if he had stripped naked. It became very apparent to Davis why Raegan was so successful. The focus of his entire staff was unlike anything he had ever witnessed, which gave him soothing assurance that he had selected the right attorney to go after Steven Fortier.

Raegan entered the room with a handshake from twenty feet away. "Dr. Davis, I'm so sorry for the delay. Please come with me. Right this way."

"Not a problem. You could have taken as long as you needed. I feel like I should pay you for this coffee. It's not Walmart coffee . . . that's for sure."

"I love a friend who appreciates a real cup of joe. I'm in the process of opening a chain that will compete with Starbucks and PJ's Coffee. What you have in that cup is my brand, picked and imported just for you."

"If this is the coffee you plan to pour, you have your first customer right here."

"How about I have my first franchise owner after we finish with the Fortier family?"

"I like the sound of that," Professor Davis laughed and coughed at the same time.

After a short walk through a maze of hallways, they arrived in Raegan's office.

"Please, have a seat. How is Cheryl today?"

"About as well as could be expected. It is so hard to watch my beautiful wife suffer, but she's strong. I would have checked out of life if the shoe was on the other foot." His head slumped to his chest.

Raegan said, "The good news is, I will do everything in my power to make her as comfortable as possible until there is a cure. You have my word."

"I believe in my heart you're the man with the plan to make it happen. That's why I hand-picked you." Professor Davis lifted his head. He couldn't help but notice that every wall of the office was a tribute to all of Raegan's legal successes, as well as his academic achievements at Tulane. However, there were no pictures of his family. In the corner of the wall to the left was a row of pictures taken with all the Republican presidents, starting with Nixon.

Raegan was a slender man; the type who woke up at five a.m. to jog five miles. His hair appeared as if he'd conceded to gray, while his arms belonged to an MMA fighter. He sported the natural tan of someone with Italian ancestry, with the Sinatra baby blues to match. Professor Davis had once smoked two packs of cigarettes a day, which left him with a chronic cough, but he could tell Raegan was a non-smoker. A half-eaten nutrition bar on his desk gave some insight into his diet. His voice was deep, like the fourth guy in a quartet—the tall one commonly standing on the far left.

"Well, Dr. Davis, those three beautiful women you saw out front have successfully served the entire Fortier family and corporation with legal notices. I expect to hear from all of them, including the Tureaud Trust, by the end of the week."

"That was faster than I expected!"

"Yes, it doesn't take long to get them all served when all of them are local and in one central location. Once I receive a response from their legal team, I'll know whether we need to prepare for a long court battle or a settlement. My gut tells me to dig in and prepare for a long and bloody battle."

"Yeah, I figured that as well, but my wife has just as much right to the Fortier fortune as Steven Fortier. I'm prepared to go all the way."

"I'm glad to hear you say that, because it will be an uphill battle at first—at least until they realize that we're not going away easily. I am going with a 'shock and awe' strategy in which we threaten to go public with a search for other unknown heirs."

"In other words, more descendants of Beatrice Fortier?"

"Correct. Currently, we're only dealing with Eva's kids, and we know of Annette's kids. But according to Brandon's portion of that dissertation, Beatrice and Steven had nine children in total."

"I see, but wouldn't that cut into our money if more heirs were discovered? I hate to sound greedy, but I'm not interested in sharing—excuse my French—a goddamn thing. Haha! *Cough, cough!* Haha, *cough!"* Professor Davis wiped his mouth again with the overworked handkerchief.

"I agree, and that is why we will only threaten them with the possibility of going public. Steven Fortier will cave before it gets to that point. The goal of 'shock and awe' is to introduce them to fear. Just the thought of that type of negative publicity might get them to cooperate faster, especially if they fear this thing could turn into a class action-type case with hundreds of descendants. The other part of this strategy is to disrupt their comfortable life and rob them of their privacy. I'm also in the process of getting court-ordered financials on all their assets on the personal side and the corporate side. From what we've pulled on the commercial end, the Fortier family is worth about six billion dollars collectively."

"Billion, as in billion with a 'B'? Did you say Steven Fortier is worth six billion dollars?"

"Yes, sir, and most of that is due to their international shipping lines and the fifty-five ports worldwide that Fortier International has under their control. You're talking about a company that has dominated the shipping world since 1824, primarily in several small countries. The three beautiful ladies we passed on the way to this office have also tracked down two manufacturing shipyards among its conglomerate. Those shipyards are currently building two cruise ships for Carnival."

"Oh, my gosh! Wait until I tell Cheryl how much money she has missed out on all these years. She might leap out of the hospital bed and cut a rug!" Professor Davis chuckled without a cough.

"Having said all that, Fortier International has enough money and resources to fight this lawsuit to the bitter end, which is why I need you to be prepared emotionally for an intense battle. In the end, I feel they will settle with us out of court in an attempt to get your wife to sign over any rights she has, along signing with a non-disclosure agreement. Is that acceptable to you?" Raegan asked.

"It depends on how much we're talking about in a possible settlement."

"At its core, this case is seeking damages for illegally re-moving Cheryl from a trust and profits left to her mother and grandmother from the Tureaud Trust. I intend to come in high, then allow them to counter from there. So, we'll set the bar at 520 million, with a hidden settlement mark set at 280 million."

Professor Davis leaned back in his chair and tried to wrap his mind around a minimum of 280 million dollars. In a split second, he envisioned the standard of care he could provide his wife with a settlement that large, and how nice it would be to finally retire.

"Dr. Davis, I usually never say what I'm about to say, but in your case, I feel very comfortable. That diary is your ticket to millions. Brandon Fortier and Sherman Campbell unknowingly included that key piece of evidence in their dissertation, proving your wife should have been a bloodline heiress. All I plan to do is read the same dissertation out loud. In the world of civil attor-neys, we call this one a 'softball over the plate!'"

"Great, that's just great! It's more money than I ever expect-ed. I know we have some ways to go, but I thank you for caring about us enough to take on this case. I appreciate it."

"Dr. Davis, your wife was my friend before she became your wife. I'm honored to do whatever I can to make her life a little bit easier. Will I see you at the lodge tonight?" Raegan asked.

"The brothers have me on the program to welcome in the recruits."

"That works out perfectly, because Judge Rowan Klein will be there as well. I called in a few favors to get your case in front of his bench. The brotherhood will all come together to support you for your years of service. I look forward to seeing you at the lodge tonight."

"I look forward to it as well." Professor Davis stood up and initiated the masonic handshake. Later, sitting in his car, he'd nev-er felt so confident in his life. The fact that his masonic broth-

NINE NOTCHES / 405

er, Judge Kline, was the presiding judge of his lawsuit was more than he'd ever hoped for. Before pulling out of the parking lot, he placed a call to his secretary at Tulane.

Shelita Burns answered. "Thanks for calling the Tulane History Department. How can I help you?"

"Ms. Burns, do you have a free minute?"

"Always for you, Dr. Davis. How can I assist you?"

"Can you mail those two letters on my desk—one for Brandon Fortier and the other for Sherman Campbell?"

"Dr. Davis, would you like me to overnight them, or send them through regular mail?"

"Please send both letters today through regular mail. Whenever they arrive is fine with me. Should either one of them request a meeting with me, I am unavailable due to a family emergency, then on vacation."

"In other words, no meetings with Brandon Fortier or Sherman Campbell under any circumstances?"

"That is correct! Please insert a little card from me congratulating them on completing their Ph.D. requirements, and letting them know we look forward to seeing them at commencement."

"So, what about me?"

"You, sweetheart?"

"Are you still coming over tonight, or should I make out one of these letters for myself?"

"I will see you around the same time I always see you."

"Okay, that works because I am having dinner with a few leaders from my sorority and should wrap up by the time you get her settled in. I love you, babe."

"I love you too, Shelita. Bye-bye."

CHAPTER 44

I t was that euphoric moment of the morning, during a hot shower, when all the knotted areas of his shoulders finally relaxed. It was the perfect sauna. Soothing, rhythmic water pressure, a deep, pulsating therapy for the aching crick in his neck—so invigorating he could've drifted to a happier place if he hadn't been standing up. It would have been a perfect shower if not for the ringing that came from the other side of his bed, where his phone was charging on a nightstand.

It wasn't one of those beds at the Hilton with the bedding tightly stretched and chained under the mattress. It was his bed, their bed; a bed he'd shared with Ronelle before she left. Everything Sherman loved about his bed ran off with Ronelle.

Like a newborn, his cell cried for his attention. Likewise, no mother could ignore her baby. The shower was cut short so he could answer the phone. His aching neck—a consequence of sleeping on the sofa—would have to wait. After partially drying off, Sherman retrieved his phone from the nightstand and noticed three missed calls from Brandon and one new text. It was a text message like none he had ever received. It was life-changing.

It is with great honor that I'm the first to call you Dr. Camp-

bell.

He blinked repeatedly. His vision was only made worse by rubbing more infused soap lather across his irritated pupils. Sherman struggled to restore his vision, but it wasn't the soap that caused the blur, though his eyes burned. It was the content of the text that left him awestruck.

It is with great honor that I am the first to call you Dr. Campbell.

He stood motionless, drip-drying until his skin itched, mesmerized by a prefix, hoping it wasn't one of Brandon's poorly-timed pranks. Today was not the day for jokes. When Ronelle left him, his lightheartedness also departed with her—rolled into a ball and stuffed in the bottom of one of her totes. Sherman dialed Brandon's number.

"Dude, what are you talking about?" Sherman asked, still bracing for the prank.

"Apparently you haven't received your letter in the mail yet?"

"A letter from the dean?"

"Yes."

"I guess I haven't checked the mail in a few days."

"Sherman, my brother from another mother, we did it! We will receive our doctoral degrees from Tulane. We are history professors! Congratulations, *Dr. Campbell!*"

"Same to you. Congratulations, *Dr. Fortier.* I wish it wasn't so bittersweet. Last week was a tough one, learning that Professor Davis and his wife baited us into that lawsuit. It's hard to celebrate right now. I want to kick his ass."

"Believe me, I share that feeling."

"And by the way, you still have an ass-whooping coming, too!"

"I know. It just all happened so fast. I just freaked out," Brandon sighed. "I still can't believe I accused your family of filing a lawsuit against my dad. I knew the dissertation was going to be rock solid. We knocked it out the park—it was court evidence solid—but it nearly destroyed our friendship."

"Maybe this is all a sign? Like a deeper purpose is going to surface as a result of this journey?" Sherman suggested.

Brandon disagreed. "How do you see it as a sign of a profound purpose? As a whole, we're not okay. Not sure if you've noticed, but I have. This is the longest we have ever gone without hanging out, shooting hoops, or just chilling. If I had to do it over again, I wouldn't. Just look at you and Ronelle or my mom and dad. I'm not sure how this is a sign."

Sherman held the phone to his ear as he dressed. Then, he headed out the door to his car, where he switched to hands-free and began to drive. At a red light, he lowered the sun visor and grabbed a portable razor out of his glove compartment. "I feel that all of this could be a sign because . . ."

Brandon cut him off again. "Dude, the discovery of this diary has been the worst thing that has ever happened in my life. It's cool that we are related and all, but my parents have fought every day since getting served. You and I have fought, you and Ronelle have fought . . . It's more like we've found a tomb and opened it. Now ancient mummy shit is all over us! The only good to come of it is the Ph.D."

"Bro, I see it differently."

"How, how is it different?"

"Brandon, poke your head out of lover's paradise with Jynika for just three seconds, and you will see this attack has brought us together like never before. Yes, this is a sign that we need to stick together as a family. Professor Davis didn't just attack your family; he attacked us too. And we will fight as one family. That is what the diary has taught me. Don't get me wrong; I feel the turmoil every day. And keep what I'm about to say between us: Ronelle ended our relationship again. Today makes a week."

"Noooooo. Are you serious?"

"The ultrasound was last week. I was there on time, but Ronelle wouldn't allow me to experience the moment. I had to wait in the lobby."

"Wow! I've never known her to go that extreme. I hope you two get it together before the babies arrive. Sherman, all the break-up-to-make-up madness . . . has to stop."

"B, I thought things were going fine . . . then she exploded. I still want to marry her; I simply asked for a moment to get over the diary."

"I know my sister; she's super-spoiled. If Ronelle sensed that you're hesitant, she would take that as rejection . . ."

"Too late, she sees it as rejection."

"Oh boy."

"And to add to it, you and Jynika are so in love, it makes everybody sick," Sherman chuckled a little. "But I am happy for you two. Have you guys set a wedding date yet?"

"Not yet, but three months after she delivers, you can count on a wedding. I would like to see you and my sister tie the knot before we do. Doing so would make her feel a lot better."

"I was thinking the same thing, but I was just about to ask her to set a date, then boom! After the ultrasound appointment, she packed a few bags and moved back in with your parents. I'm heading over there now."

"Sherman, one second. That's my mother calling now. Please hold. Be right back."

Sherman sighed as his mind flashed back to their dissertation. Though he wouldn't admit it to Brandon, Sherman regretted not going with a different topic, something more generic like the other Ph.D. students. Something like "New Orleans during the Great Depression," or "The Influence of Carpetbaggers on the Post-War South." It would have caused fewer headaches and resulted in zero lawsuits. *If only I'd taken Brandon's advice.* In moving full-speed ahead, he'd discovered more than he wanted to know about everything Fortier, everything Campbell . . . and everything about himself. Like a pus-filled pimple camped on the tip of his nose, Sherman couldn't hide his feeling of shame—but he loved Ronelle. *I love her too much to be without her!*

Suddenly, Brandon switched back from the previous call. "Oh—my—God! No, this this is unreal. Sherman, where are you right now?"

"I'm about five minutes from your parents' house. Why, what's going on? Don't tell me. Professor Davis has served you, too?"

"No, not Professor Davis. Dammit! Dammit! Dammit!"

Brandon became frantic. "Why is this happening?" he screamed into the phone.

"Brandon, talk to me! What is going on?"

"Don't go to my mother's house. Turn around and get to Touro Hospital. Ronelle's water broke!"

"But . . . but that shouldn't happen until she's nine months pregnant. She's only just about to start her fifth month," Sherman reasoned as the severity of Ronelle's emergency began to sink in. "Oh, no! She . . . sh-she is in danger of losing my sons!"

"Correct! My mom is rushing her to the E.R. as we speak. Get your ass over there! I will meet you there. Go!"

Sherman parked his car and ran into the E.R., but he couldn't outpace his guilt. Since the ultrasound visit, Ronelle had avoided him in plain sight. She and his mom had become very close, and over the past week, he had seen them together on several occasions. But after hello – silence. Because of the way he rejected her and their last argument, Sherman knew she was going to blame him regardless.

He arrived in the E.R. just as the nurses rolled Ronelle to Labor and Delivery, with Brenda by her side. Brenda never said a word to him, but she didn't have to; her facial expression said it all. *How could you hurt my daughter?* But he'd never meant to hurt her daughter; he only wanted time to process Anne Fortier's diary.

"No, don't come. Please don't come. Dear God, don't let my babies come right now. Please!" Ronelle prayed as time expired.

"Get the patient to the labor unit, ASAP! I'll meet you there," directed the E.R. doctor.

"Are you her husband?" the nurse asked Sherman.

"No, he's not!" Ronelle yelled.

"Well, you'll need to remain here in the waiting area, sir. We'll keep you updated," the nurse instructed.

"Listen, ma'am, I'm not her husband, but I am the father, and her fiancé," Sherman argued.

"If they paid me a dollar for every time I heard that one, I would own this hospital. I'm sorry, but we have to respect Ms. Fortier's wishes. Now, Mister Fiancé, if you would excuse us. You can have a seat in the waiting room, the expecting mommy is the Queen of Labor and Delivery, and she has spoken," the nurse said to Sherman before turning to Ronelle. "Tell me, Ms. Fortier, who is your doctor?"

"My mother is her doctor!" Sherman interrupted.

"My doctor is Doctor Yvonne Campbell, and I don't want this man anywhere near me. Get him out of here!" Ronelle demanded.

Sherman continued to follow the nurses as they pushed Ronelle's bed to the labor unit. Once they arrived and the nurse keyed in her password to open the door, Sherman could go no further.

"For the last time, before I call security, you will have to wait in the waiting room. Patient request. Sorry!"

"But I am the father."

Slowly the doors closed. "What you're saying does not matter. We have to honor her request. From this point, I am not even allowed to update you on her status because of the HIPAA Privacy Rule."

Sherman was kicked out of the labor unit and Ronelle's life in the span of a week. He leaned against the wall and slowly slid to the floor. Almost three hours passed.

Upon hearing footsteps, he opened his teary eyes to see his mother running down the hall.

Winded, Yvonne said, "Of all days to get stuck on a delivery, this would be the day. That girl tried her best to die on me. She even coded twice, but I told her, 'Not today. You'll have this baby and live.' She lived." Yvonne was out of breath and elated about her successful delivery; she hadn't lost a child in fifteen years. "What are you doing out here?" she asked as she entered her password to open the labor unit doors.

"I . . . I couldn't get in," he lied.

"Boy, get your ass off that floor and come on," his mother said as she raced to Ronelle's delivery room . . . but it was too late. The attending physician exited Ronelle's room just as they arrived. On the other side of the door, Sherman heard the grief.

As the physician removed his gloves, Sherman knew the look; he had seen it on television and in movies many times before. He also knew what the doctor was about to say to his mother.

"Doctor Campbell, I'm sorry. We did everything we could, but they were stillborn."

Sherman's pain was overwhelming. The doctor continued to talk, but Sherman only saw his lips moving. It felt like the day he learned of his grandmother's death, like the day the catastrophic floods of Hurricane Katrina destroyed New Orleans. He slid down another wall.

Brandon and Jynika arrived outside of Ronelle's room to the sounds of Sherman crying, Ronelle's screams escaping under the door, and Yvonne softly weeping in the arms of the attending physician. Brandon lifted Sherman off the floor.

"This is my fault! It's all my fault!"

"Don't say that, man. These things happen. It's not your fault," Brandon consoled.

"Yes, it is! My babies came too early because I stressed Ronelle out so badly. She was afraid to bring them into the world without a husband," Sherman wept. "The thought of having these babies without being married caused all this. I fucked up! Ronelle is never going to forgive me."

"Yes, she will, Sherman. In time she will. Let's go see her."

"I can't. Ronelle doesn't want to see me."

Yvonne finished getting the details of the miscarriage. She wrapped her arms around Sherman, and they all entered Ronelle's room together. Directly into her anguish and sorrow, they entered—and directly into her rage. Brenda was hugging and kissing Ronelle as she stood beside the bed. That's when she saw Brandon, Jynika, Yvonne, and Sherman slowly approaching.

"Please, Dr. Campbell, you have to respect my wishes. Get him out of here," Ronelle pleaded. In her arms, together in a blanket, were two tiny boys; motionless, blue, silent . . . as if they were asleep. It was then that the nurse informed Ronelle that the doctor was waiting to perform a final examination.

"Ronelle, I just want to see my sons before they take them away," Sherman said.

"*Hell . . . no!*" she screamed. "Take them away without him laying one eye on my children. Take them now! He didn't want us, so there's no need or reason for him to see my babies! He is not my husband! He does not want to marry me because of some stupid diary—from two hundred years ago! It's karma. God has made me pay for all of this. I'm the one losing babies now. I am Beatrice!" Her tears paused just long enough for the anger to take over. "I don't care what that book says. He is a stranger to me. Just go away!" Ronelle cried into her mother's arms.

"Someone will marry you, and you will be a beautiful bride," Brenda said as she shot Sherman the same look. *How could you hurt my daughter like this?*

Yvonne tried to defend her son. "Ronelle, try not to blame Sherman for this, please. Let him say goodbye to his sons," she begged.

"Miss Yvonne, please stay out of this! I don't want him to see them, and that's final!"

Brenda kissed both of the little boys goodbye, lifted them from Ronelle, and handed them to the nurse. Brandon supported Sherman's entire bodyweight as he walked him back to the waiting room. Sherman saw his sons only from across the room, and he didn't get the opportunity to say goodbye.

Yvonne and one of the delivery nurses rolled the babies away. Cause of death was determined to be asphyxiation due to the umbilical cord wrapped around both of their necks. Yvonne made it to the morgue and signed her grandsons in on the log. In the morgue, she was motionless long enough to say goodbye. Yvonne spoke to the dead.

"If only I could have made it here sooner, both of you would be upstairs in the nursery, fussing with the rest of the newborns. I know the two of you came too soon, but I just wanted you to know what kind of man your daddy is. Your father didn't get to hold you or kiss you, but he's here, in that waiting area. He's been here the whole time. You two would have loved him so much. He's a kind and loving man. I know you would have learned so much from him and grown up to be exceptional young men. I'm not saying goodbye. I will see you later. I love you."

With a gentle kiss for each one, she turned and left the morgue.

CHAPTER 45

The Home of Professor Davis
Later that day

It was that time of evening when the news recapped the mundane events of the day while reducing loss of life to nothing more than a red star—a graphic on a street map. A man was killed on this road, right there. During each news broadcast, a star represented a murder. If the victim were someone famous, such as a Hollywood actor, the anchor would have at least uttered his name. Today he was just an average star, so no such distinction. Then came the sports report.

Such is life in New Orleans.

But Cheryl wondered about that star. Was he one of her students in high school? What about those he left behind? She cared about the city's latest murder victim enough to wonder, which was more than the local news attempted. *It's a shame how society discards those they've deemed of little value . . . which also includes me*, she thought.

There was once a time when the aroma of smothered chops, sweet yams, and hot buttered rolls greeted all who entered Cheryl's home, but not today. Not since her feeding tube, and not since her encounter with the thief. The one who victimized her was a crook of the worst kind. Lou Gehrig's disease was the thief that robbed Cheryl of her vastness of life and her mobility, but the heist wasn't a complete success. She still maintained a range of movement in her index finger—a slight movement that became her last method of communication, and her voice.

Cheryl's caretaker, Nicole, was forty-five years old and a divorced mother of three teenaged girls. She was divorced because her husband had caught her in bed with their pastor—the climatic end of a thirteen-year sex scandal. Cheryl knew these things because Nicole spent the majority of her work day on the phone with her girlfriend—gossiping about the pastor's wife, boasting about sex in the church parking lot, and plotting how to get even—instead of attending to Cheryl's needs. Sitting in a soiled diaper for hours become the norm for her. Her urinary infections felt as if she were passing grains of rice, and her persistent rashes caused her to welcome death.

Eavesdropping also revealed to Cheryl that the pastor was the father of Nicole's youngest daughter. The pastor paid her 950 dollars per month in child support, in addition to the 1,050 dollars per month she received from her ex-husband, and the 2,400 dollar per month salary she collected from Professor Davis. Nicole had a gift for collecting checks, and Cheryl had a gift for eavesdropping and counting. Cheryl wished she could tell the preacher's wife, or at least send her an email, but the thief had robbed her of the ability to warn the innocent.

Nicole had modeled in her teens, but her dream of New York runways was discarded after the birth of her first child. She had two styles of walking, the slouch trot when it was just the two of them, and the "stripper coming to the stage" stroll whenever Professor Davis was around. Implants were tucked here and there; even her lips were artificially inflated periodically like tricycle wheels. She was a natural redhead with matching freckles and blue eyes, but the only color that mattered to her was green.

Nicole and the gym were no longer on speaking terms. Her fashion sense, despite her age, was Forever 21, but her hips told the whole truth. She snacked all day, gorged on social media all day, and schemed over how to steal Professor Davis for eight consecutive hours. Cheryl hated being her entry point into her husband's life.

Nevertheless, her index finger knew only one word. If Cheryl wanted to object to something, her finger would motion like she was pressing the top of an ink pen. If she grew tired of the cement bench of her wheelchair, she'd press the pen. If she wanted a little more time alone in a warm tub and Nicole was about to take her out, she pressed the pen. From the moment her promiscuous caretaker entered her home at seven a.m., Cheryl's index finger flicked in protest until her husband returned. He never noticed.

Long before the thief stole a heap of her life, she stood like a Creole queen, with beauty borrowed from a golden age. She possessed the presence of Vivien Leigh and the flawlessness of Joan Crawford, topped with the smile of Lena Horne. Throughout her life, she had been voted the prettiest, always deemed the smartest, and in track and field, she was always the fastest. She intimidated men, and none approached, even though she was welcoming and approachable. All her twenties and most of her thirties were spent dateless. She was living *Home Alone Part Six* until Irving Davis escorted her on a new hire tour of Tulane. She knew within five minutes of their introduction. He was bold, intelligent, chocolate, and available. As soon as he lowered to one knee and asked, "Will you?" she'd interrupted him and replied, "Yes!" Cheryl had the man of her dreams—until she was robbed.

Like a car buried up to the door handles in the snow, Cheryl sat in her wheelchair parked next to the kitchen table where Nicole fed her baked chicken and noodles, liquefied into a slop more fitting for hogs. Nicole was perfectly attuned to Professor Davis's schedule. She would freshen up her face, glide on lipstick and eyeliner, wiggle out of her work scrubs in front of Cheryl, and compress her hips into a pair of jeans. Then she would turn it on. Nicole's charm evaporated the moment he backed out of the driveway, then spontaneously regenerated the moment Professor Davis returned.

She flipped on and off just like a turn signal, a light switch, a microwave.

Peeking through the blinds, she called, "Oh, look, Mrs. Davis. Your husband is home." Moments later, he coughed his way through the door. "Good evening, Dr. Davis! We were just finishing dinner."

Nicole grabbed the mail from the center of the table and hurried over to him. "You know, I've been so busy with your wife that I forgot to ask you. How did your meeting go with the attorney last week?" Nicole stood in front of Cheryl's husband like a cheerleader greeting her quarterback boyfriend after he threw the winning touchdown.

"It went far better than I expected. It was the first of many meetings to come." He placed his briefcase on the kitchen counter. "Nicole, when this case is done, I will buy you a home health agency. You just wait and see."

"Okay, Dr. Davis. I'll hold you to that," Nicole said jokingly.

He shuffled through his mail. "Bills, bills, and more bills! When will it ever end?"

"Dr. Davis, it's almost over. Soon bills will be the furthest thing from your mind when we're sipping Coronas in Jamaica. Just keep doing what you're doing and keep a positive attitude."

"I'm trying."

"Well, you know I'm here for you, so whatever you need, I'm on your team," Nicole said in her "Happy Birthday, Mr. President" voice.

Professor Davis walked over and kissed his wife on the head. "How was everything today?" he asked Nicole.

"Today was better than yesterday. Our girl is crawling back into her own, slowly but surely," Nicole lied. The truth was, today was worse than yesterday, and the day before yesterday was miserable.

Each day, Nicole would sashay away around seven p.m. Only then would Mrs. Davis exhale the frustrations of the day. Cheryl calculated it took her husband five seconds to find a place to set his briefcase, then twelve minutes to shuffle through the stack of mail—dispersed with twenty to thirty minutes of getting his ego stroked by Nicole. After that, Cheryl would get a 1.5-second kiss on the forehead.

To blow a kiss takes longer than the peck on the head he gives me, Cheryl thought. *It's just a matter of time before Nicole convinces him to warehouse me in a nursing home.*

"Dr. Davis, I'm all done. Will you need anything else this evening?"

"Nicole, that's all for the day. I don't know what I would do without you."

"You are so sweet. I continue to say it, no matter what time of day, even in the middle of the night, if you need me, I will be here in ten minutes."

"I needed to hear that. Thank you."

Professor Davis kissed Nicole on the cheek, and they hugged. Like a koala, Nicole wrapped, gripped, and held onto him while Cheryl counted the seconds.

A total of ninety-seven seconds!

Nicole kissed Cheryl's husband on the lips, and he kissed her back—as if Cheryl wasn't even there. All the while, her index finger wept in silence and twitched in frustration.

CHAPTER 46

After five months of contentious negotiations, Steven Fortier remained determined to fight it out in court. Brenda never allowed Steven to forget her humiliation; it was reenacted nightly in the winter of their bedroom. Though she never filed for divorce, his punishment was of far greater severity—Brenda stayed. A corpse that refused to relinquish life, she walked in his midst a bluish hue.

Long before Sherman proposed to Ronelle or the discovery of Anne Fortier's diary, his marriage to Brenda was practically a Triple Crown.

Love.

Longevity.

Loyalty.

Then, they tripped and fell during the derby of life; every ligament of trust and loyalty shredded. Divorce felt like the most humane form of euthanasia for Steven's marriage. Watching a fractured Brenda was proving too painful. The Brenda he had fallen in love with was a morning person with the kind of optimism he envied. The Brenda that Steven no longer enjoyed wasn't. Their roles had reversed. Waking up to her felt like entering a funeral parlor to eulogize an old friend. That old friend was his marriage.

He missed the warmth of her body and the erotic fragrances that permeated their bedroom after her baths. On the nights he was too tired to touch her, her enticing panties provided the jolt of energy needed to separate her legs. If it hadn't been for the complications she endured with her uterus resulting in a partial hysterectomy, they would've had nine kids themselves. Brenda and Steven were the type of couple who would disappear at dinner parties only to reappear in a guest bathroom on the same floor. Then came the proposal to Ronelle and the pages of the diary.

On this morning, even her lips were blue. On his way out the door, he kissed Brenda on the cheek, and it took most of the morning commute for his lips to defrost. It was during that same commute that he understood Brenda for the first time, grasping the depth of love she had for her family. Brenda was protecting her family from men like Professor Davis. Steven finally made sense of it all.

He wanted revenge on behalf of his wife, retaliation for the audacity of the lawsuit, and retribution for ignoring their philanthropy. Vengeance for the humiliation his wife had suffered was his right, and he alone would determine when the battle was over. There would be no settlement.

The previous evening, attorney Gabriel Raegan, on behalf of Mrs. Irving Davis, aka Cheryl Gullage Davis, had submitted an offer of 422 million dollars with a nondisclosure agreement regarding the details of the settlement. Steven replied with a sticky note: *Wipe your ass with this offer.* Melvin wanted to counter with 30 million, but Steven wanted to make Professor Davis pay.

Against the advice of all his attorneys, including Melvin, Steven wanted a war with Raegan and Davis, if for no other reason than to defend the honor of his wife.

"November 12 is the court date. We will see them in court. There will be no settlement!" Both of Steven's fists pounded the conference table; a cup of black coffee spilled on the 422 million dollar settlement. With the offer rejected, the lawsuit of Cheryl Gullage v. Fortier International was set for trial.

But Melvin wanted to settle. "Steven, with all due respect, I hear everything you're saying, buddy, but you're not thinking straight. This joker Raegan is the real deal in court. I'm not saying we can't beat him, but he doesn't have a track record for losing cases when there's a large payout on the line. This is the type of case he loves. The victim is a woman, and some big corporation—Fortier International along with the Tureaud Trust—has damaged her life. I'm suggesting we lowball them on the settlement offer and get them to go away."

"Do you honestly think Professor Davis has come this far to take a lowball offer? They're in this thing for blood. Unless Sherman is in need of another donation, I'm fresh out."

"Steven, how about I get a continuance, and stall them out?"

"Melvin, it sounds like you're afraid of Mister Big Bad Attorney Raegan," Steven challenged. "Raegan is nothing but an ambulance-chasing hustler."

"Steven, I'm not afraid of him, and you know it. But if you gamble long enough, the house will take it all."

"I appreciate your concern and your legal counsel, but if I don't beat this one, the next one will be twice as bad."

"That's just it, Steven. Knowing what I know about Raegan, he has the next Cheryl Gullage waiting."

"Then it appears to me that we have no choice but to win. My only question is, can you still be part of this team, even though you feel there isn't a chance in hell we could win?" Steven asked.

Melvin removed his glasses and rubbed his temples. "I've wanted a rematch against Gabriel Raegan for five years. I never said there was no chance of winning. I just said the consequences of losing are too high and . . ."

Steven cut him off. "Melvin, I like our chances because we have a good strategy. That presentation Chantrell delivered yesterday was brilliant. 'Invasion Comes with Casualties.' I loved it. Chantrell said it so eloquently. We hunker down on Thursday and allow them to invade us. Their weakness will slowly surface. Melvin, that's what we're going to do. Hunker down."

Melvin returned to his seat and gulped his coffee. "Steven, if you remember, the second half of our presentation was side-tracked when Mrs. Jacques notified us of the settlement offer. Here's the part we didn't get the chance to present, but it's the most important." Melvin opened his briefcase and held up a large photo of Oprah Winfrey.

"Raegan will split his army into three attacking forces. The first will invade from the rear. Once the trial starts, he'll seat an all-black jury and only two men. The majority will be success-ful, educated, African American women hereby referred to as the Ten Oprahs." Make no mistake about it—he will play to the Ten Oprahs, and you will be the worst man since O. J. Simp-son."

Melvin turned the picture of Oprah over. On the reverse side was an image of Cicely Tyson in *The Autobiography of Miss Jane Pitman*. Reminiscent of a slow-walking jazz funeral, Mel-vin walked around the room, making sure every attorney saw the slave woman in the photo.

"From the North, he will deploy guerrilla tactics designed to rip at the heart of every black juror. At some point during the day of this trial, Attorney Raegan will reach in his back pocket and hold up for all to see the biggest trump card you have ever seen in your life—slavery!"

Melvin's slow-moving procession went full circle back to the seat that held the chairman. With a violent thrust, he slammed the photo in front of Steven. Every receptionist on the floor took notice. All eyes were locked on Melvin.

"I know this man. There exists an evil inside of him that will tarnish every member of your family, including Ronelle. By the end of this civil trial, Fortier International Shipping will go down in history as the largest slave trader in the history of the Southern states. I know you want to make him pay for what they did to Brenda, but Steven, it's not worth it."

"And his final attack?" one of the staff attorneys asked.

Melvin directed their attention to a monitor, and pressed play on a video from the wedding of Cheryl Gullage and Irving Davis. The video captured her looking joyous, full of life. Then the video cut to a current photo of Cheryl, secretly taken by a private investigator during her recent trip to the doctor. It was a horrifying view of the symptoms of Lou Gehrig's disease and how the disease had destroyed Cheryl's life.

"Steven, that disease she has is not your fault, but that jury will make you pay for it. Slavery was not your fault, but that jury will place the blame on you. The final attack from Raegan? His flank will come in the form of a blood test administered in open court, proving her ancestor was once a slave owned by you, Steven Fortier!" Melvin yelled in Steven's ear.

Steven stared at the photo of the slave, then angrily stood face-to-face with his lifelong friend. "Melvin, I never owned one—not one—slave, and you know it! This current generation of the Fortier family will not pay for the sins of Bernard Fortier. I'll be damned if I allow them to paint us as slave owners."

Exhausted, Melvin made one final plea. "Steven, by the time Raegan is done presenting his argument, all twelve of those jurors will believe every dime you own was a direct result of slave labor. Raegan has baited us into a reparations lawsuit, and unfortunately, Bernard Fortier was on the wrong side of history." Melvin returned to his seat. "Steven, we still have three days before this thing kicks off. Take this time to consider a settlement," he concluded.

Steven's Chief Operations Officer, Mrs. Jacques, entered the room. "Mr. Fortier, the bank just called."

"Yes, and what did they want?" Steven asked. Mrs. Jacques glanced at Melvin. "Melvin's my attorney, you can speak freely."

"It was the bank president. He called to say they just received a court order to have all of the assets of Fortier International and Tureaud Trust frozen, pending the court date on November 12."

"Well, damn," Melvin said. "And so, it begins."

"The hell it does. Catherine, find out who signed that court order. I'll have that judge's ass on a platter for this!" Steven exclaimed.

"Sir, I already know who signed it. Judge Rowan Klein."

Feeling sucker-punched, Steven walked over to one of the large windows that provided a panoramic view of the city.

"Well, Melvin, it seems your old adversary Raegan has some

friends in high places down at the courthouse, but so do I."

"Steven, please consider settling this thing."

"Absolutely not! Didn't you want a rematch with him? You just got it!" Steven stormed out of the conference room and slammed the door.

With Steven out of the room, Melvin walked around to the front of the conference table.

"Gentlemen, I gave it my best shot. The time has come to go on the offensive," Melvin said to a room of staff attorneys. "I will notify Raegan today that we plan to place Cheryl Gullage on the witness stand whether she can speak or not. Something tells me Professor Davis will not want his wife on the stand. That's when I will paint them as frauds for exploiting her."

CHAPTER 47

Cheryl sat in her wheelchair counting the amount of time Nicole was in her bathroom—a total of an hour and twenty-five minutes. In the large, oval tub in the master bedroom, Nicole soaked, covered up to her neck in a cloud of bubbles. Once her bath was done, she stepped out of the bathroom wrapped tightly in Cheryl's pink robe with *Mrs. Davis* embroidered in green across the back. Pink and green were Chery's favorite colors because of her sorority, Alpha Kappa Alpha. The robe was also a wedding gift from her mother, who had died three days after the wedding ceremony, while Cheryl was still on her honeymoon.

Nicole returned to Cheryl's bedroom and slammed the door—a clear message to stay out. Cheryl counted thirty-seven minutes before Nicole returned to the kitchen table; the place she'd sat parked all day since 2:31 that afternoon. It was now 6:15 p.m. Her husband always arrived between 6:30 and 7:30 pm—he was that predictable. As was Nicole.

Suddenly Cheryl felt Nicole behind her, rolling her to a guest bedroom where her medical bed had been relocated. The room was only ten feet by ten feet, and there was just barely enough room on either side of the bed for a flowerpot. But there were no flowers in the room. The room was stripped bare, like solitary confinement, with no television. Nicole positioned Cheryl on the side of the medical bed and raised her to its highest vertical level.

Cheryl watched as Nicole lowered the medical bed as low as it could go, disconnected her breathing tube, and repositioned it behind Cheryl's wheelchair. She knew what was coming next. It happened once a day, seconds after the tube was disconnected from her throat. Face forward she fell onto the bed, dumped out like trash from the back of a garbage truck.

As Nicole changed her soiled clothing, Cheryl couldn't help but notice that Nicole wasn't stuffed into her usual pair of jeans. Tonight, she wore a tiny red skirt, red lipstick, and no bra. The scent of Cheryl's Estee Lauder Beautiful perfume—from a bottle she had sprayed only once—was drenched over Nicole. Then something else caught her attention, something far more painful than the bedsores forming inside her thighs. Nicole's accessories were her accessories. Nicole wore Cheryl's diamond earrings and red ruby necklace.

Cheryl's index finger protested, but Nicole never acknowledged it as she reconnected her breathing apparatus. Cheryl was clean. She still felt dirty, but she was happy to rest in a fresh diaper.

"I plan to have a little alone time with Irving because a man like that deserves to have the simple pleasures in life. Don't you agree?" Nicole asked.

This time, when Cheryl's finger twitched, Nicole noticed.

"Oh, so you don't agree that he deserves a few simple pleasures? Well, what kind of wife are you?"

With Cheryl positioned in the middle of the bed, Nicole knelt over her and started taunting her with seductive movements and orgasmic moans. Then Nicole unbuttoned the front of her red dress; her breasts popped out like two helium-filled balloons— shiny, unnaturally perky, and bouncy for no reason.

Squeezing her glittered breasts together, she said, "Tonight I plan to put both of these in his mouth." She gyrated her hips. "Then pull up this skirt slowly, like this, and let Irving take whatever he desires." Nicole forced her breasts back inside the dress. "You should thank me for taking such good care of him. After all, he pays me well to care for both of you," the nurse winked.

The front door chime announced the arrival of Irving Davis.

"You sit tight while I go greet the man of the house," The home health nurse giggled as she hurried to greet Professor Davis.

Cheryl wanted Nicole out of her house but lacked the voice to express her resentment. Some of the resentment she felt for Nicole also spilled onto her husband. She blamed him.

Cheryl immediately started to count. While she'd lost all mobility, her hearing could pick up the faintest sound; on some days, she even detected words unspoken. She focused her thoughts, and that's when she heard Irving tell Nicole that Cheryl would have to testify—there was no way to avoid it.

How dare he discuss my life with that woman! I have to get her out of this house, somehow.

Nearly an hour passed before Professor Davis opened the door to her cell and kissed her on the forehead. He kissed for one second—the shortest kiss ever. As his lips retreated, she saw the glitter and smelled the scent of her stolen perfume. The twitching of her finger was so rapid, so intense, it caused the bed to vibrate, but her husband never took the time to notice. Today, he made zero conversation with Cheryl. Not even a five-minute recap of his call with attorney Gabriel Raegan—nothing.

In the corner of Cheryl's eye stood Nicole, in the hall, directly in front of her bedroom. Behind her was a candlelit room. Her bedroom.

When Professor Davis turned to leave the room, he saw a topless Nicole. Seductively, she summoned him with a finger. Though he ignored Cheryl's finger, the one that cried for help, he followed Nicole's finger without a second thought.

Her husband didn't bother to close the cell door behind him. As if controlled by hydraulics, the door to her bedroom across the hall slammed shut. It was Nicole who slammed it, to reaffirm the message she'd sent earlier: *Do not enter.*

For three hours, Cheryl listened as they had sex in her bed. It finally ended around 11:50 p.m. It was then that Nicole kissed Irving goodnight and headed home to her latchkey daughters.

As he walked back to the bedroom, his cell phone rang.

Cheryl heard him answer once he closed the door.

"Shelita, I can't make it tonight, baby. I know. You're right, I said I was coming, but I'm a little tired." A pause. "I know you have needs. Don't I take care of those needs?" Another pause. "Okay, since you put it like that. Give me about thirty minutes to take a shower, and I'll be right over. She's out for the night already. I just need a quick shower, and I'll be right there." He paused again. "Love you more."

After his shower, Irving Davis threw on a pair of jeans and a sweater Cheryl had bought him for his birthday. She heard the pop of a pill bottle, which she concluded was his Viagra. Her husband stuck his head in the door and peeked at Cheryl. She watched the entire sequence of his movements in the periphery of her right eye. Then she heard the jingling of his keys, followed by the front door chime.

And just like that, she was alone.

I've been demoted to third place behind Shelita. He didn't even say goodbye.

CHAPTER 48

Nearly an hour passed before Judge Klein took the bench—he had a very bad habit of tardiness no one dared to complain about. The last time Melvin faced Gabriel Raegan in New Orleans Civil Court, it was for a personal injury lawsuit filed one year after Hurricane Katrina. Melvin's client was a woman whose husband had fallen his death while working on the roof of the Mercedes-Benz Superdome; his fall was broken by the fifty-yard line. Raegan had been retained by the insurance company, while Melvin took the case pro bono because the client was a friend of Chantrell's. Melvin was so confident he was going to win a huge settlement that he was willing to advance the wife of the plaintiff more than 60,000 dollars. That was before Raegan dropped the Mother of All Bombs on his lawsuit.

Gabriel Raegan was able to get the best friend of Melvin's client to testify that both of them had injected heroin during their lunch break, thirty minutes before his client's husband plummeted to the ground. Though the family was able to prevent the insurance company from conducting an autopsy, Raegan was still able to obtain enough DNA from the floor of the Dome for drug testing. Once toxicology confirmed that drugs were found in his system, the case was thrown out. Then, to top it all off, Raegan sued Melvin's client for a portion of his attorney fees.

This morning, the barely-full courtroom felt eerily similar. Gabriel Raegan was wearing an ash-gray suit with a purple tie. On four of the five times Melvin faced had him, Raegan wore the same gray suit, complete with masonic lapel pins. The only difference today was that Irving Davis also wore the same colors and pins.

"All rise. The Honorable Judge Rowan Klein presiding. Please turn off all cell phones and remain quiet while court is in session," the bailiff said as the judge took the bench.

"Good morning, gentlemen! Please state your names for the record and name the client you're representing."

"Good morning, Your Honor. I'm attorney Gabriel Raegan, and I'm here representing Cheryl Gullage Davis." The judge greeted Raegan with a friendly smile and a nod of the head.

"Good morning, Your Honor. My name is attorney Melvin Campbell, and I'm the lead attorney representing Fortier International."

Melvin noticed that during his introduction, the judge never made eye contact with him, unlike the warm smile he extended to Raegan. While still looking down and appearing uninterested, the judge then asked Reagan to start off the opening arguments.

"Good morning to the court once again, and to all of the jurors. Thank you for the opportunity to present this claim to the court this morning. As I stated earlier, I am here to represent the plaintiff, Cheryl Gullage Davis, because she was cheated out of her birthright." Raegan stood directly in front of the Ten Oprahs and two black men who appeared to be college students.

"My client has a valid claim to the Fortier fortune, but she was robbed of the inheritance that was left to her by the founder of Fortier International. I plan to prove during these arguments that my client should be awarded her full inheritance with interest. I will also prove that her right to the Fortier International Board of Trustees has also been denied. We have in our possession proof—in the form of content from the diary of Anne Boleyn Fortier—that my client is the direct descendant of Bernard Fortier, which confirms our claims here today."

Raegan's voice then shifted to a somber tone, like one of

those Feed the Children commercials that runs in the middle of the night. "Ladies and gentlemen of this jury, the twelve of you can correct an injustice committed against my client. There was a real racist culture that existed here in New Orleans at that time. Her side of the family was removed from the will of Anne Fortier. Just imagine that for a second. Your grandmother left you an inheritance, only to have another family member erase you from the estate. Why was Cheryl's side of the Fortier family never mentioned in Bernard Fortier's will, you ask? If you guessed skin color, then you're correct."

Melvin stood angrily. "Objection, Your Honor! That is a race-baiting attack on the character of my client, and a salacious mischaracterization!"

The judge overruled.

"Thank you, Your Honor." Attorney Raegan continued. "Many of you are probably wondering where Mrs. Davis is today and why she's not in court. She could not be with us this morning because of her illness. It wasn't possible to bring her here, but her loving husband is here in her place while she receives care at home. As the council for Cheryl Gullage Davis, I ask you to hold the Fortier family accountable and send a message that African American women are not to be discarded like rags."

Melvin stood. "Objection, Your Honor!"

The judge overruled. "Attorney Campbell, this is Attorney Raegan's opening argument; you'll have plenty of time to even it out. Continue, Attorney Reagan."

Raegan continued. "Thank you, Judge Klein. As I was saying . . . Please send a message to the Fortier family, the state of Louisiana, and this country that the African American side of Fortier family mattered to Anne Fortier, and she made provisions for them, but those charged to carry out her wishes lacked the integrity to do so. Thank you." Raegan returned to his seat next to Irving Davis, who greeted him with an enthusiastic handshake.

Melvin took inventory of the Ten Oprahs. All of them sat with arms folded and heads tilted. Their narrowed eyes warned him not to get too close—to stay at least five feet away.

"You're up at bat; knock it out the park, Melvin. This is the rematch you wanted," Steven whispered.

Melvin began his opening in the same dramatic fashion, but the two male college students and the Ten Oprahs avoided him with their eyes, no matter where he stood. His opening spoke of how there wasn't any ill intent on behalf of his client to remove or erase the plaintiff from her inheritance, and that all the events took place before Steven Fortier became the chair. He also argued that the diary in question was part of a school project, was never independently authenticated, and was obtained without the consent of the students.

"Your Honor, may I approach?" Melvin asked.

After he received permission to approach the bench, Melvin presented a motion to dismiss the diary from evidence and another motion to dismiss the case altogether, because there was no birth record that Cheryl Gullage was related to the Fortier family. Only the sound of Professor Davis coughing into a handkerchief could be heard in the courtroom.

"I will need a little longer than normal to review these motions; therefore, we will take a quick recess. I will see you all back in court in one hour."

With the pounding of the gavel, the court was in recess. When Melvin returned to his table, Steven greeted him with a handshake of hope and the first genuine smile of the morning. After an hour, the bailiff requested that both Melvin and Raegan come to the judge's chambers.

"Gentlemen, I have reviewed both motions, and I will rule accordingly. On the motion to strike the diary of Anne Boleyn Fortier out of evidence . . ." Melvin held his breath because that diary was very damaging to his case. "I have granted that motion on the grounds of how the content was obtained. Due to the plaintiff's husband's position as a professor at Tulane, there was unfair access to the diary. It would not have been accessible to the general public. The motion to remove the diary has been granted. However, the lawsuit against Fortier International will proceed. The motion to dismiss the case has been declined."

Melvin was very relieved to hear Judge Klein agree to throw out the diary as evidence, but this was just one victory in a colossal war. Raegan took advantage of the brief moment of silence with another counterpunch.

"Your Honor, we would like to present Attorney Campbell with another settlement offer of two hundred million dollars. And my client will agree to drop all further legal claims against Fortier International."

"Mr. Campbell, are you interested in settling this case and taking the offer presented by Mr. Raegan?" Judge Klein asked.

"No, sir. My client has no desire to settle this case, and we would like to resume arguments in court at this time."

"Why not take this recess to present your client with this option?" the judge asked.

"Your Honor, we are firm in our decision to resolve this at the hands of a jury."

"That jury out there?" Raegan asked. "You'd rather risk it with ten women and two men, all of whom are African American? Do you remember the last time we crossed paths?"

"Judge, I will see you in the courtroom," Melvin said as he exited the judge's chambers.

With the rejection of the settlement offer, all three parties re-entered the courtroom. Melvin took a brief moment to update Steven on the final settlement offer Raegan had presented and inform him that the diary could not be entered as evidence.

"Looks like their invasion is already exposing a weakness. Good job, Melvin. We have a great shot at defeating this lawsuit!" Steven smiled.

"All rise. The Honorable Judge Klein is presiding. Please turn off all cell phones and remain quiet while the judge is on the bench."

Once court was back in session, Melvin and his partners watched as a staff member handed Raegan a bundle of legal documents. Then, they huddled. "All right, guys, Raegan is about to attack from the rear, but we've prepared for it, so hunker down and look for their weakness," Melvin instructed.

"Your Honor, may I approach?" Gabriel Raegan said.

"Yes, you may."

There they stood, shoulder-to-shoulder in front of the judge, with the inside voices of second grade teachers. Ever the preemptive strategist, Raegan handed the judge a motion prepared for the moment, a page torn straight from *The Art of War*—a motion that attacked Melvin from the east while he watched from the west.

"Your Honor, I would like to call my first witness to the stand to prove that my client is related to the Fortier family." Raegan half turned to Melvin. "My first witness is the attorney for the defendant, *Melvin Campbell*."

"*Objection!*" Melvin said. "Your Honor, I object to Mr. Raegan calling me as a witness. Any information I have is protected under attorney-client privilege. I ask that you strike down this motion. I am the lead attorney for Steven Fortier!"

Raegan quickly argued, "Your Honor, we have received financial disclosure from Chase Bank that the defendant cut a check to Attorney Melvin Campbell and his brother Clarence Campbell for a sum of 230 million dollars. We believe this amount was a settlement of some sort, in exchange for Steven Fortier III acknowledging their mother as a direct descendant of Bernard Fortier. Because the diary has been removed as evidence, we're left with no other choice. Your Honor, my client is entitled to the same financial reward Mr. Campbell has received, and I request that you place him under oath for questioning regarding the check from Tureaud Trust."

"Is this claim true, Mr. Campbell? Have you received funds from the Fortier Estate totaling 230 million dollars?"

"With all due respect, Your Honor, what I may or may not have received from the Fortier family is not relevant to this case. And I ask again that you reject this motion!"

Melvin felt like he'd just been hit in the face with a sack of bricks. He knew he could not lie because Raegan had already reviewed the bank statements from Fortier International. But to admit it would sink his case.

"Mr. Campbell, is this claim valid, or do I need to place you under oath right now?" Judge Klein demand to know.

"Yes, Your Honor, that is correct. But this line of questioning could damage my client's chances of winning this case. Therefore, I object to this motion on the grounds of attorney-client privilege!"

"Mr. Campbell, I will allow Mr. Raegan to call you as a witness, as the defendant has other attorneys present who could serve as lead. I will allow Mr. Raegan's motion on the grounds that he can only inquire about the funds you received from Fortier International and the reason for those funds."

"But, Your Honor—"

"Mr. Campbell, my ruling on this matter is final."

"Judge Klein, I accept your ruling, but can you issue a continuance allowing me the opportunity to recuse myself after testimony, and for my client to appoint another lead attorney?" Melvin pleaded.

"I will grant the continuance, but you will testify today. We will resume at fourteen-hundred hours."

Once both attorneys returned to their clients, Judge Klein announced his decision regarding the motion filed by Raegan.

"Jurors, I have been presented with a motion by the plaintiff to call Melvin Campbell as a witness for the defense." There was a gasp of astonishment in the court. "This motion has been granted due to a payment made to Mr. Campbell by Tureaud Trust for the total of 230 million dollars. Mr. Campbell is ordered to recuse himself as lead attorney and prepare to testify once we return from an extended lunch. I will see you all back here at two p.m." The gavel banged, and all the hope left the room with the judge.

Melvin turned to Steven with a look that said, *I begged you to settle this lawsuit.*

As he left the courtroom, Raegan shot Melvin a look that said, *Rookie.*

CHAPTER 49

M elvin's respect for Gabriel Raegan required the balance of walking on a slippery floor of hate; one poorly placed step was all it took to land flat on his back. It was there, on his back, that Melvin gained a greater appreciation for Hilary Clinton in the aftermath of two separate presidential campaigns: having to concede defeat back to back, getting reduced to nothing more than a civilian after coming so close.

In his case, he was being called as a witness against his client. Another disconcerted slip-and-fall in front of the same judge.

He was a lawyer, but he needed a lawyer to defend him against his self-inflicted personal injury. That lawyer proved to be attorney Blake Allison.

Discreetly, Melvin suppressed a bad feeling about handing the lead over to Blake, because he was the type of poker player who wore his cards on his face. A part-time staff attorney at Fortier International, Blake Allison, also a Tulane Law graduate, was a few years short of fifty. After becoming inspired by Tom Cruise's performance in *The Firm*, he had changed his major from engineering to law. A loud, vulgar guy, Blake had the Tom Cruise hair and eyes, and the same stocky courtroom presence—

right out of central casting, with the same arrogance. He was the new lead attorney for Steven Fortier.

His record against Raegan wasn't that much better than Melvin's; he'd also suffered two prior falls. Unlike Melvin, however, Blake welcomed any opportunity to jump back in the ring. The wounds from his most recent defeat were still fresh. In fact, they were hemorrhaging.

In the same courtroom six months prior, a malpractice lawsuit in the death of an infant during childbirth had brought Blake face-to-face with Gabriel Raegan. It was a case he was strongly advised not to litigate, but narcissism is the thickest form of earwax.

During the litigation proceedings, Allison flew off the handle and nearly faced contempt after the nurses testified they believed the doctor to have been under the influence and reeking of alcohol during the delivery only to have Raegan rip their testimony to pieces. Raegan was also able to show the family's history of suing physicians, which eventually caused the judge to side with the doctor. Blake Allison had been the father; that botched delivery had killed his son. Today was just as good as any for revenge.

"All rise. The Honorable Judge Klein is presiding. Please turn off all cell phones and remain quiet while the judge is on the bench."

After his session with Allison, Melvin sat silently—like a kid seated outside the principal's office. Periodically, he gazed at Steven, whose chin pressed against his chest, inhaling defeat with every breath. To his right Gabriel Raegan hovered over their drying carcasses, licking his lips at the raw meat of victory. Melvin knew the spoils of war were well within Raegan's reach, and his testimony was going to guide the way. It was then that Melvin noticed Irving Davis turn to acknowledge a woman who sat directly behind him. They touched hands, but the woman wasn't Cheryl Gullage.

"Mr. Raegan, are you ready to call your witness?" Judge Klein asked.

"Yes, sir, I'm ready to call my first witness, Melvin Campbell."

Not wanting to slip a second time in the same court, Melvin traipsed across an oily floor toward the witness box, where he was quickly sworn in. *Where in the hell is Chantrell?* His eye's roamed the court room for his security blanket.

Raegan pounced on Melvin before he even settled into his chair, without giving him even a second to sip from a glass of water.

"Melvin Campbell, did you, in fact, receive a check from Steven Fortier for 230 million dollars?" Reagan asked. "Before you answer, I must remind you that you are under oath. I wouldn't want you to perjure yourself," he chuckled.

"Yes, I'm very familiar with the implications of perjury."

"Are you now? Surprising," Raegan mocked. "Did you, Mr. Campbell, receive said amount from Mr. Fortier?"

"Yes, I did," Melvin replied.

"And what was that payment for?" Raegan asked.

"It was the total of our inheritance with interest."

"Inheritance? Interesting. And how are you related to the defendant?"

"Well, my great-grandmother was the daughter of Steven Fortier, Sr."

"And how did you come to discover this?"

"My son, Sherman Campbell, and Steven Fortier's son, Brandon, embarked on a project to trace their ancestry, and it was then they discovered the diary."

"Is your son Sherman Campbell here today? If so, could you point to him, please?"

Melvin pointed.

"Your Honor, for identification purposes I would like to have Sherman Fortier and Brandon Fortier stand, please."

From their courtroom seats, Sherman and Brandon stood briefly before quickly sitting down.

"It's Sherman *Campbell*!" Melvin snarled.

"My apologies, the family resemblance is just so striking. I will try harder to distinguish between the Fortier family and the Campbell family.

Attorney Raegan turned to face the witness box. "Mr. Campbell, are you familiar with the debilitating symptoms of Lou

Gehrig's disease?"

"Yes, I am."

"When was the last time you interacted with someone with Lou Gehrig's disease?"

He is about to rotisserie my ass. Chantrell, where are you? Melvin panicked. "I can't recall if I have interacted directly with someone who battled that condition."

"I see." Attorney Raegan stood to the right of the witness box, which caused the jury to focus solely on Melvin.

Like a magic trick, Attorney Raegan *voila'd* a television remote from the inside pocket of his suit jacket, then held it elevated above his head with great grandstanding. He topped off the performance with a dramatic wave of his hand that held the remote. That was the signal to his staffer to dim the lights. It was time for the show. It was time for death by exhibit, death by surprise witness, or perhaps death by a little-known glitch in the Napoleonic Code that was hidden away in the dusty attic of the St Louis Cathedral. It was time for Raegan to do what he'd become known for—it was time to humiliate Attorney Melvin Campbell.

It was time for the attack Melvin knew was coming. He could hardly watch, but he forced himself to sit up and take his lick like a man.

On the side walls of the courtroom were two large LCD televisions, and on both sixty-inch screens, a video appeared.

That better not be a video of Cheryl, Melvin hoped against hope.

The video was a split screen that rolled a clip of a very healthy, stunningly beautiful bride on the left. On the right Cheryl in her current condition.

Crippled!

Crumbled!

Condemned!

Dude, you are the dirtiest fucker on planet Earth, Melvin lipped.

The video captured a nurse changing Cheryl's diaper, then faded into a clip of her feeding tube procedure, then displayed a still shot of her ailing body in a wheelchair. Then, a full-screen shot of Professor Davis removing Cheryl's garter belt appeared, while the sound of Shania Twain singing "You're Still the One" in the background gouged out the heart of every single juror, anyone who ever dared to love, and every woman who dreamed of happily ever after.

That's it, that's it, twist the fucking knife in my chest, Melvin conceded from the witness box.

When he glanced at the jury pool, it was impossible to miss the tear-saturated faces of the six women seated in the front row, the multiple Kleenex noses, or Juror Number Three—the 270-pound offensive linemen-sized dude with the Don King hair who folded himself over to hide his watery eyes. It was then that Melvin braced himself for the final death blow from Raegan; that final Johnny Cochran *If the glove don't fit, you must acquit* uppercut, but it never came. Instead, Raegan allowed that still-frame photo, the sniffles from the jurors, and Shania Twain to speak for him.

"Well, I guess I have no further questions for my star witness, Your Honor," Raegan said as he smirked at Blake Allison. "He's all yours, go easy on the poor guy," Raegan said as he took his seat.

A woman around the same age as Cheryl, who resembled anchor Hoda Kotb, was the foreman of the jury pool. She was Juror Number One, and the most visibly shaken of all the jurors. As soon as Shania fell silent, she spoke. "Judge Kline, I feel it's best that we're given a fifteen-minute recess. Just a little time to pull ourselves together."

Judge Kline agreed, and court was called to recess for thirty minutes, but Melvin didn't have the legs to move. He needed the thirty minutes to recover from a concussion.

Then he saw her!

As everyone filed out of the court, she made her way upstream through the crowd—she had finally arrived. Still feeling punch-drunk from Attorney Raegan, Melvin thought he was hallucinating at first, but it was real. Chantrell entered the courtroom for the first time that day, accompanied by a woman Melvin didn't recognize. From the reactions of Brandon and Sherman, however, it was clear they knew her. Chantrell scurried to Blake Allison carrying a thick dossier of documents. Raegan and Professor Davis also noticed. From the witness box, Melvin studied her every move as she whispered in Allison's ear. Watching Chantrell and Allison felt like fingernails across his face.

Updating Allison first? I'm recused, but I'm still her boss!

There was something about Chantrell whispering in the ear of another man that made him instantly territorial, but there wasn't a thing he could do about it. Melvin was reduced to just a witness in a box called jealousy.

Blake flipped through the documents he'd received from Chantrell with eyes wide as boiled eggs—he even invited the other staff attorneys into the huddle. But not Melvin—he was a witness for the defense, and Chantrell couldn't share the juicy documents with him even if she wanted to because he was still on the stand.

After briefing the entire legal team, Chantrell took a seat on the bench directly behind Steven, folded her arms, and looked straight past him to Melvin. In a single-file line, the jurors sauntered back to their seats and the recess was over.

"All rise. The Honorable Judge Rowan Klein presiding. Please turn off all cell phones and remain quiet while court is in session," the bailiff said as the judge took the bench.

Unfortunately for Melvin, Attorney Raegan returned to the same spot and stance he held before the recess, and all eyes in the jury box locked and loaded on Melvin. Seated on the left side of the courtroom was one of Melvin's projected opponents for the mayor race next year—the shit-slinging state rep for District 99, the infamous Sheldon Copeland. He shook his head in pity at Melvin.

In the last city-wide election, I was endorsed by the Soul Ticket, and the only reason Sheldon's slimy ass is here is to dig up dirt.

Melvin's assessment was correct. Sheldon Copeland was a lifelong New Orleans politician who was more corrupt than a mafia boss—but his people loved him. Win or lose, Representative Copeland was present to make sure Melvin was hated throughout the city, and it had already begun. The jury hated him already!

Melvin felt the heat from their bloodshot eyes. He could count the creases in their brows, their nostrils that flared like cobras. He even heard their thoughts, their disgust, and every blistering criticism. For the first time in his life, Melvin didn't feel like a card-carrying member of his race. In the span of four hours, he had become traitor for simply helping a friend who would have done the same for him. As a result, he was castigated for standing with Steven. The Black Delegation offered up a trade: Melvin Campbell for Rachel Dolezal. The trade was accepted, and he was expelled from the African American race by a unanimous decision!

Juror #1: *Oreo!*

Juror #2: *You sell out!*

Juror #3: *Wannabe white!*

Juror #4: *Coon-ass nigger!*

Juror #5: *Clarence Thomas!*

Juror #6: *This is Black on Black crime!*

Juror #7: *You Chicken George-ass nigga!*

Juror #8: *How could you go against your own people?*

Juror #9: *That's the problem with our race—we don't stick together!*

Juror #10: *How you represent a slave master in a lawsuit versus black folk?*

Juror #11: *Yea, I voted for you once, but I'll never vote for your baldhead ass again!*

Juror #12: *He's one of those light-skin Seventh Ward dudes who thought they were all that!*

At least that's how it felt to Melvin, sitting helplessly in that little witness box—like the ultimate humiliation.

"Attorney Raegan you may resume questioning *your witness,*" Jude Klein said in a voice that was thoroughly entertained by the courtroom ass-whipping taking place.

"Judge Klein, we have no other questions, and if the defendant has opted to rest, I would like to address the jury with my closing arguments at this time," Raegan said. "I anticipated a long trial but looks like we can wrap this up today and proceed to the damages phase. We might even make it out of here in time to beat the five o'clock traffic," Raegan crowed proudly like a rooster.

Melvin had failed to anticipate how the check from Steven in the hands of Gabriel Raegan would become a deadly dagger, and his old adversary could taste victory in the form of a winning judgment for his client.

I guess this is my last court battle. I'm going out the biggest loser of all time.

Suddenly, Melvin noticed Blake Allison stand to address Judge Klein.

"Judge Klein, I have no questions for Melvin Campbell."

"Mr. Campbell, you may return to your seat," the judge said.

Melvin left the witness chair and deflated next to Chantrell; she immediately started whispering in his ear.

"I would like to move to closing arguments," Raegan went for the kill.

"Mr. Allison, do you have a witness to call, or do you rest?" the judge asked.

"Your Honor, I would like to call Professor Irving Davis to the stand."

Professor Davis walked as if his shoes were weighted down by sacks of sand. He raised his right hand and was placed under oath. Blake Allison stood to the side of the witness box and waited for Davis to settle into his seat, even allowing time for a sip of water. With the formal greeting of two old friends sipping wine at a private gallery, Allison eased into his cross-examination.

"Professor Davis, what is the name of the nurse who cares for your wife?"

Melvin watched as Davis winced in pain. "I believe her name is Nicole Crocket, sir."

"And where is Ms. Crocket right now?"

Gabriel Raegan stood. "Objection, Your Honor. Relevance!"

"Overruled. Continue."

"Thank you, Your Honor," Allison said. "Dr. Davis, where is Nicole Crocket right now?"

Professor Davis leaned to the left as if there were a sharp pain traveling up his left side. "She . . . she's seated right there."

"Please point to your nurse," Allison requested.

Professor Davis pointed to the woman who sat behind where he had been sitting.

"Let the record state that Irving Davis has identified Nicole Crocket," Allison addressed the court, then walked over to the witness stand. "Dr. Davis, have you hired another nursing service to provide care for your wife? And before you answer, I must remind you that you're under oath."

After a long, contemplating pause, "No sir, I haven't hired another nursing service."

"Hmm, so she's home alone, I presume?"

"Objection, badgering!" Attorney Raegan protested.

"Overruled! Continue."

Allison walked over to the edge of the jury box and folded his arms. He appeared baffled. "Here is what I don't understand, sir. If Nicole Crocket is the nurse who cares for your wife, and your wife is battling Lou Gehrig's disease, who is caring for your wife right now?"

"Ummm, ummm," Davis stuttered. His eyes found his shoes.

"Dr. Davis, who is caring for your wife right now if both you and Nicole Crocket are here?"

"Ummm, no . . . no one, sir."

"And why is that, Dr. Davis? Why is no one home with your sick wife?" Allison yelled, causing the Ten Oprahs to take notice for the first time. A few shifted in their seats as they waited for Davis to answer; others took notes. The remaining jurors looked on with faces of grave concern for Professor Davis's wife.

Like whipping up a well-prepared roux, Attorney Allison placed a lid on Professor Davis and forced him simmer in silence under the heat lamps of the juror's eyes. After two minutes, Allison removed the lid to stir—it was time for the final ingredient.

"Your Honor, I have no further questions for Dr. Davis at this time, but I would like to call to the stand an undisclosed witness," Allison said as Professor Davis was placed on a back burner next to his attorney.

Attorney Raegan leaped to his feet. "Objection! Your Honor, there are no grounds that would allow an undisclosed witness at this point in the trial. I would like to proceed to closing arguments."

"Approach!" Judge Klein demanded. Once both attorneys arrived at the bench, Judge Klein asked, "Attorney Allison, under what grounds should I allow an undisclosed witness?"

"Your Honor, we were told that the plaintiff is in poor health and could not appear, but her nurse is seated behind Dr. Davis. If the nurse is here and he hasn't hired another nursing service to care for his wife, then who's caring for the plaintiff? After all, that video proved that she is incapable of caring for herself."

"And your undisclosed witness can provide the court with new information regarding her condition?" Judge Klein asked.

"Yes, Your Honor. Attorney Raegan made this case about the plaintiff's health, therefore, I need this witness to present my rebuttal. Especially considering that our lead attorney, Melvin Campbell, was an undisclosed witness for the plaintiff."

"Your Honor, I object," Attorney Raegan attempted.

"I will allow it since the lead attorney was the first undisclosed witness. You will have your chance to cross-examine the witness, Attorney Raegan. Attorney Allison, who would you like to call?"

"Your Honor, I would like to call Chantrell Gutierrez!"

The cayenne pepper.

Chantrell was sworn in and replaced Melvin in the witness box. Once Chantrell was seated and stated her name to the court, Attorney Allison asked his first question.

"Mrs. Gutierrez, I understand you have some information

that is pertinent to this case, is that correct?"

"Yes, that is correct."

"And what information do you have regarding the plaintiff?"

"Well, this morning I was having breakfast with members of my Alpha Kappa Alpha sorority when . . ."

CHAPTER 50

C hantrell griped: "Of all the days for this trial to fall on, it would fall on our annual scholarship breakfast for teenage mothers,"
She knew Judge Klein was notoriously late for every court session, so she figured she'd have enough time to award the two scholarship recipients before hauling ass downtown to civil court. The only problem was that one of the recipients was running about twenty minutes late, and her sorority sisters were growing restless. She was distracted from the aggravation of waiting by her phone. A text message from Jony. Her first smile of the morning.

When she opened the text, it was a video of her deported husband holding a poster board with the words *Before you start your day.* Then he dropped that poster board. The second message said, *I miss us & I miss you.* The third message said, *Someday we'll be together.* The last poster board simply said, *I love you.*

As soon as I pass this bar exam, I will bring you home! Chantrell resolved.

Chantrell's best friend and sorority sister, Natokie Napoleon, was the hostess for the breakfast at Neil's Restaurant in Mid City, and Chantrell could tell from her troubled expression that something was bothering her, something far more troublesome than the tardy recipient. There was a mic stand placed in the center of the restaurant, and all the tables surrounded it like *MTV Unplugged* from the nineties. Chantrell was front and center when her friend took the mic with soaked eyes.

"My beautiful AKA sisters, I have some good news and bad news this morning. First the good news. Our second recipient was involved in a minor car accident, but she has arrived safely. Praise God." Natokie waved at the recipient of the scholarship, who waved back and quietly eased herself into one of the chairs. "The bad news that I have to share with you is I have just received information from a very reliable source that our State Vice President of Alpha Kappa Alpha, Cheryl Gullage Davis, who was also my math teacher in high school, has passed away. Please be in prayer for her family. I will keep you updated on funeral arrangements in the days to come."

What?! Chantrell thought. *Did I just hear that Cheryl Gullage has passed away?*

Chantrell bolted to the back of the room and tried as best she could to get Natokie's attention, but to no avail. It was now time to hand out the awards.

The first recipient, Tatyana Sincere, was the first teen mother to wobble through the audience; she was a full seven months pregnant. At the mic, she was greeted by three Alpha Kappa Alpha sisters who quilted her in hugs. All three college graduates shared brief stories of how they started out just like her, and with family support, they were able to continue their educations. Each sorority sister committed to helping Tatyana through the challenges of teen pregnancy—and adjusting to life as a mother and college student. The same was done for second recipient, Destiny Thibodeaux. Her baby was three months old, and she was homeless. The sorority sisters greeted Destiny at the mic with everything from baby supplies to a permanent place to live. Chantrell had even convinced Melvin to buy her a used car to get to work and school.

Chantrell's phone buzzed again. Thinking it was another video from Jony, she quickly opened it only to read another message from Melvin.

Trell! Trell! Court is about to start. Are you on your way? That text was followed by, *It's about to Go Down! Get Here Now!* She could tell Melvin was freaking out, and he had every reason to.

Finally, the award and prayer portion of the breakfast was over—finally Natokie was able to join her at the hostess station.

"*Gurrrrrl,* I am so sorry to hear the news about our Vice President!" Chantrell exclaimed as she rushed to join her friend.

"I know! It's so sad. I struggled during the presentation because Ms. Gullage was the reason I went to college and became an AKA," Natokie said sadly.

"I have to cut out a little early but needed to ask you a quick question first. Who is your reliable source? The one you mentioned during the announcement of her passing?"

"My husband. The coroner's office is a little shorthanded, so they called us to ask for help with a few pickups."

"Wait, hold up! The city coroner's office called your funeral home and Jarvis volunteered on a pickup?"

"Yes, he said in her bedroom next to the bed he found a beautiful AKA robe and then took notice of all the AKA pictures and plaques. After she was delivered to the morgue, he called me. Sent me a photo of her wedding picture, and that's when I informed him that she was my teacher and the Vice President of AKA." Natokie shared the photo with Chantrell.

"Did Jarvis notice anything else at the house?"

"Not really, other than the drama on the front porch."

"Drama? What drama?"

"He said the nurse was there when they arrived. The driver from the coroner's office knew her from another pickup, but then another lady arrived. Her name was Shelita."

"Shelita Burns! His secretary!"

"You know her?"

"Not personally, but my job is to know her now!"

"No lie, my husband said an argument ensued between the three of them as they were rolling his wife to the van. That no good dog!"

"A love triangle?"

"Appears to be! But at least wait until after the poor woman is buried!"

"Did Jarvis mention anything else from the argument?"

"Yes, Ms. Cheryl's husband left his cell phone at Shelita's house last night. On her way to return, it curiosity got the best of her and she flipped through it."

"And saw texts from the nurse?" Chantrell inquired.

"Texts and *tits!* Gurrrrl I would have risen from the dead, kicked the door off that van, and chopped their asses up like *hibachi!*" Natokie was repulsed and nauseated. "But you know my husband loves a mess, so he recorded a good bit of the argument. I can ask him to send it to you."

"Please!" Chantrell was on her tiptoes with excitement. "I'm sorry I can't stay for the entire breakfast and the presentation of the car, but I will reach out to our recipients later this week. Please give Jarvis a heads-up that I need to ask him a few more questions."

They embraced, then Chantrell was off to the city morgue. On her way, she received another text from Melvin.

We're at recess, the diary has been tossed—get here!

CHAPTER 51

The previous night, Cheryl decided to fight back! No longer would she be a victim of her husband's infidelities. No longer would she eavesdrop on his plans to support various women with money from a lawsuit filed in her name. She decided that no one was going to roll her into a courtroom and humiliate her for money she never wanted. Cheryl also decided that this was the last night she would hear the horrific sounds of her husband having sex with Nicole in her bed or taking a shower to go have sex with Shelita.

She decided that night that enough was enough, and another day married to Professor Davis was too much.

In a rush to have sex with her husband, Nicole hadn't noticed that Cheryl's breathing tube had become entangled around her hand—but Cheryl noticed. With the same finger that cried for help that never came, she wiggled and pressed on the tube as hard as she could. After fifteen minutes of twitching and pulling, her index finger finally pulled the tube from her throat. She heard a *whoosh*, then the sound of air escaping a flat tire, followed by the gurgling of her esophagus, then heaving as her air passages clogged.

It was then that she did something she knew how to do better than anything else. Cheryl counted. It took two minutes and ten seconds for her air passages to clog. It took forty-two more seconds before she started to suffocate. It was only then that she could count no more.

The next morning when Nicole entered the house, she headed directly for the master bedroom, but Irving was sound asleep. Back in the kitchen, she prepared a pot of coffee and returned to his room. She placed a cup of coffee on the dresser, then climbed on top of Professor Davis, softly kissing and licking his neck.

"Good morning, my king. Would you like some more of this?" she asked while guiding his hands inside her scrubs. He squeezed her hips.

"Good morning, beautiful," he said, struggling to open his eyes. "What time is it?"

"It's six forty-five, my king."

"Shit! Shit! I'm late for work. The alarm on my phone wakes me every morning. Where is my phone?"

His phone was on the floor next to the night stand at Shelita's house.

"Would you like a little bit more before your big day in court, my king?"

"I wish I could, but I have to hop in the shower and get to court. How about you keep it hot for me tonight—today will be the best day of our lives!"

As Davis entered the shower, Nicole walked into Cheryl's room. Cheryl's skin color, her mouth, and a slight stench of something gone wrong smacked Nicole in the face the moment she opened the door. Wrapped around Cheryl's wrist was her breathing tube. Nicole screamed and called for Irving.

In the doorway of Cheryl's little cell of hell, Nicole said, "This is horrible. Once we call the police, they could think foul play was involved."

Emotionless, Professor Davis said, "My wife has been sick for a few years now, and EMS has been to this house at least fifty times. I've prepared for this moment. It's all about how I call it in."

"What about court today? Are you going to ask Raegan to reschedule?"

Professor Davis walked over to his wife, slid his palm over

her eyes to close them, then pulled a sheet over her face.

"I don't have to appear in court until ten o'clock. Not even Attorney Raegan can know she has died, just in case there is a settlement offer this morning."

"But what do we do with her body?" Panic started to show in Nicole's face. "I can't sit with it, and if I'm not here, then I could be held responsible."

"I understand that, but I need to keep this out of the news. Any suggestions?"

"Okay, okay, then I will make a call to 911 and tell them the truth. I arrived, and you discovered your wife deceased. I know a guy at the coroner's office and will explain everything to him. As you said, EMS has been here several times. No big deal."

"Can I count on you to keep this between us?"

"Of course you can."

"Then make the call."

Nicole took hold of her phone and was about to dial when he touched her arm.

"Will you meet me at court after we're done with the coroner? It would arise suspicion if we arrived together, but I would like to have you there . . . for support."

"Of course I will," she said with flickering eyes. "When this is all said and done, will you take care of my daughters and me?" Nicole asked helplessly.

"Of course. How about you start packing up that apartment right after the funeral? If this case goes as planned, then we can buy a house together."

The entire discussion took place in Cheryl's room, next to Cheryl's medical bed, over Cheryl's dead body.

Attorney Raegan was severely wounded—his case against Steven Fortier was hemorrhaging all over the courtroom. Allison reclined with a smirk as he searched for questions to ask his undisclosed witness—who just happened to be one of the best legal minds in the office. During his cross-examination of Chantrell, he mainly asked stunned confirmation questions regarding her testimony, but in her file were certified documents that verified each statement line for line.

At the conclusion of Raegan's questioning, Attorney Allison thanked Chantrell for her testimony, then dragged Professor Davis back to the front of the stove. He turned the heat up.

"Dr. Davis, at this very minute, is your wife at home?"

"No, sir."

"At this very minute where is your wife, Dr. Davis?"

"Sh-she . . ."

"We can't hear you, Dr. Davis, where is she? Answer the question!" Attorney Allison pressed.

"The morgue." Professor Davis melted in his chair, grabbing several sheets of tissue to hide his face from the cutting eyes of the Ten Oprahs.

"When did she die, Professor Davis? When? When did she die?"

Davis cried through the tissue. "She died overnight."

"And when did you find her dead?" Allison stood over Professor Davis. "When did you find her dead? The sooner you answer these questions, the sooner we can get out of here. It's Monday Night; Saints kick off in two hours. I have tickets!"

"I . . . I . . . found her dead this morning."

"When?" Allison yelled at Professor Davis.

"Objection, Your Honor. He's badgering my client!"

"Overruled. Continue," the judge said.

Blake Allison walked back toward the jury and reiterated

"Professor Davis let me explain how we got here. Life has taught me that we live in a small world, and in New Orleans, there are only six blocks of separation. This morning, a member of our legal team, Chantrell Gutierrez, was having breakfast with a few of her Alpha Kappa Alpha sorority sisters when a condolence announcement was made for Cheryl Gullage. It was then that this member of our legal team recognized the name of the deceased sorority sister. It was Cheryl Gullage Davis. Professor Davis, who were you arguing with this morning on your front porch?"

Melvin watched as Professor Davis sizzled under the hot lights of truth. Attorney Raegan could not bail him out—he had to answer.

"Nicole Crocket and—"

"Nicole Crocket and *who*, Professor Davis? Who was she arguing with, only moments after your wife's body was rolled out of the house?"

"Shelita Burns."

"And how do you know Shelita Burns?"

"Shelita is my secretary."

"And?" Allison asked.

"And also, my mistress . . ."

"Do you see her in this courtroom, Professor Davis?"

As Davis peered out into the courtroom, Shelita Burns stood.

"Professor Davis, were you also romantically involved with Nicole Crocket?" Allison asked. "Now, I must remind you, Dr. Davis, you are under oath."

Davis looked at Nicole, who turned her head away. He then glanced at Shelita Burns—his mistress of three years, the one he'd promised to marry once Cheryl reached her life's end. Shelita flicked him the finger.

Once she arrived at the courtroom and had a chance to catch him up, Chantrell had told Melvin that she'd reached out to Shelita Burns and invited her to court this morning to verify her testimony and to witness Professor Davis testify under oath. Shelita Burns had agreed. But first, Chantrell had paid a visit to vital records, where her cousin was the Clerk of Court.

"Your Honor, I would like to enter the following certified document from the Clerk of Court," Allison said as he handed the bailiff a photocopy, and also one to Reagan. The third and final copy Allison handed to Professor Davis. It was then that Raegan requested to approach.

"Your Honor, you cannot allow this document until I've had it verified," Raegan said.

Judge Klein studied the document for about a minute, then replied, "I will allow it because this is an official stamp from our clerk, Anthony Baltimore. You may continue."

"Professor Davis, do you recognize the document in this photocopy?" Allison asked.

Davis held the copy up to the light. "Yes, I do, but . . . but . .

."

"Professor Davis, what is it you're holding?"

"It's a copy of my . . . marriage license, but I don't understand."

"It is a copy of your marriage license. It's *unsigned!*" Blake Allison said as he turned to the jury and walked across their view, allowing them to see the unsigned marriage license. One by one, the Ten Oprahs covered their mouths, dumbfounded.

"Dr. Davis for some strange reason—and I know it happens—but it appears you and Cheryl Gullage never returned a signed copy of your marriage license to the Clerk of Court after the honeymoon. You only had thirty days to do so, after that, this document would have expired. What do you think happened?"

In a trembling voice, Professor Davis said, "We went on our honeymoon after the wedding. Her mother died on the third day . . ."

"I understand her mother died, but did either of you ever get around to returning a signed copy of this marriage license to the Clerk of Court?"

"Ummm . . . ummm . . ."

"Did you return a signed copy of your marriage license to the Clerk of Court?"

"Not that I recall. We planned a funeral for her mother, and my wife was grief-stricken. So, I guess . . . I guess we forgot." Davis's eyes found his shoes once again.

"Your Honor, may I approach?" Attorney Allison smelled blood in the water.

It was then that Blake Allison presented his final motion, which had been prepared by Chantrell. It was motion to dismiss, challenging that Irving Davis was not the legal husband of Cheryl Gullage. The judge took a minute to review the motion, then addressed Gabriel Raegan.

"Attorney Raegan, has your client, Cheryl Gullage, established an estate or trust in the name of Cheryl Gullage in which Irving Davis is listed as chairman of her estate?"

"No, sir. It wasn't required because he was her husband."

Judge Klein's head oscillated from left to right like a toddler avoiding a spoon of cough syrup. "Not according to these documents. The gentlemen in court today is no more the husband of the deceased as I am."

"I present this last document to you with respect for the privacy of Cheryl Gullage and her next of kin." Attorney Allison presented the judge with a certified register entered from the coroner's office, along with a photo of the toe tag for Cheryl Gullage. Attorney Allison also handed a certified copy to Attorney Raegan.

Judge Klein lowered his voice to a hushed, clearly frustrated tone. "Attorney Raegan according to the Deceased Register from the coroner's office, your client was entered into their system at 8:12 a.m."

"It appears you're correct, Your Honor. I offer no rebuttal," Attorney Raegan said in a shattered voice.

"Then, that settles this matter. Irving Davis cannot establish that he is legally married to Cheryl Gullage; therefore, I have to grant this motion. Mr. Raegan, this case is dismissed."

Both attorneys returned to their tables. After a brief announcement to the court, Judge Klein thanked the jury. With the pounding of his gavel, it ended.

Melvin watched as Nicole was the first to rush for the exit, leaving Irving Davis still in the witness box. As Davis returned to his seat, he passed the Ten Oprahs; some spewed insults, some looked as if they wanted to hock and spit. Gabriel Raegan cleared his table and exited the courtroom without saying a word to his client. Everything he thought was certain had evaporated. Steven and his team were handed a victory.

The final victory was reserved posthumously for Cheryl. In taking control of her own death, she won the fight for her legacy and kept her promise to her mother—to never break the blood covenant officiated by Marie Laveau.

CHAPTER 52

The Toast!

S teven could hear them the moment he stepped out of the elevator. Never in a million years did he anticipate the lawsuit ending with the plaintiff passing away in the middle of the night, but it had happened. Cheryl Gullage was dead, the case against Steven Fortier was dead, and Professor Davis's dream of millions was dead. The only thing left to do was toast their unlikely victory and exhale.

The entire team gathered around the conference table in the Situation Room, hugging, cheering, and breathing deep sighs of relief. Lead attorney Blake Allison could not stop bear-hugging Chantrell; it was the first time he hadn't left the court with his tail between his legs after battling Gabriel Raegan. Allison made sure every lawyer in the room knew he hadn't had a plan to win—it was Chantrell who had made one.

"This beautiful little legal wizard was able to get a picture from the morgue, a certified copy of a blank marriage license, and type up two motions before most of you slackers brushed one ugly tooth in your mouths! Gentlemen, we are not worthy. Long live the queen!" Blake Allison announced.

"Long live the queen!" the lawyers replied. "*Speech! Speech!*

Speech! Speech!"

Chantrell, being very shy, made eye contact with Melvin first, who gave her the nod to speak. In a trembling voice, with fingers interlocked, she said, "Guys, I cannot take all the credit. If it hadn't been for Melvin having patience with me every time I cried on his shoulder after failing the Bar, I would not be here. So, as you all thank me, I would like to thank my mentor, Melvin Campbell." Melvin blew her a kiss from across the room.

"Chantrell, you have to tell us. How did you know they never signed that marriage certificate?" Allison yelled out.

"To be honest with you, I didn't, but Melvin taught me years ago to always read everything to the last sentence on the last page, no matter how annoying. Something else he taught me: As often as possible, go to the source for answers instead of depending on the internet. So, I went to the source when I could not get the exact date that Cheryl and Irving were married. My cousin Anthony Baltimore is the Clerk of Court, so that's where I went."

"Long live Anthony!" Blake Allison toasted.

"Long live Anthony!" the lawyers replied.

In the center of the conference table were several bottles of the finest wine from Steven's collection. Once he entered the room with Brenda on his arm, it was time for the final toast.

"Gentleman, I think we all can agree we just dodged a very expensive bullet. After Raegan filed that motion to call Melvin as a witness, I lost all hope of winning."

"Tell the truth, you pissed your pants," Allison screamed out in laughter.

"Yes, I did, brother," Steven said as tears of joy swelled in his eyes. "But an angel saved us. To Chantrell!"

"To Chantrell," they toasted.

"By the way, Melvin, I plan to steal Chantrell from you, so don't look for her come Monday morning!" Steven joked.

"And I will see your ass in court!" Melvin said in laughter, causing every lawyer in the room to bellow.

"In all seriousness, this is also bittersweet," Steven continued. "Because Cheryl Gullage, the plaintiff in the lawsuit, has died. I lost a family member today. A loved one I didn't have the opportunity to love or know. Some good has to come out of this, though; something more meaningful than beating back a lawsuit. In the upcoming months, my wife and I have agreed to develop a plan we hope will become a model for fourth-generation business owners like the Fortier family, a plan that makes room for those who share the same grandfathers. As for now, I just want to thank Melvin, Chantrell, and all of you who came together to help an old friend. Here's to teamwork and family." Steven and Brenda lifted their glasses and kissed.

"Teamwork and family!" the lawyers replied.

CHAPTER 53

Something old, something new, something borrowed, something pink . . . and purple?

There was still no sign of the bridal party, but Sherman couldn't help but notice Uncle Clarence in his tuxedo. He was amazed how his skin had benefited from a full year of sobriety. Clarence strutted like a new man. Gone was the signature Miller Lite he carried in his left hand. Interestingly enough, he was just as enjoyable to be around without the liquor—a small fact most of them had long since forgotten.

Clarence had recently started little league basketball team for inner-city kids at several recreational parks around the city, and even officiated high school games. Even his marriage was healthy again after a ten-year break. But his sobriety was about to face the ultimate test: An open bar at a family wedding.

There was still no sign of the bridesmaids, only a sharp cutting on his heels from the tuxedo shoes and the dawn of ever-expanding blisters. Sherman's shoes felt wooden on the inside, and with every step, his feet received another injection of splinters. A thought entered his mind, if just for the moment, of folding the backs of the shoes inward and converting them into slippers. But he feared a beatdown if his tuxedo slippers were captured in any of the wedding photos. Tonight, he would have to endure the blisters and walk it off. But the torture inside of his shoes could not distract him from the breathtaking ambiance that awaited the wedding guests; it was like nothing he'd ever witnessed.

The venue was outdoors, something that made him extremely nervous because of the rainforest climate of New Orleans. But there wasn't a cloud in the sky and nearly zero humidity. The colors for the wedding were pink and purple, and Sherman observed this central theme in every available space, including the outer walls of the surrounding buildings. It was impossible to look in any corner or crevice and not see the colors pink or purple. The backs of all the chairs were draped with a pink satin material, while the entire altar was decorated in purple and pink flowers.

Finally, the bridal party arrived. Brandon leaned over to Sherman for the first time since they'd lined up to get a nerve check on his buddy.

"How are you holding up, bro?"

"I'm good, B, but these shoes are killing my feet. As soon as we hit the dance floor, these logs are coming off."

As the wedding planners finished aligning the last groomsmen in the order they would escort their partners, a stretch limo slowed to a stop. The planner was Kyle Alfonso, who worked side-by-side with his husband, Brett Alfonso. Together, their microscope-like eyes scanned every member of the bridal party for the slightest flaw—an off-center tie, a quarter-inch thread dangling from a hem, or a displaced lock of hair swaying in the wrong direction. One by one, the bridesmaids began to exit the limo in their evening gowns, and after a thorough inspection by Brett, the ladies were paired up with their assigned groomsmen. Sherman could hear all the men gasp for air as each one of them paired with a bridesmaid.

Then a high-pitched voice said, "Listen up! All the guests are seated, and we're ready to make our entrance. Here is your last chance for a restroom break before we begin," Kyle said.

"And remember guys, this is not a racetrack, so do not pull my ladies down the aisle. Ladies, don't forget you're on a stage; therefore, stay mindful of your posture. And smile the entire time you're on my stage," Brett instructed.

Suddenly, there was another high-pitched outburst. "Guuuurl! Lacey! How many times have we covered this?" Brett said as he ran to the back of the line where one of the bridesmaids stood. With his hand right below her lips, he demanded, "Spit it out. Now, Lacey!"

Even the sun fell under the authority of Kyle and Brett; on their cue, it drifted off to sleep. More than one hundred strategically placed candles provided splendid illumination, while still allowing the night to attend the ceremony.

Sherman made his way to the arch of the altar with Brandon, where his view of the aisle was the best place to see the love of his life, Ronelle, slowly walk in his direction. Once Kyle gave the signal, the first wave of the wedding party made their entrance down the candlelit walkway, which led to the wedding gazebo.

Keeping with tradition, the mother of the groom, then the mother of the bride, were first to walk the aisle. Next, the bridal party began a graceful procession, pausing only for a photo.

Intently, Sherman looked for Ronelle. Finally, she made her entrance—the last bridesmaid, escorted by six-foot-eight Jared Joseph, center on his college basketball team. Sherman's heart slid inside his wooden shoes, where it became riddled with splinters. *Oh! I see. That's why she stopped answering my calls. She's dating Jared.*

Brandon interrupted his jealous thoughts. "I wish you two would have jumped the broom before us."

After a deep sigh from as far away as China, Sherman said, "Thanks, bro, but tonight is your night, and that is all that matters. But Ronelle does look beautiful, doesn't she?"

"I know, but I'm waiting on the star of the show to appear," Brandon said.

Brandon had spoken her into existence. Everyone who was seated began to stand as the bride was ready to walk down the aisle with her daddy. Because of the heels she wore, Jynika towered over Clarence, but his smile beamed like a lighthouse as he guided her down the pink flower-covered path that led to her future husband. In a strapless mermaid gown, with lace-over-satin organza, Jynika was truly the star of the show.

"Brandon, Jynika looks like a tall, beautiful Barbie doll, and you look like Ken," Sherman joked. "Just make sure you don't trip in front of all of these people."

Brandon chuckled discreetly with Sherman as he walked to receive Jynika's hand. They embraced midway as her dad passed Jynika off to Brandon. Then, the two of them walked hand-in-hand back to the altar. Shortly afterwards, the ceremony was underway.

As Sherman looked through all the other bridesmaids to get a better view of Ronelle, she refused to make eye contact with him.

"May we have the ring? The ring, please," the pastor requested.

"Sherman! Dude! The ring!" Brandon called out to him in a shouting whisper.

Sherman had mentally left the wedding and returned to the labor room where he had tried to see his babies. Coaching himself back into the moment, he slid his hand into his suit pocket and produced the ring. "Sorry."

"By the powers vested in me, I now pronounce you husband and wife. You may now kiss your beautiful bride."

Brandon and Jynika kissed and were officially married!

In a flash, the reception traveled back in time to an era when twenty-year-olds left their homes after dark and migrated to disco clubs that had the best mirrors, the best dance floors, and the hottest dance tracks. From "Good Times" to "Jungle Boogie" to "Got to Give It Up" and "Let's Groove Tonight," it was a Studio 54-style celebration no one wanted to leave, including Clarence.

Suddenly, Clarence swayed over to Brenda's table, where she was sipping wine with a few of her friends from the Krewe of Rex. He grabbed Brenda by the arm and led her out onto the dance floor. They swung out to "We Are Family" by Sister Sledge. Soon after, Brenda's friends joined her on the floor. The only person seated was Jynika's mom, Jackie, who danced in her chair as she held her beautiful granddaughter in her lap.

Sherman couldn't help to notice when Ronelle came into view. The entire wedding party was seated together. Ronelle was to his left, next to Jared. He looked for chemistry between the two; those little intimate indicators, those flirtatious interactions that would confirm his suspicion.

Does she love another?

Awkwardly, Ronelle and Jared sat together like strangers, pressed into each other's space on a subway, forced together by duration and capacity. Sherman could tell she was uncomfortable, but he wasn't sure if he was the source, or if there was trouble in paradise with Jared. He wanted to rescue her, but Ronelle never asked for help.

Then the atmosphere in Studio 54 shifted from disco to romantic. The reception had reached the point when the bride and groom could enjoy their first dance; that instant when cell phone paparazzi competed with the award-winning wedding photographer for the best shots, when those who never walked the aisle dreamed, and those who had divorced reflected. Brandon led Jynika to the middle of the dance floor to the song "Tender Love" by the Force MDs. His arms wrapped around her waist; her arms folded across his neck. Ken and Barbie were absorbed in each other. Somewhere around the second verse, Brandon released himself from his new bride, walked over to the DJ, and was handed the microphone.

"Ladies and gentlemen, do you know what would make this day even more magnificent?" Brandon asked his guests. "If my best friend in the entire world and my sister would join us for a dance. It's only fitting, since they introduced us. Please give it up for Ronelle and Sherman as they make their way to the floor."

Encouraging applause filled the room; the entire wedding party knew this moment was coming—even Jared.

Sherman walked over to Ronelle and whispered, "If it's okay with your boyfriend, may I please have this dance?"

Ronelle nodded and rose from the table.

Sherman and Ronelle walked out to the middle of the floor as the DJ played a different song: their song, "Adore," by Prince and the Revolution. Ronelle leaned back in his arms, her expression asked, *How could you?*

Sherman's expression responded, *I had nothing to do with that.*

They allowed the song to play in their ears, minds, and bodies. At first, they danced without saying a word, reminded of how good it felt to be in each other's arms.

"By the way, Jared is not my boyfriend, but every day he makes an effort. Not that I owe you an explanation or anything."

"Well, I'm sure your mom loves him. He's tall and white."

"Give it break, Sherman."

"Now I know the reason you send me to voicemail. Jared Joseph."

"Wrong. *You're the reason.*"

"I know, and I'm sorry."

"Let's just get through this song, okay?" Ronelle said.

"I've missed you so much." His lips moved across the surface of her ear.

"Sherman. Don't!"

"Helping Brandon with this wedding has made me miss you even more."

"What? Helping my brother with this wedding . . . made you miss me? Seriously? You changed your mind about marrying me. I gave you room to process, so please spare me the excuses."

"Ronelle, I never changed my mind . . . about loving you."

The song wasn't over. Ronelle tried to pull away, but his arms locked tightly around her back. "I love you. I allowed you to walk away from me once, but not again. Not tonight."

"Sherman! Stop it . . . just stop!"

"Since you left me, I've bought fresh flowers every Saturday and placed them in the same vase on the kitchen counter, hoping the scent would lure you home. Right now, another set of fresh flowers is patiently waiting for you, should you decide to come back. I'm going to wait for you. As long as it takes. Because without you, there is no me."

Over the speakers, Prince repeated, "There is no me." Then Sherman said it again across the surface of her ear. *"Without you, there is no me."*

It was only then, after those four precise words, that he felt the weight of her body in his arms. Then the song was over. Sherman and Ronelle's dance came to an end. He walked the love of his life back to another man, back to Jared. From the DJ speakers and subwoofers, "It's Electric," began to blare, which caused another migration to the dance floor.

At a table center court of the dance floor sat Steven and Melvin. They waved for Sherman and Brandon to join them. Uncle Clarence was also at the table, holding a yellow drink topped off with cherries. The drink was the first thing Sherman noticed.

"Nephew, don't cut your eyes at me. This is some watered-down pineapple juice in this cup. You should know me by now. If I really wanted a Miller Lite, y'all would be at the liquor store right now."

"Boys, have a seat," Steven said.

"What's up, Dad?" Brandon asked.

"You know I'm very proud of the work you two did with your dissertation," Steven said. "Or should I refer to you as Dr. Campbell and Dr. Fortier?"

Brandon and Sherman touched knuckles with the signature President Obama fist bump.

Steven then waved for Mrs. Jacques to join them, but she was in the middle of the dance floor, busy with the Electric Slide. After two unsuccessful waves from Steven, she finally decided to join in the conversation.

"*You can't see it. It's electric! You gotta feel it. It's electric!*" Singing as she danced to their table, Mrs. Jacques asked, "What, Steven? What could possibly be more important than the Electric Slide?"

"Catherine and I have been thinking a lot since that scary situation with Professor Davis, and here's what we've come up with," Steven said to the table as he took a quick sip of his wine. "We would like for the two of you to get to them before they get to us."

Sherman shot Steven a confused look. "Before they get to us?"

"Get to them, meaning we want you to locate as many of these descendants of Beatrice's as you can, and bring them into the trust before they lawyer up. I want you to find out what happened to all nine of her children, and let's welcome them into the family. I'll have you report directly to Mrs. Jacques here, who will set you up with a budget, and I'll handle the financial end."

Mrs. Jacques interrupted, "You can take up offices in the Tureaud Trust building, in a new division we have created just for this project. We'll go more into the details later, but for now, the name of this project will be 'The Nine Notches of Beatrice Fortier.'" Mrs. Jacques stood from the table. "If that's all, I need to get back to Brenda and the girls." She returned to the Electric Slide.

"Take two weeks to think it over, and let's get together at my house once Brandon returns from his honeymoon," Steven said.

With a handshake, they all agreed, and "Nine Notches" was officially a thing.

CHAPTER 54

S eated at the table next to Melvin and Steven was Chant-rell. She was there by invitation, but was not mental-ly present. Her mind was on her husband. Yesterday marked six weeks since she'd taken the Bar again, but there was no word from the Bar Association as to whether she'd failed. Again.

With each glass of amaretto and pineapple, Chantrell tried to drown out that 'just settle' voice that encouraged her to quit and accept a life sentence as a paralegal. After all, she was making double her original salary thanks to Melvin and Steven.

Panning around the reception hall only made her depressed, but all things considered, she was happy for Brandon and Jynika. At the bottom of her amaretto and pineapple juice, she devised a plan to request two drinks the next time the waiter returned— one for her and one to toast her marriage.

Please don't come over here, don't!

From across the room, she felt the third guy of the night building up the confidence to ask her to dance. He was the third one in a row she declined. Chantrell was lonely by choice and alone as a symbol of her devotion. At the end of the night, she was still lonely, but content.

"Are you just going to sit here all night while we party our asses off?" Melvin danced his way to the vacant seat next to Chantrell.

"Me? I'm having a great time. Just a little worried about the Bar. I checked the mail yesterday at the office and I . . ."

He interrupted. *"Trell! Trell! Trell!* Listen to me. I believe you will pass it, but if you never pass that Bar, you're still the *baddest* attorney in this city. Campbell Law Firm is compensating you according to your worth—not your title."

"I know, and I appreciate it, the raise really helps." A waiter came to collect her empty glass and return with another. "Can you bring two more, please? One for my boss. Thank you," she lied.

"I see you're knocking 'em down—what's on your mind?" Melvin asked.

"Just the Bar and my husband, that's about it. And earlier I was thinking about Cheryl. Do you ever think about her?"

"About who?"

"Cheryl Gullage?"

"I have to admit, I do. The medical examiner said if someone would have simply taken better care of her, she would have lived."

"I wonder if she decided to end it on her own, being that her husband clearly moved on right under her nose. In the same house! Good thing karma is a bitch!

"Yes, it is! The bitch was Brenda Fortier . . . a top donor at Tulane. They fired his ass the following Monday!"

"Yea, Shelita texted me as he was cleaning out his desk. She told me the greatest feeling was slamming the door behind Professor Davis."

"And I put a lien on his house for the rest of my attorney fees, and Attorney Raegan paid you the other half—a crisp sixty-five thousand dollars." Melvin offered a toast.

"I'll drink to that!" Chantrell said. "Thanks again for the coins, Melvin."

"Chantrell . . . you earned it. If not for you, we were doomed."

The waiter returned with her drinks. She tipped him. "Watching Sherman and Ronelle gave me life tonight." She savored the liqueur-soaked cherries the waiter had piled on top of each almond-flavored drink.

"Sometimes it takes a little separation to remind you how much a person means to you."

"I know, but life is so unfair. People who can't stand each other remain married for fifty years for survival purposes only, and then there are those who love each other perfectly . . . but are forced apart." She tossed her straw and sipped her amaretto from the rim. "But I am cheering for Sherman and Ronelle."

"I hear you, but my son has a little more growing to do. Some men know instantly that they've found the one, and others have to come full circle."

"I don't think that's it at all. That whole diary thing was a lot to deal with, then finding out that your dads are a direct blood match? I'm on Team Sherman—give me a minute to process."

"I guess you're right." It was then that Melvin became distracted from their conversation. "What is Brandon up to? If he tries to sing, I'm running out of here!" Melvin chuckled down his drink.

In the center of the floor, Brandon sat Jynika in a chair. With the microphone turned low, he serenaded her to Lenny Williams's "Cause I Love You." About halfway through the song, several of the groomsmen joined him, including Sherman.

Then Melvin stood in front of Chantrell and joined the serenade. "Cause I looooooooooooove! Cause I neeeeeeeeeeed you! *Oh! Oh! Oh! Oh! Oh! Oh! Oh! Oh! Oh! Oh! Oh! Oh! OOoooooooooh!*"

"Melvin are you drunk already?" Chantrell laughed.

His glass of gin and juice became his microphone. "Cause I looooooooooooove! Cause I neeeeeeeeeeed you!"

Chantrell was caught off guard by Drunk Melvin; she'd never seen him so relaxed and free of the perceptions of others. Sure, in the office he would kid around, but the moment he was in the public eye, it was like a steel rod clicked in his back. But she liked this Melvin, and she liked the song, too.

"Come dance with me!" Melvin pulled her arm.

"I'm in no mood to dance, but this song was my dad's favorite. I couldn't stomach it as a child. He played it all the time, especially after arguments with my mom. Now, I listen to it all the time."

"Get up and dance with me!" Melvin continued to pull her arm insistently.

I guess I better dance with him, or he will dislocate my shoulder trying.

With her hand in his hand and his arm around her lower back, Melvin swept Chantrell into a slow dance. At that moment, however, the song ended.

"*No! No!* Play it again DJ," Melvin demanded, but the DJ spun another slow song for the bride to serenade her husband. The song was "Dangerously in Love 2" by Beyoncé. Chantrell's eyes rolled white.

Not that song! Of all songs, not that song, not tonight. Chantrell tried to pull away from Melvin, but his arm was locked around her.

"Chantrell, there's something I've wanted to say to you for a very long time."

Immediately, Chantrell's eyes scanned the room for Yvonne, but she couldn't find his wife.

"Working with you every day has been the highlight of my career in law. Over the years I have gone from being your boss to your friend, and now . . ."

Don't say it, Melvin; please don't.

"I'm probably your biggest fan."

"Thank you so much, Melvin . . . I would've never made it this far without your support."

"Chantrell . . ."

". . . Yes?"

"Do you enjoy what we have?"

"Hmm, yes, and most of all, I value your trust."

"And I think you know how much I value you."

"Melvin, I do. I have never felt more appreciated." *Oh, my God . . . Melvin is drunk! Where is Yvonne?*

"I want to keep you. Really . . . keep you," he said firmly.

"I'm not going anywhere . . ."

"Say it again, but this time in my good ear," he shifted her body.

"I said, you don't have to worry. I'm not leaving the firm.

And besides, no one else is crazy enough to pay a paralegal five times the normal pay."

"*Do you promise?*"

"Yes, Melvin."

"Seriously, I need to hear you say it, because what I'm about to do could risk it all for me."

"I promise you; I will not leave Campbell Law Firm!" she yelled over Beyoncé.

"Then would you do me a small favor? It would mean a lot to me."

"Hmm, sure. What is it?"

"Could you reach inside my tuxedo jacket? There's something inside for you."

Reluctantly, she reached into Melvin's jacket and retrieved a letter. Her eyes asked, *What is it?*

"Open it and you will see." Melvin stepped away from Chantrell with a smile. And so, she opened the white unsealed envelope from his inside pocket and started to read it on the dance floor.

Dear Mrs. Chantrell Gutierrez:

Congratulations! I am happy to inform you that you have passed the Louisiana State Bar Examination.

According to our records, you have now satisfied all requirements outlined by the Board. Unless some change in your status arises between now and the time when licenses are issued, your license will be forwarded to you at the above address in the near future.

We are confident that you understand your ethical responsibilities as a licensed attorney and will conduct yourself accordingly throughout your legal career. Please also remember the importance of civility toward your fellow attorneys, court officials, and others. It is an essential component of being a legal professional.

Once again, Mrs. Gutierrez, on behalf of the Board of Law Examiners, congratulations! We look forward to your admission as a member of the Louisiana State Bar.

Best wishes,

Doug T. Bastorphen
Chairman

Chantrell read the first portion of the letter five consecutive times, just to make sure the amaretto and pineapple hadn't distorted her vision. To read such embracing words after so much devastating rejection, to open a letter of *congratulations* instead of *we're sorry to inform you,* to finally cross a mountain that nearly shattered her self-worth, was deserving of another read.

Congratulations! I am happy to inform you that you have passed the Louisiana State Bar Examination.

When Chantrell was confident it wasn't the amaretto drinks and that the letter wasn't prank, her eyes tore away from the letter. Melvin was gone. She found herself in the middle of a huge circle of cheering wedding guests. None louder than Steven, Melvin, and Natokie.

Suddenly Steven took a step to the left, and that's when Chantrell's heart stopped, her jaw dropped, and the letter dropped. She couldn't hear the clapping, the celebrations, or her own thoughts. From behind Steven, her husband stepped forward holding a letter—a work visa sponsored by Fortier International Shipping, endorsed by Catherine Jacques and Steven Fortier. Jony Gutierrez was six months and a class away from becoming a citizen of the United States.

Chantrell leaped into his arms. Jony caught her, kissed her, and held her as the DJ played "Dangerously in Love 2" from the top. Melvin had planned the entire reunion two months ago, to erase the memory of that day when Jony was deported and Chantrell's soul departed. Melvin and Steven had pulled it off, fulfilling their promise to thank her in the best possible way—by reuniting her with her husband.

"Take me home now!" She kissed the words into Jony's ear, and on their way out, her feet never touched the floor of that reception hall.

CHAPTER 55

It was nearing the end of the wedding. Most of the guests were starting to trickle out the door when Sherman noticed Ronelle and Brenda loading wedding gifts in a limo. Ronelle turned to find Sherman standing directly behind her. A few paces behind him stood Jared.

"Were you planning on leaving without saying goodbye?" Sherman asked.

"No, I just sent you a text," she said as she raised a stiff finger at Jared, asking him for one moment.

That's when Sherman turned to see Jared walking away.

"I'm not trying to impose on you. Just wanted to say goodnight. That's all."

Her mother walked over and stood between them. "Goodnight, Sherman," Brenda said firmly.

"Mother, can you give me a moment?"

"Ronelle, we have to get going."

"Mother, I will be there in a second. Okay?" she asked as Brenda narrowed her eyes at Sherman.

Once Brenda was out of earshot in the soundproof limo, Sherman turned to Ronelle. "It was so much easier when I thought she hated me because of my skin color."

"No, she hates you because you hurt her daughter. Isn't that the way it should be?" Ronelle smiled at him for the first time in what felt like an eternity.

"I guess you're right," he smiled back.

Brenda opened her limo door again. "Ronelle."

"Mother, I will be there in a second!"

"Can I have a kiss before you go?"

"Sherman, I don't want to go down this road again. So, let's just leave this as a wonderful night shared between two people who really cared for each other."

"Cared? So now I'm past tense? Wow! How quickly you deleted me from your life. And I have waited for you all this time."

"Why do you have to say things like that and ruin a fantastic night?"

"Okay, okay. I'll leave it alone and respect your space. Thank you for the dance tonight; it was wonderful to hold you again. Take care, Ronelle, and don't hesitate to call me." Sherman turned away, hurt.

As he drove home, he negotiated with his heart to release his mind at every red light, so he could finally think about something else. Each time the light turned green: *I have to let Ronelle go*. Not able to suffer the tuxedo shoes another second, he tossed them in the back seat of his car and walked from the parking lot to his apartment. Limping to the cabinet, he grabbed two wine glasses, but only poured wine for one. His second toast of the night was to Ronelle.

At least I held you tight, if only for one night . . .

After downing the first, Sherman poured one more glass of wine for the night. He could still smell her perfume on the collar of his shirt. At the end of the counter were the flowers. Right below the flowers, a hungry trash can.

I guess I'm officially single.

He reached into his pocket for his phone and read her text.

Goodnight, Sherman. Drive home safe.

As he reached for the vase to throw the flowers away, he heard trinkets and charms, mixed with the sound of a falling Christmas tree. *Ronelle?*

"I came to see my flowers and to see if it was true," she said, placing her purse on an ottoman by the door.

His hands picture-framed the followers. "Voila, fresh flowers."

"You did this for me?"

Sherman nodded. *Yes.*

"Every Saturday?"

Another nod. *Yes.*

"My mother said men only try once you quit, that it's a defect in all of them that prevents them from appreciating what they have in a woman until they're kicked out of her life. So, is this . . . that?"

"I can't speak for all men, only for myself, but I don't want to know another woman in the way I know you. I don't want to meet anyone else or invest the time in discovering her favorite song, or color, or ice cream. I just want what I had with you."

"Then why is the top of the trash can opened? Were you about to throw those flowers away?"

"Yes, because tonight it became evident you've thrown us away."

"Sherman, I can't. No matter how hard my mother pleads with me to forget about you, I can't. And, I don't want to."

"Then come home," he begged.

"I'm scared . . . of you. Scared of the rejection. The uncertainty. The hurt. All of that is the risk that comes with loving you. I don't want to feel those things . . . *only your love.*"

Sherman pulled her close to him; Ronelle melted into his arms.

"Please, give me another chance to love you the right way, please."

"Thank you for my flowers." Her head rested on his chest.

"Will you come home?" He kissed her hair.

"Sherman, I'm already home." Ronelle tiptoed to his lips for a kiss.

THE END
By: TJ SPENCER JACQUES

About the Author

Author TJ Spencer Jacques is a lifelong resident of New Orleans who uses the pages of his novels to give readers a great story, and a tour through the history of his fascinating city. TJ is the grandson of a third-generation wash lady who provided him with a treasure trove of life stories passed down through the ages, gift-wrapped for his readers. His goal is to tell stories that have never been told through the eyes of those born and raised in New Orleans.

Visit him at www.tjnovels.com